Praise for *The Good Luck Girls of Shipwreck Lane*

"Funny, original, and delightfully quirky, Kelly Harms's *The Good Luck Girls of Shipwreck Lane* shows us that sometimes, all we need to make it through one of life's rough patches is a change of scenery and a home-cooked meal."   —Molly Shapiro, author of *Point, Click, Love: A Novel*

"The characters are so well drawn that they practically leap from the page, charming dysfunction and all! A poignant, hilarious debut that's filled with heart, soul, insight, and laugh-out-loud moments. It'll make you rethink the meaning of what makes a family—and if you're anything like me, it'll make you want to pick up and move to 1516 Shipwreck Lane immediately! I'm such a fan of this utterly charming novel."
—Kristin Harmel, international bestselling author of *Italian for Beginners* and *The Sweetness of Forgetting*

"Janey and Nean each have a common name and uncommon hard luck, and when they suddenly have in common a sweepstakes house, their lives begin to change in ways neither of them could have imagined. Their quirky wit will win you over, even as they fumble through their crazy new life. *The Good Luck Girls of Shipwreck Lane* is alive with warmth and wit; I enjoyed it right through to the satisfying end."
—Kristina Riggle, author of *Real Life & Liars*

"Aunt Midge is a pure joy, and I loved Wimmer's surprising, spirited, and generous slant on what it takes to make a family."
—Nancy Thayer, *New York Times* bestselling author of *Summer Breeze*

"Warmhearted and funny . . . Harms's debut is as refreshingly delightful as a bowl of her character Janey's chilled pea soup with mint on a hot summer day."   —Meg Donohue, bestselling author of *How to Eat a Cupcake: A Novel*

"Spunky leading ladies that you can take to the beach."

—*Fitness* magazine

"Love, lies, food, and past and present triumphs and sorrows deliciously intertwine in Madison author Kelly Harms's debut novel about accepting second chances." —*Madison Magazine*

"Refreshing . . . In addition to making readers giggle, this foodie novel will leave most craving freshly baked bread, seafood, and other gourmet meals. There are no lulls in this one—Harms will have readers eager to learn how Nean and Janey come to tolerate one another without pulling each other's hair out. Also, this romantic novel has a bittersweet ending that may invoke some tears, but will leave readers smiling."

—*RT Book Reviews* (4½ stars)

"Harms has created two incredibly likeable heroines, allowing the strengths of one woman to bolster the weaknesses of the other. . . . a succession of plot twists keeps the reader intrigued and invested."

—*Booklist*

"I guarantee you'll miss this crazy bunch from Christmas Cove long after you close the cover. This story will make for some great book club discussions as well as a perfect way to spend a lazy afternoon poolside. Grab a copy, a comfortable lawn chair, and enjoy!"

—Brodart Books

"*The Good Luck Girls of Shipwreck Lane* is a charming summer read packed with humor, surprises, and lots and lots of good food. When you finish, you'll want to have your girlfriends over for a big home-cooked meal, and you'll wish you had an aunt like Aunt Midge." —*The Gazette*

"Clever and memorable and original." —Samantha Wilde,
author of *I'll Take What She Has*

"I really enjoyed this novel and felt sympathetic toward both Janey and Nean. I wanted only good things for them. Aunt Midge was quite a character, full of life and personality, as well as a huge heart. She was impossible not to love. The story is funny and heartbreaking throughout."
—Chick Lit Central

"Great for book clubs."
—*Library Journal*

"Another perfect summer diversion is *The Good Luck Girls of Shipwreck Lane*. Kelly Harms writes with love about a trio of women desperate for a change and smart enough to recognize it may not be exactly what they planned. Delicious."
—Angela Matano, *Campus Circle*

"The friction between the Janines, along with a few romantic foibles and a lot of delicious meals, result in a sweetly funny and unpredictable story that's ultimately about making a home where you find it."
—*Wisconsin State Journal*

"*Good Luck Girls* melds that female-centered viewpoint with a light, witty, and highly accessible style."
—*Isthmus*

"In Harms's deft hands, the story of two women who share the same name and both claim a gigunda luxury furnished house from the Home Sweet Home Network's *Free House Sweepstakes* as theirs is a quirky, funny, and bittersweet read. . . . Harms's writing style is warm and inviting with a soupçon of quirky humor, intelligence, and compassion. The more you read, the more you become emotionally invested."
—*Spa Week Daily*

The

Good Luck

Girls of

Shipwreck Lane

The Good Luck Girls of Shipwreck Lane

KELLY HARMS

Thomas Dunne Books
St. Martin's Griffin 🏔 New York

This is a work of fiction. All of the characters, organizations, and events portrayed in this novel are either products of the author's imagination or are used fictitiously.

THOMAS DUNNE BOOKS.

An imprint of St. Martin's Press.

THE GOOD LUCK GIRLS OF SHIPWRECK LANE. Copyright © 2013 by Kelly Harms Wimmer. All rights reserved. Printed in the United States of America. For information, address St. Martin's Press, 175 Fifth Avenue, New York, N.Y. 10010.

www.thomasdunnebooks.com

www.stmartins.com

The Library of Congress has cataloged the hardcover edition as follows:

Harms, Kelly.
    The Good Luck Girls of Shipwreck Lane / Kelly Harms. — First Edition.
        p. cm.
    ISBN 978-1-250-01138-1 (hardcover)
    ISBN 978-1-250-02264-6 (e-book)
    I. Title.
    PS3608.A7493G66 2013
    813'.6—dc23

                                                        2013003728

ISBN 978-1-250-01139-8 (trade paperback)

St. Martin's Griffin books may be purchased for educational, business, or promotional use. For information on bulk purchases, please contact Macmillan Corporate and Premium Sales Department at 1-800-221-7945, extension 5442, or write specialmarkets@macmillan.com.

10   9   8   7   6   5   4   3   2

For Griffin

ACKNOWLEDGMENTS

Thanks to my spectacular agent and true friend, Holly Root, and to my gifted editor, Katie Gilligan, to the inspiring Pete Wolverton, the estimable Tom Dunne, and the teams at Thomas Dunne Books and Waxman Literary who lent their considerable gifts to this publication.

Thanks to my family, the famous Harmses of Cedar Rapids, Los Angeles, and Rochester, and to Josh Wimmer.

Thanks to Andrea Cirillo, Christina Hogrebe, Lyssa Keusch, Lucia Macro, Annelise Robey, Meg Ruley, Patience Smith, and Nancy Yost for all you taught me about books along the way. And thanks to Maine for letting me borrow your beautiful coast for my fantasy world.

Thanks to my friends Barbara Poelle, Kelly O'Connor McNees, Jennifer Ferreter Sabet, Eileen Joyce, and Anna Rybicki. If you hate my book, these are the people to blame. It is their kindness, encouragement, and enduring friendship that made its creation possible.

HERE IS HOW YOU MAKE
RUSSIAN SALMON PIE

First you buy all the ingredients. When the only real fishmonger in Cedar Falls, Iowa, asks you what you want with an entire salmon, and you all alone and so skinny, you do not answer, because you are mortified at the mere thought of talking to strangers, even though you've been buying obscene quantities of seafood from the same man for five years now and so he is not technically a stranger. Still, you stammer and twitch and then eventually just give him the money and run, forgetting to ask him to take off the head and tail as you flee. Then you end up carting off a twenty-inch salmon wrapped in paper and get a nasty shock when you unwrap it at home and find it glaring at you accusingly. What's done is done. Rest the fish on ice in your too-small apartment fridge.

Next you must set aside a long period of time in which to work. This might be a weekday afternoon, when you've been sent home from work early by your manager, Tami, to work on your issues with customer service (e.g., talking to strangers).

Now you make puff pastry from scratch, because, let's face it, you've got nowhere to be. When it's ready, you form the dough into the shape of an enormous fish—two adjoining blobs, one large body, one small tail.

You edge the whole thing with a two-inch lip to keep the pie filling inside when the time comes. Put this masterpiece on a cookie sheet and bake it. Hopefully you have a big oven, because you must also bake a matching "lid" to go on top of the fish at the same time. If you do not, have you ever considered baking puff pastry in a toaster oven? It works, after a fashion.

While this is blind baking and filling your kitchen with the scent of butter steaming, you cook an assortment of mushrooms and end-of-winter vegetables and stir them into a creamy white gravy—you do have bacon drippings in your fridge, don't you? You'll want a lot. Oh, and now is a good time to relieve the salmon of its extremities, because it has to fit in a poaching pot with a bottle of respectable white wine and eight lemons. Cook him (or her) to just this side of rare—s/he's headed for the oven next.

When the shell is mostly baked, scoop out the risen insides and replace them with the gravy and the veggies and the deboned, chunked salmon— which may not all fit, in which case, better luck next time. Seal the lid to the shell with a beaten egg, and then cut little pretty vents where the fish's gills would be. There? Good. Bake this whole thing at the lowest temperature you can stand so that the whole mess simmers together to make something beautiful, something you will admire for a long time, and then scoop out just one portion to eat for dinner, and throw the rest away.

Serve with hollandaise, homemade of course.

PART ONE

Mix

JANEY

"Walking a mile in another person's shoes is nothing compared to cooking a meal in someone else's kitchen."

—CHARLIE PALMER,
Charlie Palmer's Practical Guide to the New American Kitchen

It is the middle of the afternoon and my phone has been ringing on and off for about ten minutes. I don't want to answer it—it might distract me from the single most important thing in my life at the moment: hollandaise.

I believe in my heart that I can make a hollandaise sauce that does not split up, like supermarket salad dressing, but stays creamy and smooth and pure like a running yellow river of butter and egg. I believe this, and yet I have not quite accomplished it to date. I feel like today will be my lucky day. Or maybe it already is: I've been cooking for hours, and I am only halfway done with tonight's dish.

The phone starts ringing again. I know who is calling. My great-aunt Midge is the only caller in my life who won't leave me a message, but instead keeps trying until I pick up. Aunt Midge knows the likelihood of me checking my messages is very, very slim. The likelihood of me returning them is zero. Aunt Midge knows me pretty darn well.

I pick up the receiver, pinning it under my chin as I take eggs and milk out of the fridge to start coming to temp.

"There you are." It is indeed Aunt Midge, her creaky old-lady voice deceptively sweet. "I tried the bridal salon and they told me you'd gone home." She is referring to Wedding Belles Too, Iowa's Premier Bridal Warehouse, where I sew hems and take in busts. "Have you finally gotten fired?"

I sigh. My job at Wedding Belles Too is a good job. I am a good seamstress, and I like the sweet smell of the oil that I use on my Pfaff machine and the blue dust kicked up by my chalk hem marker. I like the swishing sound of poly-satin as it whooshes underneath my presser foot and the methodical work of moving buttons, adjusting a row of sequins, tacking on beads. But I cannot seem to handle talking to the brides about their alterations when things go wrong, and soon, soon it is going to cost me the job.

I take out six eggs, then two more, then decide to just warm the whole dozen. You can never have too much hollandaise sauce. "No, Aunt Midge. I haven't been fired. They just sent me home to practice my people skills." Which I am clearly not doing.

"Hmph. Who needs people skills when you can sew so well, I want to know."

"Me too," I say, though I know exactly why my job is on the line. On the rare occasions that I come face to face with the brides, I scare them with the crippling social anxiety that causes me to stammer, and wheeze, and say either nothing or something incredibly inappropriate. And I would do anything to be able to change that. It's just that I know I can't.

Aunt Midge's voice cuts into my thoughts. "When are you coming over?"

I sigh as loudly as possible so I know she'll hear it. "I'm not. I'm cooking fish. You can come over here if you want." But even as I say the words, I put away my cookbook with the salmon recipe in it. Good-bye, Russian Salmon Pie. This is as far as we go today.

"You know they took away my driver's license."

I put the hollandaise-bound eggs back in the fridge. "Yes. Yes I did know that. It makes it that much easier to extend you an invitation."

That remark doesn't take Aunt Midge aback at all. She is never taken aback, not even by her hermit of a grandniece. "You just wait. One of these days I'll just hop in a taxi and show up on your door uninvited and never leave. What do you think about that?"

I smile a little to myself and wish for the four hundredth time that Aunt Midge would do that very thing. Aunt Midge is my oldest—well, my only—real friend. It is very worrying to have her on the other side of town in her little house getting very old and eating strange meats out of the freezer.

"I think . . ." I pause and try to figure out what to do with an entire poached salmon now, since there is no time for Russian Fish Pie *and* a social call. "I think that it would be easier for me to just come over."

"Agreed. Bring food. I'll provide the drink. And you have to be here by eight o'clock, because that's when the show starts."

"What show?" I know of a show that starts at eight, every night, on the Food Network, but I also know that's not the show Aunt Midge is talking about. As far as I can tell, my aunt has never watched the Food Network in her life. Why bother, when there are so many episodes of *Law and Order* to choose from?

"The 'No Place Like Home' giveaway on the Home Sweet Home Network. You know, that channel that runs *House Browsers* and *House Browsers Global*? They are giving away a big gorgeous house on the coast of Maine, and I am planning on winning it."

My eyebrows pop up. "Oh really? You're going to win this house in Maine?"

"That's right. It's a sure thing at this point. I am very excited, because the house has an endless pool that comes with."

"What is an endless pool?"

"Only the greatest old-person invention of all time. It's a tiny pool, only the length of one person—that person being me in this case—and it has a water current that lets you just swim in place for as long as you want. Can you imagine? Swimming . . . in place!" Aunt Midge really wants to hit this point home. "And the water is nice and warm, to keep your muscles lithe . . ."

"Mm-hmm." I'm not really sold yet on the idea, which is fine because I know Aunt Midge hasn't yet finished her sales pitch.

"It's great for your health, you know. All that low-impact exercise. For old ladies like me with the frail bones and achy joints. And . . ." She pauses dramatically, and I brace myself for the punch line. "And the jets are good for massage as well."

Now my eyebrows shoot up. "Like a hot tub?" I groan. From the last bit of Aunt Midge's description I now know exactly why she wants this item. My great-aunt is a dirty old bird who once got herself kicked out of a hotel pool area for "indecent use of the Jacuzzi." It's not the sort of thing I want to revisit.

"Exactly. A hot tub treadmill. The house they're giving away tonight has one, and I want it."

Oh boy. "Well, it's a good thing you're going to win it then, isn't it?" As I say this I realize nothing tastes better with cold poached salmon than potato salad. I have plenty of time to whip up a potato salad, and my fridge is full of fresh dill to boot. This is an excuse to make homemade mayonnaise. Brilliant.

"A very good thing. So I'll see you at seven-thirty then?"

"Okay. Seven-thirty. I love you, Aunt Midge."

"I love you, Niece Janey. Go cook." Aunt Midge hangs up the phone. I hold the receiver by my side, gazing at the oven, wondering if it's possible to make mustard from scratch in two hours.

It's not. The phone starts beeping and I hang it up, put on my favorite apron, which is printed with moose and bears, and go to the hallway right outside my apartment's little galley kitchen, where I've precariously balanced a small black-and-white TV on an old collapsible tray. I turn it on and set the volume up loud enough that I can hear it over running water or sizzling oil and smile when I see who's on the Food Network. Then I return to the kitchen to chop dill and boil potatoes and daydream about a dinner party with Ina Garten.

NEAN

All this time, I am at home. Trying to take a nap after a long day manning the fry station at Hardee's. Not hurting a hair on anyone's neck. I have my alarm clock set to 7:30 p.m. because, despite all the odds, I know I am destined to win the Home Sweet Home Network's "No Place Like Home Free House Sweepstakes" tonight, and I don't want to miss out on the announcement.

I am trying to nap because I have a headache. I have a headache because of all the shouting my boyfriend Geoff likes to do. Geoff is in a band and I'm pretty sure that all the loud noise he subjects himself to is making him deaf, because he never talks in a normal tone of voice anymore. If he wants to know where he put his keys, it sounds like this: "WHERE DID I PUT MY KEYS?!" And if he is hungry he will turn to me and say "BABY, WHAT ARE WE HAVING FOR DINNER TONIGHT?!" This is when I'm sitting next to him on the couch. There isn't really punctuation yet invented for the noise he makes when I'm in the other room. It's just shouting, all day and all night, whether he's angry or not, though it's usually the former. He is one of the angriest people I have ever known.

He—and his one-bedroom with a view of the interstate—is also the only thing standing between me and homelessness, though, so let us remain mum on Geoff's lesser qualities for now. He is not the first jerk-wad I have had to crash with just to have a place to live. But he will be the last. Soon, I will be the proud owner of a new, fully-furnished, Free House somewhere in New England, and then I will not have to put up with guys like Geoff ever again.

They ran a TV special about the house's features last week, as a tease for the drawing tonight, and the house is pretty damn fantastic. When I win, I won't need another thing but the clothes on my back and a bus ticket to Maine. The whole damn house is furnished straight out of an episode of *The Martha Stewart Show*, with all kinds of sofas and match-ing lamps and books already on the shelves and all the stuff you need to live already right there, and color-coded to boot. And it has a fitness area with state-of-the-art exercise equipment and a flat-screen TV for watching Oprah while you do the Best Life Challenge on the treadmill. And it has a finished basement game room with a fifty-bottle wine re-frigerator. A refrigerator *just for wine*, you understand. To say nothing of the real refrigerator that has a TV built right into the door so you can watch *Jeopardy!* while you wait for the pizza to come.

Yessir, the house is pretty fantastic. Outside, it has two matching rocking chairs on a porch in the front and a little heated pool off to the side, surrounded by pretty hedges for privacy so you can sit in it naked if you want and no one will ever know. And then the hedges open up to the back, which has a big view of the ocean and some pretty cliffs, though they are the sort of cliffs that you can imagine people getting too drunk and dashing their brains out on, so maybe I will put up a fence before my first big party. Still, the view is pretty spectacular. On the show they panned out to the ocean, and it was full of sailboats and seabirds and various other items of extreme scenicness.

I am really looking forward to living there.

Listen, I'm not dumb. I know the odds are stacked against me. But I had a very clear dream about a month ago about this house. It wasn't one of those ambiguous dreams where you have to tell someone else about it to figure out what the hell it's supposed to mean. It was a crystal clear dream—nay, *vision*. In it, I won a house, dreamed every last detail of it, and then the next day while I was watching TV I saw an ad for the sweepstakes and realized it was the exact same house from my dream. So yes, I'm pretty sure I'm destined to win.

I know it's not a sure thing until they call my name on the live winner's announcement show tonight, but it won't be much longer now, and I am a very, very lucky person, if you don't count my present circumstances, which I don't. I probably would have won last year's "No Place Like Home Free House Sweepstakes," a house in Florida (which, let's face it, is way nicer weather-wise than one in Maine) but the post office screwed up my entry postcard and it got bounced back to me after the drawing for insufficient postage. Boy was that a heartbreak. But at least it explained why I didn't win.

This year I didn't take any chances with the g-d---- post office. Those jerks are always changing the price of stamps, and they expect people to somehow know what the cost is to mail a postcard on any given day, like we have nothing better to do than think about postage prices. I say, if I go in and buy a sheet of postcard stamps—and they are specifically called postcard stamps, so I know whereof I speak—which are only useful on postcards and have exactly zero other uses, then they should keep being useful on postcards until they're all gone. You can't just all willy-nilly change the cost of postage and not tell anyone. That's the sort of thing that can bring down a civilization. You just watch.

This year I went right down to that post office with my postcard and took absolutely no chances. I waited in line for nearly a half hour, and when I got to the front counter, sure enough, they had changed the postage prices again. If I hadn't taken so much care and added a few extra dollars in stamps just to be on the safe side, my postcard would probably be at the bottom of some pile of letters to Santa or something and not where it is, which is in a big vat of postcards at the Home Sweet Home headquarters in New York City, very near the top where it will easily be selected by celebrity guest judge Carson Jansen-Smit, the hunky chiseled carpenter who is always going around knocking down people's dining room walls without their permission.

When I win the dream house, I will NOT let Carson Jansen-Smit anywhere near the property with his sledgehammer. If he wants to come over he should bring only a bottle of massage oil and some condoms.

I can't sleep. I'm too excited about the house. The announcement is not that far away. I crawl out of bed—okay, out of mattress, because it's just an old mattress on the floor I'm napping on—and teeter out a little dizzily to the main room of the apartment. I'm still groggy while I take in the mess. Geoff is not a tidy person, and I'll be damned if I'm going to clean up after a man at my young stage in life. Housewifery is for women over the age of thirty, if you ask me. For now I am just tolerating the squalor and holding on for those glorious days when Geoff's mom comes over with a mop and bucket and glares at me until I get out of the way. After one of her visits you can see yourself in the linoleum kitchen floor and there's no gritty sensation under your feet when you shower. She cleans up so thoroughly that dirt is afraid to come back for a couple of weeks, at least.

But those couple of weeks have come and gone. Geoff is asleep on the couch—maybe his shouting gave him a headache too—and the floor below him is covered in random stuff. Stickers, unopened mail, clothes, fast-food cups, and an unfathomable number of socks. It is early summer in Cedar Falls, Iowa, and Geoff wears black shower sandals pretty much 24/7, so I can't for the life of me understand where all these socks are coming from. Part of me thinks they are other people's socks, and Geoff is collecting them for some reason. Maybe he is getting his fans to give him their socks at his shows, and then planning to donate the socks to some sort of charity sock drive. I am fairly certain there are enough socks on the floor of this room to completely cover the feet of every homeless person in Cedar Falls, Iowa. Hey, that's not a bad idea.

It's an idea I want to run by Geoff right this second, in the hopes that he'll pick it up in here a little. So I sit on the couch and stare at him until he wakes up. Nothing happens. Apparently my piercing stare is not that piercing. When staring doesn't work I start bouncing on the couch a little. He keeps sleeping so I lean over and get my face down right in his, planning to scare the shit out of him when he opens his eyes, but when I'm within sniffing distance I get a big whiff of booze. Crap. I move away slightly, but before I do I take another big snootful of the smell and think hard. It isn't tequila, thank crap. Tequila is rare, but it's also scary. This smell on his breath today is Jack Daniel's, which I can totally handle. In fact, I could go for a Jack and Coke myself. I leave Geoff to sleep and go fix myself a drink.

In the kitchen the sink is full of damn near every dish we have, all covered with a layer of crusty grime that almost puts me off my drink. But I look in the cabinets and there are still three or four clean coffee mugs, the sturdy homemade kind that his last girlfriend made for him on her potter's wheel. On the bottom of each there is a heart with her and Geoff's initials in it. I take one down and pour in a finger or three of Jack and then ice, and then half a can of Coke over the top. I give it all a good swirl with the paring knife, which is mostly clean. By the time I'm done the announcement is about to start.

And here, things get tricky. There is only one TV in this apartment, and it's right next to the sleeping body of my landlord boyfriend who is stinking drunk. I have to turn it on—the TV, not the boyfriend—because I have to see the announcement. If I miss it, I won't know if I won for sure until the library opens tomorrow morning at 10:00 a.m. and I can go use the computers there to look on the HSHN website. Waiting overnight would make me crazy. And surely the HSH people will be expecting the winner to be watching tonight and provide instructions on how to claim the prize. What if I miss that?

I've *got* to turn on the TV. I'll just lean over, turn it on, and then right away dial down the volume to next to nothing and stand really close to the TV so I can hear what they're saying. Geoff will sleep right through. I pull up a beanbag right in front of the screen and plop down with my drink. Then I lean over and push the power button on the TV and watch the flash of light grow into a picture, all while trying to hit the volume down button as many times a second as humanly possible.

It doesn't work. It might have worked if we'd had a nicer TV, but this one, with it's missing remote and sticky console buttons, simply can't react in the time necessary for this endeavor. The sound blares on and it's set loud enough for Deaf Geoff to hear his favorite show: *South Park*. The noise that my drunken landlord boyfriend wakes up to is a giant cartoon fart, ripping its way across the apartment and startling him so much that it takes him several blinks to figure out exactly where he is. By the time he is sitting up I've got the sound off and the channel switched to the giveaway. I turn around and smile innocently, bat my eyelashes a little. "Sorry."

"Turn off the fucking TV," Geoff tells me.

"Okay," I say, then turn back to face the TV, where the opening scenes show a beautiful view of the coast of Maine from a boat or maybe a helicopter just off shore. Does the house come with a helicopter, I wonder?

Behind me, I hear Geoff get up. My hands clench around the drink. I will be watching this show. I *have* to watch this show.

"Hey, bitch," Geoff says. He is moving toward me. I know because I hear the detritus that covers the floor part like the Red Sea as he stumbles my way. On screen they are zooming in on the house. I'm starting to get nervous.

Geoff's leg connects with the coffee table and he shouts, "FUCK." I am trying hard to keep my eyes glued to the screen and focus on the show, but it's hard when I know he'll soon be standing right behind me. I check the clock. It will be five or ten minutes until they announce the winner. I know I can hold him off that long.

Now he is right behind me. I'm sitting cross-legged on the beanbag chair pretending I don't care about his existence and he's right behind me, standing up, and he grabs my head with his big hand and says again, "BITCH." I'm pretty sure he means me.

Then he closes his hand over my head and gets a big fistful of hair. "I said TURN OFF THE TV." I ignore him. I know how pissed this makes him, and I don't care.

He cares. He pulls the chunk of hair he's got in his fists and pulls hard. I feel myself being lifted up out of my seat by my hair. It hurts like hell. I scramble my legs underneath me and get purchase so I can lift myself up and take the pressure off my scalp. When I'm fully standing I turn around and face Geoff and see the rage in his face. I should back down, but I hate to be bullied. Besides, it's just Jack Daniel's on his breath. If it were tequila, I'd be more careful.

"Go back to sleep," I tell him as forcefully as I can. Then I put my hand over his wrist and try to wrest his fist out of my hair so I can get back to my show.

He doesn't move, but his grip gets tighter. "Seriously, Geoff," I try again, hating the pleading tone in my voice. "The show's almost over, and at the next commercial I'll order some pizza for dinner." Pizza, right? Who can be angry when tempted by pizza?

He releases my hair. Yes! But then he moves his hands to my shoulders and grabs me tight. "I was sleeping," he hisses out at me, his foul breath making my face pinch up involuntarily. "You didn't see me on the couch, right over there, sleeping?"

"Nope," I say. "I didn't even notice. Sorry!" I try to sit back down. Behind me, very, very softly, I hear the announcer introduce Carson Jansen-Smit and wish like hell I was looking at his pretty face instead of Geoff's grimacing one.

"You noticed," he accurately guesses. "You must have been *trying* to wake me up."

"Why would I want to do a thing like that? Go back to sleep, asshole." I don't know why I say that, except that I mean it.

"I'm the asshole?" he asks. "I was just trying to get a little rest around here." He moves around me, and I can tell he has every intention of turning off the TV.

"Don't you turn that off," I tell him. I step away from the beanbag chair and angle myself in front of the power button.

"Or what? Are you going to beat me up?" He shoves me out of the way and turns off the TV. The dream house shrinks to nothing. I elbow him right in the side and turn the TV back on.

"I was watching that!" I scream. Now I'm getting kind of pissed.

What will happen if I miss the announcement? Will they give the house to someone else, if I don't call a certain number on the screen within a certain time frame, just like on those radio show giveaways that I hear all day long at work?

"Too fucking bad." He tells me. He's going for the off switch again. I push him harder. He pushes me back. On the screen they're panning over the kitchen, which is so shiny and yellow and bright. The appliances are space-aged. They zoom in on the TV fridge, and the sight of it all shiny and new gives me a boost. Soon I will be able to watch whatever I want, whenever I want, even if I want to watch it on a refrigerator.

"You better sit down right now, you stupid shithead," I tell Geoff. "I'm not afraid of you just because you spent the day drinking and now you think you're some big man."

Geoff wheels around and hits me in the shoulder and I stumble back a little. It hurts but I'm not even thinking about it. I'm thinking about that house in Maine and how sweet living there is going to be. How I'm going to take off so fast and start a new life there, where no one knows anything about me. I wrestle my shoulders away from him, turn my face back to the TV even as he manhandles me.

It's making him crazy that I'm not crying or fighting back. He grabs my arm hard and spins me around so my back is to the TV. "You listen to me when I talk, bitch." Then he slaps my face. Open-handed. What a pussy he is. I tell him so, but in my mouth I taste blood.

They're about to announce the winner. Behind me I can hear them discussing the drawing rules and talk about the certified public accountants that are there to make sure the selection is on the up and up. I feel dizzy. My nose is bleeding. I just want this asshole out of my face so I can watch the show. He's yelling at me now and I can't even hear the TV anymore. I look at the mug I've been holding all this time, the Jack and Coke in the hard pottery mug with the heart carved in the bottom. He's going to hit me again if I don't turn off the TV and apologize right now, he's saying. He's going to hit me until I am sorry. I'm going to miss the announcement.

"You hear me? Apologize to me right now!" he's shouting. I hear faintly a drumroll on the TV.

"Fuck you," I tell him. Then I spit in his face. Now he's really mad. But it doesn't matter. Because before he gets a chance to deliver another hit, I haul back my hand with the mug in it and bring it down hard on his head, crack, and watch the Jack and Coke go everywhere and a tiny stream of blood trickle down his head and watch his lights go right out and see him sink down on the floor. I hear his pained scream and then the sound of him hitting the ground but I'm turning away already. My eyes are back on the television, where Carson Jansen-Smit is holding a piece of paper, an envelope with the name of the winner on it.

Carson is beaming like an idiot. "The winner of the grand prize, the fully furnished dream house in Christmas Cove, Maine, worth more than one million dollars, is . . ."

He pauses and I chant my name in my head. Say my name, Carson Jansen-Smit, you gorgeous moron you.

The drumroll stops. They zoom in on Carson's face. His lips form the words. "The winner is . . . Janine Brown of Cedar Falls, Iowa!" Confetti goes flying all around his head and a banner drops down in front of the house that reads CONGRATULATIONS JANINE and I blink my eyes hard and then start to shake and cry and scream all at once, and then I start to do a little jig right in front of the TV, careful even in my jubilation not to stomp on poor Geoff lying there unconscious and bloody on the floor.

"OH MY GOD!" I scream and start waving my fists in the air even though it makes my shoulder burn like hell to move it. "OH MY GOD!!!" I say again. I'm bleeding a little on my shirt but it doesn't matter. I'm very, very happy, and not happy for Janine "Janey" Brown, the bridal seamstress who lives across town and is right this moment staring openmouthed at her aunt Midge's flat-screen TV with a mouthful of salmon in danger of plopping right out onto the floor in front of her. I have—as of this moment—never met that Janine Brown of Cedar Falls, Iowa. I don't know she exists. She is not why I am happy.

I am happy because her name is my name too.

JANEY

"I wish I could just sit people down and give them something to eat;
then I know they would understand."

—ALICE WATERS,
Chez Panisse Menu Cookbook

After they read my name off on TV, things happen very, very fast. First
there is a brief period of time where I freeze in the exact position I was
in when they read my name (fork halfway back to the plate after a huge
bite) and stare for a while like a total idiot while trying not to panic.
This is followed by a wild celebratory dance by Aunt Midge that I feel
fairly sure will cost her a hip. Then a bunch of people come to the front
door holding balloons and video cameras.

My first instinct is to hide. This is my first instinct in any situation
that involves people I have never met, or balloons, or cameras. I have a
crippling case of what Aunt Midge calls Stranger Danger, the kind of
paralyzing shyness usually found in preteen boys with acne and a collection of twelve-sided dice. There are hives, and there is stuttering,
and, sometimes, there is sudden and extreme nausea. I'm sure shrinks
have another name for this, but to find out, I would have to talk to one,
which I cannot do, so there we are.

This particular scenario is especially acute. After all, I never entered
this contest and I'm pretty sure this is some sort of terrible mistake, and
I don't want the house anyway. But as Aunt Midge is marching to the

door she stage-whispers to me that she'd entered my name online a couple of dozen times alongside her own—for extra insurance, she told me. I'm not entirely sure when she got so handy on the computer, but I am beginning to see the danger in teaching old people to use the Internet.

She throws open the door and a film crew rushes in and they make me pretend to hear the news for the first time over and over and over again until they get every angle possible of me gasping. A complete stranger smears my flushed complexion with makeup, pulls my long wavy hair into a neat strawberry blond ponytail, applies dark mascara to emphasize my light blue eyes. I break out in a flop sweat. My jaw hurts from all the exaggerating dropping it has to do, but I'm not required to speak, and the crew seems pleased with the final result. I have plenty of real surprise available to keep it convincing, seeing as I've just won a million-dollar house I don't want in a contest I never entered.

Almost an hour later, when the filming is finished, a producer with long yellow-blond hair and stupid-looking shoes takes me and Aunt Midge back to the TV room and sits us down on the plastic-covered davenport for an interview. She asks me if I am related to anyone who works for the Home Sweet Home Network, and I say no, and she says she'll be checking into that, and I think to myself, go right ahead, you're looking at my one and only living relation right here, and she can't drive, so I don't see her working at a television network in California too successfully. Instead I say, "Sure, I understand." I stutter on the words.

Then she launches into a lot of personal questions. Am I married? Have I ever been married? Do I have any kids? Do I have any money to pay for the taxes on the house? And so forth. I get through "Are you married?" (no) without any trouble, but on the next one I pretty much shut down, just like always. There is some muttering about Ned, trying to explain how I had once been engaged, but that something had gone very wrong, and how I didn't ever plan on getting engaged again, and how I was perfectly happy on my own, thank you, and not every woman gets her own perfect life partner, and the quiet loneliness isn't that bad when you get used to it. But I say all this without using any

actual verbs or nouns. The producer stares at me with a look on her face
that translates loosely to "What the *hell* is she talking about?" until finally Aunt Midge steps in for me in her usual way.

"She's never been married," she says authoritatively. "As if it's any of
your business."

The producer balks a little. I imagine her toes curling a little inside
her pointy shoes. "I'm sorry, Ms. . . . ." she glances down at her notes,
"Mrs. Richardson. I know it seems very personal, but I'm asking these
questions of Janine because our lawyers will need to know the answers
before they can transfer the deed to the house. They'll also be inter-
viewing you independently, so you'll have to go through this a few more
times. We just can't take any legal risks with a million-dollar sweepstakes, you understand."

Like a mama bear lashing out, Aunt Midge clearly doesn't understand the nuances here, but I do. The Home Sweet Home Network
wants to make sure I don't owe any child support or alimony or mil-
lions in back taxes or something unsavory like that. And, I'm sure, they
want to figure out how much good reality TV they might be able to get
out of me now that I've won. Answer: not much. After a few more nosy
questions and my incoherent replies, I can tell that the producer is pretty
disappointed on that front. Anyone can see I am not star material. It
would take a lot more than a free fancy house I don't need to get me to
talk on camera.

Finally the inquisition is over and the producer, clearly deflated, says
to me, "Maybe our best bet is to do a sort of montage of you excitedly
walking through the house after you're all moved in. It will be useful
for next year's sweepstakes, but doesn't involve much actual talking into
the camera. How does that sound?"

I look at her all buttoned up in her smart pantsuit and think, *If I
were the sort of person to hug strangers, I would hug her.* I forgive her the
shoes. "That sounds good," I manage, ignoring Aunt Midge's look of
disappointment. Let her go on TV in front of the world. I will do the
montage.

"Great. So I know you must still be in shock from this exciting news," she pauses and I summon up my best excited face, knowing it probably looks more like a grimace, "but I've got to ask. Are you interested in living in the house?"

"As opposed to what?" asks Aunt Midge. I was wondering the same thing, only without the power of speech.

The producer clasps her fingers together, "Well, some years our winners decide to sell the house right away, because of the tax burden such an expensive property can bring. And other winners use it as an income property and stay where they are. Picking up and moving across the country can be impossible for many people, with jobs and family to think of."

"Oh," said Aunt Midge. "No. I'm retired, no kids to speak of. It's not at all impossible for us."

It is at this moment that I realize that in Aunt Midge's mind, *she* is actually the one who won this house, and I am merely the name on the deed. After all, she entered the contest, and she wants the house, not me. Maybe I should be irked by this, but instead I'm flooded with a sense of relief. Now I have an out. I can let her move there, while I stay in my little place and keep working at Wedding Belles Too and absolutely nothing has to change. Yes! It's the perfect plan. Soon the TV cameras will be gone and my life will go back to normal. I'll miss Aunt Midge, but visiting her will finally be a use for all the vacation days I've been stockpiling.

"That's great news," says the producer to Aunt Midge, and I agree wholeheartedly. Off she goes to Maine, and with my best wishes. I will hold down the fort in Iowa. My shoulders relax for the first time since they read my name on TV.

But two hours later, when it's just me and Aunt Midge in her little house, and she's racing around putting things she doesn't want to take with her to Maine into a box for the Good Samaritans, I realize I'm not getting out of this as easily as I thought.

"You're coming with me, and that's final," Aunt Midge says imperiously. I know she uses this tone of voice on me because it works, but I still hate it. I also hate the way she puts her hands on her tiny hips and squares herself toward me, like she'll take me by force if she has to. It is exactly what it would look like if the Golden Girls got into professional wrestling.

"I'm not going to move to Maine," I tell her, taking my mother's wedding veil out of her toss pile. "You go. Enjoy the place. It sounds lovely. I'll visit on every holiday and you'll make tons of friends right away—you won't even have time to miss me."

Aunt Midge sneers at me. "Of course I'll make friends. Please. I have no problem making friends." As if to illustrate her popularity, she pulls down a stack of high school yearbooks from a closet and dumps them into a recycling bin. "You, on the other hand, will sit in that dinky apartment with the plastic countertops and painted-shut windows, cooking for an army every night, and wasting all that food, and before you know it you'll be a little old lady who hasn't gotten laid in forty years."

She is my great-aunt, and I love her, but sometimes I wonder why she is still alive.

"Thank you for your concern, but I am just fine. I like it here. I like my job." I sound whiney and defensive, like someone on a reality cooking show who's just been cut.

"You are just fine? Please. You don't answer your phone, you don't eat your own cooking, you're about to be fired from your job, and you get hives just from talking to strangers."

I've heard this all before and I ignore her just like always. "I don't get hives," I say, thankful that I'm wearing long sleeves so she can't see the red welts that have popped up all along my arms and shoulders since talking to that producer.

"Fine, then stay here," Aunt Midge says.

"Fine, I will," I say, like the petulant brat I know I'm being.

"Good." Aunt Midge grabs a weighty stack of piano music and drops it with a thud into the keep pile. "I'll just get one of those life-alert bracelets like those old ladies on TV who are all alone with no one to love them or tell them how bad their hair looks. That way when I fall and break my hip someone might come to help me, after a few hours at least, assuming I keep up with the payments. I'm sure it won't be too painful, lying there on the new ecologically sound bamboo flooring, unable to do anything but moan in agony . . ."

I growl and sit down on the forty-year-old Barcalounger. Be strong, I tell myself.

Aunt Midge sighs dramatically. "I always imagined it would be your mother taking care of me into my dotage. She would never have abandoned me alone on some windy cliff in the middle of Maine. It's just not what she would have wanted."

"Oh, for God's sake." I am annoyed, yes, but my defenses are crumbling.

"Of course, if you were there with me, I'd be so much safer . . ."

I drop my head into my hands and moan. Aunt Midge sees this as a chance to go for the jugular.

"I wonder what cooking in that fancy kitchen would be like."

I look up.

"They said something about it last week on the preview show . . ." she scratches her head, pretends to think back a week, "Oh yes. Granite countertops. Does that mean anything to you?"

I can live without granite countertops. They'd be nice for making fudge, sure. But mostly they're just for show. I turn away.

"And what was the name of those fancy appliances? Sub-Zero?"

I turn back. Now I am mildly interested.

"Sub-Zero was just the fridge, though," she pushes on. "I think the ovens had a different name."

Ovens? Plural?

"Wolf. Is that the name of an oven maker?"

I stand up. "What else did they say about the kitchen?"

Aunt Midge is coy. "Hm . . . it's hard to remember. Let's see. Two great big ovens, six-burner gas range, a fancy fridge with French doors, a chest freezer in the garage, raised-bed kitchen garden out the side door, a baker's island, farmhouse sink . . ." She turns to face me, hands on hips. "Jeez, it's just such a shame that such a lovely kitchen will be going to waste. I can barely make toast. It'll just sit there unused all day long. Probably get really dusty."

I scream. "You are evil."

"Oh, calm down. Your kitchen is just fine. You've got a fridge and an oven and two lovely burners. What more could you want? Counter space is overrated, that's what you always say. You've got a lovely life here in Iowa and I wouldn't want you to give that up."

That's *it*. My dander is officially up. "I'm outta here," I announce, and start pulling on my shoes. "You *know* you are making me crazy. I don't understand why you would want to take something good—after all, you're getting the house of your dreams, aren't you?—and make it into a huge mess for me." I grab my jacket and pull it around my shoulders dramatically. No time for sleeves or buttons—I'm in a huff. "You just love to see how far you can push me, don't you? I don't want to move to Maine. You do. You should be jumping for joy, not needling me until I snap." I throw open the front door and see that there are still some bright red balloons lingering on Aunt Midge's porch. Just the reminder of all that hoopla makes my arms grow itchy and hot.

"Wait!" Aunt Midge cries before I can slam the door behind me. I see her tottering toward the door as fast as she can move. "There's something I have to tell you."

The sound of her shaky old-lady voice softens me. I need to get a grip. I take a deep breath and stick my head back in the door. "What is it?" I ask, as gently as I can in my state.

"The refrigerator has a TV built right in. So you can watch your cooking shows right there, *on the fridge while you cook!*"

ARGH. "I. Am. Not. Going." I shout out, and then whip around and slam the door behind me, knowing I might as well go home and pack for Maine.

NEAN

"The first thing to do, if you have absolutely no money, is to borrow some. Fifty cents will be enough, and should last you from three days to a week, depending on how luxurious are your tastes."

—M. F. K. FISHER, *How to Cook a Wolf*

Here is the thing about winning a free dream house on TV: You've got to *get* there somehow.

I took the bus. The ride took four days, nonstop, and my ass hurt like hell by the time I got to the last stop on the Greyhound—Damariscotta, Maine. I had to sleep overnight in the bus station in Chicago, and in Boston too. Boston was significantly dodgier, let me tell you. There's just something about East Coast bums. Not big fans of the bathroom.

But the Boston bus station did have one thing going for it: a twenty-four-hour Internet kiosk. Which, by day three of my journey, I realized I sorely needed.

You see, after they announced my name on TV, I was too damn excited to wait for instructions. I just wrapped my bloody hand up in a paper towel, grabbed my duffel bag and filled it as full as I could with underwear and wool socks and an extra-large box of Cheerios—rats can live for weeks on just Cheerios—and threw everything into Geoff's car and took off. Well, I did make sure he was still breathing first—he was, phew—and I took the time to leave a note telling him I'd borrowed his car and was leaving it in the Waterloo bus station with the keys above the wheel well, and sorry about the gaping head wound. I didn't want to totally screw up my karma. At the station, I cashed my last paycheck to buy the bus ticket and used a pay phone to let Hardee's know I was not coming back. Ricky, the manager, picked up. She was happy for me.

But I didn't leave a forwarding address. Didn't figure Geoff would want to write. So the contest people probably have been wondering how to reach me. I'm guessing they went to the house or called my cell phone—which was turned off for nonpayment weeks ago. That would only leave one method of contact: e-mail.

And sure enough, when I log on, here's what I find:

From: mmukoywski@HSHN.com
To: janinebrown@gmail.com
Subject: Congrats!

Dear Ms. Brown,
Pursuant to our conversation, here is a map to your new home (!) and the lawyer's office where your paperwork will be finalized. You are confirmed to meet at Caselwit, Stanson, and Moss at 10:00 am on the 9th of June.

If anything comes up during your trip east or upon arrival, just call my assistant Lavender at (323) 400-1449.

Again, congratulations!
Meghan Mukoywski
Executive Producer, Home Sweet Home Network

I have no idea what "pursuant to our conversation" is supposed to mean, but there's a map attached with the address of my new house: 1516 Shipwreck Lane. There's no way for me to print the map but at least I know what I'm supposed to be looking for. Besides, you know, the giant house and the sailboats and the heated pool.

. . .

After four days of bus travel, sunny, quaint, charming-as-hell Damariscotta is quite a refreshing change. They drop me off in a Walgreen's back parking lot, but it's more like Ye Olde Walgreen's, with its gray-stained shutters and green shingles. The whole town makes me a little barfy. It's pottery store this and bead store that, and of course an expanse of jewelry stores stretching block after block for all the rich tourists all over the place.

They have novelty maps of the area available for free at every store-front, and I pick one up to try to get some vague idea of where I am and where I am going. Alas, the maps have no viable scale, and were drawn giving extreme height to buildings where sponsors are located and absolutely zip detail to areas without any retailers, such as the neighborhood where my new house would be. I know I look like a drifter, with my greasy four-day-old hair and stuffed-to-the-gills duffel bag, so I don't ask for directions until I find a rundown tobacco shop on the edge of the main drag. Inside is a weathered old man smoking a pipe carved in the shape of a grizzly bear. Bingo, I think.

"Hey," I say, holding my body in my best, "I'm not here to shoplift anything" posture, arms open wide. "I'm looking for Shipwreck Lane. Do you have any idea how I'd get there?"

The old man scratches his thick gray beard. Seriously. I pray my immune system will be strong enough to survive the quaintness poisoning I am surely getting a hefty dose of.

"Well," he says at last, in a voice that sounds like this isn't his first grizzly-bear pipeful. "You can't get there from here."

"Very funny," I say, eyebrows raised. "Is it far?"

The man straightens up, smiles, and holds out his pipe to me. "Not far. Here, smell this."

I take a deep whiff of the burnt leaves in his pipe. Weed. How classy. I cross my arms in front of me and shake my head.

"Good stuff, though, right?" he replies, even though I have said nothing. "I've got a fisherman buddy who's bringing it in from the seaport in Boston. None of this Vermont-grown organic bullshit."

"Nice," I say, just hoping the guy still has the brain cells left to get me to Shipwreck Lane. "But seriously, how do I get there?"

"Get where?"

Oh for God's sake. "To Shipwreck Lane? I know it's close to a light-house," I say, thinking back to the preview show.

"Oh yeah. Shipwreck Lane. . . . That's gotta be on Pemaquid Point. Just take Main Street and follow it until it's not a main street anymore but just a long winding road—that's Highway 130. When you get to the yarn store, turn right on Mariner's Way. Shipwreck Lane is off there somewhere." He jabs at the cartoon map and shows me exactly where I'm going. I'm thrilled.

"Can I walk there?"

"Why would you want to do a thing like that?" he asks, resuming work on his pipe.

I shrug. "Maybe because I don't have a car?"

"Ah. Then my sister will drive you. Any excuse to get to the yarn store, that knitting maniac. Lemme call her. Are you in a hurry?"

Not even slightly. "Sort of," I say, trying not to sound too demand-ing, but still rushed.

"No problem. Hang on."

The salty old stoner turns his back on me and finds a cell phone. A few moments later he turns to me and says, "She's on her way down," and points at the ceiling. "Don't tell her about the pot. She's particular about that sort of thing."

"Sure. I'll just wait outside. Thanks for all your help. Oh—and hey, can I get a pack of matches while I'm in here?"

"No problem," he says, sliding a box across the counter to me. *Bud's Tobacky and Gifts*, the case reads. "Nice meeting you."

"You too." I open the shop door and push my way back into the fresh air and sunshine. My pockets are now full of a novelty pipe of my own, two packs of American Spirits, and four cigars of unknown qual-ity. I can't wait to get to the house and check them out. I didn't think to steal a cigar cutter, but the kitchen should have a good strong knife that will do the job.

Thirty minutes later I am standing in the shared parking lot of a small cluster of dilapidated buildings. One houses the yarn store, into which Bud's sister has obligingly disappeared after giving me a friendly smile and taking the five dollars of gas money I offered. One is clearly a corner store, with windows full of beer signage and toilet paper displays. Good. That means I won't need a car anytime soon, if we really are within a decent walk of the house. The third building is, near as I can tell, some sort of garden supply center. Really, it's a bit of a mystery, with nothing on its sign but a cartoon mushroom surrounded by hovering fairies. Maybe this is where the town gnome lives. Who knows. Maine is weird.

I set off in the direction Bud advised and after an easy ten-minute walk I find Shipwreck Lane, and when I do, I get a feeling in my chest—sort of a tight, breathless feeling, the same one I felt right after they called my name on the winner's show. A lucky feeling. Sure, I knew I was going to win, but even so, hearing it confirmed was pretty freaking exciting. I feel that excitement again the closer I get to my new address. It builds in my chest cavity and on the back of my neck and right behind my eyes, where it burns like uncried tears.

When I get to 1514, one house away, I have to start telling myself to breathe—my automatic bodily functions seem to be shutting down. Then I see a big boat-shaped mailbox marked 1516 Shipwreck Lane and I break out into a gasping run—let's face it, I'm not exactly a fitness buff—and hurtle my way up the driveway, up the garden path, up three little porch steps, and across the porch, thinking "home, home, home" on every hard exhale. I press my body flat up against the red front door, a one-way hug, and pant like a lost puppy. For a few minutes I just stand there and hug the shit out of my new house while I try to catch my breath.

Then I realize I don't have a key.

JANEY

"For most cooks, recipes served primarily as aids
to prompt the memory."

—TERESA LUST, *Pass the Polenta*

I lost my deposit when I broke my lease, but the super was all too happy
to see me go—too many cooking smells coming from my apartment,
he said. Truth be told, the reaction was similar at Wedding Belles Too,
although there was no mention of smells, at least. But they did get me a
little cake on my last day, and there was a cute frosted zipper on the
top of it. I was always really good at moving zippers, everyone said. It
was nice.

As for Aunt Midge, there's a FOR SALE sign in front of her house.
The listing price is a stunningly cheap sixty-five thousand dollars,
though Aunt Midge reminds me that she bought the place for two hundred bucks and a big smile about a thousand years ago when she was just
eighteen. Still, I didn't know you could even buy a house for less than a
hundred thousand dollars anymore. The Realtor tells us it's a "scrape,"
which means that somebody is going to come along and buy Aunt
Midge's house just for the privilege of knocking the whole thing down
and building something bigger and more fabulous on the property.
She's lived there for seventy years, and soon it will be like the house
never existed. The concept makes me a little sad, but Aunt Midge is

not at all upset by this. "Take the money and run," she says. "That's what I say!"

And running is exactly what we're doing. It's a race against time to make the twenty-three-hour drive from Cedar Falls to the house on the southernmost coast of Maine by June 9, and I'm the only legal driver in our U-Haul, not that it stops Aunt Midge from trying to talk me into letting her drive. We've got three days to make the trek before we're due at the lawyer's office in Maine for the last piles of paperwork. Or so I assume, because the confirmation of that meeting that was supposed to come via e-mail from the producer never arrived. But then again, she did read my e-mail address back to me wrong about eight times. How hard is Janine dot Brown at gmail dot com, I ask you?

I suppose my stuttering didn't help.

The first day's drive is a breeze; we make it as far as Sandusky, Ohio, and find a Super 8 with plentiful vacancies for the night. But the next morning I wake up feeling significantly less enthusiastic about driving and have to make frequent stops for candy and coffee and to get out of the car and do some of those full-body shivers every now and then. We make it only to Scranton before I go stark raving mad and demand a hotel with a TV that carries the Food Network.

That night, we stay in a luxurious Holiday Inn, and I watch three straight hours of *Iron Chef* before conking out and dreaming about yellow lines and construction zones. When we get into the truck the next day I pass the hours by thinking of the most outrageous things I could cook with one of last night's secret ingredients: sturgeon. Sturgeon ice cream, that's the obvious one. But what about sturgeon flan? What would that taste like? Or sturgeon cheesecake? That could actually be good, in the right hands. I ask Aunt Midge if she'd ever eat sturgeon cheesecake as we make our way through the winding roads of Maine.

"A cheesecake made out of doctors? I don't get it."

"Not *surgeon* cheesecake. Sturgeon. It's a kind of fish. They have it at that deli downtown that has the bialys you like."

"Oh, right. The Jewish fish."

"I'm not sure the fish itself subscribes to any particular faith," I say, glad that we are in a private, enclosed space.

"You know who loved those bialys? Ned. He liked cheesecake too."

Maybe I have been driving for too long, but for some reason I don't snap back the way I usually do when Aunt Midge forces Ned into the conversation. "I was just wondering if you'd eat sturgeon cheesecake if I tried to make some," I say again. "It would be savory. Kind of like a quiche."

"He was such a nice boy," she says.

"And he would have been a wonderful husband," I say in a singsong voice, finishing Aunt Midge's oft-repeated eulogy.

"That's what I was going to say!"

"I know. It's what you always say whenever Ned comes up. But honestly, he's been gone a long time. I've let him go. Maybe it's time for you to do the same."

Aunt Midge is silent for a little while. I know what she is thinking: that I never really let Ned go, that I'm living my life like I died instead of him. She's said all these things to me before, and I'm good at ignoring them, because really, for all her platitudes and euphemisms, she hasn't been able to explain how a person goes about getting over something as wonderful as what Ned and I had. Nor can she explain why I would want to do a thing like that. It's not like something better is coming along.

When Aunt Midge speaks at last, she surprises me. "You're right. Maybe I should let him go. It's just that you're my only family, and I liked seeing you happy when he was alive. I wish I could see you that happy again."

Her unusual earnestness takes me aback. I feel tender and teary-eyed all of a sudden. The purple tinge of Aunt Midge's hair bobbles in my periphery and I wish I could pull over and give her a bear hug. Instead I keep driving, not trusting myself to speak.

"Maybe," she goes on, "it would be easier to move on if you didn't have all that insurance money just sitting there in the bank."

My soft feelings dissolve in an instant. "What, exactly, do you think I should do with all of it?"

"Use it! What better chance could you have than now, when you're starting your whole life over again? You could do anything you wanted! Start a catering business. Open a kitchenwares store. Travel to Italy. Go to culinary school. The possibilities are endless."

"I already said I'd use it to pay the taxes on the house."

"But that's only a fraction of what you've got. It kills me that you're just leaving it lying there to do nothing, even now when you've got nothing holding you back."

I raise my eyebrows. *I've got one thing holding me back,* I think, but do not say. "I don't need the money. I've already got a lead on two bridal shops within driving distance of the new house. After we get settled in I'll go see them and see if they need seamstresses. Good zipper movers are in short supply, you know."

Aunt Midge harumphs. "Fine. Waste your life tatting lace. But don't try to hold me back from having a good time."

"I wouldn't dream of it."

"Good. And don't complain when our house becomes party central."

"Don't worry, I won't," I say, imagining a house full of geriatrics snoring away in the living room at 8:00 p.m. "Just don't turn up the volume on *Matlock* too loud or the neighbors will complain."

"I don't watch *Matlock*, thank you very much," Aunt Midge sneers. "I watch *Columbo*. And only for the stud factor."

After that I am too squeamish to talk further, and we drive across New York in silence.

NEAN

"Wine is essential with anything!"

—JULIA CHILD, *The Way to Cook*

Here is a concise history of all the places I've lived: a shitload. I have lived in two trailers, both times with my mom. I have lived in the Y, both with her and without, since, believe it or not, they frown on meth use there. I've lived in eight foster homes, the longest for three years, the shortest for two days. But mostly, I've lived with men. The first was when I was sixteen and he was twenty-eight, and the last was Geoff. And the ones in between, eh, they don't really bear mentioning, except to say that they all provided a roof over my head. And they always made it known that I owed them gratitude. Or more.

Needless to say, this beautiful, painstakingly restored estate on the coast of Maine pretty much beats the pants off all those places. It's perched above the ocean and surrounded by a sea of manicured lawns, winding stone paths, flowerbeds in full bloom and towering silver birches, and yet, there's no taking your eyes off the house itself. Somehow it is grand and understated at once, with its pointed gables, weathered gray shingles, perfectly whiter-than-white trim, and two-story front porch. And all the windows—it must have more windowpanes than that fancy house from the Keira Knightley costume drama.

So I would really like to get inside and start living there, instead of standing here on the porch all day berating myself for being an idiot and not figuring out how I was supposed to get a key to the damn door.

I sit down on a beautifully carved rocking chair, one of a pair that are placed on either side of the front door with little matching lemonade tables standing ready and waiting right next to them, and have a think. I could probably get a hold of that Lavender person by finding a pay phone—there might have been one in that little cluster of buildings near the yarn store, but if not, I suppose I could try to hitchhike back to town—if she is still at her desk, *and* she knows how I can get a key, and fast.

But that could take forever. And I'm already at the house. There has to be an easier way.

So I leave my duffel by the front door and case the joint. The front of the house is just a long stretch of porch centered around the beautiful lipstick-red front door, which is solid and has a deadbolt on it. There's a planter and a doormat—but neither yield a spare key. I look through the yard for twenty minutes, and find nothing that even remotely resembles a fake rock or a ceramic turtle key holder. The windows are that vinyl weatherproof sort that have real locks on each side and double-paned glass. All the energy-efficiency improvements the design team made to my house are looking a little excessive right now.

On the left side of the house—north if the setting sun is reliable, which I think it is—there is a thick row of hedges and that little rectangular pool, looking incredibly tempting for a refreshing splash, and a sliding glass door leading to it that is just as solid as the windows. The place is sealed up pretty tight, and I'm starting to panic about whether I'm going to get in tonight. I move around to the back of the house, where the ocean meets a huge wall of rocky coastline, and find the extension they called the "three seasons room" on the preview show. A wall of long-paned windows stretch the distance of the entire house and curve outward on stilts, and inside I see a host of potted plants on every surface and a pair of plush loveseats angled to face the water. Boy, I bet the view from that room will be spectacular on a stormy day. Not that I will ever see it at this rate.

But when I move to the right side of the house I hit pay dirt. A kitchen door, either as old as the hills or just designed to look that way. I'm hoping for the former. First, there's a locked screen door, and that's no problem, I just use brute force and some creative jiggling to pop open the little wire hook at the top of the door and then stick my hand in the crack and unlock the latch on the handle. Then there's just a hollow-sounding wood door behind it. I whip out my driver's license and go to work on the lock, hoping it's as flimsy as it looks.

It gives me a satisfying bit of resistance before it slides down and the door pops open. I'm in! My license is mangled, but who cares? I'm a terrible driver anyway. I take a few steps into the kitchen and glance around at the shiny appliances and fancy countertops, and then my eyes latch on to the thing I was wishing for most just a few minutes ago: a phone. Within seconds I am dialing up the number from the e-mail I memorized back in Boston. Lavender answers on the first ring.

"Meghan Mukoywski's office."

"Lavender?" I pant. I realize now that I am out of breath. It's not from the forced entry so much as it is from the excitement of being in my first real home. A house more beautiful than anything I have ever even seen before.

"Um, who is this?"

"Lavender, this is Janine Brown," I hear myself bark, as though I am someone important, instead of just lucky. She says nothing. "Of the sweepstakes? I won the free house." I really need to calm down.

"Oh of COURSE," Lavender exclaims. "Sorry, duh. I mean, I totally knew who you were, but I'm like an intern so it's like, you know?"

It's a good thing I've watched so many marathons of *Jersey Shore* because I so totally know what she is trying to say, you know? "Don't worry about it," I tell her. "Listen, I'm wondering where I might get a key to my new house."

"Huh? You mean you lost yours? Didn't Meghan give you one, um, last week?"

"What? No. Meghan who? What?" I am only partially listening because the house's shiny newness is so distracting. "Isn't there a hide-a-key in this place somewhere?" There are about four bazillion wine glasses in the china cabinet. I may never have to wash dishes again.

"Um, let me check the e-mail, okay?" I hear shuffling on the other end, as though she is rifling through paper, not e-mail. "Okay, the gardener? He put a key? In the mailbox? Which I'm pretty sure he was totally not supposed to do."

I do one of those overwrought-comedian forehead slaps. Jesus Christ, of course, the mailbox. Why didn't I look in the mailbox? "That is great, thank you."

"No problem! So . . . you're kind of like, early, right? I thought you wouldn't be there until the ninth."

Again, no idea what she is talking about. No interest, either. "Yeah, whatever," I tell her. I probably missed an e-mail on my exotic bus tour of America.

"Could you like, not mention that to my boss? Because Meghan said I was supposed to send you a fruit basket for the day you arrived. And flowers for your aunt?"

"What aunt?"

There is confused silence on the other end of the phone. This might possibly be the stupidest conversation I have ever had in my life, and I worked the drive-thru at Hardee's.

"Um, never mind! So you're good, for the lawyers and everything?"

"Yep," I tell her, remembering the e-mail. "Caselwit, Stanson, and Moss. I'm good. Thanks a lot. Bye!" I hang up the phone before she can say bye back, and imagine her staring at the receiver, wondering what just happened, and, for that matter, what does this "phone" thing do?

And then I realize I am starving and exhausted and this is all mine, mine, mine.

Making sure the door won't lock behind me, I run out to the mailbox, grab a set of keys on a plastic Home Sweet Home Network key ring, and run to test it in the front lock. When it works I stride in, prop a dining room chair up against the doorknob of the vulnerable kitchen door and proceed to make myself totally and completely at home.

JANEY

"And, if worse truly comes to worst, you can always order
Chinese takeout and serve it on your best china with
a glass of champagne, and you can all have a good laugh
about it for years to come."

—INA GARTEN,
Barefoot Contessa Family Style

After New York, after Connecticut, Massachusetts, and New Hampshire, and after a whole hell of a lot of Maine, I pull the truck off a narrow street onto a long winding driveway that is only partially paved. This is it: 1516 Shipwreck Lane. Better not to contemplate the significance of that street name. I am relieved to be done driving but also a little chagrined, since my overenthusiastic left turn into the driveway has cost us our new mailbox and, most likely, the deposit on the U-Haul. As soon as we hear the telltale crunch, Aunt Midge starts doing her silent laugh, the whole-body-shaking one that makes me laugh too, even though I'm mad at myself for mowing down the first thing I've seen of our new home. I hit the brake, and the moment the truck comes to a rest she unbuckles and bounds out of the car to survey the damage. Through the windshield I see her run around to the front of the truck and look the grill up and down with a grin so big it must hurt a little and a big thumbs-up and then move on to the shards of gray-stained wood that was once the mailbox.

After a few moments, she comes up to my window and signals for me to roll down the window, which I do.

"It was shaped like a whaling ship!" she says, now laughing so hard it's difficult to understand her at first. "You ran over an entire boat!" There is some snorting, and now I start to giggle too. I can't help it— I'm punch drunk from three days on the road. I let myself out of the cab and step to the earth below, and see what was once an elaborate mast reduced to splintered firewood with miniature tattered sailcloth still attached.

Aunt Midge leans down to pick up pieces of the hull and finds a pointy plastic thing sticking out. "Is this a tiny harpoon?" she asks between snortles (half snort, half chortle). She bends over and grabs her sides, howling with laughter. "God, it's a good thing I wore my Depends today." Ah. That explains why we didn't have to make so many potty stops on this leg of the journey.

"*The Eagle's Shadow*," I read off the side of the fractured hull. "Well! I felt bad about my driving at first," I tell her, as I survey the ruins. "But now I realize I'm actually the savior of hundreds of tiny white yard whales."

"At least! But oh, those poor tiny whaler's wives. The tiny widow's walks will be crowded tonight, I promise you that."

"Lost at tiny sea. It's the circle of tiny life," I say, shaking my head in mock philosophical objectivity. "But honestly, I do feel bad for ruining our fancy new mailbox."

"Oh please," says Aunt Midge, regaining her composure at last. "If you hadn't run over that thing, God knows I'd have been out here with an ax before the week was out. We may live in Maine now, but we're still landlubbers. We still have our Iowa pride."

"So are you planning on replacing it with an ear of corn then? Won't that make us the most popular folks on the street?"

"Maybe so. We'll see. Whatever I choose shan't be as seaworthy as this fine rig. We'll drink a pint of mead in its honor tonight." She drops the little harpoon and a few other bits of boat with a dismissive thud. "Avast, me hearty! Shall we be headin' up to the great grand house at last?"

"Aye. But since when did whalers talk like pirates?" I ask.

Aunt Midge ignores me and scrambles toward the house as fast as her eighty-eight-year-old legs can carry her. Right on her tail, I pass a stand of tall pine trees and come into an opening where the house stands. When I see it, I nearly fall down out of awe.

NEAN

"If you don't like to cook, you should have the very best equipment."

—LYNNE ROSSETTO KASPER AND SALLY SWIFT,
The Splendid Table's How to Eat Supper

I am sitting in an old gray T-shirt and a pair of black cotton underpants on a fancy-pants version of a La-Z-Boy in front of my new flat-screen TV when I hear a crunching sound from outside that is louder than the rerun of *Melrose Place* I am watching. Which is saying something considering this is the episode where Kimberly blows up the apartment complex. Almost a week has passed since I moved into Free House, and I have gotten used to the stone silence that surrounds me out on this desolate rock. I rather like it. So I ignore the noise outside and hope it will go away. It does.

But a few minutes later I realize I have to pee like a racehorse. And that's when the shit hits the fan, pardon the expression.

From my perch on the toilet, door wide open so I don't miss my show, I hear the unmistakable sound of footsteps on the front porch. At first I think it's another fruit basket from Lavender, just what I need because I am living on gourmet pâté, imported herring, and perfectly chilled wine. But then, instead of the doorbell, I hear a key turn in the lock. Of my house. That's when I realize: someone is breaking into my house! With a key! I feel like I'm going to barf or pee again or both. In a panic, I slam the bathroom door shut and then immediately curse myself, because now I'm trapped in this little bathroom with no escape, and no way to call the police, and all I can hear is footsteps on my fancy tile entryway and Heather Locklear telling it like it is.

And then I hear the sound of the TV switching off, and two voices, clear as day, sounding just as puzzled as I feel. It's definitely women, two of them, and they're talking about how someone's been in the house. Um, duh! Maybe the person who owns the house, perhaps? The person who is presently cowering in the bathroom wondering if she can get the basin part of her marble sink free to use as a weapon?

"Maybe the construction workers were in here, and they left it on," says the first voice. It sounds meek. Like I could take her with just the towel bar.

"Why would construction workers be watching TV?" asks the second voice, much older, kind of creaky. Great. I'm being robbed by Betty White. Doesn't that just figure.

"Maybe to make sure the wiring worked or something?" says the first voice. "I don't know. We better take a look around." The footsteps grow closer. My heart starts racing.

"What's in here?" The older one asks, and footsteps get closer to the bathroom door. Oh so surreptitiously, I lean over from the toilet and depress the door lock. It makes a loud click. Dammit.

"Someone's in there!" The knob starts to turn and jiggle. "Hey! Whoever you are, open up!"

I do no such thing.

"Are you sure someone's in there?"

I start sizing up the skinny little bathroom windows. If I stood on the vanity . . .

"I just heard someone lock the door. Open up! I know you're in there!"

"Maybe we should call the police, Aunt Midge."

"Did you hear that?" the older woman shouts. "My niece is going to call the authorities if you don't open up right this second." And tell them what, I wonder? That they broke into my house and I rudely refused to greet them?

The window within reach is painted shut. Damn these sloppy home giveaway people. If they were actually living here they'd have done a better job. I climb down and consider my options. It doesn't take long, since I don't have any.

"You have five seconds to open that door before we break it down," yells the granny. "Five, four, three—"

I throw the door open and walk out as casually as I can, considering I'm brandishing a toilet plunger. "Jeez, can't a girl take a private pee in her own house?" I ask, but when I see what I'm dealing with, all bravado falls aside. I don't need it.

Two wide-eyed frumpsters stand in front of me. One is old as dirt, about four feet tall, pleasantly plump, and purple-haired. The other is closer to my age, skinny and tall, wearing a baggy Mickey Mouse T-shirt and mom jeans. I always wondered who bought those godawful embroidered cartoon T-shirts in the mall, and now I know. I just wish she'd get out of my house.

"Your house? This is *our* house," says the old one. "How did you get in here?"

"Through the door," I say, feeling more detail would be cumbersome. "How did *you* get in here?"

"With the key that the producers from the Home Sweet Home Network gave us, when we *won the house*."

I try not to process this tidbit of information. They're lying; they've got to be. "You didn't win the house. I won the house. They said my name on TV. I'm Janine Brown of Cedar Falls, Iowa."

This strikes the women silent. Ah hah! I think, feeling victorious. These two are con artists or something.

Then the skinny one speaks to me for the first time, softly, meekly, a quiver in her voice. "*I'm* Janine Brown of Cedar Falls, Iowa."

Oh, no. Oh no, no, no. This cannot be. "Prove it."

She pauses and looks at me hard and then fishes out a Velcro wallet from her handbag. Out comes a driver's license and I study it hard. Of course, we all know exactly what it says. I go into panic mode.

"It doesn't matter. I got here first. The house is mine, fair and square."

"Oh really?" asks the old one. "Did a camera crew come to your house and film your reaction to winning?"

"Yes," I lie, but now I am starting to sweat profusely. I mean, I did have a moment when I wondered why there hadn't been a camera crew. But then, I did talk to that girl at the office, and they knew I was here already . . . "Did you get an official e-mail from the network?" I counter. "Cause I did. Scheduling an appointment for me to sign the deed and everything."

The old one glances at the other Janine Brown skeptically. "A likely story," she says. "We can't have both won the house. You'll have to get out."

I think back to a piece of wisdom I've gleaned from Judge Judy. "No way. Possession is nine-tenths of the law. I'm not going anywhere." Take that, old bag.

"Well, neither are we," the old bag barks back. "Tomorrow morning at ten a.m. we're meeting with the lawyers who are signing over the deed. To us. They'll send you packing."

It's the mention of this meeting, tomorrow morning at ten, just like the e-mail I got back in Boston, that gives me that horrible shiver in my spine and pit in my gut. This is not good, I think. Not good at all

"It's you who will be sent packing," I say, feeling stupid and hamstrung even as I make my empty threats. "So if I were you I wouldn't get too comfortable." But as I speak I am making contorted faces and squinting my eyes to try to keep back tears. Because now I am really scared. What if I *didn't* really win the house? What if these horrible people did? What if my entry postcard never arrived? Or what if there was some sort of mistake in the contest, and the first Janine Brown to sign the deed will be the one to get the house? I *have* to be the first Janine Brown to the lawyer's office tomorrow morning. It has to be me. But I don't even have a car, and the office is miles and miles away. Up to now, I was just planning to try to hitchhike in whenever I could. Which, I now realize, could be too late.

Right then I know exactly what I have to do. And looking at the angry wadded-up face of the old woman and her bright-red-cheeked, stuttering friend, I don't feel bad about it, not even for a second. "I'm going outside for a cigarette," I tell the other Janine Brown in a weird, scrunchy voice. "Don't even think about locking me out, because I have a key. And besides, I'll call my lawyers and they'll have you on the street so fast your head will spin." With that I make for the kitchen, throw aside the dining room chair that was supposed to keep me safe, and slam the door hard on my way out.

JANEY

"Keep your knives sharp."

—JULIA CHILD,
Mastering the Art of French Cooking, volume 1

"Quick, put something heavy in front of the door." Aunt Midge is already moving toward the kitchen before the screen door has even stopped banging. I am bent over at the waist, elbows on knees, trying to get a good breath of air.

"I'll do nothing of the kind," I tell her, straightening up and putting my arm out to clothesline her before she gets much further. "Sit down. Let's think this over logically." I steer her over to the long, narrow three-seasons room that extends the full length of the back of the house. Maybe the gorgeous ocean view will help us think more clearly. Already I feel the dizzying spin of panic start to slow.

"What's to think over?" she asks, as she plops down on a plush red and white loveseat, utterly unmoved by the scenery. "There's a con artist squatting in the house that we won, fair and square. Either we lock her out now, or call the police, or both."

"Maybe she's telling the truth. Janine Brown isn't the most unique name, and Cedar Falls is a big enough city that she could have been living there her whole life and I might not have ever run into her. Maybe she was the real winner of the contest and I was some sort of mistake. Like, a clerical error."

"Hah! If her name is Janine Brown, then I'm the Queen of Sheba. Hang on . . ." Aunt Midge struggles her way out of the cushy chair and disappears back into the main part of the house for a second, then reappears holding a battered-looking string purse. "Here!" she says victoriously. "She left her purse inside."

"Please tell me you're not going to go rustling through her things," I say, knowing full well that's exactly what she's planning to do.

"You better believe it," she answers with a wicked grin. She starts digging in the purse. It's not exactly vast, but it is stuffed to the brim. A couple of used tissues fall to the floor, and a can of mace topples out with a clatter. Then Aunt Midge pulls out her hand triumphantly holding a rubber-banded stack of cards. She drops the purse with a thunk on a side table and pulls the rubber band off and starts sorting through them.

"Bruegger's Bagels, CVS, Walgreens, Hy-Vee," she says, reading the names off of the plastic affinity cards as she sorts through them. "No credit cards," she says to me. "Seem a little suspicious?"

"No, it doesn't, Sherlock. Plenty of people don't use credit."

"Plenty of people who don't want to have a traceable record of where they've been," she says. I silently vow to cut her off from *Law and Order* reruns.

"Aha!" She pulls out a mangled driver's license. I recognize the look of it instantly. It's from Iowa.

"Here, you read it," says Aunt Midge, forcing it into my hands though I want no part of this sordid business. "I left my glasses in my purse."

I hold the card up close and scrutinize it. It looks like she's been using it as a crowbar or something. But it's definitely the real deal, goldfinch hologram and all. "Janine D. Brown. 1851 Tom's Terrace, Cedar Falls, Iowa, 50613." I ponder the address. Isn't that a trailer park out by the interstate? I'm pretty sure it is.

"It's a fake," Aunt Midge says, even as she plops back into the love-seat looking a little taken aback.

"Looks real enough to me. And her birthdate makes her . . ." math, math, math, "twenty-four years old. Twenty-four. We're not turning a twenty-four-year-old Iowa girl out into the street in the middle of rural Maine. She'll stay here until we've gotten this all sorted out and she has someplace else to go." I realize as I speak that I don't need to summon my authoritative voice. It is already in use. I look out over the cliff and to the ocean in wonderment.

Aunt Midge looks at me a little wondering herself. Has she too heard the new resolution in my voice? "Did you hear that?" she asks.

"You mean, what I just said?" I think, eager to get some praise for asserting myself, something she lectures me about on a near daily basis.

"No, no, I'm ignoring your nonsense. I mean that sound outside. Sort of like an engine turning over."

I flush with embarrassment and then train my ears for the noise. "It sounds like a car is pulling into the drive."

"Or pulling out." Aunt Midge blinks at me hard a couple of times, and then smacks her forehead. "Where did you put the keys to the U-Haul?"

"I think I left them in the truck when I hit the mailbox. Why?"

Aunt Midge sighs dramatically. "You go look outside. I'll call the cops."

Like a ton of bricks the realization dawns. "Oh *shit*," I cry and rush out through the great room, past the elegant limestone fireplace and the fifty-two-inch LED TV and the handcrafted driftwood chandelier, through the entryway, and out the big red front door onto the porch, where I see the very upsetting sight of our U-Haul in reverse, lights blaring, pulling out of the long, tree-lined driveway. I scream in horror, and the driver looks out at me with an absolutely evil smile and gives me the finger with a flourish just before she disappears from sight. I hear a squeal of wheels and the crunch of gravel, and then the unmistakable sound of the engine gunning up the main road.

I stand on the porch, powerless, clenching my fists and seething in

THE GOOD LUCK GIRLS OF SHIPWRECK LANE   47

fury. All this just moments after sticking up for that . . . that devious little *bitch*.

I turn on my heels and march back inside, to find Aunt Midge already on my cell phone giving a description of the other Janine Brown. "Mangy, scarily thin, about five foot four or so, hair dyed sort of purplish red. Burgundy. A gray T-shirt. No pants. That's right, no pants. We just watched her pull away five seconds ago. Yes, that's right."

I tap Aunt Midge on the shoulder and she looks at me, holds up one finger to say hold on. Then she says into the phone, "Hang on, officer. What is it, Janey?"

But when I get the chance to speak, I'm speechless. I look at Aunt Midge in utter desperation. I feel like crying but I'm not much of a crier. Still, everything was in that U-Haul. Including my faith in humanity. My eyes stay dry but my throat swells up, and my face feels hot, and I know if I open my mouth no sound will come out.

"I know, sweetheart." Aunt Midge says to me, wrapping her cool arm around my waist and pulling me close to her. She pats my hip with her hand and says again, "I know."

Then she turns back to the phone, with just a hint of John Wayne drawl in her voice, and says, "Detective? Tell your men we want her dead or alive."

It's two hours before a pair of not-terribly-concerned police officers come and take our statement and then another few uneventful hours pass while we wait for word. I know we should be spending this time touring the house, taking in the wonderful décor and beautiful architecture of our new place, but I feel too shaken up and bitter to enjoy anything. Aunt Midge is banging around the house, saying things like, "This is where I'll put my Elvis commemorative plate collection. If I ever see it again . . ." and announcing the names of each empty wine bottle she finds strewn throughout the house. "Lamothe de Haux Bordeaux Blanc," she calls out, pronouncing the words "La Mothy dey Hoax Bore-doescks." She sighs with enough drama to get her a role on one of her soaps. "I wonder what that would have tasted like. I guess we'll never know."

A few minutes of this has me headed for the hills. I tell her I'm going to check out the grounds of the house and slip out the front door, locking it behind me to be on the safe side. It's dark now, but there's just enough light from the porch lamps for me to step carefully down the stairs and around to the left side of the house. There, behind a thick row of piney hedges, I find the legendary endless pool, making a slight purring sound from under its heavy cover. Tomorrow, assuming we still own this house, I'll try to cheer up Aunt Midge by setting up the pool.

I walk along the inside of the hedgerow, following it around the pool to where it meets a tall garden gate and the side of the house, which I open with a little jiggle of the old-fashioned latch. Through the gate is the backyard proper, about a quarter acre of birch trees and tall grasses that cover the distance between the house and the outcroppings of rock that form cliffs. Looking out past them, I hear the sounds of the ocean lapping and lunging, but see only darkness in every direction. And, I suddenly realize, I also see stars.

Enough light is leaking from the house to dim them a little, but the expanse of ocean stars still glows bright enough to enchant me. I sit down as close to the edge of the cliffs as I dare and begin to follow the brightest ones in circles around the sky, getting my bearings. I see the glowing haze of the Milky Way, streaming across the sky in a great arch, and down closer to the water I find Cygnus flying south, neck stretched out and wings extended as if she's caught a nice thermal and is coasting her way to the nest.

The rest of the night sky is a blur to me, but a beautiful blur. A transporting blur. I forget about the house and the U-Haul and the woman who stole it and let myself remember the last time I saw stars so bright. It was on a camping trip with Ned in the Ozarks. I close my eyes tightly, and when I open them, I am there, on a bluff with a campfire at my back. I feel Ned's hand where it always came to rest, right at the top of my neck, cradling the heaviest part of my head, hands buried in my hair.

"Ned," I ask him. "What am I doing in Maine? Did I really even win this place, or is it all some colossal mistake? And if it is, what am I supposed to do now?"

I wait a beat, somehow expecting him to reply. But instead of Ned's voice, I hear soft squishy footsteps coming up the lawn toward me. The gait is fast and confident, definitely not the short-stepped shuffle of Aunt Midge. I stand up so fast I get a little dizzy and shout, "Who's there!" like a crazy person. My heart is racing and I feel my armpits go damp. It's the goddamned social anxiety, made worse by the fact that just a second ago, I was with the person who knew me better than anyone.

In the distance I see a figure open his arms wide and make a sort of shrugging gesture, like a zookeeper approaching a wild animal. "Hey there. Sorry I scared you," he says as he moves in closer. His voice is cool and relaxed, one step away from singing, and my shoulders drop down an inch and my heartbeat slows slightly at the sound of it. "I'm Noah Macallister, from up the road? Are you Janine?"

I blink a few times. The stranger is standing between the light that's coming from the three-seasons room and the dark of the ocean, and it gives him an eerie halo. It also makes it entirely impossible for me to make out anything more than his solid shape.

"I'm sorry . . ." I start to say. My palms are sweating. I don't know what to say. I start to stumble backward.

"Janine?" he says, and moves closer to me. I feel my eyes bulge. "Wait, be careful."

Suddenly I remember that I'm standing on the edge of a cliff. A slippery cliff. I look for a way to move forward, away from the ledge, without walking straight into the strange man. It will take a little sidestepping to the left, but I'm not above a little creative sidling to avoid contact. I hold my arms up in front of me, palms out, the international symbol for "stay back," and start making my way in a wide leftward arc.

The man looks at me curiously but doesn't move closer. "You okay?" he asks.

I'm scared of him, as I'm scared of every stranger I run into, but for some reason—maybe his low singsong voice—I don't feel truly threatened. Just in danger of humiliating myself. "I'm just going to go inside," I say warily. I know this poor man will think I'm a lunatic, but I just don't care, that's how badly I don't want to talk to him. I keep edging my way around the lawn. I'm getting closer to the light of the house, ever so slightly.

"Um . . ." he says, clearly registering my lunacy, "all right, that's fine. But you might want to see who I have with me before you go . . ."

Puzzled, I drop my arms and start looking around for another person.

He sees this as an invitation and takes a small step in my direction. "Did you lose track of a U-Haul truck at some point today?" he asks.

I whirl back around to face him full-on. Now I can make out his shaggy dark hair and broad, straight shoulders. He's wearing blue jeans and an unbuttoned chambray shirt over a light-colored T-shirt. On his feet is a pair of serious-looking work boots.

"Because if you did, I think I know where you might find it. C'mon up here," he says casually, like it's no big deal. Now I am starting to get truly worried.

I lower my head and take another big step to the side. He takes two toward me. I freeze in my tracks, shaking a little.

He tilts his head, like he's having a think. Then he tilts it the other direction, and says, "It's so dark out here, and you don't know me from Adam. Why don't you go on up to the porch, where there's plenty of light, right near the door in case you want to go inside. I'll get my friend and meet you up there." He pivots his body so I have a safe path to cross past him and get to the house.

"Okay!" I say too loudly, relieved to get away from the crashing waves and steep cliffs and my formerly private darkness. I make a bee-line up to the house, climb those three porch steps, and sit on one of the rocking chairs, psyching myself up to talk to this guy, to find out what he knows about our U-Haul. He's just a nice guy from Maine, I tell myself. He's not an angry bride or a reality show producer or a moving-van thief. Still, I feel dizzy. I lean my head over, between my legs, and take deep breaths for what feels like a very long time, until I've calmed down quite a bit and replaced most of my terror with curiosity. It is only then that Noah Macallister rounds the corner and comes into the light. Behind him, still lingering in the darkness, is another figure, a slighter one.

"That's better," he says, as he settles into the rocking chair opposite mine. "Much more comfortable up here." Finally I can see his face. It's square and a light tan color, with a good scruff going on his chin and heavy eyebrows over soft green eyes. His dark hair is unruly, yes, but in a sort of sweet disheveled way, more tousled than shaggy. I feel something twinge inside. A long-quiet part of me registers it as attraction.

"So. You're the big winner of this house, eh?" he asks. I nod, rather than explain that I really have no idea. By now I'm calm enough that I think I could talk if I wanted to. But maybe not just yet . . .

"Is it nice?" he goes on. "It sure is big."

It's not a compliment, exactly, but at least it doesn't require a response.

"Right, well. The purpose of my visit." He leans back in his rocking chair like he's about to tell a good story. "I was driving up Highway 130 to town and I saw a U-Haul truck pulled aways off the side of the road about ten miles north of here. Kind of an unusual sight. I pulled over to see if anything was the matter, and found this young lady . . ." he uses the arms of the chair to push himself up halfway, and calls out into the darkness. "Get up here, Nean!" Then he plops back into the chair, watching my face carefully all the while.

From the shadows a very sheepish version of the woman who stole our truck emerges. Her posture is crumpled over, and her head is tilted downward like a naughty puppy. She's wearing an enormous pair of athletic shorts rolled up at the waist several times and a pair of plastic flip-flops, the kind they sell at every gas station and grocery store. It makes her look even younger than she is. I roll my lips together and inward, shutting up as tight as the locked house.

"No pants, no shoes, just a run-out-of-gas-U-Haul," the man goes on, as the other Janine Brown gets close enough to the light of the porch for me to make out her dirty feet, the dark puffy bags under her eyes. "Well, I said to myself, something here is awry. She said she was moving here but I put two and two together when she didn't have any ID or idea where she was. Plus, she seemed awfully interested in not seeing you tonight, didn't you, Nean?" he calls back to the girl. "So I figured this was the first place we should go," he adds with a wily smile. "And she didn't have a lot of options, it being pretty quiet out here on Pemaquid Point, except for the coastal wolves."

At the ridiculousness of the phrase "coastal wolves," I feel a totally involuntary contraction in my cheeks, and before I know it I'm cracking a full-on smile. I nod solemnly, and say in a surprisingly solid tone of voice, "Oh yes, the wolves. Very dangerous."

"And powerful enough to break right through the glass on a windshield, did you know? Especially when they're hunting in packs." Somehow he is keeping a totally straight face. "Well, after the whole story came out about the stolen truck and the contest confusion, I told her I was sure you'd let her stay here for the night, so long as she returned the truck and didn't pull any more funny business. I mean, it's that or out here with the wolves. I didn't suppose you'd be that heartless, though I guess it's totally up to you."

The joke stops being funny when I consider letting this person, Nean, I guess she's calling herself, back into what I'm hoping is my house. I shake my head.

"No, she can't stay here," I tell the man, Noah.

"See, Noah?" Nean whines. "I told you they were horrible."

I shoot her the dirtiest look I'm capable of before I turn back to Noah. "Can't she stay with you? We've had our issues, to put it mildly."

A shadow crosses over his face so dark I recoil a little bit. "Sorry, no." He shrugs and his tone lightens just a little. "No room at the inn."

"A hotel then."

"Are you paying?" Nean asks me, arms folding over her chest.

I grit my teeth. "Sure. Fine."

Noah frowns. "It's kind of late for that, I'm afraid. There's nothing but bed and breakfasts out here, and they're all shut up tight at this hour. But there's got to be a spot for her in this big old house, just for one night. She'll be good, won't you, Nean?" He turns back to me. "And even if she feels like doing a runner, it's not like there's anywhere for her to go that's safe . . ." he raises one of those thick dark eyebrows and a little playfulness returns to his countenance.

". . . from the wolves," I finish. To my great surprise, my shyness seems almost entirely gone.

"Exactly."

"Well . . ." I think this over. I know I should go inside and wake up Aunt Midge, but I'm too embarrassed to admit in front of these two that I have to go to my eighty-eight-year-old aunt for permission. And anyway, I have to say yes. Because if there's even the tiniest chance that this house really belongs to her, what right do I have to keep her out? "Fork over the car keys," I say, stretching an open palm toward Nean.

Noah smiles and digs around in his pants pocket. "I thought I'd just hold 'em for you while we straightened all this out. Here you go."

Noah reaches over and sets the keys, warm from his pocket, into mine. All at once I feel anxious again. I channel it into the interloper.

"No smoking in the house," I tell her. "And tomorrow if the lawyers say we own the house, you're out."

Nean's eyes slide away from mine off to the darkness. "Fine. But they won't."

"Great," says Noah. "Tomorrow, when it's light, we can get some gas out to the truck and bring it back where it belongs, sound good?"

"Wonderful, thank you. And thank you for finding the U-Haul. Everything we owned from before is in there. It would have been a big loss."

"Anytime, Janine." He holds my eyes for just a moment, but it's enough.

I think about telling him to call me Janey, but the phrase sounds so overtly flirtatious in my head that I can't get the words out. I turn away from him instead and unlock the front door.

"See you tomorrow?" I finally call behind me, when he is already down the porch steps and heading to his car.

"Can't wait!" he calls without turning back. I think I hear a smile in his voice, but it's too dark out to know for sure.

NEAN

"Civilization began with the invention of the cocktail hour."
—ROY FINAMORE, *Tasty*

Coastal wolves? Please. They must think I'm some sort of moron to buy that nonsense. As anyone who has the National Geographic Channel can tell you, Maine has been wolf-free and lovin' it for over a hundred years.

But, as I lie in the cozy bedroom I used to think was mine, watching the sunrise light the room pink, I have to fess up: I needed an excuse to get back here somehow, and letting those nimrods think I was afraid of coastal wolves was as good as any. Before Noah the Wandering Mountain Man found me, I was utterly lost, out of gas, facing a long night in a cold moving van cab and not exactly relishing the idea. After all, Maine may not have wolves, but they do have serial killers, just like anywhere else. More, if one is to believe Stephen King.

And . . . though I shudder to admit it, in the far recesses of my dark, dark heart, I was feeling pretty terrible about what I'd done. Not that I'll ever tell those two that. They're probably down the hall dreaming about stringing me up by my toenails and lashing me with macramé plant holders. But I know they must have packed their whole lives into that moving van, and I was already regretting the loss of my duffel bag enough to be sympathetic to how they must have felt about losing everything. Forget the duffel bag. What I really missed was a pair of pants and some shoes. Why do I do things like this?

I guess my junior high guidance counselor was right: I do have trouble predicting the consequences of my actions.

Although, the minute I swiped the truck, I realized just how dumb a move it was. The clock on the dash informed me that it was well past lawyer's hours, not that that stopped me from wasting the last of the U-Haul's gas to drive into Damariscotta anyway. And when I got there, and found the lawyer's office right on Main, it was shut up just as tightly as I'd expected, with my deed trapped inside.

At least, I hope it's my deed.

And if it isn't?

As Noah pointed out in the car ride back here, I may be able to talk the real Janine Brown out of pressing charges tomorrow. She seemed like a forgiving sort—or if not truly forgiving, at least spineless enough to let me get off with a slap on the wrist.

But then what? I don't have any money left, and I don't know a soul on this side of the Mississippi. Even if I could get back to Iowa, it would be unwise to run back into Geoff's arms, what with our earlier difference of opinions regarding his skull and my coffee mug. In the roof-over-my-head department, winning this house was pretty much as far as my planning went. If I've unwon it, I'm out of ideas.

Of course, there's probably a shelter nearby where I could stay. God, I hate shelters. They are hard on everybody, but they are hell on girls. I'll do just about anything to get out of relying on them—and I have. Let's face it, it's not like I was dating Geoff for my health.

Maybe, once I get to town I can find a job right away and save every penny until I can afford to get myself my own apartment. Yes! Then I could go to night school and get a degree so I can make more money. Maybe I'd even meet some nice guys for a change. It would be a whole new Nean. Nean on the straight and narrow.

But . . . don't you need a credit check to get an apartment? And how long would I have to work at a min-wage job to save up enough for first month's rent *and* a deposit? Let's see. . . . If I can wrangle ten bucks an hour and find a three-hundred-dollar apartment, that's . . . hey—that's just two weeks of work, with a little extra for taxes. I could do a shelter for two weeks. No problem.

Oh, right, that's two weeks assuming I don't eat or do anything or go anywhere the entire time. Shit.

I just have to have won this house. That's all there is to it. After all, it was my name that Carson Jansen-Smit read on national television, and me who got to the house first. I'm the one who figured out a way in. I'm the one who got an e-mail from the HSHN producer.

I'm the one who ate the congratulatory fruit basket.

It's my house. And I'm not going to hide up here like some sort of squatter waiting to find out something I'm already perfectly sure of. I'm going to go downstairs and eat something in *my* kitchen and watch something on *my* TV and swim in *my* pool and do whatever the hell else I want until I can find a way to get rid of those two gate-crashers once and for all.

When I get downstairs around six-thirty that morning, the first thing I notice is a loud humming sound, like a refrigerator on steroids, or an alien spaceship. It seems to be coming from outside, making the space-ship option even more likely. Flummoxed, I slide open the poolside door and slip outside to investigate. The hum is definitely coming from the pool—from *my* pool, I remind myself. And the contents of my pool? One naked old lady. Really old. Really naked. Really splishing and splashing like the day she was born.

She seems to be doing something close to a breaststroke, if you can do a breaststroke with your breasts bobbing up under your arms like that. I now realize the pool is some sort of streaming water conveyer belt that forces a current through in one direction, so you can swim con-stantly without ever getting anyplace. Huh. And I thought it was just a very large hot tub.

The pool continues humming loudly, and I'm sure she can't hear anything with all that water rushing past her ears and the enormous smacking sound that her arm flaps make every time they hit the water. But maybe she senses me or something, because after a few seconds she lowers her arms and comes to a stop and then fumbles to turn off the current.

Before she's even turned around to verify my existence, she says, "Well, well, well, look what the cat dragged in."

"More like dragged out," I say, watching her surprisingly nimble movements as she takes the stairway out of the water. She's stark naked, but doesn't seem self-conscious at all. "This is my house, after all," I remind her. "I can come and go as I please."

She rolls her eyes. "I don't care if this is the pope's house; you sure as shit better have a U-Haul with you if you want me to call off the dogs. Hand me that towel."

I pick up the fluffy beige towel from the dewy grass near my feet and gently toss it to her. "I'm sorry about that, really," I say as earnestly as I can. "In fact, I was trying to return it to you last night. I knew you would need it to leave today."

She ignores the last bit as surely as if I hadn't spoken it. "And?"

"I got lost and then ran out of gas. I left it about ten minutes away."

The old lady rolls her eyes and begins toweling off with vigor. "You've got some nerve, missy," she says in the shaming way only a woman this old can muster. "Stealing our car and then just waltzing back here like you own the place."

"I do own the place. They said my name on TV. That means I won."

She squints at me. "But there were no producers with balloons there when you found out? No paperwork to confirm it?"

I shake my head, feeling that pesky shadow of doubt again, but refusing to show it. "Not exactly. But I did get a confirmation e-mail from the network producer, Meghan Mewcow-something. And—"

"Meghan Mukoywski?"

"That's right," I say. "And I've spoken to her assistant *several* times."

"Well, we'll see where that gets you. Now stop checking me out like a sex-starved teenage boy and help me cover this pool."

Embarrassed, I realize I have been staring. Now that she's back on land, her body is plainly displayed and it's oddly beautiful. I mean, don't get me wrong, I love the menfolk pretty exclusively, but really, she looks good for an old bat. She'd be downright attractive if I was a guy. An old guy. She's got some muscle tone going on in her arms and legs, despite a wrinkly covering of skin, and though there's a certain sag happening in every direction, her big grandma hips speak of fresh-baked cookies and hours spent in the easy chair knitting.

"How old are you?" I blurt.

She harrumphs. "None of your damn business, Little Miss Grand Theft Auto. Grab the corner over there." She gestures to the hard-sided pool cover, and I scramble to follow her instructions, damn that old-lady authority thing. "Right over here to this edge. No, more to the left. There." I grunt and groan as I try to force the cover up and over the pool. "It's heavy, ain't it?" she asks, and I look up to nod and catch her face softening. "Not that a lady would ever confess her age, but I will say that it rhymes with 'matey-hate.' You'd never know it to look at me, though, would you?"

"No. No, you wouldn't." I'm not exactly telling the truth, but I'm not exactly lying either. Weird.

"Pull it tight so no critters get in and drown themselves," she instructs, and while I struggle to do so, she cools her heels. "So you figured you'd just steal our truck and head for the hills, is that it? Sell our every possession for drug money and cheap hamburgers?"

I think back to that moment when I crawled inside the high cab of the U-Haul and turned the key in the ignition. I just wanted to have that deed in my hot little hands as soon as possible. Now I'm worse off than if I had just sat tight and waited. "To be honest, I hadn't really thought things out too well."

She squinches her face at me. I feel like she's trying to read my mind. Good luck to her.

Finally she lets her eyes slide away and says, "Have you had breakfast? Let's go get Janey to feed us. Do you think this place came with bacon and eggs?"

"Uh-uh. Just prop food. Fancy cans of fish and jars of marinated vegetables and some stuff from the sponsors. But there's coffee . . ."

"It's a good start. C'mon, you." She leads me through the sliding glass doors, still dripping, and once inside trades her fluffy towel for an even fluffier-looking robe. It's way too big for her, and when she puts it on it makes her look tiny and a little frail, despite the solidness I just witnessed au naturel moments ago. As her thin white hair starts to dry it stands up on her head in patches. Now she looks eighty-eight. I fight the urge to offer her my arm to lean on.

We walk in through the great room, past the big leather sofas draped with snuggly quilts and plush pillows, past the built-in bookcases filled with high-minded novels and grouped vases, past the antique sailing maps, framed one atop the other in a high stack to the vaulted ceilings. I know it wasn't designed for me, and yet, if I closed my eyes tightly and imagined my wildest dream of home, this is what it would look like.

"The place is a palace," she says, reminding me that I am not the only one who knows how to dream big. "Did you see the size of the steam shower in the master bedroom? I could have a tea party in there."

"I was thinking it would be a good place to raise an alligator," I reply. "They love the damp, I hear."

I get a smile for that, and the warmth of it hits me hard. It will be hard to watch her dream go up in smoke. Maybe, after I sign my deed, I will let her stay for a few days, just until she's had time to come up with a plan B. Yes, I think I will.

"An alligator. Not a bad idea," she says. "I wonder what my niece would think of that."

"She's your niece?" For some reason I assumed the other Janine Brown was the old lady's granddaughter. She only seems a few years older than me.

"*Grand* niece. Her grandma was my sister. Her name was Janine too. She was quite the lady." Her voice gets a little misty and I think we are headed for a trip down memory lane. But before she can go any further into the old days and how it snowed every day in May and they had to eat SPAM and turnips to survive, I hear footsteps on the stairs. Through the banister rails I see the long, skinny pajama-pant-clad legs of the Other Janine Brown.

"Aunt Midge?" her drowsy voice calls, and then grows closer and closer as she descends the stairs. "I left a message with the lawyer's answering service. They said they'd buzz Mr. Moss, whatever that means. Oh! And someone found our truck! Remind me to call the police and tell them to stop looking. If they've actually started." By the time she finishes talking, she's in the living room looking at me with a narrow stare. I try not to look as doomed as I feel. "I see you've found the perpetrator."

"Morning, Janey," calls the old woman. Aunt Midge, I guess that's what we're calling her, walks past us both to the three-seasons room and disappears from view.

Janey—she really is more of a Janey than a Janine—tilts her head at me. "Are you all packed to go?"

"Sorry to disappoint you, but I'm not going anywhere. The house is mine, and I'm going to live in it." I give her a big smug smile. "But thanks for calling the lawyers—just saved me a step."

Janey looks appalled, but before she can get a word in edgewise, Aunt Midge chimes in from around the corner.

"I thought we should feed her before the lawyers kick her out on her criminal little heinie. Everyone deserves the Janey Brown treatment at least once . . ."

While I wonder what the Janey Brown treatment is, exactly, she twists her mouth around and chews things over, looking from the kitchen to me and back. "Fine. Hang on." She turns around and disappears to the kitchen, and the atmosphere of the room clears in her wake. What a Debbie Downer that one is.

Aunt Midge sighs and calls out, "This sure is some view," in a way that indicates I am to come appreciate it alongside her. Obediently, I move into the three-seasons room and see she's gotten good and comfortable on the striped loveseat. She's got her legs propped up on its enormous ottoman and is slouched down enough that it's not clear whether she's actually even sitting up anymore. I sit down on an equally cushy armchair, but remain in an upright position so as to gaze out at the water. I like the view just slightly to the north, where you can see a constant cycle of waves bashing their brains out on the cliffs and then regrouping to do it again. Sort of reminds me of myself.

"It's a lot prettier than the Jetway at Waterloo Regional," I say, thinking of the view from Geoff's place, then immediately regret my words. I don't want to sound pathetic. I want to sound like the sort of person who wins million-dollar houses.

But she seems to ignore my comment. She's probably lost in some wise old lady thought. Thinking about all the friends she's known and lost, each a swelling wave on the sea of her life . . . or something like that.

"Is it too early for a drink, do you think?" she asks me out of the blue.

My eyebrows pop up like they're on springs. "Well . . . shoot. It's got to be at least eight a.m. by now."

She growls a little and sneers. "You're just like my niece, always disapproving the slightest bad behavior."

That's a laugh. "I am *nothing* like your niece, I promise you," I say bitchily.

"No," says Janey, who has suddenly appeared behind us, the hurt apparent in her voice. "She is nothing like me." We both whirl around guiltily.

Standing there in her pj's holding a tray of elegant mugs, with brown cubes of sugar and nondairy creamers set out in pretty matching bowls, I feel a pang for this poor woman. Look at her waiting on us hand and foot. She may be a bit of a drag, but she is nothing like me, and that is a compliment.

"Ooh, coffee," I gush a little too eagerly. "Where'd you find the creamer?" I know there wasn't any in the house—I was looking for something to make a white Russian with a few nights back and came up empty.

"My purse," supplies Aunt Midge, sounding quite pleased with herself.

Janey looks at me a little wearily as she sets down the tray and hands us our mugs. "She got us kicked out of a Dunkin' Donuts in Pennsylvania yesterday when she emptied the entire bucket of creamers into her tote bag. God knows why she does this. I think it's a Depression thing."

"You're depressed, Aunt Midge?" I ask nosily, and get a snort in response.

"As if," Aunt Midge huffs.

"The *Great* Depression," Janey clarifies. "It's still going on in her mind."

"Huh. Too bad she didn't get stuck in Prohibition," I say.

"A fine criticism from a woman who managed to drink her own weight in wine in less than a week," Aunt Midge says. "Anyway, those creamers are looking pretty good right now, aren't they?"

They are, and I'm about to say so, but before I get a chance there is a loud banging at the door. Even without looking, I know, in my bones, exactly who it is.

Mike Moss, attorney at law, looks less like a rainmaker and more like a grandpa. He's wearing a tweed suit coat over Dockers, and I definitely catch a glimpse of suspender when he reaches out to shake our hands. The handshake is warm and doughy. I feel sure my fate is in good hands with this guy.

"My answering service tells me you were having some car trouble, so I just thought I better swing on by, get our business taken care of so the network bigwigs would stop their caterwauling. Hope it's no imposition, Ms. . . . er, which one of you two is Janine Brown?" he asks, because Janey and I beat Aunt Midge to the door by a mile.

"I am," I say confidently, while I hear her stutter out "we both are" in the background. Rube.

"Nice to meet you, Ms. Brown," he says, since he heard only me. "This is my secretary Sharla," he says, gesturing to the frumpy woman next to him on the porch. "She's a notary, and she'll witness the signing of your deed—"

"Now hold on one fat second, Mr. Moss," I hear Aunt Midge say from behind us. She pushes up between Janey and me and grabs the lawyer by the arm, pulling him inside. "There are a few things we need to discuss before any deed gets signed. A little matter of mistaken iden-tity."

Mike Moss looks mystified, but he lets himself be ushered through the door and gestures for Sharla to follow. "Mistaken identity?"

I resist the urge to push the old lady out of the way. "Not exactly," I say. "I won the house. It's my name on the winning entry. I got here first, fair and square. These two"—I gesture with the top of my head to Tweedle Dee and Tweedle Dotty—"are trying to swipe it out from under me."

Aunt Midge makes an outraged coughing noise. "Actually, my niece here is the real winner," she tells him with so much confidence that if I were him, I might believe her. "We've spoken to the sweepstakes pro-ducer in person. The house belongs to us."

Mike Moss looks from her to me and back again. "Why don't we all sit down," he says, as though this sort of thing happens every day. "Do I smell coffee?"

"Janey," says Aunt Midge. "Go get a couple more mugs, would you?"

I look at Janey. If anyone ordered me around like that at a moment like this I would be pitching a fit, but she looks only grateful to be sent out of the room. That girl is some kind of shy around strangers.

When we are all settled around the coffee table, coffee at hand, Mike Moss opens his worn leather satchel and pulls out a thin manila file. "Well, Ms. Brown, Ms. Richardson, Ms. Brown," he says with a tip of his head to each of us. "This is all very easily solved."

"It is?" I ask in surprise.

"Of course. I have a copy of the winning entry form right here." He closes his file with a flourish. "I just need both of you to tell me exactly what you put on your contest entries and we'll have our answer just like that."

Janey begins to stutter frantically. "I didn't . . . I mean, I don't . . ." she stammers. "I mean . . ." She looks near tears.

Aunt Midge puts her hand on Janey's shoulder. "I'm the one who entered her name. I did it online, using my own address, since I can never remember hers. So her entry form would have said something like, Janine Brown, in care of me, Maureen Richardson. And my address is—well, was—7411 Bradwood Drive, Cedar Falls, Iowa, 50613."

My face breaks into a wide grin. Surely this is hard-and-fast proof that I'm the real winner of the house. After all, Janey's entry wasn't even really hers.

"And your entry, Ms. Brown?" Mike Moss says, and it takes me a few seconds and everyone staring at me to realize he's speaking to me.

I rattle off Geoff's old address. "It was a postcard, by the way, and I *know* I used plenty of postage."

"Right, then," says Mike Moss. And then his face turns somber and he reopens his file wide on his lap. "Ms. Brown," he says, looking more at me than at Janey, "My client, the Home Sweet Home Network, provided me with this notarized copy of the winning Sweepstakes Entry, as chosen by random integer generation by the folks at Price Waterhouse. I am at liberty to tell you that the winning entry was submitted online, not by postcard, and belonged to a Ms. Janine Brown in care of Maureen Richardson, 7411 Bradwood Drive, Cedar Falls, Iowa, 50613. As the publicly posted rules of the contest delineate, the winning entrant was notified in person by an employee of the Home Sweet Home Network—heretofore the Network—as well as by certified mail to be posted on the evening of the drawing or no later than three p.m. on the following day. I take it you were not notified in person, Ms. Brown?"

I stop listening after he gives the address. I know he is handing me something important, a sheet of paper on which he is pointing something out, but my eyes are blurry, covered, as they are, with swelling salty tears.

"You're lying," I tell him, taking the paper and wadding it into a ball. "It can't be true. This is a trick."

"I am sorry for the misunderstanding, Ms. Brown," Mike Moss says to me with a wave of a hand, but I can tell he doesn't care one bit. He doesn't care that I have nowhere else to go. He doesn't care that I'm homeless. "I'll just need to see your passport or other government issued ID, uh, Ms., uh . . ."

"Call her Janey," says Aunt Midge.

"Very good, Janey. Your passport and then we can get that deed signed." It is as if I'm not even there anymore. As if I never happened.

"Wait!" I call frantically through my tears, standing to stop Janey's progress toward her purse. "This isn't fair. Possession is nine-tenths of the law!"

Moss shakes his head at me piteously. "I'm sorry, Ms. Brown, but it really isn't. The house belongs to this Janine Brown here," he gestures to Janey. "Her entry was chosen per the rules stated online at Home Sweet Home dot com. Participation in the contest qualifies as acknowledgment and agreement to the posted rules."

"Tell it to someone who cares," I say to him lamely. "I'm getting my own lawyer." Right. What lawyer wouldn't jump at the chance of a sixty-eight-cent retainer?

"In that case, I will wait to be contacted by your representation," says Moss. He is as cool as a cucumber. That's because he can see right through me.

"Good!" I shout. I sound like I'm seven. "Because you will be!" Shut up, Nean. Just shut up. "And you'll be sorry! You'll wish you never messed with me! I'll take you for every penny you have!" Frantically I start tearing up the copied contest entry. "There! Now you have no proof!"

I start to look for more things to destroy, grabbing at nothing, spinning around desperately, knocking things off shelves. Sharla looks a little scared, and I realize just how wild-eyed and hysterical I am acting when she asks Janey, "Maybe we should call the police?"

While Janey looks from Aunt Midge and back I blurt out, "Yes, do call the police, and tell them you are involved in a scam to rob me of my rightful winnings!" Now I know I sound like a lunatic. What am I doing? They're going to haul me away in the padded wagon.

But Aunt Midge, through the deep-set frown she's been wearing since the moment I stood up, stops me, puts her hand on my arm just the same way she did with Janey a few moments ago. "That won't be necessary. Nean is just going to calmly collect her things and move along. Aren't you, Nean?"

I look from the lawyers to Aunt Midge. They are all looking at me like my head could start spinning in circles at any second. Ashamed, I nod. "I'm just going to collect my things," I hear myself say robotically.

Everyone looks so relieved. And what did I expect? Of course they don't want me here. Of *course* I didn't win the house. Why would I have believed something so good could happen to me, even for a second? What a total idiot I've been, thinking I would win, thinking I *did* win, dropping everything and spending every last cent I had to get to a place where I have no real right to be.

What an incredible fool.

I head up the stairs and grab everything I can carry and shove it in my bag, violently, wildly. I leave some of my crappy old clothes behind in favor of the big, soft, multicolored quilt that covered "my" bed. It's not technically stealing, I think. They won't want it anyway, now that it's been tainted by me. Wherever I go next, I can keep this quilt as a reminder of that short magical time when something good seemed to have happened to me.

Wherever I go next. I just wish I had some idea of where that would be.

I wait to go back downstairs, until I know the lawyers are gone. I find Janey and Aunt Midge still around the coffee table where I left them, but now they have stacks of documents in front of them. Janey is still holding a pen. They look a little worn, like this ugly business of winning has been too much for them. And they look wary of me, like I am a criminal, and not simply the unluckiest woman in the world.

"So . . ." Janey's voice starts strong when she sees me, but then it begins to trail off.

"So when am I leaving?" I bark back. Even as I say that I am looking around, glancing around the room like I might find within it some last-ditch way to stay here. I don't know what the point is. It's time to face facts.

"I know when you're leaving. As soon as possible. Sooner. But, uh . . . what's your plan?" Janey asks.

"I don't have a plan," I admit. "Maybe I'll go find that Noah guy and see what he can do for me." I say that just to make her jealous—she obviously has the hots for this guy—but then instantly feel guilty. "I mean, where he'll drive me. If he can drop me off in Damariscotta, or what."

Janey's face seems to twitch a little. "And from there you can make your way back to Iowa?"

I decide to spare them both the little details. They already find me pitiful enough. "Yeah, sure."

But Aunt Midge won't leave it at that. "How are you going to do that exactly?" she asks. "You can't rent a car without a credit card."

"Same way I came. Greyhound bus."

"Don't you need some money for that, too?" she asks.

"How do you know I don't have any?" I shoot back. I don't, but that's not the point.

"Because I looked."

"God, have you been rooting through all my possessions?"

"Of course," Aunt Midge says. "After you stole ours, I didn't feel you were entitled to any privacy."

That shuts me right up. I cross my arms in front of my chest and sulk.

"Maybe we could lend you some money," Janey suggests. "Just bus fare to get you back to Iowa."

"Don't worry about me," I say, taking a gulp of the lawyer's leftover cold coffee for fortitude. "I'll be just fine." But I won't be fine, and they probably know it. My next stop will be some crummy shelter. And then after that, if I'm really lucky, another Geoff.

Geoff. I think of him, lying slumped on his apartment floor, the shards of pottery around him, as my name flashes across the television screen. I think of that sweet, sweet feeling in the moment when I first thought I'd won this house and truly believed I would never see him or anyone like him ever again. When my old life seemed to be over forever. When I was free.

And that's when a lightbulb goes on in my mind. A big one. The sort of lightbulb that only turns on when you are looking down a really nasty tunnel and you are trying to find any possible way to avoid going into that tunnel (because there are probably bats in there) even if it means telling a colossal whopper and probably damning your eternal soul to hell in the process.

For a moment I hesitate. Despite everything that's happened, this Janey person has been generally nice to me. She even offered me money, even after I stole her truck and threw a tantrum and threatened to sue her for everything she's worth.

And her aunt is a defenseless little old lady. If I go down this road, I am pretty much the most despicable human being ever.

But if I don't . . . I think of the uncertainty that waits for me the minute I walk out these doors. And for the first time in a long time, I feel scared. I do not like feeling scared.

"Before I go . . . there is one thing you could do. A little favor." I say in my sweetest, meekest voice.

Janey furrows her eyebrows at me. "What kind of favor?"

"Could you . . . throw the police off my trail?" I ask as innocently as possible. "I know it seems weird, but if they follow up about the U-Haul, maybe you could tell them you made a mistake, and I was just taking it out to be washed or something, so that they don't put me into the system? I mean, if it's not too late . . ."

Janey looks at her suddenly very interested aunt and then turns just her eyes to me. "Why would we do that?" She sounds very suspicious. Good.

"I . . ." I pretend to stutter. "I can't tell you. Just trust me. I really can't let the police find me, no matter what."

Aunt Midge sits up straight at this. "Are you on the lam?" she asks.

I say nothing for a moment, for dramatic effect, and then pinch my lips together, as if I'm holding in a secret. A horrible secret. "Please don't ask any questions," I say in a distraught voice. "It's too awful to speak of . . ." My eyes start getting glassy with tears. Yes! I am the master. I should think about a career in the thee-ay-tah.

Now both women are staring at me with wide eyes. "You better talk, missy, if you want us to do any favors," says Aunt Midge.

I look back and forth between them, pretending to weigh my options. "I just don't know who to trust . . ."

Janey looks truly concerned and I push back a twinge of guilt. "If you're in some bad trouble, maybe you should talk to the police. They'll help you," she says.

"Or just tell us," says Aunt Midge with a greedy expression. "We won't tell a soul, will we, Janey?"

I look to Janey for confirmation. She looks at Aunt Midge. "I don't know. . . . Maybe it's better if she goes to the authorities with whatever it is."

"I could never do that," I tell her. "It's too, too . . . *dangerous*." Then I purse my lips and look off into the distance as though I'm trying not to cry.

That does it for Aunt Midge. She is frothing at the mouth with curiosity. "Janey, tell her you won't tell anyone. Swear it." Her voice is authoritative enough that even I would obey—so I know reliable Janey will do as she says. She nods.

"Fine. I won't tell anyone. But I still think you could go to the police."

I wait another moment for the anticipation to build even more, then take another swig of cold coffee. When I've swallowed, I look straight at them and deliver the clincher.

"I killed a man," I wail, and burst into tears. In the ensuing shocked silence, I congratulate myself on my diabolical brilliance.

JANEY

"Do not make loon soup."

—recipe for loon soup, from *The Eskimo Cook Book*, 1952

"Oh for Pete's sake." Despite her so-called frailness, Aunt Midge leaps off the sofa with great indignance. "Would you listen to this horseshit?" she asks me. "I'm sick of these lies."

Aunt Midge storms into the sunroom and, like a bolt, Nean follows her. I trail behind them both, forgotten but nonetheless dying of curiosity.

"No, wait," says Nean, chasing after Aunt Midge. "It's true. It wasn't on purpose, but, but . . ." She slows and begins to falter. "But I *had* to do something to stop him . . ." then she collapses onto the love seat and buries her face in her hands. Her shoulders begin to shake.

I want to cross over to her and take her in my arms. It's the damnedest thing: I hate this woman, truly. She's ruining everything for Aunt Midge and, by extension, for me. She stole all our stuff, which includes my cookbooks, and trapped us for the night in this house without any real food or personal belongings. Then she stormed her way back in and went to great trouble to keep us from signing our deed, effectively trying to steal the house right out from under us. But I have learned this in the five years since the shyness took over: the one thing that can overcome my fear of people is someone more pathetic than me. I blame this on some quirk of female biology—I would probably try to pet an injured grizzly bear if I got the chance.

I look at the shuddering creature on my—yes, my—couch and then to Aunt Midge, hoping she'll somehow give me permission to just temporarily befriend the enemy, calm her down, stop her crying. She looks back with hard eyes and shakes her head firmly, and I sigh.

But then Aunt Midge looks back at Nean, or rather Nean's scalp, since all that is visible of her in her miserable state is the top of her head and her two little fists clenched over her eyes. Aunt Midge's mouth opens in a little *o*, and she walks toward the sofa. "What happened to your head?" she demands, when she is standing right over her.

Nean's weeping slows to sniffles, and she lifts her face up to imposing Aunt Midge. "What do you mean?" she asks, her voice thick.

"There are patches of bare scalp, did you know that?" I dart my eyes to Nean's head. Sure enough, there are missing chunks of hair right at the crown. "Are you sick?"

Nean instinctively moves her right hand up to touch her hair and I see for the first time that it's covered in ugly cuts. They're old and half-healed, but nonetheless in the bright natural light I can see lacerations all over the knuckles and cascading down the back of her hand. Aunt Midge sees it too. She grabs Nean's hand in hers and yanks it closer, squints. "Janey, get my glasses."

I obey and bring them to her, and take the opportunity to sit down next to Nean and rest one hand on her back. "What happened to you?" I ask softly, while Aunt Midge is peering through her readers at the injuries on Nean's hand.

Nean trains her eyes on my face. She's watching me closely, sizing me up. I try to look open to whatever it is she has to tell me.

It must work because words start to spill out of her. "It was self-defense," she says. "When they announced my name in the sweepstakes, he got so upset. He'd been drinking, and he . . . he didn't want me to leave him, to come here. He said I had to be with him forever. I could never leave him, or he'd kill me. I was so scared . . ."

Aunt Midge sits down on the other side of her and grabs her knee. "And? And?"

"I just knew I had to get away from him. He was so strong. If I didn't escape then, I never would. It was the only way."

Aunt Midge gasps and covers her mouth with one hand. Her eyes are in danger of popping out of her skull. "Nean?" she asks, her voice barely above a whisper. "Did he hurt you? Did he do this to your hair?" She sounds dramatic enough for the Lifetime network, but she's asking what I want to know too.

Nean nods in solemn silence.

"And did you hurt him back?" Aunt Midge asks, leading her down a scary path.

Nean nods again.

"Did you kill him, Nean?"

Nean lets out a wail and curls her legs into her body like a child, not answering. There's no need.

"It's okay," Aunt Midge singsongs. "It's okay. Whatever happened, it's over now."

Nean says nothing coherent, but the crying slows a little. "I didn't mean to hurt him," she says at last, in a quiet little voice I haven't heard from her before. "He wouldn't let me come here, and I just wanted to be free. . . . It was so awful . . ." She seems to be regaining her composure as she speaks.

"I know, sweetheart," says Aunt Midge. She rubs Nean's back comfortingly and Nean falls into her shoulder. Still reeling with shock, I try to ignore a twinge of jealously at Aunt Midge's tenderness but fail miserably.

After a moment, Nean sits up. "So you see why you can't tell the police anything?" she asks, suddenly all business. "I don't know what happened after I left . . . if they found him . . . if they know it was me . . ." she chokes up a little again. "I just have to find someplace safe to hide for a little while. That's why I was so desperate for this house. I can't go back there and there's nowhere else to—"

Nean is interrupted by the sound of car wheels on a gravel driveway.

All three of us jerk our heads toward the front windows and gasp a little like we've been caught at something illicit. Which maybe we have. What if it's the police? What if they've figured out what happened to Nean's boyfriend and are coming after her—and us too, for harboring a fugitive?

Suddenly I feel red-hot angry. If Nean is telling the truth, I do feel sorry for her, really I do. But she should have gone to the police right away, not come up here and put her problems on my aunt and me. If we're in trouble somehow for letting her stay here . . . I clench my fists, hating all the grouchy energy surging through me like too much sugar on a hot day.

While I think these bitter thoughts, we sit frozen like woodland creatures while we wait for something to happen. When we hear nothing further we all start to relax and turn back to each other. And then the doorbell rings.

I look at Aunt Midge. "The doorbell plays 'La Cucaracha'?"

She just shrugs, like this is the most natural thing in the world. "You go answer it. If it's the police don't tell them anything."

The walk to the door feels like the green mile. When I get there I peer out the side windows and smack my forehead in the universal sign for "duh" when I realize who it is.

"It's Noah," I hiss to the other two.

"Who?" asks Aunt Midge, too loud as ever.

"The guy who brought Nean back last night. Maybe he can give her a ride back into town." I unlock the deadbolt with relief, more than ready to see the back of this girl and all the drama she's brought with her.

"Like hell he can," I hear Aunt Midge say as I'm opening the door, and my stomach drops. Behind me, her comment has scared the poop out of me, and, in front of me, Noah is standing there looking really, really good in the same thing he was wearing yesterday, only now his shirt is unbuttoned and a fresh white crewneck T-shirt shows through. Blue jeans and white cotton. My mouth goes dry. I motion into the house and try to figure out what to say. "Come in?" I finally try.

"Good morning," he says, sounding as jovial as ever, but he doesn't actually step inside, hovering instead right in the doorframe. "Muddy shoes," he tells me, and I nod, following his easy gesture down his body to his work boots. I am distressed to find that he looks just as rugged and charming in the daylight as he did in the dark. "How was the houseguest?"

At the mention of Nean, my head snaps around and I see that the woman in question is no longer in view. Aunt Midge has probably spirited her away someplace, possibly under the floorboards or in a secret passage behind the bookcase. This is not good.

"Um . . ." I try to focus on the braided rug on the floor and not my aunt or Noah. "She's just fine?" Well. That didn't sound authoritative at all.

Aunt Midge pipes up and crosses the foyer to Noah. "Good morning! We haven't met. I'm Janey's Aunt Midge. Janey tells me you were a big help with our U-Haul?"

Noah smiles and shakes her offered hand. "Well, I did think there was something odd about the situation when I found her by the side of the road. After all, even in Maine most people wear pants for long drives."

Aunt Midge waves an arm in front of her face and goes into full bluster mode. "Oh, ha ha ha, well, no, nothing odd, just a silly miscommunication. She was taking the truck out to fill it up with gas for us, but we didn't realize just how low the tank had gotten. Silly old me, I forgot to explain the situation to Janey."

Noah looks from me to Aunt Midge and back, eyebrows raised. "I see," he says at last, clearly not buying her nonsense anymore than he should. "But I thought there had been some sort of mix-up over the ownership of this house?"

Aunt Midge chuckles. "Oh, it's the funniest thing." I narrow my eyes at her. I haven't been laughing. "Another miscommunication. My fault! I really need a fresh set of hearing-aid batteries." She puts a finger to her eardrum, where a hearing aid would go, if she had one, which she doesn't. I cast my gaze heavenward. The woman has ears like a bat, when it serves her.

Noah furrows his brow. "That is funny."

Aunt Midge does another one of her creepy forced laughs. "Oh, ha ha ha! Isn't it just? No matter, it's all sorted out." My mouth pops open in surprise.

Now Noah looks truly perplexed. He must think we're crazy people. "It is?"

"Oh yes. There's a perfect solution, you see. She's moving in with us."

My heart stops and I grab Aunt Midge by the arm and drag her out of the hallway. "She's doing what?" I hiss the moment we are out of sight. Anger is pushing on the backs of my eyes, hotter and hotter.

Aunt Midge looks at me like I'm the one being ridiculous. "Don't get your knickers in a bunch," she says in full volume, as if Noah isn't ten feet away wondering what the hell is wrong with us. "We'll just let her stay here until she's back on her feet and the heat has died down."

"The *heat*?!"

"Well, would you rather turn her in and let her rot in jail?"

"She's not going to rot in jail. It was self-defense," I whisper.

"Is that a chance you're willing to take?" she asks.

"Yes."

"Well, *I'm* not sending the poor thing to Sing-Sing," she tells me. I resist the urge to point out that Sing-Sing is a long way from here, and a men's prison. "And besides, we have plenty of room. It'll be fun."

I think living with a woman who might at any time steal my car sounds about as much fun as snake handling. Not to mention the fact that, God help me for being skeptical, but her story does seem awfully convenient considering. I mean, if it were really true, wouldn't she have avoided trouble at all costs, rather than risk us going to the police? Although, something has to explain the clumps of missing hair and bloody knuckles . . .

I turn away and walk further into the house, buying a moment to think. Is Aunt Midge right? Should we do the neighborly thing and house her until a better solution comes around? I press my eyes tight and a vision of Ned comes to me, as it often does when I'm feeling steamrollered. I ask him for help but he doesn't move or do anything besides pose there in the front of my brain in his blue parka and ski goggles, and I know in my heart that it's Ned from a vacation photo I kept of him. Not real, alive, dynamic Ned from my memories, but a flat image that's beginning to replace them.

I open my eyes and level my best glare at Aunt Midge. "No," I say. "She is not staying here." But though I say that, I have already capitulated. I am just putting up the appropriate level of fight now, an "I told you so" worth of struggle in case I need to point it out later.

Aunt Midge knows this—I guess she can read it on my face. "Just for a little while," she says, her voice now gentle and warm. "We'll be three women against the law, just like Thelma and Louise and . . . Brad Pitt. Think of it this way: she's one more person for you to cook for." She turns away from me, discussion over, and marches into the foyer where Noah has undoubtedly been listening all this time.

"Son, you willing to give my niece a ride to our truck? We'd like to start getting unpacked and settled in."

"Of course, ma'am," he says in a way that makes it impossible to tell if he's been charmed by her old-lady wiles and is eating out of her hand or if he's just obliging to get out of this crazy house. "You sure you don't need me to drop off Nean anywhere?"

Yes! I think from the hallway, wishing for telepathy or at least the guts to say what I want. *Yes, get her the hell out of here and leave me alone in my fancy new kitchen so I can try out my new recipe for All-Day Bolognese.* But I don't actually say anything, and Noah doesn't seem to be able to read my mind. I come round the corner and Aunt Midge is giggling and telling him she'd like to hire him to help us move our stuff in, all the while feeling his biceps like a sixteen-year-old cheerleader. I sigh and go look for Nean to tell her the good news.

Thirty minutes later I am riding toward our U-Haul in a slightly odiferous Honda Accord built in the year of the Lord's birth. The Maine landscape is a dense one, and the moment we pull away from the house, all sights, sounds, and especially sweet smells of the ocean drop away and I find myself looking out at a forest that looks not unlike the sort you'd find in Iowa, except with a few more evergreens. This is home now, I tell myself. Soon I'll get a car and find a job sewing hems somewhere, and it will be just like Cedar Falls, only with a much nicer, much larger kitchen. No big deal. Normalcy is returning, I promise myself.

Except for the fugitive houseguest. And the fact that I am trapped in a vehicle with a stranger. Noah and I haven't said a word to each other since we got in the car, which is just fine with me. He is a good arm's length away from me, plus we've got a gear shift and two broken cup holders to keep us apart, and I thank the gods that he isn't driving the beat-up pickup truck with the slidy bench seats that I thought all mountain men were issued at age sixteen. If he were, I would probably have to jump out of the moving vehicle.

Since Ned died I have not been in a car with a man. Period. I haven't really been in the car with anyone besides Aunt Midge and this hyper-attractive blond girl from Wedding Belles Too whose VW Bug was always in the shop. She didn't make me nervous; she made me sad. Now it's been ten minutes of riding in a car with Noah, and I am already neck to toe in little-bitty hives. I know they are going to show above my V-neck T-shirt when they mature in a few minutes. I rest my hand over my neck as subtly as I can until I realize it might look like I am rubbing the place where a dog collar once was. Wearing a collar has to be weirder than getting hives around strangers, so I drop my hand and go for the lesser of two humiliations.

"You're flushed," says Noah. My hand goes right back up to my neck without my telling it to. "Is it too hot in here?"

Cool air sounds like a wonderful idea, so I nod and he starts rolling down his window with an old-fashioned crank. I do the same and feel fresh piney air fill the car. "Better," I say, hoping the redness in my cheeks will go down now.

"We're not far from where she left the truck," Noah says. "Maybe five more minutes. It's actually kind of a lovely spot, in the daytime. The road gets close to the bay, and you can see the sailboats coming by."

I nod again. But now my head is filled with thoughts of standing arm in arm with Noah on the banks of the bay watching the boats go in and out. God, where did that come from?

"I know it's none of my business," he goes on, and my stomach clenches at those words, "but Nean seems kind of fishy."

I tilt my chin to him. I'm loathe to voice the persistent doubt I feel about the whole situation to him but am actually kind of pleased that he saw through Nean's blustering. "Well . . ." I say at last. "It's complicated." Then I start coughing. It's just a few gentle "excuse me" coughs at first, and then my lungs start heaving like a TB patient's.

Noah turns his eyes from the road to me, looking deeply concerned before turning his head back to drive. "Hey, are you okay?" In response I keep coughing. It's more of a hack now. I feel like I have something in my throat, but I haven't even eaten today. What could it be? Am I choking on my own spit?

I try to answer him, tell him I'm fine, but I can hardly get air in. My throat is burning now and I feel my head getting lighter. Yes, I'm actually choking on my own spit. Or not even spit. Drool from sitting in the same car as an attractive man. What the hell is wrong with me?

"I've got some water in the trunk," Noah says. "I'll pull over." I nod frantically. I feel like I'm going to pass out. I keep rasping out a cough and start to wonder which will take me faster—death by choking or by embarrassment.

Noah pulls over and pops out of the car with vigor. I crane my head around to see the trunk pop up and notice for the first time that his backseat is littered with detritus. It looks like he's ready for Armageddon, considering what he has back there. Blankets, pillows, two thermoses, and a bargain box of peanut butter crackers. Is he one of those lunatic survivalists like they have in Montana? Great. First man I've been attracted to in umpteen years and he's preparing for the rapture. That figures.

While I'm taking inventory of the unholy mess, the trunk slams and I spin back to my door and open it, try to get out before I realize I'm still buckled in. Before I can unlatch myself, Noah comes to my side of the car and does it for me. Just reaches down right by my hip and feels around for the seat belt button and presses it. Though he never touches me, I feel the warmth of his hand, moving past my thigh, loosing the belt, and guiding it out of my way. While he's doing this I freeze completely—even stop coughing, stop trying to breathe. Nothing moves and there is no sound.

But as soon as I'm free and he pulls his arm away, I'm back to the gasping wheeze, and he hands me out of the car and gives me a water bottle and starts whacking me on the back with vigor. I make him stop long enough for me to get a good drink of water in, and finally my throat relaxes and my lungs stop seizing. A few more shuddering coughs and slow sips of water and then I'm done, coughing fit over. My breathing goes heavy and panting, and I realize with some disappointment that I'm going to live and thus must face Noah again. My chest caves and I slouch my way over to an old rock wall on the side of the road and sit down, dropping my head between my legs to keep from passing out.

The view from down here is somewhat obstructed, but I still see Noah's shoes moving toward me, then his legs lining up to sit on my left. I feel him put his hand gently on the small of my back and move it upward very softly, to the space between my shoulder blades, and then back down again. My breathing starts to return to normal. My heartbeat starts to slow to the rhythm of his hand.

We sit there like that for a very long time. I am wondering if I can stay still long enough to just die and decompose on the spot, without ever having to look at Noah—my savior from death by choking on nothing—in the face again. Noah is probably wondering what the hell is wrong with me. But he just keeps gently rubbing up and down, never going any lower or higher than the little pathway he's marked out on my back. It feels really good. I wouldn't mind dying right here, right now, I decide.

But Noah seems determined to make me live. He takes me by the shoulders at last and pulls me upright and says softly, "You okay?" And when I nod, he says, "you sure?" and I nod again. Then he looks me right in the face and I go red from forehead to shoulders and wish I could plunge my face in a bucket of cold water.

"You're really shy, aren't you?" he says.

I nod. Suddenly I feel like crying.

"Huh." He scratches his beard and looks at me inquisitively. "Usually beautiful girls are too confident."

To my horror, I lean over the back of the wall and throw up.

PART TWO

Simmer

NEAN

"Anyone can cook, and most everyone should."

—MARK BITTMAN,
How to Cook Everything

"So I heard you barfed on the mountain man." It's been a day and a half since Janey and Aunt Midge decided I could stay, and I'm starting to feel a little bolder. After all, I did help them move in yesterday and carried a metric ton of groceries into the house this morning. They're getting their money's worth out of me, that's for sure.

Janey looks offended and embarrassed when I bring up Noah. But then, that's her usual expression. "I didn't barf *on* him," she says, as if this is a crucial distinction.

"Whatevs. I'm just saying it's probably not the sexiest thing you could have done in that situation."

"I am not trying for sexy," she huffs. Well, that's a good thing. "Pass me the olive oil."

I am sitting on the countertop in the far corner of the kitchen, using my heels to push a lazy Susan cabinet below me back and forth, back and forth, while I watch Janey cook. The kitchen is luxe as hell, just miles and miles of granite and stainless steel as far as the eye can see. I like the way the pot rack dangles from the ceiling on thick brass chains, like a chandelier, only instead of lightbulbs and crystal, it's sparkling with copper pots and pans. The TV in the fridge is tuned to the Food Network on mute, and on screen an impossibly thin middle-aged woman is pretending to enjoy a cannoli. The closed captioning marching across the bottom of the screen reads "Mmmm." But the look in her eyes says "Cut away from me, dammit, before I accidentally swallow!"

"How many calories are in a cannoli?" I ask.

"What?" says Janey. I notice that when she is in the kitchen she only half listens to anyone. "In a cannoli? How would I know?"

"Well, you're the food diva. Look at you," I say, gesturing to the massive pile of flour she's made into a little volcano on her wooden cutting board. "You're making pasta *from scratch*."

"How else would you make it?" she asks.

"Seriously?" I look at her to see if she's joking. She smiles enigmatically, and I put my head in my hands in mock exasperation. "I'll tell you what. If you're very, very nice to me, I will show you how to make a little thing called Kraft macaroni and cheese. It's my specialty." I wiggle my fingers a little to show the specialness.

Janey raises an eyebrow. "I'll pass. But if you like macaroni and cheese, I'll make my grandmother's recipe for you tomorrow night. Six kinds of cheese, and bacon too. It's got tomatoes though, so you're going to have to stomach some vegetables."

Janey apparently thinks I'm a twelve-year-old boy. "I'll survive," I say, and go back to watching her work. She's got this relaxed thing going on that I don't usually see from people in the kitchen, like she could stand there all day playing with the flour and not care whether or not a meal ever got cooked. How different from her usual scared squirrel imitation.

There are three big brown eggs standing on the countertop, and she picks up one and walks over and hands it to me. "What do you feel?" she asks me.

"Nothing," I say. "An egg."

"What temperature is it?"

"It's no temperature. I mean, it's the same as the air."

"Right. So it's ready to be used." She plucks the egg out of my hand

and whacks the hell out of it on the granite countertop next to me. I'm thinking we're having floor eggs now, but instead she somehow keeps the fractured shell shut tight until she's right in the lava pit part of the flour volcano, where she opens the egg and lets it slink down like a drunken cowboy through swinging saloon doors. And of course she does all this with one hand. I haven't seen someone cook this fancy since I washed dishes at the hibachi restaurant in Waterloo. Two more eggs go into the volcano, and then she whips out a fork and starts beating the yolks as if she were using a real bowl with hard sides. I watch the eggs turn golden yellow all over and then fade lighter and lighter as they start to gobble up the dry flour, until she has a pale dough exactly the color of a downy chick. She smudges it around her board a few times until it's a respectable rectangle and then turns her back to the dough and leans back with her messy hands on the counter and looks at me. "It's resting," she tells me.

"Should we keep our voices down, then?" I ask her facetiously.

She raises an eyebrow at me. "If you could refrain from speaking entirely, I think that would be best."

I smile. In the three days I have known Janey Brown, she has been funny exactly twice and both times it has delighted me. I'm not an idiot—I know she can't wait to see the back of me. For two women with the same name, we could not be more different. But there is something about her that makes me wish I could make her like me. I wish I knew what it was, so I could actively ignore it.

"Have you ever peeled a tomato before?" she asks me, her mind already on the next thing. I shake my head. "What about knife skills? Can you chop?" I shake my head again.

"Peel garlic?"

"Nope."

"Have you ever cooked *anything* that didn't come in cardboard?"

"Not a thing," I say. She does that thing where she twists her lips around and juts her chin to the left. Her thoughtful face. I'm getting pretty good at reading her.

"Maybe . . ." She takes her apron off and begins tying it around my waist as I sit on the counter. "Hey!" I say. No one said anything about kitchen duty.

"I know you are going to be leaving soon." *Gulp.* "But until then, you will bake," she announces. "That is what people who cannot cook must do. Hop down."

For a moment I hang there, resistant to the idea that I should have to do anything at Janey's request. But I have to do something useful if I want to win her over. Something besides help Aunt Midge cheat at crossword puzzles. I jump down.

"Bakers start with cookies," she tells me when I'm standing in front of her. "Go into the pantry and find a bag of Toll House chocolate chips. The bag will tell you what to do. When it comes to chocolate chip cookies, the bag is always right."

That night, I belly up to the dinner table like I'm part of the family, setting myself a place and helping myself to a generous serving of wine. Eyebrows raised, Janey serves a ridiculously good meal of fresh pasta, which tastes like regular pasta only more so, and a plate of tomatoes and mozzarella drizzled with something tangy. I notice she eats hardly at all, maybe three or four bites, and when I say something to her about it, she tells me she is saving room for my cookies.

I love cookies, don't get me wrong, but I am stuffing myself to the gills now and worrying about them later. Long after Janey and Aunt Midge have set down their forks I am still going. There is a salty, almost meaty cheese dusted down over the top of the pasta that I could eat by the bushel and strings of very thin sliced ham running through the noodles that tastes like some kind of super-bacon. When it starts hurting to swallow, I push back from the table and groan a little bit.

"I take it you were hungry," says Janey drily, but I can tell she's pleased. "If you like it that much, I can put a little away for you to snack on tomorrow."

I look at the big blue pasta bowl in the middle of the table, still heaped with enough food for at least two more people. "What else would you do with it? There's tons left."

Aunt Midge laughs, and it's kind of a weird barking sound. "Same thing she always does. Tosses it out so she can start from scratch to-morrow."

I look back and forth at both of them to see if they're joking. "Seri-ously?"

Janey nods. "I hate leftovers," she says.

"But that's crazy. There's *tons* of food left. Delicious food. And it took so much work."

Janey shrugs.

"Come on," I say. "I watched you actually shell the freaking peas. Peas that you can buy frozen for a buck ninety-nine, you shelled by hand instead. It took you *hours*. I'm pretty sure people stopped shelling peas at home around the time of suffrage." Aunt Midge laughs at this. She's such a good audience, for a bitchy old broad. "You can't just throw away all your hard work."

"Well, it won't keep forever, and besides, I've already planned out tomorrow night's dinner."

"And the night after that," adds Aunt Midge.

"Maybe I have," says Janey. "I like to cook," she tells me. "I like shelling peas." She stands up and starts clearing our plates.

"Aunt Midge, is this true?"

Aunt Midge nods her head, clearly long resigned to her niece's bi-zarre behavior. "She cooks like this all the time. Everything from scratch, big elaborate dinners. Sometimes she feeds me, but most nights she just eats what she wants and tosses the rest."

"That's not true," interjects Janey, and I am relieved for a moment, until she goes on. "In Iowa, I didn't have time to cook every night, because of my job. It was maybe one night a week, two, tops."

"That's two nights a week too many," I say.

"That's what I told her," says Aunt Midge.

"Think of the waste! Why don't you just make smaller quantities?" I ask.

Janey stops loading the dishwasher and gives me a hard look. "Because I don't."

Whoa. Guess I won't go there. She straightens up from the dishwasher and returns to the table for more dirties. Absentmindedly I've been scraping and stacking bowls and plates and silverware in neat piles while we talk, and I hand her a stack now and she smiles at me. "Thanks."

"You're batshit," I tell her in response. "This is the craziest thing I've ever heard."

"Coming from you, that means a lot," says Janey. She comes back from the sink and moves to pick up the serving bowl of pasta. Before she can, my hand shoots out and grabs the rim tightly.

"Don't touch that," I snap at her. I yank it closer to me on the big wooden table and wrap both arms around the bowl like I'm cradling a baby. This close to the food, my nose fills up with the smells of cheese and sharp ham and butter again and I find myself wondering if I can eat the entire rest of the bowl myself. "You'll throw away this food over my dead body."

Janey tilts her head at me like I've gone mad and shrugs. "Okay. Suit yourself. Eat until you explode if you want to. Just don't clutter up my fridge with leftovers that are just going to go to waste. Need I remind you that your stay here is temporary?"

I roll my eyes. "How could I forget?" But I'm not thinking about my tenuous housing situation for once. I'm thinking about the food. Cooking up a plan, if you will.

Janey pulls out a pair of thick rubber gloves from the pantry and grabs the bucket of pea shells and then fishes around in the fridge for a few moments and pulls out a large tub with opaque plastic sides and a tight-fitting lid.

"What's that?" I ask her.

"A little something from the bait shop," she answers, and then turns the tub around until the words WORMS LARGE written in black Magic Marker face forward. "I'm going to go try to get that composter going. Wanna help?"

Well. Clearly she wants to be alone. "Um, no thanks. Knock yourself out."

She disappears with her slimy friends through the kitchen door, saying, "Oh, and don't let me forget we need to get a deadbolt on this door," as it closes behind her.

"We wouldn't want any more unexpected visitors, would we?" Aunt Midge turns to me, watching as I eyeball the huge bowl of pasta warily. "So, are you planning to eat until you die of gluttony?"

I laugh. "Hardly, although I can think of worse ways to go. I'm thinking. . . . There's got to be a little shelter around here somewhere that would take in a few extra hot meals every night. Maine must have homeless people. We'll just divide everything she cooks into two portions: one to eat and one to deliver." I pause, wondering over the logistics of this idea. "What we've got to do is find out if they'd rather have leftovers the next morning or if they want the food the same night, in which case we'll have to persuade Janey to get the meals ready a little earlier so we can deliver the extra before we eat."

She looks at me, a shocked expression on her face. "Of course! Why didn't I ever think of this?"

Maybe because you've never eaten shelter food, I think. "Because I'm a genius. We'll figure out the details tomorrow. For now what the hell am I going to do about all this pasta?" I ask.

Aunt Midge looks from the bowl to me with a new light in her eyes. Is it possible I've earned her respect with just one totally obvious suggestion?

"I'll finish whatever you can't eat. I've been ruining my figure on Janey's leftovers for years."

It turns out Maine has lots of homeless people, or at least enough hungry people to snarf up whatever deliciousness Janey feels like cooking on any given day. The next morning Aunt Midge gets on the horn—her turn of phrase, not mine, I assure you—and strikes up a deal with a place called Hopeful Helpers. The name makes me vomit a little in my mouth, but other than that it sounds like a decent outfit. They run out of a shut-down YMCA twenty minutes from here, providing temporary shelter for men and emergency meals for all comers, plus a food bank. They have some community classes too, vocational and GED-type stuff, and I can tell Aunt Midge is into it because she starts pestering Janey to let her borrow the car they've been renting while waiting to hear about the deed.

When I offer to drive her myself, the two of them look at me like I'm speaking that clicky language from Africa. Bantu. Whatever. They don't want me to drive, I won't drive. I'll just hang out here and watch the grass grow.

While the two of them bicker about what would happen if Aunt Midge got caught driving without a license (I know *I* would like to find out), I go out to the backyard and start investigating the property. In the high late-morning light, the ocean is a lighter color blue than usual, and it's doing that diamond sparkle thing through the scattered birch trees. I gotta hand it to the Home Sweet Home Network, they've got great taste. If I wasn't so jaded, I could spend hours gazing out on this view.

But I am very jaded, and therefore instantly bored. I survey my options. When I stand with my back to the house, I've got the hedges that conceal the endless pool on my left and the burgeoning compost pile on my right, and in front of me is nothing but the kind of dark, shiny cliffs that one would go to if one wanted to commit suicide in a really exciting and messy sort of way. The kind of cliffs that sailors would be lured by sirens to sail too close to, only to reduce their ships to splinters and drown in the churning seas.

It hits me that it's time I scaled those cliffs. I size them up.

Sure enough, there's a sort of staircase of rock that has been knocked into the cliff wall to my right. You have to really be looking for it, but once you see it there's no question that humans put it there. It kind of curls back and forth and looks just treacherous enough to be fun, so I sit down with my butt on the edge of the grass and scoot myself down to the first real "stair" of rock.

From there the stairs are closer together, and I get about fifteen feet down with no problem whatsoever, using my butt-scoot technique whenever necessary. Now the house is out of sight and it's just me and the cliffs and a bunch of seabirds who are squawking like mad on the rock about twenty feet away, feathers flying as they try to get their beaks on a small pile of something interesting. After about twenty minutes, I get to a rock-stair so steep I'm going to have to get down on my belly and lower myself down backward. Past it is a gradual slope that layers right into the water—I am definitely near the home stretch. The ledge gives me pause, but now that I'm this close, I want to go all the way. I want to put my feet in the ocean water to see what saltwater feels like and if it's cold like the Mississippi or warm like Lake Okoboji. I get down on all fours and then lie on my tummy and sort of slither as slowly as I can down the edge to the next tier of rock, using my hands and arms outstretched to drag against the smooth rock and slow the fall down. I end up on my ass, but it's with dignity and only minor abrasions. When I stand up, I pump my arms up and down like Rocky and listen for the roar of the crowd.

The rest of the way to the water is a cinch. Once the rock truly levels out, I leave my shoes, a pair of sneaks I've had since forever, up as high as I can and wander a little closer to the spot where the puny waves meet the rock.

Ten seconds later I'm drenched head to toe. Turns out ocean waves can be all kinds of different sizes. And apparently no one has informed the Atlantic Ocean that it is the middle of June. The water is *extremely* refreshing and I am shivering everywhere. My goose bumps are shivering. I'm having my own private wet T-shirt contest out here and definitely winning in the Nipple Division. It is time to retreat.

Only, my shoes have apparently decided to go surfing. The rock where I had left them high and dry now glistens from a fresh bath. Gah. At least I still have my pants, moist though they may now be. It seems I am learning my lesson one item of clothing at a time.

Shoeless, I make my way back over the sloping rocks until I'm finally well out of the reach of the waves and then take my time picking over the steeper and steeper steps until I'm almost crawling on all fours. Then I reach the big drop off that slowed me down coming here.

Only now gravity isn't on my side. It's just a big wall now, and, though I can definitely get my hands over the top, I can't seem to find anything to grab on to up there. If I could, I could probably get my feet under me and walk myself up high enough to throw my body weight over the ledge. But all I feel is smooth stone in every direction within reach. I'm going to have to go around it somehow, but there don't seem to be that many safe-looking options once I leave the makeshift stairway.

Well, shit. I might have seen this coming. I sit down for a while on the lower step to have a little think about what to do next, then lie down flat on the smooth rock and listen to the ocean. It occurs to me that I'm not smelling the salt and sea as much anymore—finally my nose has gotten accustomed to the briny air, I guess. Too bad; I like that smell. I inhale big through my nose and still manage to get a little whiff of seawater, but mostly I smell the metallic odor of wet rock, like the way old silverware tastes when you are licking it clean of ice cream. I see a few fishies splashing around in the distance and then disappearing into the sparkling waves, and the fishing birds are circling the water again and again in this hypnotizing pattern, and the sun feels so warm on my wet skin that I think about a little nap. Nothing better to do, is there? When I wake up, refreshed, surely I'll figure out a way up from here.

I close my eyes and fall into a weird dream about swimming pools and birch trees.

After a while, one of the trees starts shouting at me. "Hey, hey you!"

In my dream, I tell the tree to leave me alone, but he keeps shouting. "Are you okay?" Finally I wake up. When I see who's really doing the shouting I nearly roll off my rock ledge. It's a scuba diver, fully outfitted in head-to-toe neoprene, stomping around on the rocks below with those ridiculous pink flippers divers wear. His head is nothing but goggles, snorkel, and bright blond hair. It's a regular Jacques Cousteau.

"I'm fine. Just stuck is all," I call down to Jacques. "You don't know how to get up from here, do you?"

"What?" he shouts. "Come on down here, I can't hear for the waves."

Grumble. I am going to lose all the ground I covered. But I scramble back toward the shore anyway. Maybe this guy can go get me a ladder after he gets done hunting for the elusive giant squid or whatever.

When I'm close enough to see blue eyes behind the neon yellow goggles, I repeat, "I'm fine. I'm just stuck—can't get back up to my house."

Jacques looks up at the cliff and then back at me. "You came down here *that* way?" he asks, incredulous.

"Is there some other way I should know about? Besides, there's practically a staircase leading down. Until that one spot." I gesture to where I was napping before and he nods.

"No kidding. Must have been there since the Indians. That would explain the huge leap in the middle. Probably a step washed away over the last thousand years or something. Cool. I thought I had this place figured out, but I never knew about that. And you only got here, what, a week ago?"

I nod, feeling a little intimidated by the network of gossip going on out here. "I guess the house giveaway was pretty big news?" I fish.

"Well, maybe. But I only knew because I had to come in the day after they made the announcement to spruce up the yard a little and turn on the pool. I'm the groundskeeper there. Or I was."

"No kidding! So you know how to get me back up there?"

Jacques looks from me to the huge wall of cliffs between me and the house, and when I follow his eyes even I can't believe I made it down here without severe head trauma. "Well . . ." he says, and then there's a long pause. "Sure. Can you swim?" He looks me up and down and sees the state of my clothes, which aren't dripping anymore at least, and adds. "Or did you just learn the hard way about tides?"

"I can swim," I say. I lived in a Y off and on from ages seven to ten. I swim like a dolphin. "But yes on the tides. They don't have those where I come from."

"Where's that?" he asks.

I think about saying Iowa but rule that out for sheer lack of glamour. "Texas," I tell him. "The landlocked part." How that is more glamorous, I cannot say.

Jacques tilts his head at me and peels off his goggles, revealing a pretty, sun-tanned face with two lighter circles around his eyes like a raccoon's. "You don't have an accent."

Oh great, Jacques is also a detective. "Okay, not Texas," I concede. "But someplace without an ocean. I thought the waves were less, um . . . wavy. That's how my shoes ended up in Davy Jones's locker out there." I gesture grandly to the vast water.

Jacques laughs and then surprises me by unzipping the miles and miles of neoprene that cover him and peeling off the wet suit, starting at his shoulders and working down until the whole shirt part is hanging around his waist.

"Humminah humminah humminah!" I say, as I watch him expose first one tawny muscled arm and then another, followed by a stunning swimmer's chest. "Keep going!" I am kidding, but also not. Thank you, Jesus, for putting this extremely interesting man in my ocean.

Jacques laughs harder. "Well, you're giving quite a show yourself, Miss Wading-in-the-Ocean-in-a-White-T-Shirt." He gestures to my boobs, and sure enough, my little size As are giving an eyeful. I immediately cross my arms in front of me.

"Eyes up, buddy!" I tell him. But I am thinking: take off your pants.

"Yes, ma'am. Here," and then as if I have direct dialed heaven, he starts working at the legs of his wetsuit. Yes! I watch as he gets one leg out, then sigh with disappointment when it becomes clear he's got a pair of swim trunks under his suit. Bummer. He peels the other leg out but I am losing interest fast. Then he foists the whole drippy mess over to me. "Put this on."

"Um?" I say, as I hold the heavy suit at arm's length. "Why?"

"We can swim over to the inlet back there," he points to the left, "and walk up the hill from there—there's a put-in for boats. As impressed as I am by your mountain-goat-style descent, there's no way up from here that doesn't involve at least a mild concussion."

I smile but don't move. "It's going to be too big on me."

"Sure, but it's stretchy. Trust me, the water is pretty cold for a girl from not-Texas, even in June," he wiggles his eyebrows. "I'll snorkel in front so I know where I'm going; you just stay close right behind me. If you feel overcome by waves, grab my leg or something. Do you want these?" he gestures to his silly-looking flippers.

"I think they really will be too big," I answer, zipping my way into the cold wet suit. Just the neoprene on my skin feels like taking an ice bath, so I can't imagine how the water would feel without it. I guess my feet will soon find out.

"Yeah, probably." He looks at me and sees my shivering, I guess, because he stops wading into the water and stands there hip deep, shivering a little himself. "Hey look. I can swim back and get someone to come pick you up on a boat. Wouldn't probably take more than a couple of hours. Or I can—"

I dismiss him with a flip of my hand. "Please. I'm fine. How far is the swim?"

"Not far at all. Three lengths of a pool, maybe four. We can break if you need to."

"I won't need to," I tell him, and then wade into the water to my shoulders and get used to the bobbing sensation of the up-and-down waves, imitating Jacques's relaxed arms-out posture and sticking my butt high to get my float on.

I see him smile at this, and then he waves one arm high and shouts, "Come on!" and we start swimming to the break in the waves, about sixty feet from the shore on a leftward lean. I get a snootful of saltwater at the break, then manage to cough most of it up on the smooth plane that follows and keep a close distance behind Jacques all this time. He swims well, better than me, and doesn't look cold at all, though without this suit I know I'd be suffering. It was pretty sweet of him to give it to me. Plus I got to see his abs.

As I watch his hands dip into the water like seal fins I realize that he must have grown up here. Probably has lived on this coast his whole life. I wonder what that makes him. Extremely rich or part of a fancy old family, maybe? Since he's mowing our lawn, I sincerely doubt it. He must be a native son, living in one of those little houses inland that I saw on the drive here, with the yards full of cars on cement blocks and rusty swing sets. I bet his family is a lot like mine was, before I gave them the old heave-ho. It makes me tingly to think we might be in a similar social stratum. I find myself suddenly wishing I was wearing lipstick.

A few minutes of swimming and I start to understand where we are heading. Though I didn't realize it before, our house is set on a point, and around the side of it the cliffs taper off and mellow into a low easy slope to the ocean. There's even some grass growing on the hill. But it's farther than I'd hoped, and my nose is running like crazy, and the taste in the back of my throat is this salty-vomit flavor that I keep choking on. Jacques keeps swimming like it's nothing, so I keep kicking away, but I'm getting that weeble-wobble in my stroke that you get as you get tired. When we're just thirty feet from the shore I have that sinking feeling, literally, and start grabbing at his leg and sputtering and waving my arms in distress.

Jacques stops and rights his body and swims over to me, where he puts his arms underneath my body and lifts so all I have to do is just float there and recover. He hardly seems to be even moving to tread water, and I'm starting to wonder if this is one of those part-dolphin people from the *Weekly World News*. "How are you doing that?" I ask him after swallowing way too much seawater.

"Doing what? The water is shallow here, I'm just bouncing on my tiptoes."

Oh my God. "What? Why am I trying to swim, then?" I wiggle out of his hold and let my feet reach for the gravely bottom, feeling like a total moron as I find the comforting surface.

"No idea. You okay? I thought maybe you were going to go be with your shoes."

"I'm fine. Let's go, this water is freezing."

Jacques splashes toward shore, shouting, "Told you so!" I half walk, half swim in behind him.

Jacques's name turns out to be John Junior. Seriously. And there is no John Senior. His mom, he tells me during the short walk back to the house, is and always has been wildly in love with the Kennedy family. I understand exactly where he's coming from, considering my middle name is Diana. When I tell him so, he laughs and then looks at me sideways. It is the "is she for real?" look, and I get it all the time. Mostly, I am not for real, but right now I am extremely for real and want J.J. to know this thing we have in common is pure and true.

"My mom shared Lady Di's penchant for bad boys," I explain. And her habit of leaving the kiddos behind to chase after the good life, I think.

"Are you into bad boys too?" J.J. asks, and I get that thrill I get whenever a guy flirts with me. And that tingle of apprehension, too.

"Nope," I call as I race ahead ten feet, energy pumping through me, bare feet smacking on the pavement. "I like *all* boys. Did you do all this gardening?"

By now I am standing at the turn from the main road to that long gravel driveway that leads to the house. J.J. picks up speed into a light jog and joins me there. There are two stands of trees flanking each side of the drive, and then at the base of the trees are flower beds curling around them grandly, welcoming all to the manor. They're really pretty and elaborate-looking, and if he did plant them I'm impressed.

"Sort of," says J.J.

"Sort of how?"

"The network, they brought in a celebrity landscape designer from one of their programs. Some brawny Asian dude. He drew all these maps and plans and whatnot. Then they hired a bunch of local kids, me included, to execute his plans. When it was all done, they kept me on for maintenance. "

"Well, it's beautiful. You did a great job."

He shrugs. "I don't know anything about landscaping." J.J. leans in to examine the leaves of a blue-green plant as he speaks. "I'm just the gardener." He plucks a little black bug off the broad leaf and squishes it between his fingers.

A thought hits me. "I bet they stop paying your salary now that we've moved in, huh?"

Another shrug. "Last week was my final job at this house."

"Who's going to take care of all of this, then?" Besides the expanse of grass to mow, there's got to be about four bazillion flowers to water and prune and whatever. Janey has put out little pots of herbs all over the place but she clearly has no interest in growing anything that she can't cook.

"You, I guess," J.J. says this with a smile. Somehow he already knows this is the last thing on earth that is going to happen.

"I don't think so. I'll talk to Janey. Maybe I can convince her to keep you on."

"Who's Janey?" he asks. "Your mom?"

"Hardly. She's my . . . cousin. Sort of. I'm, uh, letting her stay with me in the house." Oh, this lie isn't going to blow up in my face in a matter of days or anything.

"And it's just you and she up there?" He tilts his head up the long driveway.

How does one explain to a very cute guy with a great body that one has conned one's way into living with a near stranger and the near stranger's great-aunt? Is there a Hallmark card for that?

"It's Janey, me, and Janey's super-old aunt. Her name is Midge. She's actually pretty hilarious." An evil thought hits me and I go for broke. "Hey, speaking of, would you be able to come in pretty early to trim the hedges around the pool one day? Like maybe around six-thirty a.m.? We'll pay you."

J.J. looks at me cross-eyed. "Seriously? Why so early?"

I think quick. "Because that way it would be all done and gorgeous by the time everyone is up and they'd love it so much they'd be sure to hire you permanently. Just this once?" Please, please let him say yes. I fight back the urge to cackle manically.

"Sure." I get one more of his patented shrugs, which are growing more and more adorable. "Whatever you think."

"Cool!" I impulsively give him a big wet hug and then a weird high five too, managing to be both overly touchy and ridiculously chummy at the same time. Whoops.

He gives me another sideways look and echoes, "Cool. I can probably come over on Thursday. I'll see you then?"

"Of course! I wouldn't miss it for the world."

This is a weird answer and his raised eyebrows tell me he thinks so
too. "Oooooo-kay. Well, bye, then." I watch him walk away, his still
dripping wetsuit over one arm, looking both absolutely scrumptious
and completely clueless. I wait until he's round the bend and well out of
sight before I check the corner of my mouth for drool.

JANEY

"However wide ranging our culinary interests,
however sophisticated our palate and talents in the kitchen,
we usually return home for breakfast."

—CHERYL ALTERS JAMISON AND BILL JAMISON,
A Real American Breakfast

This kitchen is a palace. It's the Taj Mahal, and Versailles, and the Hearst Castle all wrapped into one shining shrine dedicated to the culinary arts. I am fairly sure that if I could just be left alone in here to my own devices, I would die and ascend to heaven. Where I would sit at the right hand of Julia Child.

First, there are the appliances. The vast side-by-side fridge that fits everything imaginable twice over. The two ovens, both of which can crank up to 550 degrees in fifteen minutes. The two-drawer dishwasher large enough for a family of seven—no, eight! And the stovetop. Six gleaming gas burners set flush into the counter like it grew right there in the granite. And over the stovetop is the best feature of all: a hood! I have never had a kitchen with a hood before, not ever. When I look at the hood I can actually hear the sound of sizzling meat, searing right there on a big hot grill pan, forming a delicious crisp crust and perfectly rare meat inside. Not filling the room with smoke, not setting off the fire alarm, just sizzling away like it's nothing at all. A big juicy filet, a cast-iron pan, and a healthy wallop of brandy: Steak Diane, sans fire department.

Then there are the countertops. The gleaming blue granite counter-tops extend in every direction, as far as the eye can see. I'm not sure there is anything I know how to cook that could require this much counter space. Maybe if I was making pasta, pie, sushi, and fudge all at the same time—then I *might* use up all the counter space. But it's hard to imagine that scenario coming to fruition, short of my opening some sort of fusion restaurant. And sitting on the countertops are all manner of modern convenience. Food processor, stand mixer, blender, espresso machine. I right away took the bread machine out to the garage where it wouldn't be in the way, along with all the geegaws that the designers spread about to make the place look fancy—iron antler candlesticks, a bamboo cookbook holder, a glass trifle dish full of polished rocks. All things that would be hard to clean if covered in, say, a thin coating of splattered vichyssoise. But I must admit I have been eyeing the pressure cooker with some interest. What would happen, I am wondering, if I put short ribs in there?

I close my eyes and try to think of something I would want in my kitchen but would never go out and buy. Copper pots and pans? Enam-eled Dutch ovens? A diamond knife sharpener? They are all here, and they brought friends. Yes, I suppose I could have bought any of these things for myself in the past out of Ned's life insurance money, but then how would I be sure I had enough in the bank for a lifetime of beef Wellington and paella?

Or, perhaps, more honestly, how would I keep ignoring that money and pretending it—and the reason for it—wasn't there?

Now, for the love of this kitchen and Aunt Midge, I am going to have to crack that nest egg open. Though I have visited every bridal salon in a thirty-mile radius to deposit my résumé, I've received very little actual interest. I have to assume it has something to do with all my stammering. At a little storefront in Damariscotta, the elegant British owner took mercy on me and offered to let me take home a few brides-maid's dresses that need hemming and the straps shortened, but here is no way I can support the two of us (I am not counting Nean, as she will be leaving soon) and pay the enormous property taxes on this house with in-home hemming jobs. I just have to hope that they'll see my good work and hire me full-time. Until then, I might as well enjoy my kitchen.

These thoughts pull me out of bed much too early in the morning. The wood floor in my little bedroom is cold, so I put on my shearling slippers and pad downstairs and find the kitchen exactly as I left it last night. Pristine. The sink is gleaming in the early light and the air smells clean and just a little lemony. The spotless blue counters and matching backsplash welcome me, say, "Good morning, Janey. How about some coffee?"

Thank you very much, Kitchen, I would like some coffee. And maybe some made-from-scratch cinnamon rolls. What day is it?

It's Thursday, I realize with a start. Are you allowed to bake cinnamon rolls on a Thursday? I'm not sure you are. Thursdays are toast, or maybe a bowl of oatmeal if you're ravished. Nobody makes cinnamon rolls on a Thursday. It's against the laws of nature. I really need to find a job soon, or I'm going to lose all hope of order in my life.

As if to prove my point, Nean materializes out of nowhere. It's not even 6:15 a.m. and the wanted woman I'm living with is awake. These last few days since we've given her the okay to stick around, she's slept until noon and then come into the kitchen to eat everything that isn't nailed down. But today the sun is barely up and she is standing in the wide entrance to the kitchen, wearing see-through cotton shorts and a skin-tight camisole. Her hair is sticking out in weird angles all over the place, including in front of her eyes. She yawns.

I'm annoyed. I was just about to commune with my new kitchen. In private. Maybe she will just get a glass of water and go back up to bed. Maybe she will go outside and be hit by a truck.

"Is there any coffee?" she asks.

"No," I say. But I am holding a mug of coffee, plain as day, hot enough that the steam and fragrance are wafting all over the place like a Folgers advertisement. She ignores me and shuffles over to the coffeemaker to help herself. Then she crosses to the fridge and takes out the cream, sniffs it, and then pours half a cup into her mug so it is roughly the shade of a camel. *Now go away,* I think.

"Whatcha making?" she asks.

"Nothing. Go away." I am irritated just looking at her.

"The oven's on."

So it is. I might have preheated it just a little, just in case someone needed some muffins or a frittata in a hurry. Definitely not for cinnamon rolls.

"I'm cleaning it." I am a terrible liar.

Nean crosses over to the top oven and looks at the setting. "It's not set to 'clean.' It's set to three fifty." she says. "Are you baking something without me?"

"What do you mean without you? This is *my* kitchen."

"You said you were going to teach me how to bake, remember? When I made those cookies?"

I roll my eyes heavenward. "I said no such thing."

"It was implied."

It's interesting that the person who is most annoying to me in the whole entire universe is also the person who shares my first and last name. "Go away," I say. It comes out really whiney and petulant.

"Come on. Just let me watch. Think how handy it would be if I could bake things for you."

Huh. She has me there. I love to cook, and cooks need baked goods from time to time, but I don't actually love to bake. I like slopping and stirring and tasting and the smell of warming olive oil. I do not enjoy trying to figure out whether the item in my canister marked FLOUR is all-purpose bleached, all-purpose unbleached, cake, bread, or pastry flour. Good bakers use things like scales and pH strips and know what's in cream of tartar. They are always standing around holding a pizza peel and looking world-weary. I eye the wall next to the oven, where an alder pizza peel hangs like wall art, then picture Nean, stooping over a 450-degree oven at five a.m., sweating and tired, hair covered in flour.

"Fine. We're making cinnamon rolls, but then you have to leave me alone." It's a win-win, I tell myself. "This might take awhile."

Cinnamon rolls use a yeast dough, so I take out the jar from the fridge and get Nean going on blooming. She stares at the Pyrex glass of

warm water and yeast like she expects ducklings to hatch, and when I
get that warm bakery smell that tells me the yeast are alive and ready to
start their belching, I show her how to add them to the flour, and then
the eggs and butter and buttermilk and absolutely embarrassing amounts
of sugar. I give her the option of the stand mixer but she wants to knead
by hand, so I set her to it on the large butcher block island and get a
bowl oiled up for the dough to rise in.

She is just calling me over to check the dough's elasticity when I
hear a piercing series of screams from the other side of the house.
They're coming from the sliding glass door that leads to the pool. I race
across the house in a panic, imagining as I run that Aunt Midge is
drowning in the pool or has gotten her hair caught in one of those current jets or is otherwise deeply endangered.

So when I stop suddenly in the open sliding glass door and see her
standing up on her own two feet unscathed and clutching a towel to her
breast I am greatly relieved. Whatever has happened, she still has all
four appendages. It can't be that bad.

"What is it? What happened?" I ask.

Aunt Midge utters another piercing cry in response, so I make a
move toward her, but before I can get very far she rushes over to me and
pushes us both inside the house. "Close the door! Lock it!" she tells me.
"There's a perverted ax murderer out there!"

Well, I didn't expect her to say that. "What?"

"A man with a chain saw!" She is panting hard and shivering at the
same time, so I try to get her robe wrapped around her, but it is hard
with her dramatic hand gestures. "He came out of nowhere! He must
have been peeping on me while I was swimming! Naked!"

I am looking at my great-aunt naked right this moment, and something about this scenario strikes me as odd. "Are you sure?" I ask her. "I
don't see anyone out there."

"He ran for it when I started screaming." She grabs my shoulders
and shakes me hard. "I think he was planning to slice me up with his
chain saw, and now he's still out there somewhere!" A theatrical silence
falls.

And then the doorbell rings. La Cucaracha, again. We have to find out how to change that if we're going to keep having these dramatic moments.

"That must be him!" Aunt Midge cries. "Where do we keep the shotgun?"

I look at her sideways. "We don't have a shotgun—that I know about. I'll go see who it is. This is probably some big misunderstanding . . ."

Aunt Midge clutches my arm, terror in her eyes. "Be careful, Janey," she tells me, before roping the sash of her robe tight around her like its a karate belt. "Don't open the door unless it's someone we know. If he threatens you, call the police."

She scoots off, locking windows and doors around the house as she goes. I move to the hallway, preparing myself as best I can for human interaction, but find the door already standing open wide and Nean inviting in a young blond man wearing overalls, holding garden clippers and looking about as dangerous as Mr. Rogers. He is clearly incredibly spooked. This must be our chain-saw murderer. What a relief.

"Holy shit, Nean," he's saying, and I can tell they are not meeting for the first time. "She scared the living daylights out of me. I thought you told me no one would be awake at this hour." Oh, hello. I should have known Nean was involved in this. I step back out of sight.

"I'm so sorry, J.J.! She doesn't usually get up this early," says Nean, and I find myself incredulous at her bald lie. "If I had known she'd be in the pool, I would have warned you to stay clear."

That little capricious . . . bitch! I'm going to take away her cinnamon rolls!

"I was just trimming the hedges like you asked," J.J. continues. "But then I heard someone in the pool and wanted to make my presence known so I didn't scare anyone, you know? So I crawled through to the other side to give the heads up. I had no idea she'd be so . . . *naked*. And she screams so loud . . ." J.J. shakes his head, and I can't help it, I start to giggle at the thought of this strapping suntanned youth innocently emerging through the hedges, garden shears in hand, to find a naked eighty-eight-year-old broad having her morning splash in front of God and everyone. The giggle becomes an unstoppable guffaw as I picture the look on Aunt Midge's face when she told me he had a chain saw, and my hiding spot is exposed. Nean and J.J. come around the corner when they hear me.

Nean sees me trying to hold it in and starts laughing too, and her laugh is loud and snorty, and only makes me laugh harder, so Aunt Midge comes into the front hall to see what on earth is going on. She takes one look at J.J., with his dopey good looks and shocked expression and pretty soon the three of us girls are bent over with tears in our eyes howling. I can't stop giggling and gasping for air until I realize I might actually pee my pants and run off to the bathroom to stop an accident. While I'm in there I hear Nean introducing J.J. to Aunt Midge through chortles and snorts, and J.J. stammering out a heartfelt apology that only makes them both laugh harder.

I'm so overcome by the silliness of it all that I almost forget to be afraid of J.J. Almost. But when I open the bathroom door I feel that familiar hesitance return and wish, not for the first time, that I could be like everyone else. No hives, no stuttering, just one normal person meeting another for the first time.

"J.J., this is Janey," says Aunt Midge between giggles when I emerge. He sticks his hand out to shake mine and I feel my arms start to get prickly. "J.J. is our gardener, Nean tells me."

I keep my arms at my side but give him a nice big smile. I'm sweating uncontrollably, but it's a hot morning. Maybe no one will notice. "Nice to meet you," I say, my voice surprisingly clear.

"Nean tells me he was employed by the Home Sweet Home Network until we won the house. I'm thinking we should keep him on. There's just too much out there for us to take care of on our own, and he knows the place already."

All faces look to me expectantly, and I notice Nean's is especially bright. She's already invested in this J.J. character being around a lot, which makes me want to say no, but the idea of mowing that vast lawn is slightly less appealing than the idea of annoying Nean.

"Sure." I say. "But come the winter, there might not be that much for him to do around here." Not to mention we'll be broke by then.

"No problem," says J.J., very, very quickly. "Let's just plan on me sticking around through August. Then we can take it from there."

Nean grins, and dammit, but her smile is infectious. "Sounds good," I tell J.J., and then excuse myself to the bedroom to put on a long-sleeved shirt and some itch ointment. The hives are killing me. As I leave I hear Aunt Midge tell him he's going to have to stay clear of the tall hedges from 6:00 until 8:00 a.m. "That's when I swim every day," she says, and I smile to myself to think that Nean's been so incredibly busted.

That afternoon, after Nean and J.J. have decimated a tray of cinnamon rolls and wandered off to some nearby put-in to cool their feet in the water, Aunt Midge starts working on me to go into town again. She wants to meet with someone at the homeless shelter about my cooking, but the whole thing makes me very uncomfortable. I'm usually cooking for eight, not for a hundred, and I don't like the idea of these poor people being subjected to tiny portions of whatever it is I feel like cooking that day. More to the point, the whole thing feels like too much pressure.

But there's no talking to her. I give in, making her promise to let me stay in the car, and we head north on the long cape, through the pine trees and past the stone wall where I had my little episode in front of Noah. Just seeing the spot makes my face turn hot with embarrassment, and I find myself hoping that I never see the guy again. It would be more than my epidermis could handle.

After we've been driving about twenty minutes, we pull into a little village called Little Pond. This town isn't quaint like Damariscotta is, and, if not for Aunt Midge the human GPS, I might have driven right past it, it's so small. Its tiny downtown is a crossroads with a stop sign and four bars, one on each corner. There's also a bank, a Pizza Hut, and a little grocery store with about three cars in the parking lot.

Aunt Midge turns to me as we're driving through and says, "World's greatest fried clams."

"Huh?"

"That bar," she says, pointing to a place called the Drunken Sailor that looks absolutely disgusting. "They have a sign in the window."

I look closely and see it: WORLD'S GREATEST FRIED CLAMS. $ 3.50 4.00 There is no visible substantiation for such a claim, nor are there any cars in the parking lot enjoying these famous clams.

"I'm skeptical," I tell her.

"Let's stop. It's lunchtime, and I'm starving. And thirsty."

It is indeed after one and we haven't eaten anything but cinnamon rolls today. I don't like eating out, though. It's one fewer meal for me to cook, and there are usually too many people around, although that's certainly not the issue here.

"I can fry clams," I tell Aunt Midge, though I've never done it before. "I'll pick some up on the way home from that fishmonger near the yarn store."

"I'm hungry now," she says. "And besides, no offense, but are you planning on making the world's greatest fried clams? Because if not, it would be kind of a letdown, don't you think?"

I sigh and pull into the parking lot of the Drunken Sailor. Inside, we find a surprisingly bright, cheery dining room with checkered vinyl tablecloths and faux Tiffany glass chandeliers from another time. My spirits lift. The place is completely empty.

"Sit down anywhere," the pleasant-looking lady at the bar calls, so we move around to a table by the window. As soon as my butt hits the chair she shouts, "You two want clams?"

Aunt Midge looks at me and I nod, so she shouts back, "Two clams. And iced teas too, please." She waits as long as it's decent, then adds, "make mine a Long Island."

I roll my eyes but smile indulgently. "Aunt Midge, are you going to drink yourself to death?" I ask. "You're not getting any younger, you know."

She narrows her eyes at me. "I'm as young as I feel. And besides, I haven't held back from a tipple at any point in my life and look at me. I'm as strong as an ox."

"No denying it. I just want you to stay that way for another thirty years."

"Thirty years?" She shakes her head at me. "In that case I might need two Long Island iced teas."

I'm about to tell her how many Long Island iced teas I'm going to need to get through thirty more years with her when the bell on the door jingles and who should walk in but Noah Macallister. All six feet of handsome and denim. I send a silent prayer of thanks that I haven't had my clams yet. I think of how easily they would come back up if I had.

"Ladies!" he says, as though there is no one in the world he'd rather see. "What a wonderful surprise."

"Well, hello there, Noah!" says Aunt Midge. "Are you having some of these world-famous clams?"

He raises his eyebrows at the phrase and then gives us a big grin. "Well, I believe I am. May I join you?"

"Of course!" Aunt Midge is overcome with delight. I am beginning to think she has a little crush on Noah Macallister. *Too.*

"Hi Noah," calls the woman from the bar. "Same ol'?"

"Actually, Nance, I'll have the clams today, please and thank you." He crosses over to us and sits down next to Aunt Midge. Across from me. My armpits send out a geyser of sweat.

"So what brings you girls to this corner of civilization?" I notice he's dressed almost exactly as he was the last time I saw him, blue jeans, white shirt, long-sleeved button-down open over it with the sleeves rolled to his elbows. I wonder what he does that he can dress like this in the middle of a weekday. Also I wonder when it got so hot in here.

Aunt Midge doesn't know about my little barfing incident, but she seems to understand there's no way I'll be talking and covers my slack. "There's a shelter and a soup kitchen nearby. We were coming in to see if they need any help."

This seems to take Noah aback slightly, and I stop panting and sweating for a moment to consider why that might be.

"What kind of help?" he asks.

"Oh, well," says Aunt Midge. "My niece here's some kind of cook, and I'm an old lady with nothing to do all day. I need a mission, and feeding the hungry's as good as any I can think of."

He smiles at this and I watch his demeanor return to his normal relaxed chumminess. "That's very neighborly of you," he says in an Andy Griffith sort of voice. "I'd be happy to show you there myself after lunch. I work there."

At this revelation, the bar lady shouts "Order's up!" at us, and I see three red plastic baskets and three large soda glasses sitting on the bar directly in front of her, maybe a foot out of her reach. Apparently it is self-service here. I start to stand up, but Noah beats me to it and gestures for me to stay put. "Allow me," he says and gallantly whisks away to fetch us our clams.

In the two seconds his back is turned, Aunt Midge leans over with a wad of napkins in her hands and swabs my dripping brow, God bless her. I'm so busy choking to death on anxiety that I forget what a mess I must look like. "Deep breaths," she whispers. I inhale deeply and try not to hyperventilate.

"Clams, clams, and clams," Noah announces as he returns to the table, arms brimming. I'm expecting little bite-size nuggets, but the baskets are heaped with enormous, squiggly blobs, glistening through their grayish batter with oil and whatever slimy goo clams excrete. I'm not sure I'm going to be able to eat these. I reach for my iced tea and take a huge gulp.

Aunt Midge, fearless as ever, breaks off a small chunk of clam and leans her head back to lower it in. After a long bout of chewing, she lowers her head, and looks back at us. There's a grin on her face. "Mmmugh," she says, and swallows. "Huh! Tastes good!"

I incline my head. Is she serious? Before my eyes she breaks off another piece, bigger. "Hardly chewy at all," she adds, and then gets down to chewing.

"These aren't your basic fried littlenecks," Noah tells us. "They're a variety of long skinny soft-shells called gooey ducks. Nancy cuts 'em down to what *she* thinks of as bite size," he gestures to the tennis-ball-sized chunks, "and lets them rip in the fryer. Like nothing else, I can tell you that."

"Gooey ducks?" I ask, sure I've heard wrong.

"Yep. G-E-O-D-U-C-K," Noah spells. "Gooeyduck. You don't want to see them whole, let me promise you that. Make eels look appetizing." Noah opens wide and plops in a big piece like it's a piece of candy.

My stomach turns over. I start taking the deepest breaths I can muster.

"They taste so . . . *interesting*," says Aunt Midge, still working on her basket with a look of determination. "A little piece of authentic Maine flavor, right here on our table."

"Actually," says Noah, when he's swallowed, "they're West Coast clams. Parts of them are considered delicacies, but these are not those parts. Nancy ships 'em in here frozen, once a week. I guess she figures the locals don't order 'em and the tourists don't know any better."

"Seriously?" she says, and violently pushes away her basket, dropping the clam she was holding like a hot potato. "Then why am I eating these things? They're disgusting."

Noah laughs and laughs at this, and it kills me, that sound, that long low bubbling laugh. It sounds like a hot bath.

"Well," Noah leans in to us, like a conspirator. "You did notice this place was empty, didn't you?"

Aunt Midge looks around in both directions, like she hadn't noticed. "So it is! But *you* came to eat here . . ."

Noah shakes his head. "I did no such thing. I just came in to discuss something with my pal Nancy, but then I saw you in here and . . ." he looks right at me, "suddenly clams sounded delicious."

I melt into a pool of embarrassment under the table.

"Plus," he adds, more lightly, "I was impressed that Janey was up to fried clams, so soon after having that nasty stomach bug."

Aunt Midge slowly turns her head to me. "Stomach bug?"

I go looking for my voice. "I'm not sure what I was thinking," I hear myself say. "As soon as you brought them to the table I took one look and regretted ordering them."

"People do that even when they're not sick," Noah laughs. "You know, Nancy and I go way back. I bet she'll understand if we ask for something else . . . grilled cheese, maybe?"

"Oh please yes," says Aunt Midge, and I nod too, a little fervently. Noah pops up and walks over to Nancy at the bar. Without taking her eyes off the home shopping network, she calls to us, "Couldn't handle the clams, could ya? Tourists." There is quite a lot of disdain in her voice for a woman who has clams FedEx-ed to *Maine*.

She waddles off to the kitchen to get us some grilled cheeses and I heave a sigh of relief.

When our sandwiches come, Noah tells us about the real reason he came in here. He's the "produce guy" for the shelter, he tells us. He runs the Little Pond community farm—the bulk of which goes to the food bank and shelter kitchen—and was here to try to rope Nancy into buying some of their extra produce for the Drunken Sailor. He's tried four times and hasn't had any luck—apparently there are absolutely zero vegetables on the current menu.

"But this morning I saw a huge stand of celery in the garden and got an idea," he leans back and tells us, eyes lit up. "Buffalo chicken wings. All the swankiest restaurants serve buffalo wings with celery on the side, right?"

Nancy materializes at our table. I have to respect her keen hearing. "Go on, I'm listening."

Noah grins, and I know this is exactly how he planned to get her interested. "Think of it, Nancy, dear. Celery." He waves his arms in the air as he paints a picture for her like he's selling her a used car. "How many wings you putting on a plate these days?"

"A dozen," she answers. I notice a little grease glistening on her chin and contemplate the fate of the clams we sent back.

"Make it ten, add a goodly helping of celery stalks, and you've got a fancier dish that costs you less," he says. "You'll save, what, seventeen percent on chicken wings, and the football crowd will appreciate the new gourmet approach and the reduced heartburn."

Nancy snorts. "I don't know about that, but I like the way you think. I could call it the 'lighter side menu.'" I nearly cough up a nose-ful of iced tea.

"Perfect!" exclaims Noah. Then he turns to face Nancy full-on. "I'll tell you what. Buy my celery for one month. If you don't see the glory in it by then, we'll call it a day and I'll stop pestering you about celery for an entire year."

Nancy narrows her beady eyes at this. "I'll bet you only harvest this celery of yours for a month."

Noah opens up his arms and gives her the most adorably disarming shrug I have ever seen. I have the sudden urge to go sit on his lap. "You got me there, you clever thing. But it'll be a good month for wing sales, I can promise you that. And then we can talk *tomatoes* . . ."

"Fine, fine." Nancy waves him off with a smile and a shake of the head. "Go on, you rascal. Take your harem of lovely young ladies and let me watch my show."

Aunt Midge preens at this, and I know now that, despite her dubious menu, Nancy has a new customer for life. And, as much as I try to avoid it, I let my heart soften toward Nancy, just the teeniest bit. I think of all the strangers I've met lately . . . lawyers, cops, bar owners, and, yes, Noah. It seems that in the most isolated place I've ever been, my world is getting bigger.

NEAN

"Ducks and squab are notable for having dark, flavorful breast meat,
abundantly endowed with myoglobin-rich red muscle fibers,
thanks to their ability to fly hundreds of miles a day with few stops."

—HAROLD MCGEE, *On Food and Cooking*

When Janey and Aunt Midge come back from the shelter in Little Pond, they are women on a mission. I am nothing but an innocent bystander, caught in the crossfire of that mission.

"We need bread," says Janey as she stands over the club chair I am draped in at the moment. "Or rather, the shelter needs bread. Four loaves a day." She looks at me expectantly, like that is supposed to generate some response in me besides the course of action I've already decided on, which is to keep watching *Deal or No Deal* repeats until she goes away.

"Uh huh," I say. I am hoping the hairdresser on the show takes the suitcase full of money she's been offered, but I can tell by the greedy look in her eye that she's going to keep playing.

"You're the baker in this house," Janey goes on.

"I made some cookies."

"And cinnamon rolls, which are made with a yeast dough. Just like bread."

"They sell bread at the grocery store, don't they?"

Janey sighs like I've just insulted her mother. "Four good loaves a day would cost a fortune. And besides, baking bread is fun."

"Then you do it," I tell her. Take the deal, lady, I mentally urge the woman on screen. Don't be crazy . . .

"I don't want to do it," Janey says. "I don't like baking. Baking is *your* job."

"I don't want a job," I say quickly, and then immediately realize the mistake I've just made.

Janey jumps on it. "Exactly my point. You want to stay here, rent free, you'll bake the bread. And drive Aunt Midge to the shelter every day to drop it off, along with whatever I cook that day. If you'd rather not, you can get your things right now and I'll drop you off at the bus station."

I raise an eyebrow. That's no way to talk to a woman who's been deeply traumatized after killing her abusive boyfriend in self-defense. Not that I actually am that woman, but nevertheless. Sullen, I turn off the TV. "I'll bake the bread. Jeez. When did you get so bossy?"

Janey shakes her head at me and makes for the kitchen, but my question wasn't rhetorical. When *did* she get so bossy? I liked her better meek and mild.

In the kitchen, Janey is pulling out cookbooks from the tidy shelves that hang near the table. One, called *The Bread Bible*, is bigger than the Actual Bible, and looks equally boring. She plunks it down in front of me where I'm perching myself on a bar stool at the island. "Read and learn," she says, and then turns back to her books like I'm not even there.

I flip open the book and glance at some of the voluptuous photos of bread, then slam it closed. "You expect me to learn how to cook from a book?"

Janey whirls around on me. "Not cook. Bake. And yes. Everything you need to know is in that book."

I sigh. First, because my rule of thumb is that any book with a brown cover is going to be boring. And second, because I was kind of

looking forward to another kitchen tutorial from Janey. The girl is a
social freak, yes, but I kind of like hanging out with her. When it's just
us in the kitchen, she has sort of a calming presence. She's like Mr. Mi-
yagi only with food instead of kicking. I push the book aside.

"Why don't you show me one bread recipe that you like, and I'll
start there. Then when I'm ready to hone my techniques I'll refer back
to the book."

Janey turns to me and then looks heavenward. "Because I'm busy,"
Janey says.

"Busy how? I'm not the only unemployed person in this household."

"Busy cooking. And sewing dresses. And looking for a real job,
which I will find, eventually."

I smile. "Me too. Eventually."

Janey looks at me squinty-eyed. "Sooner than eventually, I hope.
You can't stay here forever."

"I know, I know . . ." I say, but I am thinking, *Why not?* "But not
yet. It's not really practical, right now. I don't have a car or anything
and we're so isolated out here . . ."

Janey thinks on this. "Yeah, we are, aren't we," she says, slowly, and
it suddenly occurs to me that she's looking to justify her life of leisure,
same as I am. "So let's start with baking for now, and we'll worry about
real jobs later." She puts down the book she's been holding—*American
Cookery*, it says on the spine—and walks toward the island where I'm
sitting. "How about we start with a basic French bread—just flour,
yeast, and muscles. Sound good?"

When she's gotten me started with the food scale and I'm deep into
weighing out an enormous pile of flour, she disappears out the kitchen
door for a moment. When she comes back, she's holding a duck. No
really, she's holding a big dead bird, wearing nothing but its goose-
bumpy naked skin, by the neck, like you or I might hold a plunger.

"What is that?" I ask her, forgetting what ounce of flour I'm on.

"It's a duck," she says, as if that explains anything at all.

"I know it's a duck." Okay, honestly, I did think it was a giant
chicken at first. "But where did you get it?"

She tilts her head at me and I know she is trying to translate my human question into her weird chef-y language. "The butcher shop?" she tries.

"Okay, that's a start. But just now. You were standing here with me, and then you left for five seconds, and when you came back you were holding a duck."

"Oh!" she finally understands. "I got it out of the second freezer. You didn't know about that?"

I look at her sideways. Why would I know about that?

"I guess not. I'm defrosting it—the duck, not the freezer," she tells me, and then moves over to the smaller sink right across from me in the island and dumps the poor duck in. It's head spills over the side and looks at me accusingly. "We're having duck and white bean casserole tomorrow."

"Um, that sounds disgusting," I inform her.

"You'll love it," she tells me, and I believe her because so far I've loved everything she's cooked for me. She plugs up the sink and pulls a tray of ice out of the freezer, then another, and carries them over to the sink.

"And what are we having tonight?" I ask, gesturing to the sink. "Duck bill soup?"

"Very funny. Although I think I do have a recipe for that somewhere . . ."

"I'm eating out tonight," I say quickly, and Janey laughs.

"You worry about your bread over there," she tells me as she dumps the ice into the sink, then submerges the duck in water. I watch her add enough salt to choke a deer and then some leaves of something or other and use the duck's head to swish the whole mess around. She's not really allowing the duck much dignity.

When she turns to wash her hands and work on something else, I start over weighing my flour. I work away, mixing flour and a little salt in a big bowl, waiting patiently until Janey seems totally engrossed in another one of her cookbooks. Then I pounce. "So I hear that Noah guy works at the shelter."

Janey's whole body gets rigid and I know I'm on to something here. She turns around slowly. "Where did you hear that?"

"J.J. He told me Noah was the other kind of gardener. The food kind."

"The useful kind," she says with a dreamy smile. Then she straightens up and snaps out of it. "Sounds like you and J.J. did lots of talking."

"Some," I say. A lot, in fact, but I don't want to let her get me off track. "J.J. says Noah just showed up out of nowhere a few months ago, just in time to plant stuff."

"Did he say where he came from?" Janey asks, forgetting herself again.

"Nobody knows," I say. "At least according to J.J. He seems to be something of an authority on everything that goes on here. He grew up on this cape and apparently he knows everyone and everyone's mother. He says the house sweepstakes is the most exciting thing that's happened in months. Which is pretty sad, considering how boring you people are."

Janey doesn't say anything for a second, and I think she's lost in her crush on this Noah guy. But then she says, "You didn't tell J.J. anything personal, did you? About . . . the circumstances that brought you here?"

"You mean that I thought I won the house? No way." There is no way I'd let him know what a dolt I am.

Janey shakes her head, looking genuinely upset. "No, I mean about . . . what happened *before* you came here. With your boyfriend?"

Oh shit. For a moment I'd forgotten all about my little tall tale—I've got to be more careful about that or she's going to figure out that Geoff was actually alive the last time I saw him. "No, no way," I tell her, looking as earnest as I can. "I figure with all the people around here paying attention, I've got to be extra careful."

She exhales, and I'm kind of touched that she got so worried about me. Touched, and a little guilty. "Good. Keep being careful. We just want to mind our own business," she tells me pointedly, "in all matters. How's that bread coming?"

"I've got the dry ingredients here. Now what?"

"Now Cuisinart," she says, and gestures like Vanna to the food pro-cessor. "Everything goes in there, then the yeasty warm water, then the ice water through the tube. Run the machine the whole time, until it starts to come together."

Sounds easy enough. I get to work. "So. Is there something going on between you and Noah?" I ask her, right after adding the yeast-water to the bowl of the processor.

"What?" she says, all aghast, and I know she's about to go into full denial mode. "Why would you—"

Annoyed by her resistance to spill, I hit the pulse button and drown her out with the whirr of the food processor's motor.

"What's that?" I ask when she's done talking and I'm done pulsing. "Sorry—the Cuisinart's so loud that I didn't hear you explain what's going on between you and Noah."

She grimaces. "I said, nothing is going—"

I hit pulse again. I've discovered a new interrogation technique!

I take my finger off the button. "Nope, no, didn't catch that. You'll have to speak up."

"I said," Janey is yelling now. "There is nothing happen—"

Pulse.

She screams. I stop pulsing. "God, you are annoying," she says. "He told me I was beautiful."

I turn away from the Cuisinart, impressed. "Really?"

"Is that so hard to believe?" she asks.

"Yes," I say enthusiastically, and she sneers at me. "But what a cute thing to say."

She sighs. "I know. But weird, right? I mean, I've said next to noth-ing to the guy to make him think I'm interested—which I'm not. And every time he comes around I start sweating and choking, so it's not like he should be getting the wrong idea."

"Maybe he's into that sort of thing," I say with a shrug. "Different strokes, and all that."

"That would be a pretty unusual stroke, if you ask me."

I think things over. "So, are you going to hit that?"

"Excuse me?"

"Noah. Are you going to hook up with him?"

"No, I am not going to *hook up* with him," she says, all indignant. "I hardly know him. And I don't expect I'll have the occasion to see him again anyway."

I roll my eyes. "Please. That's the biggest bullshit excuse I've ever heard. Call him up. Just because we are in the middle of the woods doesn't mean you have to live like a nun."

"I'm not living like a nun," she says, and throws the kitchen towel she's been twisting down to the counter. "You and Aunt Midge. Powerless to mind your own business. I'm so glad there are two of you to pester me now." She's getting huffy all of a sudden. What's the big whoop?

"Jeez, calm down, why don't you. You really do need to get laid. How long's it been?"

"None of your business! Christ!" she says, and she's visibly upset now. "Why do you find my sex life so interesting? I don't try to meddle in yours."

"You don't have to—I was just getting to that."

She sucks in a big gasp of air at that and her face turns bright red. "This is *my* kitchen," she cries, and I realize that this is about the five jillionth time she's said something like that since she got here. "No one can bother me in here." Waving her arms, she makes a circle around her body like a force field, like there is some sacred space around her that no one can penetrate. She looks frantic, maybe a little manic even.

"No one is trying to bother you, crazy lady." I'm not sure if I'm mad or not, but I can tell she is, and I don't understand why.

"You may not be trying to, but you are driving me nuts!" she exclaims. "I just want to come in here and cook a duck, okay? But you can't leave me alone. You have to ask me what's going on with Ned, and why am I not having sex, and—"

"Ned?" I ask. "Who's Ned?"

"GAH!" she screams, clutching her hair in her hands. "Ned is NO-BODY!" Her eyes look wild and glassy like she's about to burst into tears, but for some reason I can't leave it alone.

"No, I want to know who this Ned person is. Is he some dreamboat you left behind in Iowa? Did you try to get him to come with you to the house but he wouldn't propose and make an honest woman of you? Or maybe he ditched you for someone else—some brat who can't cook at all?"

Janey's face is a color of fuchsia that isn't seen in nature. She is taking great gulps of breath like a dying person. "Do NOT say another word about Ned, do you hear me," she says, in a scary low voice.

"Or what?" I ask. "Are you going to throw up on me?"

Janey screams. She screams, and then she moves so fast I can't tell what she's doing until she's grabbed that dripping wet frozen duck by the neck and hauled it behind her like a tomahawk. Next thing I know, the duck is whizzing through the kitchen, missing my head by about a foot, thank God, and crashing into the blue-tile backsplash behind me with a shattering thud. I look at the tile, cracked and broken in hundreds of places, and then Janey, who is standing there with her eyes wide open staring in amazement. She looks like she is the one who almost got hit in the head with a frozen duck. No, she looks like she *did* get hit in the head with a frozen duck.

"Holy shit," I say into the stunned silence. "You almost hit me with a waterfowl."

For a while she doesn't say anything. She just looks at me, and at the place where the tile is shattered, and then at the duck, which bounced onto the floor and is lying there looking much the worse for its little posthumous attempt at flight. At last she speaks. "Yeah, I did," she says, and not with any kind of real remorse, either. "Sorry about that." She moves over to scoop the bird up and place it lovingly back in the sink, and I realize she was apologizing not to me, but to the duck.

After the flying duck incident, Janey retreats upstairs and slams the door of her bedroom like a lovelorn sixteen-year-old girl. I stand there torn between being impressed with her and writing her off as a total nutso. The whole thing makes me wonder why I couldn't have shared a name with someone stable, and normal, and perhaps way more fun. Why

can't the other Janine Brown be more like Cameron Diaz, for example?
She and I would find the nearest dance club and work it all night, wearing satin tank tops with sequins and drinking champagne. Then maybe
the next day she would buy a boat for us to hang out on. We would put
on string bikinis and cruise for guys, literally. Furthermore, I bet Cameron Diaz buys bread at the store just like everyone else in the entire
universe. Except for the other Janine Brown.

In the end I decide to clean up the shards of broken tile and finish
making the bread. Cleaning up is actually relaxing, and I think with a
little glue the broken tiles will look, if not brand new, at least mostly
unnoticeable. But without instruction, I'm kind of hopeless when it
comes to the baking. I try to figure out where I am in the process from
a recipe in *The Bread Bible*, but there's no mention of a food processor
there, so I just dump the wet dough on a floured countertop and start
banging away at it, imitating the illustrated pictures of hands pushing
tight, neat dough around. But my dough is incredibly sticky, and my
hands are covered in edible putty within about two seconds. I wash
them off and flour them up again but end up right back where I started,
two hands covered in bread taffy that refuses to come off. In the end I
get as much of the dough as I can into a greased bowl and cover it up
and hope for the best. Easily a third of the dough is stuck to me or the
counter and it takes a good twenty minutes to clean everything up.
Flour and water, I'm discovering, act a lot like glue.

Exasperated, I leave the dough on the counter to rise and beat it
outside for a much-needed cigarette. But I've only just fished out a
cigarette from the pack when I see the unmistakable sight of J.J. coming
up the driveway, pushing a wheelbarrow full of gardening supplies. He
lets go of one handle to wave, causing his load to veer dangerously off
to the right. I stash the pack out of sight between the rungs of the porch
fence and then wave back. When he gets close enough for me to see his
smile, I get a little melty and then bound down the stairs like a puppy to
greet him.

"Hey," I call. "How's it going?" As soon as I've spoken I cringe. I
saw him this morning, after all. It's probably "going" similarly.

"Good!" he calls back. "It's finally getting cool enough to mow the lawn. Is that okay?"

"Of course," I say enthusiastically, not wanting him to treat me like I'm his boss. I couldn't be less in charge of anything around here, and anyway it's not sexy. "I mean, I'm sure it's fine for you to do whatever. You're the expert."

He raises his eyebrows and gives me a puzzled look and I realize just how giddy I'm acting. "Okay. Well, then," he gestures toward the garden shed.

"Actually," I say, trying to think of some reason J.J. should hang out and keep me entertained until the bread is done rising, "everyone else is in the house doing their own thing right now. Want to go for a walk?" Lame, I know, but there's not a lot to offer by way of entertainment out here with no car.

J.J. considers this with that puzzled look still on his face, and I'm starting to wonder if it's always there. Then he shrugs. "Okay."

We walk around to the shed and he stashes his stuff in there and then turns to me. "What about the lawn?" he asks.

"Mow it tomorrow," I helpfully suggest. He shrugs at this, as if it doesn't matter one way or the other, and I'm pleased to find at least one person on this cove with a work ethic similar to mine. "I have to be back here in an hour. Where can we go from here?"

"How about to the farm," he says. And though the idea of visiting a farm sounds no more exciting than watching the dough rise, I will follow anyone as adorable as J.J. anywhere. I fall into step beside him as we walk down the driveway and take a left, walking away from the little specklets of civilization that are down the road aways to the right.

"This is where we get our chickens," he says.

"You raise chickens?"

"Nope—but we eat them," he says with a smile. "They sell their eggs here too."

"Cool," I say. Maybe I can bring home some fresh eggs for Janey and make her forget her previous attempt at murder by Ducksicle. "Can I just pick up eggs whenever? How much do they cost?"

J.J. scratches his chin, where a beard would be, if he didn't have such a baby face. "Normally you could just swing by and meet the owners, but they're up at the farmers market today, I'll bet. My parents see them there every week. If you need eggs, we can always pop in and leave a few bucks on the table. It's not like the house is ever locked."

"What is this, Mayberry?"

"Pretty much," J.J. says, smiling. "By the time you get this far out on the cove things are pretty darn quiet. Just wait until September, when the summer people go home."

"Wait—it gets *more* boring? I'm going to lose consciousness," I say. "Just slip into a coma and never wake up. Maybe I should make a living will."

"Oh come on, you're from Iowa. How much more exciting can that be?"

"I had a little more mobility in Iowa," I say, though thinking it through makes me realize how much better life has been since I got here. Regular meals, someone to talk to, less shouting, and zero hitting. But I stick with my story, as always. "Plus, I didn't live in the middle of nowhere like this. They have real cities in Iowa, you know." Even as I say this I realize we've been walking right smack dab in the middle of the road for ten minutes, and haven't had to get out of the way for a car once yet.

"Then why'd you come here?" he asks. It's not a confrontational question, but it's not rhetorical either.

I consider the proper answer. "Well, for the house, mostly," I say at last. That seems accurate without spilling any meaningful details.

But J.J. is the curious sort. "What do you mean, for the house? I thought you said it belonged to your cousin."

Cousin. Right. "It does," I say, haltingly. "But I needed to get away," *sort of,* "and she has all this space . . ." I really am going to have to start writing down all my various lies and vagaries if I'm going to keep living in Maine. "And I'm helping take care of Aunt Midge."

Note to self: Start helping take care of Aunt Midge.

Luckily J.J. leaves it alone at that so I don't have to dig myself in any deeper. He's not exactly the disclosing kind himself, I discovered this morning when we went down to the water. We talked about all kinds of stuff, the neighbors, the cove, the ocean, and he had encyclopedic knowledge about all those things. But I didn't get, for example, such intimate details as his last name.

Or whether he has a girlfriend.

I will not be coy here; I'm hoping he doesn't. He is cute and nice and has a truck. In short, he is everything I am looking for in a friend right now. That's right: *friend*. Remember how I said two seconds ago that life had been better in Maine? I think that is because my exes are in Iowa. I don't need to go there again, at least not while I have a nice place to stay.

But it doesn't matter what my intentions are toward J.J. If it turns out he's taken there's no way his girlfriend will let him hang out with someone like me (I wouldn't let my boyfriend hang out with someone like me either), and my life will only get more boring.

"Are you going to stay a while?" he asks me, kind of out of the blue. "Or go back to Iowa at some point?"

Good question. "Stay awhile," I say, hoping that, by saying it, it will become true.

"Then you'll get used to things and start to know your way around. And plus, I can drive you into town on some weekend and I'll show you the sights. I'll even take you to Reds for a lobster roll."

Um, squeal. "Sounds good," I say nonchalantly. "What's a lobster roll?"

J.J. stops in his tracks. "Seriously?"

"Seriously."

"I have so much to teach you," he says, then takes my hand and pulls me into a driveway on the right side of the road and for a split second I think he's taking me into the woods for a little afternoon delight. Then I see the farm. "We're here."

"I see that."

The farm is a long stretch of gravel road dividing a large clearing with a house on one side and assorted animal housing on the other. On the side of a big red hen house are painted in block lettering the words THE FARM Just like that, capital *t*, capital *f*. I guess that differentiates it somehow from other farms? The chickens are having a high old time in the yard, pooping and pecking and flapping their little hearts out. I notice with some surprise that behind them seems to be another pen with what I'm guessing are turkeys. Looks like we're covered for Thanksgiving.

"Wanna see the llamas?" J.J. asks, like it's his big pickup line. Lucky for him, I do want to see the llamas.

"I'm not sure I've ever seen a llama before," I admit, nodding vigorously. "Honestly, I have a little trouble even spelling llama."

"Well, then, you're in for a treat." He leads me to another outbuilding, a shed that looks like it's made out of the same stuff as Tupperware, with a skylight and a big garage-style door, surrounded by high mesh fencing.

Once we're standing by the fence right outside the door of the shed, J.J. whistles. Two furry beasts come loping out bobbing their heads as they walk. I know in an instant that these are llamas, not just because J.J. just told me they were, but also because they look like the word "llama." They have long necks and a sheep's face set into the hairiest mane and big long eyelashes that seem skeptical. I expect one to open his mouth and sarcastically ask, "Can I help you?"

"This is Nana," he says, gesturing to the smaller llama in the rear, "and this is Boo Boo." Boo Boo is fatter and looks more cantankerous. I instantly love him. "Go dig in that garbage can for some treats," J.J. says to me. Honest to God. He gestures to a metal trash can like it's nothing, like he thinks I go rummaging through other people's trash every day. Flies are investigating the area, which means I should not be. I put my hands on my hips but don't budge, and he shrugs and says, "Don't you want them to like you?"

"I bet they would like me better if I gave them something from the nice, clean refrigerator."

"Not likely," J.J. says. "Go on." I lower him a look but go over to the garbage and try to wrench off the tight-fitting lid. I mean, it's that or lose the llama popularity contest.

I yank on the lid for a while without success. "Bears," J.J. says as he watches me struggle with getting it open.

"Yeah, right," I grumble to myself. "Bears." I finally get the lid off and am hit with the strong smell of onions. Inside are stems full of bushy leaves of various shapes and sizes. "What do I take?"

"Anything," J.J. answers. "They're mostly onion tops. Some leeks, I think. Smells, doesn't it?"

Wow, this guy really knows how to win over a woman. But then, he doesn't exactly have to try with his adorableness brimming over as it is. "A little," I say, trying not to appear squeamish. I grab a big handful of greens and walk back to the fence.

"Here, buddy," I say to the fatter llama, my left hand outstretched, holding one plant toward him on my open palm.

"Might want to toss that in and let him get it himself. He does spit a little."

"He won't spit on me," I say. Sure enough, the llama purses his lips like he's about to give my hand a big smooch and then slurps up the greens and uses his tongue to smush the whole plant inside his mouth. It's not pretty, but he looks happy enough, and I am un-spit-upon. I move around and share the wealth with the other llama, who does get my hand a little wet, but nothing dramatic. I wipe it off on my jeans and then put my hand back slowly to her face and give it a little pat.

Her fur feels like kittens and puppies and baby chicks all at the same time. "Whoa, that's soft!" I say.

"Right?" says J.J. "I basically just come around and feed them so they'll let me touch their fur. It feels like Care Bear clouds."

Interesting comparison. I smile and rub Nana a little more. "That's good stuff."

"They use it to make sweaters I guess. Do you knit?"

"What do you mean, do I knit? What do I look like?"

"I dunno," he says, shrugging again. J.J. uses shrugs like punctuation. I wonder if he ever comes home at the end of the day and wonders why his shoulders are so tired. "I just thought, maybe."

"I don't knit," I say indignantly. But then, afraid that I'll seem

uncomfortable with the homemaking arts, I add, "but I can bake."
Small exaggeration . . .

"Oh yeah?"

"Yep. In fact, I have to get back kind of soon because I have some
dough rising in the kitchen." Note to self, do not let J.J. come into the
kitchen and see the gooey blob that no doubt awaits me. Or perhaps has
already taken over the house.

"Oh, okay," he says, and I am thrilled to see he looks a little disappointed. I hope it's because of me, and not Nana and Boo Boo. "Let's
get your eggs then, and head back."

He leads me into the side door of the house, which is not the tradi-
tional big farm house but a weathered-looking cottage, and through the
mudroom to the bright yellow kitchen. There're two big fridges whir-
ring next to each other, and in one is a small supply of egg cartons in
stacks. "These are from this morning, I'll bet," J.J. says. "Take one and
leave maybe three bucks? But you have to make sure to bring back the
carton, okay? They are always saying they don't have enough cartons."

"Okay," I agree, and pick out a dozen eggs. When I open it up I find
eggs of every shade of tan and some dark brown, all quite small. Janey
is going to love these, perhaps so much that she never throws anything
frozen at me again. I can hope.

I leave five dollars on the counter by the fridges—I know what good
eggs cost and these seem extra fancy—and J.J. takes the eggs from me as
we head back down the road. The whole walk goes by and still we see
no cars, no bikes, not another living soul all the way back to the house.
But I am starting to see the upside of living out here in the boonies with
more llamas and chickens than people to keep me company.

At the house, J.J. hands me back the eggs and tells me he's glad I
liked the llamas and talks about how he thinks the llamas are very good
judges of character and he wouldn't want to hang out with a girl that
the llamas didn't like. And then he says, "I think the llamas really like
you. So, we're good."

JANEY

"Peas have a gentleness about them that is reminiscent of
a warm spring rain."

JULEE ROSSO AND SHEILA LUKINS,
The New Basics Cookbook

I spend the next couple of days basically hiding in my bedroom working on dresses while Nean is around, trying to avoid her at all costs. I tell
myself it's because I despise Nean and want her to move out, but the truth
is I'm mortified that I accosted her with a duck. And even more than
that, I don't want to have to explain why I got so upset over the whole
Noah/Ned thing. In Iowa everyone knew about Ned, how he died,
the whole kit and caboodle, and I got a lot of "poor Janey, destined to
be alone for the rest of her life now" looks. In Maine I have a chance to
start over with no one knowing a thing about my engagement or what
happened to me after—how I started working at the bridal shop to pay
off the enormous deposit on the wedding dress I would never wear, or
how it turned out that Ned had taken out all that life insurance on himself and named me the next of kin. How I've never really been the same
since.

I don't want to ruin that anonymity by telling Nean everything, and
I'm not sure I would be able not to tell her if she asked. She has ways of
making me talk. Annoying ways. So I hide out until she's gone off with
Aunt Midge to deliver the better part of a pot roast and two trays of

stuffed potatoes, or whatever is waiting in the fridge, and then try to get a burst of cooking in while they're gone. But after a while, it seems like all is forgiven, and finally I let down my guard, hanging around the kitchen to finish up a cold watermelon soup even when I hear the car crunching on the gravel outside.

When Nean and Aunt Midge blow in through the front door making a great ruckus as always, I'm standing there pushing hot-pink melon through a food mill and getting more of it on me than in the mill. Nean marches in and puts a finger in the bowl of juice at the bottom, licks it off, and says, "Janey, you've got to start driving Aunt Midge to the shelter."

"No," I say. "I don't. You're doing a great job." I go back to cranking my watermelon, hoping the mess will shoo her away.

"Yeah, yeah, but now she wants to spend a couple hours a day in there doing good works and boring everyone to tears in the process with stories of how she was a nurse during the Revolutionary War and invented color TV. I don't want to hang around every day for two hours in Little Pond, waiting for her," she jerks her thumb to my poor, maligned old aunt, "to get out her charity ya-yas."

Aunt Midge huffs. "*She* is, incidentally," she says, picking up the third person, "perfectly capable of driving herself, if you ask me." With that, both pairs of eyes turn to face me expectantly, waiting for some verdict on the subject.

"How is it I've become the mother of two in such short order?" I ask them. "I must have had Nean when I was eleven, and you"—I level a finger at Aunt Midge—"when I was . . . minus fifty-three. It's a miracle!"

"Oh, can it," Aunt Midge says. "You're just crabby because you've been all cooped up in your room for days. You're just like a set of summer sheets. You'll feel better after a nice airing out."

Well, she has a point there. "Maybe," I say, letting a little friendliness into my eyes and setting down the watermelon. "Okay, start over from the beginning. What's going on, now?"

"I'm going to start helping with lunch service," Aunt Midge says, crossing around to sit at the breakfast table and pick at the bowl of berries I keep there. "I'm bored to tears and I need to make myself useful. I have to be in there by eleven and I'll be out by one, weekdays only."

"Is it hard work?" I ask. "Will you be on your feet for the whole two hours?"

"I'll be fine," Aunt Midge says in the same gruff tone she gets every time I try to take care of her. "You don't need to worry about *me*."

"That's right," chimes in Nean, sitting down too and plucking up a big handful of raspberries. "Worry about me. What am I supposed to do that whole time?"

"Get a job?" I suggest, watching with amazement at the number of berries she can cram in her mouth at once.

"Ignore her," Aunt Midge says to Nean, putting her hand over Nean's protectively. "You're just fine. You don't have to pay your way here. We're happy to have you for as long as you need."

I raise my eyebrows and consult the ceiling at this but say nothing. "Anyways," Nean says, still chewing, "I have a job. The bread, remember? Everyone is loving it."

"Really?" I think of the dough-bricks she took out of the oven a few days ago and wonder just how bad the shelter's patrons have it if they're enjoying *that*.

"No, not really," she answers. "But today for the first time so far it all got eaten. So I think I'm getting better. It turns out it's easier to make just using your hands, no special tools or appliances," she says with a meaningful look at the Cuisinart.

"Most things are," I agree, and I can't help but feel a little proud at the way Nean is taking on all this baking with such fervor, even if I did try to kill her with a duck the last time we shared the kitchen. "Just keep at it. And keep at driving Aunt Midge," I say. "You're doing well at that too."

Nean's hand closes into a fist. "Seriously? You can't even drive her every other day?"

"Seriously." I watch as she looks to Aunt Midge for an alternate ruling, but Aunt Midge just shrugs.

"If it was up to me, I'd drive myself," she says. "But I like having you for company."

Nean sighs dramatically and heads outside, presumably to stink up my porch with disgusting cigarette smell. I go over to the table where Aunt Midge is sitting, looking for a little of the comfort she had to offer Nean just a moment ago. But when I sit down she says, "You know, Noah is at the shelter. . . ." Exasperated, I pop back up again and heave the biggest sigh I can muster.

"Not you, too," I say.

"What? I thought you'd want to know," she says.

"I did know—remember? He said he worked there when we ran into him at the clam bar."

"No, I mean—"

"I know what you mean," I interrupt. "If I drove you to the shelter I could see him every day, right? And then maybe we'd fall in love and have six kids and you wouldn't have to worry about me being all alone anymore?"

Aunt Midge sits quietly for a moment, then sighs. "I do worry about you being all alone. After I die," she says.

"Then don't die," I respond, sitting back down right next to her, so I can put my arm around her little shoulders and let her know I'm not really mad. Nor do I want her dwelling on death, not when she's as strong as a mule and twice as ornery.

"I'm trying not to," she says, and all of a sudden I hear so much tiredness in her voice that I am overcome with worry. "But I'm eighty-eight years old. At some point I'm going to have to go be with your mom and Ned, and leave you behind all by yourself."

My eyes fill with tears. "No. I don't want to talk about this," I say. "You're borrowing trouble."

Aunt Midge puts her hands on both sides of my head and looks in my eyes and I see the same fear I'm feeling reflected in hers. "I'll stick around," she says at last, like she's giving in to the demands of a ten-year-old desperate for a pony. "I'll make sure you're taken care of."

"I'm taken care of already," I say, not sure if I'm referring to the new house, or the insurance money sitting in the bank, or Aunt Midge sitting at the table with me with her age-spotted hands balanced on my head so carefully. "I have everything I need. I'll be just fine."

Her mouth twitches. "Of course you will," she says, and if she is being sarcastic, I pay it no mind.

Aunt Midge starts her volunteering the very next day. When she and Nean get home they rush into the kitchen to find me and debrief me on the day's excitements, which I can see is going to become a nasty little habit. Today the big news is Nean's bread. Last night Nean and I worked a little on the bread together and there was an unspoken truce in the air—she didn't ask me a single personal question and I didn't throw anything at her head. She's been getting a really sticky dough, so I explained that the flour measurements aren't a science, and change depending on where you live and what the weather is like on a given day, and basically just to go with the flow. This morning they took in four loaves of bread that looked like actual bread. Apparently it got rave reviews at lunch, and Nean is now strutting around like she grew an inch overnight.

"I'm going to open a bakery," she tells me.

"Oh good. Does that mean you're leaving?"

Aunt Midge chuckles like I made a good joke. "What would we do without her, Janey?" she asks me. "Think of all the baking she's doing. And she took some of your hemming jobs back to the shop and got you another stack of dresses to shorten, saving you a trip and a human interaction."

"Lucky for her . . ." I say, but I know I don't sound even remotely menacing. How can I when I'm genuinely grateful? "It's gorgeous outside and I've been cooped up sewing all morning. Want to go to the backyard and gaze at the ocean?" I am addressing Aunt Midge—after her weird out-of-nowhere comments yesterday about mortality, I've wanted to get her to myself—but Nean jumps up from her perch at the island and rushes to the kitchen door like a puppy with a full bladder.

She spins around, waiting for us to follow, and then says, "Hurry up! J.J. is out there right now mowing the lawn with no shirt on."

Aunt Midge springs up from the table so fast that I forget all my worries about her health. "Come *on*, slow poke!" she says and I untie my blue-striped apron and follow them out the back, stopping to grab a tray I've made up full of summery treats for exactly this purpose.

By the time I get out back with the grub, Nean has repositioned a row of padded teak lounge chairs so that they face the ocean on an angle, by way of the back lawn, where J.J. is appearing and then vanishing again as he pushes the mower in long rows. We plop down on the chairs, Nean, Aunt Midge in the middle, and then me, and take in the view.

"Ahh, this is the life . . ." Aunt Midge sighs the next time J.J. comes into view. I see what she is saying. He's your ideal twenty-something male specimen in so many ways: tan skin, bright blond hair, not an ounce of fat on his body, and plenty of that lean boyish muscle from all the landscaping. The sun, which is out in force, seems to gleam off his body with the same intensity that it twinkles over the breaks in waves out on the water.

"This is a very nice view," I say, feeling a little silly but enjoying the camaraderie nonetheless.

"Isn't it just?" says Nean on a lustful sigh.

"Nean," says Aunt Midge, "you need to go break yourself off a piece of that man-candy."

"Oh my God, Aunt Midge," I say, aghast. "You are a disgusting old lady."

"What?" Aunt Midge turns to face me with a saintly expression that quickly turns wicked. "Did you have dibs?"

"I don't have dibs," I exclaim.

"I have dibs, if anyone has dibs," says Nean. "But I'm not going there. We're just going to be friends."

Even I am a little taken aback by that. "Just friends? That seems like an awful waste."

Nean laughs. "I knew you had a pulse! He's all right to look at, I agree. But I haven't had much luck with men lately . . ."

The three of us get quiet as we think about this, the understatement of the century.

"J.J. doesn't really seem very . . . aggressive," Aunt Midge says delicately.

"He's as gentle as a llama," says Nean.

"Huh?"

"Never mind. I'm just saying, it's good to have friends sometimes. I'm in a friends place right now."

"Fair enough," I say, thinking of Noah. Could I be friends with him?

"Maybe . . ." says Aunt Midge. "But I'm not sure that J.J. is in a friends place." She gestures to him as he pushes the mower forward into view and sure enough, he's trying to surreptitiously sneak peaks at Nean.

Nean grins. "Maybe I should go put on a bikini."

"Don't you dare," I say.

"Chill. I don't even own a bikini. Is that sangria?"

"Yep. And mini-frittatas made from the last of those eggs you brought me." I pass her the tray.

"You're welcome," says Nean, pouring herself a glass of sangria and taking four frittatas. Aunt Midge and I exchange a look. No matter where she's been or what she's done, I'm glad she's getting fed now; she clearly needs it. Already she's put on a couple of pounds and lost that gauntness about her chin. No wonder J.J. is smitten. "Speaking of gifts that keep on giving," she says, "Noah gave us something for you today from his garden. I left it in a bag on the kitchen table."

"What is it?"

"Vegetables." Nean shrugs. "If you ask me, that makes it the worst gift ever."

"Not for Janey," says Aunt Midge.

"What kind of vegetables?" I ask.

"Dunno, something green," Nean replies. "Peas, maybe?"

Peas? I shudder with excitement. I don't think I've ever had fresh garden peas before. They're supposed to be so sweet if you eat them right away. Do I make a soup with them or would that be a waste?

No matter what I'll need some mint.

"Wow, that's a pretty big grin for a bag full of veggies," Nean says.

A chilled pea soup with yogurt, I think. Chilled! "I hope there's enough . . ." I say aloud, but mostly to myself.

"It was a pretty big bag," says Nean, and I shiver with happy anticipation. "I guess Noah has you pegged, then. He said to expect more tomorrow."

"What else did he say?" I ask as nonchalantly as possible.

Nean shrugs. "Nothing," she says. But I don't miss the look she gives Aunt Midge. A conspiring look. Those two need to be separated.

"Well, tell him thank you for me tomorrow."

"Okay. Or . . . if you want, I'll let you drive Aunt Midge in and you can tell him yourself."

"How generous of you. No thanks." An idea comes to my head. "But I will send him some pea soup so he can taste the fruits of his labors."

"Aww, so romantic. Love via produce."

"It's better than love via ogling," Aunt Midge says, and even as she does Nean looks over to J.J. and we watch as they exchange a glance that could be classified only as "longing." Before our eyes, he turns off the mower and comes strolling over to us, slowly, like he's in a perfume commercial. I wait to see if he'll toss his hair.

"Ooooh," says Aunt Midge on a gasp of air. "He's coming over here!"

"This is our cue to leave," I tell Aunt Midge, tearing myself away from the excitement.

"No way!" she says. "Hello J.J.!"

"Hi there, Mrs. . . ." he searches around for a moment, "Mrs. Aunt Midge." I crack a smile. What a cutie. He hardly gives me hives at all.

"Would you like some sangria?" she asks, already pouring him a glass.

"Aunt Midge!" I say, scooping the glass out of her hands. "Don't just feed him liquor! Are you even twenty-one?" I ask Adonis Junior.

"Twenty-two," he says with some pride. With a sigh I fork over the glass and he takes a big slurp. "It's hot out."

"Yes it is," says Aunt Midge, waving her hand in front of her face like a Southern belle. "Care to take a break and join us?"

"Actually, we were just leaving, weren't we," I say, grabbing Aunt Midge and trying to heft her out of her lounge chair.

"That's okay," says J.J. "I've got to get back to it pretty soon. You just stick around and enjoy the view." With that, J.J. brings his arms up and flexes his biceps in classic muscle beach fashion. Aunt Midge cracks up.

"We are, believe me!" she tells him. He hams it up, turning around and moving through a variety of Mr. Universe poses, adding exaggerated grunts for effect.

Nean starts applauding wildly. Aunt Midge has dissolved into a fit of giggles. "Stop, stop! I'm an old lady! I can't take the excitement!"

At this J.J. kneels in front of Aunt Midge's lounge chair gallantly. "Since when does forty-five count as old?" he asks, and then takes her hand and plants a kiss on her knuckles. Aunt Midge swoons. I roll my eyes but I am grinning too.

"And now, fair ladies, I must take my leave of you." He doffs an imaginary hat and then backs away in a low bow. When he's gotten about ten feet, he stops, and says, "See you later, Nean?"

"Um," she stammers. "Okay."

And then he's back to the lawn mower leaving us all dazzled in his wake.

"Wow," I say. "Good luck staying *just* friends with him."

Nean nods. "I'm in trouble," she says, and then crams another frittata in her mouth.

NEAN

"Bread is the most forgiving of foods."

—LYNNE ROSSETTO KASPER,
The Splendid Table

It's not long before J.J. is visiting us every day, coming up with some gardening task or other that requires him to wander by right when I'm sitting on the porch reading a book or taking a load of compost out for Janey. I'm pretty sure he's in love with me, which is nice, but kind of derails my "just friends" thing. J.J. doesn't seem like the type of guy to hang around forever waiting for some girl to see what is right in front of her. Which is good, because guys like that are weenies. J.J. is much more no-nonsense. In the last week he has told me about four times that he doesn't have a girlfriend. He has also taken me out swimming twice and driven me into town once to see the new comic book movie, a subject on which he is the utmost authority. He is also incredibly honest, and I feel terrible whenever he asks me any personal questions because I'm so full of shit these days I don't know which side is up. I can tell that eventually he'll get sick of me avoiding his attempts to get closer and move along, but until then I will try to enjoy what we have. Which is nothing. But still.

Janey and Aunt Midge think I'm keeping J.J. at arm's length because I'm afraid of men after what happened with Geoff, and I'm not about to disavow them of that notion. I know the only thing that's keeping me here is the completely bogus threat that I'd be unjustly thrown in the slammer if they turned me away, and I don't care. I love it here. Janey is a spaz, but she makes the best food you've ever tasted, day in and day out. It's like living above a five-star restaurant and never having to pay your tab. And seriously, I am turning into the best baker ever. I'm some kind of idiot savant with bread—I just lay my hands on it and somehow it gets better every day. I am making two kinds a day now—two fluffy white loaves with a nice hard crust at the request of the shelter's guests, and two with flaxseed and all kinds of whatnot for extra nutrition, that makes for an awesome sandwich. I can do rolls too, and I'm working on submarine loaves, though they are still too dense and chewy. And I found out that if you pour hot water into the oven when you put the bread in you get an impressive display of steam in a big whoosh, and it makes the crust awesome and crackly. J.J. was in the kitchen when I did that one day, and I swear I actually saw his heart melt a little. I'm pretty sure he salivates every time he sees me now, like one of Pavlov's dogs.

Right now my plan is to keep rocking the bread and chauffeuring Aunt Midge around, try not to piss off Janey too much (it's just so damn tempting though), and then hopefully, after enough time passes, they will forget the reason they let me stay in the first place and I will just become a permanent fixture around here, like Aunt Midge, only spryer. Weeks will pass and I won't have to pretend to be on the lam anymore and the whole lie can just melt away in the sands of time. Maybe I will find a way to earn some actual money and save up for a car, and then I can get a full-time job and start paying some rent here—I'm sure that would win over Janey once and for all. I could even work at a bakery— there's one in Damariscotta, I know, with beautiful displays of cupcakes out front and lists of dozens of different kinds of breads available. How cool would it be if I knew how to make all of them? Especially the chocolate sourdough loaf. That sounds amazing. I bet that would keep J.J. around a little longer.

But for now I've just got to keep him at arm's length. There's no way

I could tell him the whopper I delivered unto Janey and Aunt Midge and let him believe I was some poor abuse victim turned violent—I feel guilty enough about that already. And I can't tell him the truth either—that Geoff is alive and well and probably pushing some other girl around by now—because he'd think I was a terrible person for lying to my only friends.

And he wouldn't be wrong.

Dammit, why don't I ever think these things through? Now I've got a completely un-Geoff-like, cute, sweet, smart, thoughtful person panting after me and there's absolutely nothing I can do about it. I've spent my whole life hoping a guy like J.J. would come along and rescue my sorry ass, and now when he does, I don't want to be rescued anymore. I want to stay here, on the cove, for as long as humanly possible.

And to do that, I've got to keep my stories straight.

It turns out, Janey's got a few stories she's been keeping close to her vest herself. The whole sordid tale comes out when I get Aunt Midge talking on one of our drives to the shelter. We've gotten into the habit of driving to the yarn store, parking in the lot, and then switching sides, so Aunt Midge can "keep her driving skills sharp." I feel like sharp is not a word that will apply to her driving skills any time soon, but I love living dangerously. We switch seats and I watch, teeth gritted slightly, as she starts the car, backs out of the lot with little more than a cursory glance backward, and then realizes she needs to adjust the seat and does so while still trying to drive. The car veers dangerously toward a parked jeep and then jolts out of the way at the last minute. It's all very exciting. I'm not sure I would let her do this if Janey hadn't sprung for a car with dual airbags.

We always talk a lot on these drives—Aunt Midge isn't the sort of driver who can bear to put one hundred percent concentration on the road—and they have become one of my favorite parts of living here. She is hilarious, and though she looks like a grandma, she swears like a sailor and has a sex drive to match. She tells me about her husband and how he used to get down on the piano, playing slow torch songs that she would sing along to while gyrating all over the room until, as she put it, "they had to stop singing and start making music, if you know what I mean." Foreplay has sure changed in the thirty years since he kicked the bucket. Since then she's been with "a lot" of other guys, but she says her husband was the best she ever had. It's sweet.

I ask her if she's met anyone new since she's been in Maine, and she tells me she's taking a sabbatical on men right now to "focus on her girls." At first I think she's talking about her breasts, but then she looks at me meaningfully, long enough for the car to drift off the road and give us both a good scare. When we've righted things I ask her, "Am I one of your girls?"

"Of course, honey," she says. "You and Janey are my main responsibilities right now." And I feel like I'm going to cry. I must be getting my period to let something like that get to me so much. I don't say anything while I try to collect myself and Aunt Midge starts whistling to herself in the silence. I recognize the tune from a musical we put on in middle school, when I was in the foster care system. "Little Girls" from *Annie*.

Poor Miss Hannigan.

"I hope we're not too much of a handful," I say at last.

Aunt Midge shrugs. The wheel jerks left, and an oncoming pickup lays on the horn and swerves out of the way. "I'm up to the challenge. What are you going to do today while I'm off saving the world for our friends at the shelter?"

The way she says this makes me smile a little. I was a hop skip and a jump from living in that shelter a few weeks ago, and I like to think that even if I hadn't told my terrible fib, Aunt Midge still would have found me there.

"First the dress shop. Janey is a sewing fool. And then I'm going to the hardware store to look for some really super superglue," I tell her.

"Superglue? What for?"

"Those broken tiles in the kitchen. I saved all the bits and pieces, and

I think with some serious glue and maybe some matching grout I can pretty much make it look like it never happened."

"Like what never happened?" Aunt Midge asks, and suddenly I wish I hadn't said anything. Janey and I have been bickering like jealous sisters since the day we met, but for some reason I feel guilty about ratting her out. Too late now.

"The tile got hit. With a duck," I say vaguely.

Aunt Midge looks at me down her nose, and I watch the car weave again, so I grab the wheel to steady it. She lets me do the steering while she wiggles her finger at me. "A living duck?" she asks.

"Nope. A dead one."

She revs the gas and the car accelerates suddenly, forcing me to grip the wheel even tighter. "In my experience," she says, "ducks don't fly as much when they're dead."

"Whoa, Aunt Midge. We're coming up to that stop sign you missed yesterday."

She turns her attention back to the road and takes the wheel, and I am relieved to see she intends to come to a full and complete stop this time. After looking both ways exaggeratedly, she starts up again and accelerates to her previous speed as though she's drag racing.

"Was the duck . . . used as a projectile?" she asks, keenly.

"Perhaps," I say, warily, keeping one eye on Aunt Midge and one eye on the road.

"Were you on the pitching or receiving end of said projectile?" she asks.

"Receiving end. But it missed me by a mile."

"Hm," she says.

I say nothing.

"Janey's not usually the type to hurl poultry," she says, and I nod.

"It did seem to be an anomaly, when it happened."

"Someone would've had to really upset her to make her do something like that."

Oh great, now I'm the one who's going to get in trouble. "Someone would have," I agree. We're coming into town, and if I'm just obtuse enough, maybe I can get out of explaining what happened.

"Why would anyone want to upset Janey that much?" Aunt Midge asks.

"Surely that person didn't do it intentionally," I say. "Oh look, the turn's coming up."

She signals and slams on the brakes simultaneously. We roll slowly up to the corner and take it at about two miles per hour.

"So. After my errands I'll just come back and read until you're done," I say, suddenly anxious to get her out of the car.

"Fine." She pulls into the parking lot of the shelter. "I'll see you in a couple of hours." She hands me ten bucks. "For the glue," she says. "And the extra is for a paperback romance. Get one we'd both like." As if I don't know what she means, she adds, "You know, *steamy*."

"Aye aye," I say, and wave her off, thinking the odds are good that she'll forget this conversation by the time the lunch service is over and she's holding a juicy bodice ripper in her lap.

But two hours later I'm loading the bouquet of brightly colored flowers Noah gave me to give Janey into the trunk of the car when Aunt Midge says, "About the duck."

I sigh and get into the driver's seat. "Aren't you supposed to be at the age where you start forgetting things?" I ask her when she's buckled in on the passenger side.

"I only forget things when it's convenient," she tells me. "What did you say to Janey to make her throw a duck at you?"

"I can't tell you," I attempt.

"Oh, you'll tell me. Was it about Noah?"

"Maybe."

"Listen, missy, this is my niece we're talking about. You stop being coy."

I sigh. "I asked her why she wasn't working it with Noah,"

"Mmhmm . . ."

"And she got upset at me for bringing it up, really upset. And I should have left it alone, but I was so curious. I mean, he seems nice, and he's cute and everything, and Janey is single as far as I can tell . . ."

"Sort of," says Aunt Midge mysteriously.

"You mean Ned?" I ask. She swivels around in her seat to look at me. "She told you about Ned?"

"No, not really. I mean, when she was good and mad, his name slipped out. I think she meant to say Noah, but then she got so red in the face about it when I asked her who Ned was. She looked like a to-mato. A killer tomato. That's when she threw the duck."

"I see," says Aunt Midge, and then she is quiet, contemplating for a moment. "So she didn't explain who Ned was?"

"Not really. Who was he?"

Aunt Midge pauses dramatically and then announces, "He was her fiancé," and, I'll admit it, I gasp.

"Seriously? She was engaged back in Iowa?"

"A long time ago," she says, her voice getting that same faraway quality she uses when she talks about her late husband or the endless pool. "They met in community college," she began. "He was in techni-cal school for engineering, and she was working on her teaching cer-tificate."

I blink at this. "No way. How did she expect to be a teacher? She gets hives every time she meets someone new." And then thinks she can cover them up with long-sleeved shirts and oddly placed scarves.

"She wasn't always like that," says Aunt Midge. "She's always been shy, but functionally shy. There were times—when Ned was around—that she was downright social."

Again I blink at her in disbelief.

"Just take my word for it," she tells me. "They dated pretty casually at first, Ned and Janey. But then her mom—my niece—died, a few months after she met Ned, and the two of them formed a very tight bond after that. Ned never let her wallow too much—but he was always there for her, always ready with a shoulder when she needed it. He al-ways had some fun way to pass the time, to get her mind off of her grief for a little while. Walks, camping, trips out to eat at the most unusual, off-the-beaten-path sort of places."

Aunt Midge sighs. "He loved to take her out on these bike rides, down to a little dive on the river trail that had the best pork tenderloins in all of Iowa. Great big dinner-plate-sized loins balanced on a tiny little bun, like fat men wearing bowler hats. Janey would come back from their bike rides with enough love inside her for the whole world over and tell me all about how she wanted to marry Ned and teach sixth grade and have three babies. I told her she should name them all after me just like that weird George Foreman Grill man."

"What happened?" I ask, hoping we're not going to segue into kitchen appliances right when things are getting interesting.

"After about six months, they moved in together, and then, another six months later, they went off on one of their bike rides and came back engaged to be married. I threw them a nice big engagement party with a cookbook theme, and everyone we'd ever met came and brought them all kinds of nice cards and all those books she keeps in the kitchen. After that, she was too busy to do much socializing, with all her studying and working waiting tables and then planning the wedding. But she had a few good friends lined up to be her bridesmaids, and she went to parties from time to time, and came over and cooked for my girlfriends when we had Scrabble nights. And Ned was so popular, he always had a friend at hand. He had such an easy way about him, and he came from a big close-knit family, wanted to take over the family dairy someday. In the end, they invited almost one hundred people to their wedding, on beautiful shimmery blue stationery with dark pink writing."

I think of the Janey I know standing in front of one hundred people taking her vows. She'd never make it, I know for a fact. "So did they? Get married, I mean?"

"No. Ned worked for a cell phone company, doing repairs on the towers and such, part-time to pay for school. There was an accident and he fell and died right away." This hits me like a ton of bricks, but Aunt Midge is so matter-of-fact I try to lighten the mood.

"No wonder Janey doesn't go in for modern technology."

"Don't be crass," Aunt Midge snaps, and I recoil in shame.

"Sorry. It's awful. I don't know why I'm making jokes."

"Because," she says, "you care about Janey and it hurts to hear about this sad thing she went through."

I shrug. "Maybe you're right," I say.

"Of course I am," she says back. "Anyway," she casts her imperious gaze on me. "Ned died just two weeks before the wedding. Janey was in charge of the funeral—his poor mother was in pieces—and then after all the mourners were gone, she moved into a little apartment not far from my house and just stopped answering her phone. She quit her student teaching and took a job as a seamstress at the bridal salon where she'd bought her dress—she still owed a lot of money for the wedding deposits and she needed to scrimp and save to pay them off by herself. She didn't want to see anyone from before Ned died, or talk about him, or take any help. She just wanted to be on her own, and the girl has a very strong will, as you know."

I think of this and my heart hurts. And I feel angry—strong will or not, shouldn't someone have been there to help take care of her? What about all Ned's family and friends? They couldn't have expected Aunt Midge to do it all alone.

"What did you do?" I ask her.

"Well." She looks back to the road and squeezes her hands in her lap. "I wasn't quite sure what to do," she admits. "I should have put my foot down with her, but she was just so devastated and lost. I thought she needed her time and space to come around, and I tried to give it to her. It's not a mistake I've made with her since."

That's for sure, I think. "In the end, I was selfish. She was always there for me, always took my calls and came over whenever I needed the slightest bit of company. It took a long time for me to realize that I was the only person she talked to anymore, and by then it almost seemed normal." Aunt Midge pauses for a long time. "But now, I think, she'll talk to you."

I find this statement so shocking I very nearly pull over, but it would be pointless because the turn for the driveway is on my left in seconds.

"Are you kidding? She's not going to talk to me about anything besides baking bread and how to tell when a chicken is cooked." I pull into the drive and shut off the car.

"Then you'll talk about bread and chicken," Aunt Midge says, her voice suddenly stern. She unbuckles the seat belt but makes no move to get out. Instead she turns to me and gives me a terrifying stare, sets her jaw like a tiger about to strike. "Listen up, young lady."

The look scares me enough, but it's the cold low tone she's using that makes me freeze, hands still on the wheel, stomach clenched. This is not the normal jokey Aunt Midge voice. This is something serious. I'm in trouble.

She narrows her eyes at me. "I know how to use Google as well as anyone else, and I know there were no homicides in Cedar Falls, Iowa, in the last two months."

I suck in.

"Oh calm yourself," she says. "I'm glad you didn't kill anybody, and I'm sure as hell not going to kick you out. At least not yet. But there's a condition: You better be a good friend to my grandniece, you hear me? For years she's needed someone like you to open up to, and now that you're here, you better not blow it. Capiche?"

Gulp. The eighty-eight-year-old woman in the seat next to me is scarier than the scariest mob movie she could have learned that word from. "Capiche," I say, wondering how on earth she got the crazy idea that I would be good for anybody, but too freaked out to tell her otherwise.

"I'm glad we cleared that up," she says, and opens her car door and gets out. "You'll deliver the flowers, won't you?" she asks, suddenly all sweetness and light, but before I answer, she's slammed the door in my face, leaving me sitting in the car, shocked, awed, and utterly stupefied.

JANEY

"Mussels are sometimes called the 'oysters of the poor,' which only
goes to show that there are various definitions of poverty."

—IRMA S. ROMBAUER, *Joy of Cooking*

One day while I am working on dinner, Nean comes in from her daily
shelter trip looking like she's seen a ghost. Well, that's not it exactly. She
looks like her dog got run over, and then came to her as a ghost, and
then bit her on the leg. She's holding a huge bouquet of flowers wrapped
up in newspaper, which is what I would be mainly interested in, except
that Aunt Midge is nowhere to be found.

"Where's Aunt Midge?" I ask her.

She stammers something unintelligible.

"Huh?"

"Um . . ." she tries again. "I think she went for a walk or something."

This is odd. Every day for the last week at least, the two of them
have come into the kitchen after their drive to graze and gossip. I've
even gotten in the habit of putting snacks out like a mom waiting for
the kindergarten bus. "Are you all right?" I ask. She's not making a move
toward the warm maple and chipotle popcorn sitting in a big bowl in the
middle of the kitchen table.

"Oh yeah, I'm fine," she says, still standing awkwardly in the doorway. "I think I'm just going to hang out with you this afternoon, if that's okay."

I find this weird for two reasons—one, she wants to hang out with me, and two, she's asking. But I'm not about to discourage her behavior, because what I'm working on is boring. "Sure. I'm doing mussels à la Belge, and later I'll be frying up some potatoes for *frites*. Wanna help debeard?"

She looks at a mesh bag of mussels I've held up as illustration and shudders a little. Yeah, I knew that wasn't going to happen. "Maybe I could bake something . . . for dessert?" she asks. She heads toward the cookbooks, pulling down *Baking from My Home to Yours* and flopping down at the island bar.

I'm surprised by her offer. "That would be great. Make something nice, because J.J. is coming over for dinner tonight."

Nean looks up at me. "Seriously? Tonight?" She does not look happy about this.

"Yes, seriously." Her reaction isn't exactly what I was expecting. I wonder what's up with her—but I'm not going to pry. I'll be damned if I'm going to be as nosy as she is, no matter how curious her behavior. "He told me he's never eaten a mussel before. All these years living in Maine, can you believe it? So I'm cooking this especially for him."

"Whoa," she says. Then, "I've never had a mussel either. They look kind of disgusting."

"You'll love them," I say. She shrugs doubtfully.

I ignore her, knowing full well she'll eat anything that holds still long enough. "I'm making a double batch, so we have plenty for all four of us tonight, plus enough leftover to make a dinner for the shelter to-morrow. Mussels in their shells don't keep so well, but I'm thinking we can toss out the shells of the extras—actually, I bet they'll compost well—and dump them in a pot with a bunch of cream and potatoes and bacon, and get a nice chowder-y stew thing going on."

She looks at me like she doesn't know what I'm talking about and shrugs again. "You're spending too much time with J.J., with all that shrugging," I say. She blushes ever so slightly, and then shrugs again with comic flair.

I laugh. "Listen, I have an idea. Why don't you make something for dessert that we can fry now. Then when it's time for the *frites*, the oil will be old and yummy."

"What are *frites*? And why do we need old oil?"

"*Frites* are . . . well, when you eat French fries with mussels, they're called *frites*. And trust me on the oil. Potatoes love old oil. But not too old."

"If you want French fries, wouldn't it be easier to just go to McDonald's?"

I sneer at her. "Oh, wow. I'd never thought of going to McDonald's. What a genius idea! You're going to save me so much work."

This gets a little smile out of her and I'm glad to see some sign of perk. "You can thank me later," she says. "In the meantime . . ." She pushes the bouquet, which I have been careful to pretend to ignore all this time, across the island to me and says, "Guess who these are from."

"You bought me flowers? You shouldn't have." I look down at the bouquet and see a beautiful riot of foxgloves, honeysuckle, and three big delphiniums right in the middle. My heart gives a big squeeze. "These are beautiful. I can't believe he sent them." Even as I say that, I know I'm giving Nean an opening to ask me about Noah again, but to my surprise, she doesn't take it. Now I'm starting to wonder if Aunt Midge drugged her or something.

"They are nice," she says, admiringly. "Do you want me to put them in a vase?"

Something really isn't right here. Nean is being polite, and helpful. I am wary. "Um . . . are you feeling all right?" I ask her.

She squints her eyes at me, looking shifty. "I'm fine! Just trying to help out," she says anxiously.

"Well, okay. That would be good. There's a vase that came with the house that would be perfect—it's out on the sun porch in the back."

She goes to fetch it and I dump the third pound of mussels into the big colander in the sink and think. *What's going on with her?* She is not being herself, and as pleasant as this new personality is, I prefer the old one. Too-nice Nean is making me nervous. I know it can't last.

She returns with the vase just as I am deciding that's it something to do with J.J., and I should just ignore it. She probably just wants to stay busy and think about something besides a man for a little while. I can relate.

"Check it," she says, and when I turn around she's holding the vase full of flowers, which she's arranged beautifully. "Let's eat on the sun porch tonight and use this as the centerpiece."

"Sure thing, Martha," I tell her, her new interest in domesticity confirming my J.J. theory. "How'd you learn to do that?"

"Geisha school," she tells me, with a little smile.

"I see. Well, Lotus Blossom, when you're done over there, shuffle over here and learn how to tell if a mussel is alive," I tell her.

She folds her hands into prayer position and scoots on over. "These things are actually alive?"

"Yep. If you give them a good tap or poke them gently, they should close up on you. See?" I pester a poor mussel with the dull side of a butter knife, and he slowly tightens up his shell.

"Cool. Gimmie," she says, and takes the knife from me and proceeds to harass several mussels. Interesting how poking things with a knife seems to bring her back to life.

"Okay, okay, I think you've got the drift. Stop before someone calls PETA. Unless you want to help me get all this gunk off their shells?"

"I'm good," she says, dropping the knife and the mussel into the sink with distaste. "Thanks though." I turn the cold tap back on and get back to rubbing the little guys together to knock them clean.

"What kinds of desserts do you fry?" she asks as she watches me work.

"All kinds," I say over the running water. "You can fry just about anything, if you believe the Food Network. Apple fritters, doughnuts, anything in puff pastry. Candy bars and cheesecake, even."

"Go on."

"Okay, here's a thought," I say, still rubbing the mussels. "What if you made little cherry pocket pies and then fried them? How good does that sound?"

"Oh my God. Yes."

"Right?" I say. "And we've got tons of cherries in the fridge." I shut off the water and wipe my hands down on the towel I've tucked into my jeans. "Okay, first step is pastry dough. Hang on. The best recipe is in that *Joy of Cooking* over there." I point to the big white spine, un-missable on any cookbook shelf. "Grab that down and look for 'Pâté Brisée.'"

I hear her go over to the shelf and grab the book. "Where did you get all these cookbooks?" she asks. "You have, like, a thousand."

"They were gifts," I tell her, feeling no need to elaborate.

"From who?" she asks, incredulous. "You don't actually have any friends, as far as I can tell."

Ah. There's the Nean I've come to know and be annoyed by. "More friends than you have. Before you do anything else, cube up the butter and get it into the freezer so it's nice and hard."

She grumbles but takes a pound of butter out of the fridge. "Noah told me you make the best food he's ever tasted."

"He should try it warm," I say, a little proud of myself.

"He should! He'd die and go to heaven."

"Well, I don't know about that," I say, preening my feathers.

"You know, he always looks kind of sad when I show up at the shelter to get Aunt Midge. I think he's hoping it'll be you one of these days."

I keep scrubbing, but I feel my insides flip over. "Tread carefully," I warn her. "I've got five pounds of living breathing shellfish over here."

"All I'm saying is, it might be nice to give the guy a chance. He seems really nice, and you like his produce."

"I'm not really looking for love right now," I say.

"I hear that." Quick study that she is, she's already chopped the butter into little squares and is moving them to the freezer and starting in on the rest of the dough. "But Noah might make a good friend. And he's probably lonely, hanging around the garden all day. A visit would be a nice way to say thank you. Remember when he sent all those peas?"

I do remember. They tasted so green and sugary-smooth. My mouth waters, thinking of them. And then there was the day when he sent the very last of the asparagus, and I wrapped it up with prosciutto and placed a fried egg on top, then dusted it all with Parmesan.

"Remember the asparagus?" Nean asks, reading my mind. "My pee smelled funny for two days."

"Yes, you were pretty excited about that. Sorry we wouldn't come smell it."

"That's okay," she says, reflective. "After a while I realized you probably had your own funny-smelling pee." She turns back to the cookbook, tracing her finger thoughtfully down the recipe, moving her lips as she goes.

I turn back to the sink and watch the mussels coming clean, thinking of how good they're going to taste once they've been steamed with olive oil and white wine and the bright white and green scallions Noah gave Nean yesterday. I think of serving big bowls of them to my growing makeshift family, with newspaper-lined juice glasses full of *frites* on the side and a big bowl of discarded shells in the middle, getting fuller along with our bellies.

No matter what happens with Noah, I know these people will still come back and eat dinner at my table again. Especially after they taste the *frites*.

"All right," I say, resolute. "I'll take Aunt Midge in. Tomorrow."

"You will?" Nean sounds absolutely incredulous.

"Yes. To thank him in person. Just this once."

"That's awesome," she says. "He'll be stoked." She returns to the fridge and takes out another pound of butter. "I better make a double recipe of pie."

Dinner is a grand success. By the time we sit down at the kitchen table, Nean is fully back to her usual snarky self, and J.J. eats it up, along with four pocket pies. We drain two bottles of wine and everyone comes into the kitchen to help me make the stew for tomorrow, tipsy but willing. Despite Nean's insistence that she and J.J. dice the onions together, no one loses a finger. The next morning I taste the creamy sweet-salty dish before packing it up and find it surprisingly delicious, considering it was made by four drunks.

Then, when the food is all packed up and the pastry box full of leftover pocket pies has been tied up with string especially for Noah, I get nervous. What if Nean was lying when she said he wanted to see me? It would not be the first time she's pulled a fast one on me. Maybe I'll get up there and he'll take one look at me and turn around. Or maybe I'll go to say thank you and lose my lunch again, right there in the shelter parking lot. This was a terrible idea.

But there's no getting out now. Aunt Midge comes down the stairs in her slow methodical way, and I know she's not getting in that car with anyone other than me. When she gets to the kitchen she takes a long hard look at me, taking in the plain blue sundress I'm wearing and the white cotton sweater that's tied around my waist, which I'm bringing as hive-coverage if necessary, and says, "Lose the sweater when we get into town, okay? Otherwise, you're a knockout. You look just like I did when I was your age. Except less slutty."

"Thanks," I say. "Are you ready to go?"

"You bet I am. Are you?" she asks meaningfully.

I don't answer, because whatever I say, the outcome will be the same.

In the car we talk about easy things, the people she's met at the shelter and how the food preparation rules require her to wear a hairnet and it's not good for her permanent, which is what she calls the tight curls she sets every other night with Aqua Net and plastic rollers. I concentrate on breathing deeply and keeping an eye on my skin, which is as of yet hive-free. I run conversations through my head, imagining what I might say to Noah. Here's what I've got so far:

"Hello there, Noah. I came here today to say thank you for giving me all of the produce and flowers. Okay, bye."

He's going to be dazzled by my witty repartee. But when we pull into the parking lot, it's empty. No sign of Noah's Honda.

"We're early," says Aunt Midge. "Help me get all of this into the building."

I sherpa in the heavy casserole dish and today's fresh bread, but there's no sign of Noah anywhere. Aunt Midge doesn't seem to notice his absence and scoots me away. "Nean usually just toodles around doing errands or eating lunch," she tells me, herding me out of the building. "Come back at one, okay?"

"Okay," I say, wandering away feeling both relieved and dejected at the same time. What a bunch of hullabaloo over nothing. I go back to the car, roll all the windows down, and get out a book I've read and reread so many times I had to duck tape the binding: Laurie Colwin's *Home Cooking*. I always read her essays in order, and I am on the chapter about creamed spinach, lost in her little New York City kitchen in a matter of words. I'm on to red peppers when I see a shadow fall over my book. My heart starts pounding before I even look up, because I know who it is.

"Janey!" Noah says, and there's an excitement in his voice that knocks me totally off kilter. "How nice to see you."

I look up and see that he's leaning on my passenger side window like he's taking my order at the A&W. "Hi, Noah," I say, moving my eyes back and forth, from the sight of his floppy brown hair falling over his eyes to my arms to make sure I don't need my sweater. They are goose bumpy, but rash-less. I smile. "Hi Noah," I say again.

His smile cracks me wide open. "You look pretty today. Want to take me to lunch?" he asks. My head starts spinning and I feel dizzy.

"I came here today," I blurt out, "to say thank you for the vegetables and the beautiful flowers."

He opens the car door. "And what better way to say thank you than having lunch with me." While I reel, he slides into the car and buckles his seat belt. "I know just the place."

He slams the door closed, but I don't make a move, just stare at him sitting there. He's so . . . *delicious*-looking. He makes me think of ravioli stuffed with artichoke hearts and ricotta cheese, and fresh summer peaches, and wine—big, lip-smacking red wine that tastes of cherries and chocolate. And I feel like I've had about three glasses of that wine.

He looks back at me a little puzzled, and I know I should turn on the
ignition and pull out of the lot and have lunch with this man, but I seem
to have forgotten how to go about that exactly. My mouth feels dry.

"Aren't you hungry?" he asks, giving me the opening to get out of
this, an opening I do not want at all, and yet am seriously considering
taking.

"I'm starving," I say after a little tussle with myself, though my
stomach is telling me eating is not a good idea. "Where to?" God, I
sound casual. Go, me.

"Let's go to a little place I know of down the way," he says. "Take a
right out of the lot, and go straight at the four-way stop."

I start the car, feeling drunk but reminding myself that Driving
While Infatuated isn't technically illegal, and follow his directions. After
the stop sign, we drive about a mile, me going a little too slowly to be
normal and him saying nothing about it. "Okay," he chimes when we
get to a little diner-ish-looking place called Bambi's. "Turn in here and
park anywhere you can find." Sure enough, the parking lot is packed,
and I say so. "You'll see why it's so crowded in a few minutes . . ." he
says with great promise, while I circle to a spot in a neighboring business's lot, and successfully park between two enormous pickup trucks.

Bambi's itself is little more than a shack with about twelve counter
seats, which are not only completely full but also have a standing-room-
only crowd behind them, people holding their car keys and watching
the waitress behind the counter hungrily as she packs up to-go orders.
Outside the building are countless picnic tables, bustling with happy eat-
ers all working on stacks of something in waxed paper wrappers. "You're
not a vegetarian, are you?" Noah asks me with some trepidation, and I
shake my head no, thinking that even if I were I'm not sure I'd be able
to disappoint him by admitting it now. "Phew. You go find us a nice
table outside, one with a good view, and I'll take care of lunch."

I go outside and start noodling around the tables, unclear about exactly what he meant by a good view. The tables in front of the building
look out on the road and the parking lot, and the ones on the right are
surrounded by fields. I pick the field side, and wait anxiously.

When Noah reemerges, he's carrying a red cafeteria tray full of whatever it is that's in those waxed paper bundles, and two tall cups with straws.

"Get ready," he says, as he plops down the tray. With great flourish he hands me one of the cups, which is covered in a frosty condensation. "I wasn't sure if you were a chocolate or vanilla sort of woman, so I got you a black and white."

"Yum," I say, and my tummy seems to relax at the idea of a milkshake, much to my gratitude. I take a big slurp and get the most delicious mouthful of chocolate malt and vanilla ice cream. "Wow." It tastes so good my whole body seems to come untied. "It's like liquid Xanax."

Noah nods. "But just you wait." Then he unwraps one of the waxed paper bundles and reveals a tiny little hot dog, covered in mustard and bright green relish. He presents it to me like it's diamonds. "Bon appetit!"

"It's a little hot dog," I say like an idiot.

"It's an *awesome* little hot dog," Noah says, a dog already lifted to his mouth. "Bambi's serves two things: hot dogs with mustard and hot dogs with mayo. I got you three of each."

"Six hot dogs?" I exclaim.

"If that's not enough I can always go back for more."

I laugh and consider the little wiener in my hands. It's about three inches long, nestled into a pale tan-colored bun, and it looks like you eat it in just a few bites. I take a tiny nibble and then a bigger bite when Noah scrunches up his face at me teasingly. It tastes terrific, with skin as snappy and crisp as a Chicago red hot and a big beefy juicy flavor inside. But the real stunner is the mustard and relish, combining to form a tangy wash of deliciousness over the whole thing.

Noah is watching me all this time, watching my reaction. "Whoa," I say when I've finished chewing. "That is one amazing hot dog."

"Now try the mayo," he says. "That's my favorite."

I unwrap another dog—this one in a reddish waxed paper wrapping—and taste. I can see why the condiment choice is such a big deal—this one tastes totally different, creamy and kind of lush, and the relish doesn't seem hot anymore so much as bright and smooth. Thrilled by the contrast, I taste the mustard again, and then the mayo.

"Mustard," I announce, after I've killed four hot dogs. "Mustard is the best."

"Wrong-o," Noah says, and then to punctuate that, he shoves an entire mayo dog into his mouth in one bite. It's both disgusting and silly, and I crack up. "What are you doing?" I ask mid-laugh, though it's too late for him to turn back now.

His eyes bulge out and I watch him chew intently, trying to get his mouth around the whole hot dog. He's definitely struggling and there's a long moment where I wonder if he's going to have to spit the whole thing out, mortifying us both in the process. But he soldiers on. "Mmmm," he manages to get out. I see him swallow once, and then, with his mouth still indecently full of hot dog, he mutters "Tastes better this way," and then chokes a little. After a fit of coughs, he swallows again. "Concentrates the flavor." He's bright red and I realize he's a little embarrassed about what he just did, and it makes me feel so much better to know I'm not the only one here who knows how to blush.

"Oh yeah?" I ask, and then take an enormous bite, not the whole dog but as much as I can get in my mouth. "Mmmpfh!"

"There you go," he says, swallowing again and then taking a huge slurp of milkshake.

"It does taste better," I say when I can speak again.

"Right? And if you think that's good, you just wait. I bet I can do two at once."

"Don't show me! Seriously."

"Are you kidding? I'm saving that for later. It's the lynchpin of my seduction technique."

Seduction technique? It is unquestionably hot out, but at that I get a whole epidermis full of goose bumps and feel a chill down my spine. Noah is talking about seducing me. Would I like to be seduced by Noah? I can think of worse things. . . . But am I even capable of starting a new relationship anymore?

And then it hits me: maybe I could be. After all, I've made a new friend in Nean. I've talked to all sorts of new people since we moved here. Maybe, with the right motivation, I could try to put myself back out there. And if Noah isn't motivation, I don't know what would be.

Now if I can only think of something to say to fill the growing awkward silence. I channel Nean, searching for something appropriately light and flirtatious to say back. "What time is it?" I say at last. In my mind's eye, Nean is crossing her arms and shaking her head at me in disappointment.

"Noonish. Do you have to get back?" Noah asks.

"Not yet, but eventually. I have to drive my aunt home after her shift," I say. "I'm taking Nean's place today."

"Oh really? How come?"

To see you, I think. "Because, um . . ." I say.

"Just to see me?" Noah asks around the straw of his milkshake. I gulp.

"I mean," I start to stutter. "Kind of, well . . ." I think back to my speech preparation. "I wanted to give you some pies," I say. "And thank you for all the food you've been sharing with us."

Noah grins, that smile that breaks his whole face wide open and actually makes his green eyes twinkle. Twinkle, I tell you. It's unreal. "It's my pleasure. You don't have to keep sending things back, you know. I love everything you've sent, but—"

"Do you really like it?" I blurt out.

"Like what?"

"The food. My cooking, I mean."

Noah groans and then inhales so deeply I'm a little afraid he's mad at me for asking. "Are you kidding? It's the best food I've ever tasted."

I die—actually expire right then and there—and ascend to heaven. "Thank you."

"You couldn't be more welcome. Where'd you learn to cook like that?" he asks.

"From books," I say. "I have a lot of cookbooks."

"No training? No learning the art at your mother's knee?"

"My mom wasn't a cook, really. She kept me fed, but that's about it. I ate a lot of Kraft macaroni and cheese and SPAM on toast growing up. But when I—"

I stop myself because I realize I've somehow gotten the harebrained idea that I should tell this near stranger very personal things about my life. About how I came to own so many cookbooks and how the first time I used them was when I cooked for the hundreds of mourners who came to bury my fiancé. How the very first big meal I ever fixed was a spiral-cut ham and six quarts of potato salad, eaten on paper plates by people dressed all in black, milling around Ned's parents' house, saying nice things about Ned and forgetting my name.

Thankfully the feeling passes and I chastise myself for such a silly idea. He doesn't need to hear about some old drama lurking in my past. "When I got my own kitchen, I just learned on my own," I say with finality.

"Impressive," he says. "What's your favorite thing to cook?"

"I honestly have no idea," I say, frowning a bit at the question. "I've never thought about it before."

"Okay," he replies. "I'll wait over here while you think it over."

Yikes. I think through my mental recipe file frantically, knowing I have to say something but blanking entirely. I like cooking everything. I can't think of what I like cooking the best. Trying to choose seems childish somehow, like picking a favorite color.

But then it comes to me. "Sauerbraten," I announce proudly, and with great relief. "My favorite thing to cook is sauerbraten. It has a million ingredients and takes three days at least. It has more aromas than any other food on earth, one of them being juniper, which makes your whole kitchen smell like the Black Forest. And you serve it with spaetzle, which you can make a billion different ways. Horseradish spaetzle, and mustard spaetzle, and herbed spaetzle, and spaetzle with cheese. . . . When you are done, you have this enormous pile of tender, melt-in-your-mouth beef and potato dumplings drowning in gravy, and you are full in two bites."

"You're making me hungry, and I just ate seven hot dogs."

"The power of sauerbraten," I say. "I also like making tamales, but I'm not as good at it."

"I'd like to taste this sauerbraten of yours," Noah says. "If you'd like to cook it for me sometime."

Up until this moment, I've been feeling more and more relaxed over lunch, so much so that it's been almost like eating with Aunt Midge—if Aunt Midge were very handsome. But when he says this I recoil a little. I can't help it; I'm not ready. I don't want him coming to my house and eating at my table. I hardly know the guy. Why is he pushing me?

He must see the resistance in my face because he adds, "I mean, after we get to know each other better." This is a little reassuring, but I still feel overwhelmed.

"Maybe," I say, and try to think of a way to change the subject. I summon up the golden rule of men, at least according to the wedding magazines we had at the bridal salon: Ask them about themselves. "How long have you been gardening for the shelter?"

Noah tilts his head at this, and I know he can tell I'm sidestepping the dinner idea deliberately. "Not long," he says. "I moved here early in the spring, right when most things need to go in the ground."

"Did you move here just for this job?" I ask.

He pauses and scrunches up his face. "Not exactly. It just kind of fell into place."

He doesn't elaborate and I don't pry. "Do you like it?"

"I do. It's not my own farm, but it has a ready-made demand from the shelter, and the people who eat my food seem to genuinely appreciate it. As long as the grants keep coming in for the whole operation, I'll have good work to do," he says, and when he finishes talking I realize I recognize that matter-of-factness about hard work from back home, from the farmers I'd shop from at the green markets every week. I suddenly feel ashamed that I haven't found a full-time job yet. If he knew, surely he'd think I was lazy.

"So you want to have your own farm some day?" I ask, desperate to keep the vocational conversation focused on him, and also curious about his ambitions.

He smiles a little. "I actually did have my own farm once, in upstate New York. I grew arugula. Organic arugula." He shakes his head, looking a little sad. "I don't even really like arugula. Rocket. That's what we called it before the marketers got to us."

"What happened to the farm?"

"I sold it," he says. "To a gentleman farmer from the city who wanted to get away on the weekends. It's a long story, but basically I wasn't making any money at all, for a long time, so I had to let it go and try something else. It was a hard thing. I'm not sure I want to go back to that kind of pressure ever again."

I think of that pressure, and remember something I haven't thought of for a long time. "I was going to be a teacher," I blurt out. "I was going to teach middle school."

"Oh really?"

"Yeah. But then I realized there was no way I could do it."

"How come?"

"I'm shy," I say, as if this isn't abundantly clear by now.

"There are no shy teachers?"

"Not shy like me. There's no way I could get in front of a class and teach anything. I don't know what I was thinking, getting my teaching certificate in the first place."

"Maybe you were thinking that you had something important to share."

I shake my head. "I don't."

"So you say," he says, thoughtful. "So what do you do instead of teaching?"

Whoops. Now I'm stuck. "Seamstress at a bridal store. Or I was, when I lived in Iowa."

Noah raises his eyebrows at me. "No kidding? You can cook and you can sew and you're certified to teach. Huh . . ."

"What?" I ask. "Are you going to ask me if I can mix a good martini too?"

"Not exactly," he replies, a little too quickly, leaving me curious about what's on his mind. "Hey, did you know there's a bridal shop in

Damariscotta? I bet they could use an extra pair of hands, now that so many city girls are coming up here to get hitched. The caterers have been knocking down my door for fancy salad greens and berries all summer. There's got to be some kind of crazy demand going on. Where that demand was when I was trying to unload organic arugula, I'll never know."

"Actually, I've been doing sewing work for them, contracting out of the house. Stuff I can do by hand or on my machine at home. Nothing full-time though."

"So you're stuck just sitting around that big house all day?"

"Not sitting around," I say. "Sewing. And cooking."

"I can't have that. You'll get all moldy. There are only maybe twenty other houses out there on the cove, and The Farm. You need more society than a handful of summer people and some chickens."

I smile wryly, and say, "Then it's a good thing I'm having lunch with you." I give myself a mental high five for that one.

He grins and nods his head at me. "Definitely. Definitely. You'll have to keep coming to see me if you want to avoid turning into a mole-person."

For a moment my inner schoolgirl dances in a circle and sings, *"He likes me, he likes me."* I hush her up. "I can be persuaded."

"Good!" He puts both hands down flat on the table and looks right at me. "Next Monday. That will give you four days to get excited about seeing me again," he wiggles his eyebrows. "Is it a date?"

A date. With someone who is alive, and a guy. Maybe, with someone who will say nice things to me, and listen to my hopes and fears, and take my hand across the table, and kiss me at the end of the night. Someone who will make demands on my time, and fight with me, and keep secrets, and complain about how much I spend on groceries.

And, let's face it, someone who could leave at any time and never come back.

My stomach turns over again, but I can't say no. "It's a date."

NEAN

"[Lobsters] also have the discomforting distinction of being
just about the only food we cook live."

—PAM ANDERSON, *The Perfect Recipe*

Janey is in love. It's the most obnoxious thing you've ever seen. For the
last two weeks she's been going into town with Aunt Midge more and
more frequently, leaving me stuck here miles from everything and going wild from boredom. Every second that J.J. is off gardening somewhere and unavailable to entertain me feels like a lifetime. But Janey is
oblivious to my anguish. When she comes back from Little Pond she
hums to herself like Snow White. I keep expecting squirrels to come
into the house and fix her hair.

And she's been falling down on her cooking duties, which is the
most upsetting part of all. The other day she came home holding a
bucket of fried chicken from some roadside shack north of here. She
actually served it to us like real food. It was the craziest thing you've
ever seen—Janey Brown putting down a cardboard bucket in the middle of the table and saying, "Dinner is served." Of course, she made
coleslaw from scratch to go with, so it's not like she's had a lobotomy.
But it's the principle of the thing.

The worst part is she won't talk about it at all, to anyone. You can
tell she's way into this guy, it's as plain as the egg on my face. But she

won't tell me anything, no matter how much I pester her, which is a lot. Aunt Midge says she doesn't know anything either. She seems annoyed that I'm in the dark about all this, and I know I'm falling down on the job as Janey's confidante. What if Aunt Midge gets sick of my ineptitude and tells me to take a hike? You heard the woman: I'm here to be a friend to Janey, and that's it. If she stops needing my company, I'm obsolete.

I've got to find a way to make her talk. Maybe if I hide her chef's knife.

I'm plotting this when I see J.J. coming toward the house. He's wearing the holey jeans and baseball cap that are his uniform for garden work, so I know he's not here just to see me. But nevertheless, my heart does that little leap thing when I see him. I try to ignore it. It's irritating how cute he can be.

I greet him and tell him about what's on my mind: Janey's reticence to spill the beans. His eyebrows go way, way up. "Maybe she doesn't know how she feels yet, and she just needs time to sort it out privately," he conjectures, and I wonder if he's talking about Janey or himself.

"All the more reason to talk to her confidante, *moi*, about it. Besides, she owes it to me to explain why she's hogging all the drives into town."

"I thought you told me you didn't want to have to drive Aunt Midge all the time," he says.

"You really should consider experimenting with more illicit drugs," I tell him. "With a memory like that you're never going to be able to keep any friends."

He makes a face. "Hm. So you wanted to get out of the daily drives, but now that you're stuck out here with me, you've reconsidered?"

If I were stuck out here with him, as in *with* him, we'd have no problem with boredom. But I'm in boy-toy purgatory. I can see the bare-chested blond man-child, and I can talk to him for hours, but I can't run my tongue along the lines of his six-pack stomach. Oh, the irony.

After a little back and forth, J.J. tells me he thinks I should give her space, especially since all of this is my doing. He also has no sympathy when I complain about being stranded without a car or a job to keep

me occupied. But he is picking up some of the slack in getting me out
and about. Yesterday he asked me if I wanted to go out to dinner. I
wasn't sure if he was asking me *out* out, or just out. But I said yes. If he
tries to smooch me at the end of the night I can always play dumb. *"Oh,
J.J., I had no idea your feelings toward me were of a romantic nature! I feel just
terrible that I gave you the wrong idea!"*

"So," he says when the subject of Janey's sex life is put to rest—at
least in *his* mind. "Are you excited about tonight?"

I'm not sure what the right answer is here. Of course I'm excited, for
a myriad of reasons. But do I want him to *think* I'm excited?

"Meh," I say but with a smile. "Where are we going?"

He grins. "I'm not telling, but know this: There Will Be Bibs."

"You know just how to make a woman happy, don't you?"

At that, J.J. gives me an absolutely wicked smile, and says, "Oh, believe me, I do, and bibs have nothing to do with it."

Why, John Junior, I had no idea you had it in you! I get a chill that
goes down my spine and around to other regions that have been cruelly
ignored for some time. *Quiet, you,* I mentally whisper to my vagina.

J.J. grins, too proud of himself. "And with that, I must leave you.
The shrubbery ain't going to water itself."

Not wanting him to have the last word—or the last tease—I wave
good-bye and, just as he's turning to go, I say, casually, "Okay, see ya
later. I guess I'll just go put on my bikini and hang out by the water."

He turns back and gives me exactly the kind of reaction I was going
for—a mix of wide eyes and gaping mouth, with just the hint of lolling
tongue, while I scamper back into the house as flirtily as possible.

Luckily for my ego, I have actually acquired a bikini of late. Aunt
Midge gave it to me from one of her boxes; it's a bikini she actually
made herself back in what she calls her "heyday." It's macraméd from
thick cream-colored cord and lined with flesh-tone fabric that offers
modesty for the wearer without looking modest at all to the observer.
It's also got reddish-brown wooden beads on it, hanging off the strings
that tie the bottom closed, and sewn into a triangle pattern on each half
of the bra top. When Aunt Midge first pulled it out of tissue paper she

was storing it in, it looked huge, and I thought there was no way it would ever fit me, but apparently my butt has come into its own over the last month here at reverse fat camp.

I tie it on and look down and am shocked and delighted to find myself in possession of actual boobs. Not huge boobs, but at least B cups, I think. Now that I have some body fat, I really do look a lot more normal and healthy. I'm probably the only woman in America who feels that way, but so what? I'm hungry, so lay off, Anna Wintour.

Now, clad only in string, I go looking for a snack to take out to the backyard with me and am surprised to find someone already headfirst in the fridge, taking in the breeze while moving around containers of chicken stock and God knows what else.

"Aunt Midge?" I ask, recognizing that expanse of tushie anywhere. "What are you doing home from the shelter?"

She shuts the fridge and whirls around on me. "It's Saturday. I don't do lunches on Saturdays," she says, and I already know this quite well—I just had no idea what day it was until this very moment. "You really do need a job if you can't even keep track of the days of the week anymore."

There might be some truth to that. "But I saw Janey take the car out right at the normal time," I say. "Was she just going for groceries?"

Aunt Midge lowers her eyes at me. "Was she? Or maybe was she going into Little Pond to see someone, do you think?"

"On a Saturday? This thing is more serious than I realized," I say.

Aunt Midge growls at me. "What good are you if you aren't keeping track of her?" she asks.

"Jeez! I'm not her mother," I snap back, though her words only confirm my own fears. If I'm not going to be needed to bring Janey out of her shell anymore, what exactly am I needed for? "Anyway," I explain, just as much to myself as to her, "all my usual interrogation techniques have failed. I'm not sure what to do short of waterboarding."

Aunt Midge softens, and smiles. "She is one tough cookie, that girl," she concedes. "Nice bikini, Miss Bardot. Let's get some food and go work on our tans."

I find some slices of ham and Muenster cheese lurking in the fridge and cut us off a stack of thin slices of my latest creation, olive-rosemary bread, and follow Aunt Midge out back to the lounge chairs. She's trying to heft one over closer to the edge of the cliffs, and I set down my platter on the little table between them and take the chair from her, and then the other, and get us all settled in. The view is incredible today, the sun high in the sky turning the ocean into a diamond mine.

"She's been humming a lot," says Aunt Midge when she's comfortably seated. "I think the humming is a sign."

"Obviously," I say. "She's crazy about him. Which is what worries me."

"Why would you be worried?"

Well, not because I'm worried that she won't need me anymore. Certainly not that. "She's so vulnerable," I say. "And she hardly knows the guy."

"That's for sure," says Aunt Midge, a little too enthusiastically.

"What do you mean by that?" I ask.

"Oh, nothing," she says, clearly fibbing. "But I don't think you need to worry. He seems like a good sort of man."

"Well, they all look good from a distance," I say.

"Hmm. Does that include J.J.?"

"Of course it does. He seems nice and smart and fun and whatever, but you don't really know about a guy until you've known him a long time." And seen him drunk, I mentally add, thinking of Geoff for the first time in a nice long while.

Aunt Midge shrugs. "I knew about Albert right away." Albert was her husband, the one that stuck for thirty plus years and then keeled over when he was still in his fifties.

"How?" I ask.

"I've never told you this story?"

I shake my head, feeling just as surprised as she sounds. In the drives to and from the shelter every day we've covered quite a lot of ground in Aunt Midge's life story. And though I know she loved her husband, many of her tales have been from the "other men I've known and loved" department. I guess we never went this far back.

She sinks into her chair a little lower and takes a deep breath before launching in. "Me and my best friend at the time, this awful woman named Roberta, went to see *Casablanca*. Roberta was already pretty well into Humphrey Bogart, but I had never seen him before. That *Maltese Falcon* picture seemed like such a guy movie at the time. Well, believe me, I've seen it forty times since. Dear God in heaven, I've been a good woman. When I die, all I want is Humphrey Bogart and Matt Damon feeding me grapes, all day long. Or not grapes. Bonbons. The ones that look like nipples, with the maple crème inside . . ."

"Focus, Aunt Midge," I remind her.

"Focus on what? Oh. Right. So that night, when Bogart came on screen, I took one look and fell right in love. Oh, that hat. Who else could wear nothing fancier than an old brimmed hat and a raincoat and still look so good you think your teeth are going to fall out?"

I nod, though I have no idea what she's talking about. Note to self: look up *Casablanca* on Wikipedia.

"When the movie was over, we got up and were about to leave our seats, but it was a double feature, and the movie after . . . what was that movie, I can't remember . . . well, it was intermission, I know, and the town theater still had an organist come in at intermissions and play a couple of numbers, just like when I was a kid. But this time the lights came up and there was no organist there. Just dead silence. Well, a few people were probably wondering where he was but most of us didn't even realize what was missing—it was such a silly old holdover from the days of silent movies—until the theater door banged open and a man in a tan hat and a raincoat"—Aunt Midge's voice turns urgent—"*just like the hat and raincoat Humphrey Bogart had been wearing in* Casablanca, came barging down the aisle, running in that downhill flop-flop sort of way past all the seats, and down to the organ. And then he sat down on the organ bench, sopping wet, didn't even take off his raincoat, just pushed it behind him on the bench, and started playing. Oh, I wish I remembered what he had played that night. He made plenty of mistakes, all flustered and dripping as he was. But he still sounded great to me. Just great. He played for about ten minutes and then the music for the next movie started to come up and the lights went down. He stood up from the bench and stretched a little and walked back up the aisle to go. I didn't even see his face as he passed by. I just got up and I told Roberta I had to take a tinkle, and then I followed that raincoat out of the theater and into the pouring rain and we fell in love with each other as soon as I tapped him on the shoulder and said, 'Excuse me.' Nothing clever, just 'excuse me,' and we were both done and dusted just like that."

I'm rapt. "So then what happened?

"We went to his mother's place for pie," Aunt Midge says, as though that is the most natural answer. "And I kept trying to get him to put that hat back on the whole night, I remember."

"And then what?" I ask, hoping we are getting to the first kiss, at least.

"What do you mean, then what? Then we got married. Haven't you been listening?"

I sink back in my chair and sigh. "Never mind." But I am enchanted all the same.

We share a moment of companionable silence. I try to imagine what J.J. would look like in a fedora.

"Not all love happens like that, you know."

"I know," I say.

"For example, sometimes love happens when a young woman has been lying her pants off left and right to everyone who cares for her, and then she meets an interesting guy but she's in so deep that she can't trust him with the truth so she pushes him away."

"Oh, really?"

"Mm-hmm. Happens all the time."

"Just like that, huh?"

"Just like that."

"And in how many of these situations does the guy in question happen to be a sexy gardener?"

Aunt Midge purses her lips, pretending to be in deep in thought. "I'd say about a third," she says, grinning at me. "You could try telling him the truth."

"Maybe later," I say.

"Practice on me," she says back, too fast for me to believe she hasn't been steering this conversation here for some time. "Tell me what really happened to you before you came here."

"Nothing happened," I say. "I entered the contest, so of course I watched the TV show announcing the winners, and I really thought I had won, so I came here and broke into the house. I made up the bullshit about killing someone so you'd let me stay."

"Did you pull out your own hair just for our benefit too? Slice up your own knuckles?"

Her saying this makes me look down at the bands of scars I have on my hand from where the coffee cup broke when I beaned Geoff. They look so old already, even though it's only been a little over a month. The ones on the inside of my hand are longer, and have a milky whiteness to them, and without thinking I trace one with my other index finger, like I'm reading my fortune in them. My finger stops on a pale cigarette burn—a souvenir from the boyfriend before Geoff.

Aunt Midge catches me at it and sighs loudly. "A little honesty wouldn't kill you, you know. You wouldn't have to make a habit of it or anything."

I turn to her and give her my best carefree Nean-the-Free-Spirit look. "Nothing left to tell," I say, and then I pull my barely covered butt off the lounge chair and see myself back inside.

Hours later, I am still thinking of Aunt Midge's questions. *Did you pull out your own hair? Slice up your own knuckles?* But I am determined not to let any trace of uneasiness pollute my time with J.J. Janey still being absent, I go digging through her underwear drawer, hoping to find some lacy bra to cover up my newly budding ta-tas. After all, it may not technically be a "date," but a gal still deserves to feel sexy from time to time, right? But apparently Janey doesn't share my philosophy. All I find is a pile of tightly folded cotton briefs and the kinds of bras they sell in boxes. I don't want an eighteen-hour bra. I want a thirty-minute bra. Leave it to the girl who thinks everything is unmentionable not to own a single actual unmentionable.

In the end I go with the same ol', same ol', and put over it a pretty yellow sundress I've lifted from another half-unpacked box. It has tie-straps and elastic around the bust so I tie it as low as I can and hope I'm more Bunny Ranch than Sunny Brook Farms.

Aunt Midge sees me on my way out, and nods in approval. "Nice dress!" she calls after me as I bound down the porch stairs toward the road.

"Thanks," I call back. "It's yours."

I hear her laughing even as I make my way around the bend of trees to the end of the drive. J.J. and I have planned to meet at the boat put-in that's halfway between us, but I don't get two steps before I see his truck coming up the road. He beeps and I jump.

"Going my way?" he asks, and for a moment I consider saying no, just to see what he'd say. Instead I hop into the cab and start cranking down the window before I've even said hello.

"You look nice," J.J. says, and he uses that same damn neutral voice that I'm always trying to use on him. It means, "We are just friends, and a friend can compliment another friend without it meaning anything." It drives me crazy to hear it from him now, when I'm deliberately trying to be hot.

"You too," I say, without looking over at him. "Where are we going?"

"It's a surprise," he tells me.

I frown at him. He looks from me to the road, and when he looks back at me again I am still frowning.

"It's a seafood restaurant," he says. "On the water."

"Ooh," I say in my best upper-crust old lady voice. "Is it Chez Fancy Pants? I have been dying to go there ever since I read the reviews in the *Globe*."

J.J. laughs at me and tells me that yes, we are going to Chez Fancy Pants and getting a reservation there is a killer.

"Are those your actual fancy pants?" I ask him, noticing for the first time that he is wearing not just a button-down shirt and khaki slacks but also a red-and-gold-striped tie.

"Yep."

"Nice tie."

"Thanks," he says. "I borrowed it from my dad."

This makes me turn my head with a start. "Your dad lives with you?" Up until now he's only mentioned his mother in conversation. I sort of assumed that like me and most people I've spent any amount of time with, he didn't have a dad.

"Of course," he says, laughing. "What did you think?"

I blush, and not in a coquettish way. I'm truly embarrassed. "Sorry, I didn't know. I just figured . . ." I don't know how to complete this sentence, so I let my voice drift off. I guess I figured that since he's a gardener, and a townie, he'd be pretty much the same as me in most ways. I hope he's not offended.

But he doesn't seem to realize the nature of my mistake, and he sits there looking pleasantly oblivious until he helpfully contributes, "My parents have been married since time began. I'm the baby of the family."

"Wow," I say, unable to think of anything more intelligent. I am starting to wonder if maybe our home lives haven't been just a teensy bit more different than I realized. Starting with, you know, having a home.

"I take it your parents aren't still married?" he asks.

Well, that's a startling understatement. "No," I say, and decide not to clear up the misconception that they were ever married in the first place. I like to think I came about my trailer trashiness all by myself, but my mother shares the same attributes of frequent homelessness and bad taste in men. Happily we do not share her love of meth.

J.J. seems to notice I'm feeling a bit rattled by this little line of conversation. He takes mercy on me and changes the subject. "So, ever had a lobster boil before?"

"I've never even had lobster before."

J.J. slams on the brakes and the tires shriek underneath us. "Please tell me you're joking."

"Some of us think Bumblebee tuna is good enough, Daddy War-bucks."

"Well, you would be wrong about that." He shakes his head disap-provingly. "This explains everything."

"Explains what, exactly?"

"Everything. Why you are so skinny, for one thing. And why you seem so unsure about staying in Maine."

"I seem unsure about Maine?"

"Yes! You could not be more noncommittal if you tried. I keep thinking I'm going to come by one day and you'll have gone back to Iowa."

I don't tell him how much that thought scares me. Or how very likely the scenario is, sooner or later. "I think . . ."—I mentally start tap dancing—"that I've been waiting to see how things go here, yes. But I do like Maine."

"Say you love it," J.J. says, starting the car back up slowly.

"I wouldn't go that far."

"SAY IT."

"Fine, I love it. I love the ocean, and the silly accent, and the smell of birch trees in the morning. Are you happy?"

J.J. brings the car up to a normal speed and nods happily. "Yes, ma'am, I am. I knew you'd come around. And if you think you love it now, just wait 'til you've had a lobster boil."

We pull into a long driveway and up to a big building surrounded on all sides by forest. The sign reads "Darcy's on the Water" in swirly script. When we get inside, I find myself in an enormous and elegant dining room filled with dark oak and burgundy booths. Soft classical music is playing. I thank the heavens I wore my good flip-flops. The place looks like that scene from *Point of No Return*, when a feral Bridget Fonda starts her new life of ass kicking. I wonder if I will be called upon to shoot someone during the dessert course.

"Reservation for two," says J.J., looking cool and utterly comfort-able despite the grandeur. He's been here before, that's for sure. I note with relief the slight hesitation in his voice when he adds, "I requested a table outside?"

We get shown to a small glass door at the back of the restaurant, and through it to a wide wooden deck filled with tables and diners. Out here, people look casual, and a few are actually wearing bibs as promised. But even in jeans and plastic bibs they have an expensive look about them, like they eat lobster all the time and think nothing of it. I see big diamond rings sparkling and handbags out of *Sex and the City* draped on the back of chairs. "Look good?" J.J. asks, as he pushes my chair in and takes his seat across the little round table.

I look out at the dark ocean and the big sky in front of us—nearly the same view I'd see at the house—and try to forget the fancy white tablecloth and the array of wineglasses and candles and flatware stretched out atop it. Just like sitting out in the backyard with Aunt Midge eating ham sandwiches, I tell myself, and nod. "Looks good."

I start to open the leather-bound menu in my hands and J.J. says, "Order whatever you like, but I strongly recommend the lobster boil. They'll only do it during summer, and only then if you're sitting outside. Too messy for the dining room."

Okay, then. I close my menu and tell him the lobster boil is it. But not before I get a peep at the prices for the appetizers. Jesus H. Christ.

He orders a bottle of wine (I don't want to think about how much that costs) and the lobster boil for two, and then I get up and hit the toilets, trying not to look panicky. He suggested this place, so he should pay, right? I've got seventeen fifty to my name right now and I was feeling pretty flush about it until I discovered that my sum life savings won't even get you a shrimp cocktail in this place. Even the bathroom is posh. There are tampons just sitting on the counter for anyone to take—the good kind too, with the Satin Touch applicators. I think of pocketing a purseful, but if they have a security system in here they'll see how uncouth I am.

But wait. Who cares if they see me? It's not like the guys from security are going to call down to the table and tell J.J. I just ripped off a pile of tampons, are they? Bolstered, I shove about twenty into my purse and then toss in a bottle of hand lotion and two handfuls of mints for good measure. I wash up and head back for my table, reminding myself that I have every right to be here, and J.J. wouldn't pick a place where he wasn't comfortable. And if he's comfortable, I should be comfortable too. It's just J.J.

Encouraged, I sit down and find myself starting to relax and have a good time. J.J. is being awfully cute tonight, what with his standing up when I rejoin the table and then pushing in my chair. I wonder if he's been watching that dinner scene in *Pretty Woman* on repeat, the way I did when I was little and still convinced that knowing the right fork for snails would get me where I wanted to go in life. I ask him if that's where he got his manners, and he laughs and tells me he hopes he can do as well as Richard Gere on a date with a beautiful woman.

"Well," I say. "She *was* a hooker."

"I was talking about you, stupid," J.J. says, and I flush bright pink. This is a date, isn't it? I mean, look at this place, these flowers on the table, this view. I'd have to be an idiot not to realize this is a date.

But just as I'm thinking this, the waiter arrives back at our table holding a pair of thick plastic bibs. He ties the first around my neck, and then hands J.J. one to fix himself, and when he's done, I see that he's got a giant picture of a happy dancing lobster on his chest. Suddenly it's not a date anymore. I unclench.

"This is a really good look for me, I think." I pull the edges of the bib down, to show off the lobster to his best advantage.

"It is. It really is," J.J. replies. "In fact, I'd like to see you in just the bib."

I pull my head back and give him a shocked look. It's easy to pull off, because I'm truly shocked that he just said that. "J.J.!" I say, scolding, wondering if I should be reading him the riot act or if we are still the innocent flirtation territory. "Are you being fresh with me?" I deliver this with all of the overwrought primness of Marion the Librarian and purse my lips to boot. Keep it light, I tell myself.

"Maybe I am. Have some more wine." He slides the base of my wineglass toward me. I hadn't even realized we'd been served yet. All this time the wine's been sitting there glowing a rich creamy yellow in its crystal vessel and I've been too busy with J.J. to notice. I take a mighty swig to make it up to the wine's feelings. Thus fortified, I launch into the story Aunt Midge told me earlier about how she met her husband—after all, I think old people in love should be a good distraction from the sexual tension I'm trying desperately to ignore. I explain to J.J. that I've never seen *Casablanca*—he hasn't either—but that there's some guy with a tan-colored fedora in it, and that hat proved very important in Aunt Midge's life.

"What if it had been a fez?" J.J. asks. "After all, Casablanca is in Morocco, isn't it? Think how different Aunt Midge's choice of husband would have been. She'd have married a Shriner."

I laugh. "Or a monkey who can play the accordion."

We lose a lot of time contemplating the different hat-related fates Aunt Midge could have had. J.J. is just theorizing on how elegant it would have been if Rick from *Casablanca* had worn a top hat (if Aunt Midge married Uncle Scrooge, would their children be called cousins?) when the food comes—two large traylike plates, each with a waxed paper liner under a whole lobster, a few clams, a half-ear of corn on the cob, and some little potatoes, naked and rolling around among the seafood like starchy pinballs. In the middle of the table the waiter sets up a miniature Crock-Pot with a burning candle underneath it. This, J.J. tells me, is full of butter.

Outstanding.

I tuck in with enthusiasm. J.J. shows me how to get into the lobster, and I do my best to extract every bite of bright white meat I can, loving the creamy sweet taste and, let's face it, the butter delivery system it provides. He doesn't laugh too hard when I break open the tail too vigorously and shoot green lobster pus across the table. He's very polite when he wipes a little of it out of my hair. And he eats all of my clams when, after choking down just one, I admit that their somewhat, uh, *sweaty* texture is more than I can bear.

Then, when all the food is gone and the vat of butter has dwindled to nearly nothing, J.J. gets really quiet. I get myself ready, knowing the admission of love is coming and there's nothing I can do to stop it. My mind starts racing with excuses for why we can't be together. I get my face prepared to rearrange into a surprised and flattered, yet dismayed expression. He clears his throat and then speaks.

"Janey is supposed to be your cousin, right?"

Well, that's not what I was expecting. "What do you mean, supposed to be?" Maybe it's the wine, or maybe I'm a little bit disappointed about the turn this conversation almost took and then didn't. Either way, I get defensive right away.

"You told me on the first day we met that Janey is your cousin. Doesn't that make Aunt Midge your aunt too? But when you first introduced us, that morning I came to clip the hedges, you said she was Janey's Aunt Midge."

I pause, knowing there are plenty of outs to this. "She's from a different side of Janey's family," I say, and then refill my wine, helping myself to the last of the bottle.

"What side exactly? The paternal side?"

I take a big swallow. The wine tastes too dry now, and my mouth feels like I just licked a tree. I try to think back through the last month of conversations. Has anyone ever told him that Janey never knew her father, or is that something only I am privy to? Does he know that Aunt Midge only had one sibling? "Why do you care?" I ask him at last. I want one of those smoke bombs that ninjas are always using to escape dangerous situations.

J.J. doesn't back down. "It just seems like, if you were part of the family, per se, you would have heard Aunt Midge's story about how she met her husband before this afternoon. I mean, she's already told it to me twice."

I gulp. "She has?"

J.J. leans back in his chair and takes off his bib. "I know you think I brought you here to put the moves on you, but you couldn't be more wrong."

Ooh—that burns.

He goes on, ignoring my flinch. "What I'm really after is some kind of straight story. One that bears some sort of scrutiny. It really bugs me that after hanging out every day for the last month you still don't trust me enough to tell me, say, your full name."

I look down at the tray where my battered and broken lobster carcass lies. It's disgusting now, and my stomach turns over and I think for just a moment that I'm going to be sick. Is this how Janey feels when she talks to strangers? Like she is utterly cornered, with no place to run and hide? If it is, it's no wonder she hangs out alone in that kitchen all day. Utter seclusion is far preferable to this.

I start digging for something funny to say—for a sarcastic response or a way to turn this conversation around on him. But my smart-ass self deserts me. I can think of nothing but the string of lies that I've left in my wake. I start following one strand backward to the place where it rejoins some semblance of truth, but it just dovetails with another lie, and then another. I keep unraveling and unraveling backward, looking for one solid truth I can tell J.J.—one true thing I can tell him that will make him believe in me again so we can drop this nonsense and get back to the fun part, to the talk of hats and innocent flirtations and breaking open lobster claws and pulling out long strips of delicious meat. I will the lobster in front of me to become whole again.

In the end I come up only with this: "My full name is Janine Diana Brown, and I really did live in Iowa."

J.J. lets out a deep breath. Does he know I'm telling the truth? "Okay," he says, leaning forward in his chair again like Matt Lauer with a particularly reticent guest. "Janine Brown of Iowa. It's a start." He sounds understanding and encouraging—too much so, like he is expecting me to unleash some pitiful life story and sort of looking forward to hearing it. "Go on."

"It's a finish, too, okay?" I throw my napkin down over the mangled lobster body. I've got to get out of here now. Now, before I make a scene. Before he gets disgusted with me and leaves first, sticking me with the check. "Sorry, but I don't really feel like going to confession right now." I stand up, knocking my purse off the chair and onto the floor with a crash.

It empties its contents. First a paper-clipped wad of dollar bills, the change I've been squirreling away from errands for Aunt Midge. Then, along with the detritus of my life—cigarettes, matches, lipstick from a five-finger discount, and two AA batteries—spills out what seems like hundreds of tampons and mints, scattering themselves across the deck, covering every available inch of space between our table and the railing with pink paper and blue cellophane. The tables go silent as everyone's heads swivel toward me, then to the array they must all know I lifted. At last the large bottle of hand lotion—just a drugstore brand, I now realize with shame, something I could have asked Janey to pick up for me any day of the week if I'd wanted it—comes rolling out and makes its way to the railing between two tables of gaping diners. It rolls under the railing and falls to the rocks far below silently. I feel the urge to roll myself out of here the same way.

"Fuck it," I say, under my breath, but I might as well scream it. I know every person on that deck is watching me now, has seen the unmistakable movements of my lips forming the words even if they haven't heard. I lean down to the deck and grab up the money, the shrimp cocktail's worth of cash, and throw it on the table right in front of J.J. Then I head for the hills.

The walk home is easier than I would have guessed. The cove curls back on itself, so by keeping the full moon above my right shoulder—I remember where it was from the backyard last night—I manage to stay on course while keeping far enough from the road to avoid J.J. running me down like the dog that I am. As punishment for my horrible behavior, I try to imagine the bill coming at the restaurant. Everyone would be whispering the moment I left the deck, and then the waiter would discretely approach the table to make sure J.J. didn't join me in my runner, leaving one of those vinyl wallets right in front of him with a polite cough. What would the total be? Seventy-five dollars? A hundred dollars? And will they also bill him for all the crap I stole? I wouldn't blame them if they did. The shame for sticking J.J. with such a huge tab sits on my chest like a fat five-year-old.

But there's nothing I can do about it now. And really, he shouldn't have cornered me like that. He led me on—made me think that he was into me, when he really just wanted to figure me out. Like a puzzle you buy at a garage sale and then get annoyed with when you see how many of the pieces are missing. I am not some garage sale puzzle, I tell myself, and it's only by replacing some of my shame with righteous indignation that I am able to keep walking, instead of lying down right in the middle of the road.

When I finally get to the house, his truck is there, so I keep going. I remember the way to the farm pretty well, even in the dark. I pick my way down the road and think about what he must be telling Janey and Aunt Midge about what I did. The jig is so seriously up now. There's no way Her Righteousness Janey Brown is going to leave this alone. At first she'll be totally pissed and tell Aunt Midge it's the last straw and I have to go. Then, that decided, the three of them will open a bottle of wine and laugh about how crazy I turned out to be and pour strawberry sauce over the shortcake biscuits I made this morning and tuck in. I hope they taste like bile.

At the driveway to the farm I start choosing my steps more carefully. I still don't know the people who run this place, even though I've skulked around here more than a few times on farmers market days to visit Nana and Boo Boo. The lights are off in the whole house except for the telltale flicker of the TV on the right side of the house. Looks like it's movie night. They won't notice a few llama footsteps with that kind of distraction.

With my arms full of onion tops I make my way to the llama house and start cooing. Boo Boo comes out first and makes right for me, letting out a weird bleat that makes me freeze for a moment. The TV keeps flickering and I relax and give him the booty he's after. He lets me stroke him and I sigh deeply at the touch of his fur. It really does feel the way clouds look. Only warmer, and with more of a surrounding odor. Quietly, I start telling him about the evening. With Boo Boo I find it easy to stick to the facts. I tell him the worst part of the whole night is realizing that J.J. is not quite as madly in love with me as I'd convinced myself he was. In fact, he probably doesn't like me at all anymore. Boo Boo leans his head down as I tell him this. My head sags too.

I don't know how long I've been communing with Boo Boo when I hear footsteps on the gravel. My gaze shoots to my left and then my stomach sinks. It's J.J., of course. Who else would it be? He looks utterly annoyed, and I can hardly blame him. I rest my head for a moment on Boo Boo's long thick neck and sigh. Why can't there be more flying llamas in this cruel world? Escaping Maine on a flying llama would be so sweet right about now.

"You're trespassing," J.J. says, in a hissy whisper.

"You're a dick," I say, matching his tone of voice.

He shrugs, damn him. "How's Nana?"

"This is Boo Boo."

He pauses, takes a closer look. "So it is. We've been having a little trouble with identity issues today, haven't we?" I hear the smile in his voice but it doesn't stop my wanting to punch him in the junk.

"I'm sorry," he says, after a long silence during which I've contemplated the possibilities of hiding a body in a llama hutch.

"For what?" I ask. It's a fair question: besides being a dick, he hasn't actually done anything wrong but bear witness to my humiliation.

"For buying you lobster and asking you to be honest with me?" he tries, making it clear that he knows he shouldn't have to apologize for this, but he's doing it anyway.

"You are forgiven," I tell him sanctimoniously. I wave my hand in a quick little "wax on" circle to show he can go with God. When he doesn't turn to leave I add, "What did you tell Janey and Aunt Midge?"

"I told them that we had a nice dinner and I dropped you off by the road so you could see the stars away from the light of the house."

"Wow," I say. I am impressed enough by this masterful lie to soften a great deal. "Did they buy it?"

"Janey will believe anything." So true. "But Aunt Midge had that look. She told me you had been, and I quote, 'a crabby patty' earlier today."

I roll my eyes, hoping it's not too dark for J.J. to see.

J.J. takes me gently by the arm and I'm stunned to realize how close we're standing. "Listen, Nean. I shouldn't have pushed you like that, and I'm sorry, truly. You don't have to tell me anything you don't want to. But please don't lie to me anymore, okay?"

I swallow hard. "Janey's not my cousin. The only thing we share is a name."

"I know."

"I only just met her right before I met you. She and Aunt Midge are letting me stay at their house just to be nice. They don't know me from Adam."

"I see."

"They could kick me out any time. Then I'd be out on my own."

"Huh," he says, taking this in stride.

I think back to the whoppers I've told him since we've met. "I was never a hand model. I don't have any brothers or sisters. My mom doesn't really have webbed toes."

J.J. looks at me openly, a smile bouncing around his eyes. "Well, that's a relief. Anything else?"

I wrack my brain, knowing there's no way I've gotten it all. "And I've never been to Syracuse."

"Lucky girl."

"I've lied a lot to everyone. Not just to you," I tell him. "To Janey and Aunt Midge too."

"You can make it right. If you stop lying now."

It sounds like so little to ask. "Haven't you ever been less than honest with me?" I ask.

"Sure," he says, but doesn't elaborate. Then he adds, "I'd say we're about even now," and gives me a wink. "Come on. We need to get out of here before the Parkerberrys finish their movie." He takes me by the hand, and the effect is exactly like taking off heavy boots and wet socks and putting your feet by the radiator and letting the feeling come back while you wiggle your toes. My heart wiggles its toes.

We go back up to the road now, but instead of going back toward the house, we walk right and follow the road into darkness. There are no more houses after this, I know. The farm is the last driveway before the road loops around and starts heading back up the cove on the other side. We walk to the bottom of the loop and then J.J. guides me to a trail that's cleared through the woods, a trail I've never noticed in the daylight that now seems crystal clear. He pulls me through the woods and down a steep-ish embankment, then past a stand of evergreens that have lain a thick, soft coating of needles on the ground, mashed on top of one another in layers upon layers.

"It's slippery here," he tells me, and holds tighter to my hand.

I stop walking. "And cushiony," I say, and he circles back to me and looks me straight in the eyes. I can't help it, something instinctive inside me makes me bite my lip. It's a little thing, but it's enough right now, what with all the moonlight and the lapping ocean. J.J. puts his hand under one strap of my yellow sundress and unties it, and then the other. His hands are hot and leave trails on my skin. The dress falls to the ground and then J.J.'s striped tie flutters down beside it. The soft cotton of his shirt becomes a sheet on the forest floor, with just enough room on it for our bodies tightly stacked together. And we say nothing else to each other, true or false, for a while after that.

JANEY

"Use some restraint, but not too much."

—JASPER WHITE,
Cooking from New England

My mind has been taken over by a sixteen-year-old girl. I no longer have the ability to hold a thought in my head without applying it somehow to Noah. I get up in the morning and put on something and think, "Would Noah like this outfit?" If the answer is no, I change. Over coffee I catch myself wondering what Noah is eating for breakfast. While driving into Little Pond I practice talking to Noah in my head. "How are you?" I ask him. "How are things in the garden?"

By the time we actually meet for lunch most days, I have already been talking to him for hours, exhausted every line of conversation and told him everything I've ever done, thought, or thought about doing. I can think of nothing further to say to him. Sometimes I repeat myself, only to a live audience, but other times I don't even bother. Luckily he doesn't seem put off by my quietude. He excels at companionable silence.

Noah—or rather, the wild crush I've developed on Noah—has forced me to dine out on a regular basis. My beautiful kitchen stands unused for hours every weekday while I sit in restaurants and dingy bars and once, when Noah was totally out of new ideas and I couldn't eat another tiny hot dog to save my life, a McDonald's.

That food was execrable, let me tell you.

To think I would rather be eating a sandwich with the word "tasty" in its name than home making something that is actually tasty. But I find that I don't mind at all. Being with Noah is easy. Easier than being alone, even. When I do talk, I like telling him things about me, I discover to much surprise. I like the way he reacts when I tell him something. He has a way of processing without judging—like there's nothing I could tell him about myself that he hasn't heard a million times before. It's like going to a doctor with an embarrassing rash and having him tell you, first, that it will clear up on its own in just a few days, and, second, that he's seen much worse before. All that angst, it just dissipates so fast that you actually feel the whiplash as it goes.

In one of these bouts of confessional insanity I have told Noah about the full extent of my shyness, the hives and the stuttering and how much trouble I had in my old job because of it. He is sympathetic and kind at the moment of disclosure, but this knowledge doesn't stop him from introducing someone new to me every time he gets the chance. He calls it immersion therapy. To prove his point, he's been conducting a scientific study in which he counts my hives after every new encounter. Sure enough, they are getting fewer and fewer in quantity by the week. I am beginning to believe it won't be long now before I can go out in public without a sweater. And I am so, so glad about this.

So yes, I am falling for him. He is freeing me from long sleeves in the summer, after all.

I meet Noah this afternoon at the same place as always, the parking lot of the shelter. Today he asks me if lunch can wait. "We have an errand to run," he says. He's grinning from ear to ear.

It's not unusual for Noah to wear a tiny smile for no reason. Last week I got a flat on the way back from lunch, and I watched him hop out and put on the spare without the slightest hint of displeasure, though it was raining and he returned to the car sopping wet and covered in road grime.

But when he mentions this errand today it's not his usual twinkle I see. It's a silly ear-to-ear smile that makes me smile back at him, like this trip to the drugstore or whatever it is we're about to do is actually an all-expenses-paid vacation in Belize.

"Where are we going?" I ask. "Someplace exciting?"

"Oh yes," he says. "Quite."

"What's in the bag?" I ask, gesturing to the paper grocery sack he's nestled between his feet.

"Boots and soap" is all he says back.

He directs me down the main street past the bars and the bank and off onto a side street lined with homes. They are modest and not all in the best repair, but they are clearly lived in, and kids spill out of a few of them, with their Big Wheels and scooters and bubble wands. I see one little girl dressed, inexplicably, in a blue rayon gown, with a tiara on her head and wings strapped onto her back. She is twirling around her driveway with such vigor that I feel dizzy on her behalf.

"Left here," Noah tells me, and I pull into a parking lot of a boxy brick building with a small plastic sign that reads LITTLE POND RECRE- ATION CENTER.

"Where are we?" I ask, hoping he won't say "Little Pond Recreation Center."

"Janey, do you know what a hornworm is?"

I put the car in park and shake my head.

"A hornworm is a nasty little caterpillar that can get out of control in a hurry. It eats tomatoes and peppers faster than you can say DDT. Be- lieve it or not, we are right in the heart of Hornworm City," he tells me, and then hops out of the car before I can ask him what that's sup- posed to mean.

Mystified, I follow him to the side door where a sweet-looking young woman is waiting. She's in her mid-twenties, I'd guess, and looks at ease in her red bandanna and muddy jeans. I'm instantly jealous of her, though I'm not sure why.

"Hi, Noah," she calls. "I've got the jars."

"And I've got the soap," he replies. "And I brought a trusty assistant. Melinda, this is Janey. Melinda teaches summer school here in town, and the students are doing their own organic salsa garden this year, learning about sustainability and botany and all kinds of good stuff. Janey's got her education degree too, Melinda."

"Oh, so you're a teacher?" she asks me, turning her bright blue doe eyes on me.

I blush red and shake my head no. My skin feels prickly, but I don't know if it's the beginning of hives or vexation at Noah forcing another new person upon me without warning.

"Oh no? Did you wise up in time?" she asks with a wink, and then goes on, not waiting for an answer. "The kids were pretty resistant to gardening at first. I think they were afraid I was going to make them grow brussels sprouts. Actually, I was. Growing the ingredients for salsa was Noah's idea. Peppers, tomatoes, cilantro, onions. All utterly doable and kid-friendly. We're going to learn about canning at the end of the season. I have a whole mini-unit on botulism all ready to go."

I am starting to feel like I have botulism. I look at Noah, trying to communicate my mounting anxiety through my eyes.

Maybe he sees it. "You go get the kids, Mel, and Janey and I will get geared up."

The moment she's inside again, Noah turns to me. He takes both my hands in his. My mouth gets even drier. "Ten middle school kids so noisy you wouldn't get a word in edgewise even if you wanted to," he says. "Melinda, who is probably too busy with them to notice anyone else. And me. Just boring old me."

"There's nothing boring about you," I hear myself say softly.

"You should hear me talk about heirloom tomatoes," he replies. But he's wrong. I could listen to him talk about tomatoes all day long. "Anyway, we've just got to dispatch some hornworms and then we're free to go."

It turns out that Melinda's students are loud and brash but also sweet and easy. Hornworms are eating huge holes in their tomato plants, and the kids seem bereft about the situation and grateful when Noah tells them eradication without chemicals isn't as hard as they've feared. It's just slow.

Apparently, you have to pluck the huge green buggers off by hand, one by one, and drop them into jars of soapy water. Until all the horn-worms are gone.

I hang back at first, watching the kids listen enthusiastically to No-ah's unappealing instructions. The girls gaze at him like he fell out of a *Twilight* novel. I see him through their eyes: tall, rugged, well-built, and confident. And from mine—all those things, and also happy to spend his lunch hour showing other people's kids a good way to grow. I could stand here and watch him do this all day, with his patient way of easing each student into a task, his effusive encouragement at the slightest progress, his skilled hands checking the moisture of the soil, fixing the staking of a pepper all the while.

But once I see teenage girls picking enormous slimy caterpillars off plants with their blue-manicured hands just to impress Noah, I realize I might as well get in the game.

I pick up a jar, add a squeeze of dish soap and a few ounces of water from the hose, and steady my stomach. Noah shows me how to hunt under the bottom-most leaves of the plants, where it's coolest, and use my fingernail to dislodge the slimy buggers into the soap jar, watching out for their bite. I drown my first hornworm and Noah gives me a heart-melting smile and a thumbs-up and moves off to help a student.

"This takes patience," he tells him. "And persistence."

"It's actually kind of satisfying once you get over the ick factor," says Melinda. I can't help but agree. I lose myself in the hunting, the pluck-ing, the drowning.

"Why soapy water?" a boy asks while I am particularly lost in the rhythm of the process.

"Maybe because the soap breaks through the waterproof coating many insects have on their bodies," someone says. "The coating might be insoluble in water—that means it won't wash away on a rainy day. But soap bonds itself to things water can't, like grease on dirty dishes or oil on clothes, making it easy to rinse them clean."

I look up, startled. It wasn't just *someone* talking just now. It was me. I spoke before I had a chance to panic about speaking. I just reflexively answered a question of a student. Like a teacher might.

Noah is looking at me with a bemused expression. I know in an instant that he realizes what just happened, what I did. "That's right," he says, after a long second. "Water alone won't drown them. You need extra ammo."

The moment passes. We finish the day's debugging and Melinda takes the kids back inside. We clean our hands, get back in the car, drive to lunch, talk about middle schoolers and garden pests and the best salsa we've ever eaten. Noah doesn't mention my breakthrough at the rec center and neither do I.

But I can't stop thinking about what it means—what it could mean—for me if I could always talk in front of a class of students the way I did today.

Or that, thanks to Noah, I even believe such a thing is possible.

As the summer has progressed, Nean, J.J., Aunt Midge, and I have gotten into the habit of regular Sunday brunches together—what Nean calls our "family time," though it is no secret that what she and J.J. are doing under the table is often not appropriate for families. After a brunch of crunchy French toast made with Nean's latest bread—a quite impressive challah—and caramelized bacon, I persuade her to join me in the three-seasons room for a postbrunch Bellini. J.J. has skipped off to his own house, where no doubt he will eat another meal as large as the one we just shared, and Aunt Midge is in the living room snoring off her Irish coffee. Her snuffles make for a welcome sort of white noise as Nean and I gaze out on the ocean in welcome silence.

Which of course lasts for mere seconds.

"Just so you know, I have completely and totally lost interest in whatever's going on between you and Noah," Nean announces. "So I'm not going to ask you anymore."

"You have? You aren't?" This would be wonderful news, if I believed it for a second.

"Yep. I realized yesterday that I'm far, far more interesting than you. So whenever I find myself curious about what is happening between you and Noah, I'm just going to relive my own life in my mind. Like, right now? I'm thinking about the amazing sex J.J. and I had last night. And will probably also have tomorrow." She closes her eyes and lets her head roll back in mock ecstasy.

Of course she's off having amazing sex. Maybe I should be asking her for advice on how to get things to the next level with Noah. "So I guess you're over 'just being friends' with him?"

"I'd say so," she says lightly. "Unlike you and Noah." She shoots me a supercilious smirk.

"I'm working on it," I say.

"Whatever. I don't care about your love life anymore."

"Is this some kind of reverse psychology?" I ask, perturbed.

She wiggles her eyebrows. "Why, are you feeling the urge to tell me something?"

I shrug. "Maybe." I turn away from her to look out the great glass windows, where the skies are getting dark and gray for the first time I can remember since we arrived in Maine. The cloudy weather doesn't make me sad, for once. Instead it feels safe—the same way I would feel so safe when Ned and I would go camping and zip our sleeping bags together into one giant cocoon. It's like Mother Nature is telling me to zip up inside this snuggly house and stay cozy with my people.

Does that make Nean one of my people?

She sets her champagne flute down with a loud clink on the glass table and stands up. "I think . . ." she says as she moves to the padded wicker seat closest to where I'm standing. "I think you'd feel better if you just talked it out. What's going on? Are you two officially an item? Has he sown his passion seed in your garden of love, if you know what I mean?"

I turn around, showing her just how revolting she is with my grimace. "I know what you mean. A home-schooled seven-year-old would know what you mean. Jeez, Nean, is sex all you think about?"

"Right now it is, yes. You should see J.J. naked. Here, I'll give you a mental picture: Imagine him mowing the lawn, only with no pants on." Her twisted little smile grows to beauty pageant proportions and makes me laugh.

But then she turns in her chair and says, "Wait . . ." and I see the gears turning. "Something's not right here. You're dating this sexy un-kempt farmer and you can think about something besides sex? Are your girl parts broken?"

"My parts work fine," I say. "I don't know about his."

Nean's jaw drops. "You mean he's not . . . functional?"

"No!" I shout, appalled that I could have suggested that even by ac-cident. "I mean, I haven't, um, well, we haven't . . ."

"Ah." Nean leans back in the chair and tucks her legs up under her. "Is the woo getting pitched a little on the slow side?"

I roll my lips together, taking a moment to understand what the hell she's talking about. Pitching woo—who says that anymore? "Right. He isn't wooing me as fast as I might like, I think." I prop my butt on the windowsill, turning my back on the building storm so I can focus on Nean.

"How much wooing are we talking about here?"

"Not a lot. Maybe a third of a woo?"

"A whuh?"

"Exactly. Some kissing, some romantic talk. That's it."

"What sort of romantic talk?"

"Um, like, he tells me I look lovely, or that I have a beautiful way of expressing myself. That sort of thing."

"Hardly nine-hundred-number material."

"Probably for the best, considering we are only ever together in public places."

Nean's eyebrows pop up. "No shit? Like, never alone together? Not even a walk down the shoreline together hand in hand?"

"Never. Nothing after sundown, either. It's lunches only. He's like a reverse vampire."

"Huh."

"Exactly." I look at her expectantly. Here is the part where she tells me what to do to get Noah's blood racing. What to say, how to wear my hair. Anything.

Nean sighs deeply. "Let me guess, you want me to tell you what to do to get him to make a move. I see how it is. You didn't want my help for weeks, but now it's all, 'Help me, Obi-Nean Kenobi. You're my only hope.'"

"Who is Obi-Nean Kenobi? What's that supposed to mean?"

"Seriously?"

I nod.

"For the love of GOD," she says, exasperated. "Didn't you have a childhood? I spent my teen years living with foster parents who didn't believe in electricity, and I still have more pop culture knowledge than you."

This tiny unexpected confession makes me forget my love life altogether. "You were in foster care?" I say, trying to disguise the wash of sympathy that's come over me. Life with just me and my mom was sometimes lonely, but it was a real, permanent home.

Nean rumples her face. "From ten to fourteen," she says. "Those people were nuts. But stop trying to get me off the subject at hand: your womanly needs."

"Where did you go when you turned fourteen?" I ask, wondering if ten years ago Nean looked as skinny and rough as she did when I first laid eyes on her at twenty-four.

"That was when I got a gig singing and dancing in the Tomorrowland Chorus in Disney World. Thirty kids from all over the U.S., doing two shows a day. It was a quite a thrill. But a lot of hard work, too."

"Really?"

She sighs loudly and tips her head to the ceiling. "Not really." She collects the now-empty champagne flute from my hands. "Stupid J.J. and his big campaign for truth. He's ruined all the fun of lying," she grumbles. "When I was fourteen my mom came back. We moved into her boyfriend's trailer. It wasn't exactly Disney World, but he had a TV." She turns to leave, saying, "If we're going to be talking about this shit, I'm going to need more booze," clinking the flutes together in one hand as she goes.

While she is refilling our drinks, I begin to think about Nean's life before she came to Maine. I realize that over the last months I have invented my own history for her based on the shorthand stereotypes used in one-hour police procedurals. In my imagination, she fell madly in love with the football hero in high school, they were together for years happily, then one day he started drinking and got more and more possessive, until finally the abuse started . . .

I am embarrassed now to discover that this isn't actually Nean's life history, but the plot of a 1993 TV movie starring that girl from *The Wonder Years*. When Nean returns, glasses full, I fight the urge to apologize to her out of the blue.

"Did he beat you up?" I hear myself ask instead. "Your mom's boyfriend, I mean?" I can't believe I'm being this intrusive. I want to shut up, but I also want to know.

"Why? Did you read somewhere that women who stay with abusive guys were usually abused in their childhoods?" she asks, her voice sharp.

"Uh, well, yeah."

She tilts her head, letting her shoulders fall. "Yeah, I've read that too." She takes a swig of her champagne. "I guess it's sort of true. He was touchy-feely, but I wasn't there long enough for anything truly dramatic to happen. My mom did a runner about four months after that. He offered to let me stay, but he was kind of a handsy douche so . . ." her voice drifts off.

"So then what?"

"Eh, I'll let you fill in the blanks," she says. "But here's a hint—I stole that TV." I look at her, and she's grinning—not even a shadow of self-pity or regret crosses her face. "Anyway, we were talking about Noah vis-à-vis your vagina, remember? Stay on topic."

I have, for the first time in six weeks, completely forgotten Noah. I look at the wooden floorboards for a moment trying to regain my train of thought, then back up at Nean. "You're actually kind of an amazing person, you know that?"

Nean scowls. "Are you going to kiss me now?"

"Also, you're kind of a bitch."

Nean laughs and gives a little curtsy in response. "You've summed me up in so few words," she says, still grinning.

"The point is, living with you is, well, it's not as bad as I thought it would be."

She looks at me hard for a moment. Like maybe she's trying for a flippant retort. Then her features soften. "I think you and I might be friends or something, you know?"

"We might be," I agree. Fancy that.

For a moment we look out over the water. It's dark as night over the ocean, but some sun still manages to backlight the clouds closer inland.

"Too bad Noah's not on his way over right now," Nean says. "This would be the perfect weather to make love. Rain pounding on the roof, nothing to do but lie around in bed . . ."

"My great-aunt watching TV in the room next door . . ."

"Oh, you'll get over that, trust me. Call him—see if he wants to come over for a game of Scrabble." She puts Scrabble in air quotes.

"I can't. I don't even have his phone number."

Nean looks taken aback. "Seriously? Not even his cell?"

"He doesn't have a cell, as far as I can see," I tell her. "And I have no idea where he even lives. He never talks about his house, or his life outside the work he does at the shelter."

Nean absentmindedly plays with her hair as she thinks this over. I know what she is thinking: there is something fishy about the whole Noah thing. I am thinking this too. But what could it be?

"Is he married?" Nean asks out of the blue.

"No way," I say, but now that she says it, it does make some sense. "I mean, I don't think he is. . . . But then, on the other hand, how would I know?"

"Exactly. They don't tell you until you're hooked, you know."

I look at her sideways. "You seem like an authority on this subject. Was *he* married?"

"Who?"

"Him," I say with feeling. "The guy who . . . died."

"Oh, him," Nean says. "Look, about him."

Suddenly Nean looks very serious, and I fill with dread. What if he *was* married, and his wife is still out there wondering what happened to her husband? Why he never came home one day? What if they had children together? "Oh my God," I say. "You killed a married man?"

Nean shakes her head violently. "No, no!" she says quickly. "He wasn't married. It was just him and me. Nobody else was involved."

I heave a huge sigh of relief. "Thank God. Oh, Nean," I reach out and grab her hand before she can jerk it away, hold it for a moment before giving it a squeeze and letting go. "I'm sorry I jumped to that conclusion. It's bad enough what you had to go through, without me always thinking the worst about you. I've got to stop doing that."

Nean is looking into her lap, and I see that she is sniffling a little. She smushes up her face, closing her eyes tightly for a moment. When they open again, she looks up, and her eyes are bright and wet, but the tears have stopped. "No problem," she says thickly.

"I am sorry," I say again, trying and failing to hold eye contact.

She coughs. "Noah's not married," she says, forcing a change in the subject. "He's too annoyingly decent to be cheating. You're just looking for any excuse to avoid putting the moves on him."

"Nean!"

"Well," she shrugs. "I'm just laying everything out there."

"What would you have me do? Jump him in the middle of the lunch rush at the Drunken Sailor?"

Nean thinks on this for a moment but before she can answer we hear a familiar voice from the living room shout, "OH FOR THE LOVE OF PETE. IT'S NOT ROCKET SCIENCE."

"Aunt Midge?" I stand up and go into the living room, Nean following not far behind. "You're awake?"

"It's hard to nap through such utter stupidity," she says, sitting up and fluffing her curls. "You two are such amateurs. Here is what you do. Tell him you have been wanting to try out a new such-and-such recipe. Does he like such-and-such? He does? Oh, well, you could bring it in to lunch the next day. But it's really so much better hot. I suppose . . . well, I mean, if he'd be interested in coming to see the house now that we're all moved in . . . he would? That's great. No, he doesn't need to bring anything but himself. Okay, well, great. Until tomorrow!"

She puts out her hands as if to say, "Ta-da!" and looks at me superiorly. "Got it?"

Why, considering it came from Aunt Midge, it's actually a perfect idea. It's so easy even I can do it. "I got it!" I chirp, springing up from my seat to give her a quick hug. "You're a genius. I've got to go get some cookbooks."

Aunt Midge sighs and I catch a sarcastic look bounce between her and Nean. "Of course you do, dear. You've got to cook exactly the right thing if you want to win his love."

I pause for a moment and shake my head at both of them. "I know you are being sarcastic," I call as I walk to the kitchen, "but I don't care. I'll show you doubters the power of the perfect meal. I'll have him eating out of my hand before I've even served dessert." Can that be true? Has the answer been in my kitchen all along?

"That's the idea," calls Nean. "Except it's not your hand you're after, exactly . . ."

Aunt Midge and Nean break into depraved laughter. I tune them out as I pull down cookbook after cookbook, but a half an hour later, when I've flagged at least thirty recipes, I notice my cheeks are achy. I've been grinning all this time.

NEAN

"Opening an oyster is strictly a matter of leverage."

—JASPER WHITE,
Cooking from New England

The next week is a blur of tastings. Every time I pass the kitchen I see Janey in there, covered in food splatters, muttering to herself. The timing couldn't be better for me. She's made J.J. promise to eat at our house every night until the Big Date, so she gets more palates to judge her food. So, without even having to plot or scheme, I've got the object of my affection within arm's reach constantly. Which is perfect because I'm a J.J. junkie. I love kissing him and talking to him and doing nothing with him. And the sex is so easy and relaxed and cool. No head games, no pretending I want to when I don't, no doing that fake snore thing so he thinks I'm already asleep. It's heaven. Somehow I have hit the jackpot. Well, the John-Junior-pot. I totally don't deserve a guy like him, and it's not just my low self-esteem talking here. I may not have actually won this damn house, but I am still America's Luckiest Person.

Except. It is one of life's few sureties that about five minutes after you announce you are America's Luckiest Person, something will go wrong and make you feel much less lucky.

I am in the kitchen, helping Janey make a watercress salad with goat cheese and thinly sliced peaches when I hear the doorbell ring. I don't even look up. If Aunt Midge doesn't answer the door sooner or later, J.J. will just walk on in—we only lock the front door at night now, or when nobody's home. But Aunt Midge is nearby, and I hear her greet J.J. and say, "My, my, you look awfully spiffy tonight!" and that makes me arch my head back and try to get a look at him coming in, without being obvious about it, of course. I can't see him, so I give up and after about three seconds I've forgotten the whole thing anyway. I'm too busy watching Janey try to open up oysters. This is clearly a first for her, and I enjoy watching her try to figure out how to do it from the hand-drawn illustration in her copy of *Joy*. To me, oysters look exactly like a blond version of a mussel, but clearly they are very different. She keeps muttering to herself as she works and she's gleaming with sweat, like a prizefighter.

"I thought you were only supposed to eat oysters in months that end in '-ber.' Since when does August end in '-ber'?" I ask her, and she murmurs something intelligible under her breath and sets down the funny little knife she's wielding.

"That's only for raw oysters," she says, sounding annoyed. "And I'm frying these, in case you didn't notice." She points her knife and the oyster she's holding at the bubbling cauldron of oil on the stove with what I now recognize as a breading station next to them. "If I can ever get them open. Can you check the thermometer and tell me how hot the oil is?"

"It looks pretty hot," I say, just so I can watch her get pissy. After she huffs a little I lean in and take a real gander. "Almost four hundred degrees, it says,"

"Shit!" she cries, and I think it's the first time I've ever heard her curse in the kitchen. "It's supposed to be no higher than three seventy-five. How was I supposed to know these fricking things would take so long to get open?" I look at the pile of oysters she's wrestling with—about three are open in their shells and the rest are closed tightly, so tightly that even after she jams her knife into them and wiggles it up and down like mad they stay closed.

"Let me try," I say, and hold out my hands.

"Be my guest." She makes me put on a thick leather glove first, but then lets me go to town, which is what I do, sliding the curved tip of the knife between the shells about a millimeter and feeling around inside the oyster for what, I don't know. It seems like there's no way in deeper. Eventually I try sheer force, and crank my hand hard in one direction to make the knife blade turn while it's still in the oyster. It works—we hear the hinge of the oyster snap and the thing loosens up in my hands. Now the knife slips all the way through and I understand instantly the usefulness of the glove.

"You did it!" Janey cries, and immediately begins to back away from the oysters. "You keep doing what you're doing and I'll get the oil ready."

"Oh no. Don't leave me here with all of these!"

"I trust you," Janey says, laughing.

"But what do I do when they're all cracked open?"

"Run the knife along the top of the inside and then try lifting off the top shell. The oyster should stay in the bottom . . ."

I open the oyster like an Oreo, and sure enough, there's a little nugget of meat lying slimily on top of the shell. "Eww. Looks like female parts."

Janey winces and says, "I think that's why they're supposed to be aphrodisiacs."

Eyes wide, I swing my face around to her. "Is that why you're thinking of serving these to Noah? Because they look like your vagina?"

"What looks like Janey's vagina?" asks J.J., choosing the perfect moment to saunter into the kitchen.

I watch Janey closely, a little worried she is going to attack us with a vat of boiling oil. She turns a dark, dark shade of red, but no tears, no hives, no attack. That girl is really mellowing. "I'm making fried oysters, and that is all I am going to say about that. J.J., would you open the wine?"

She gestures to a side counter, where three bottles are standing at the ready.

"Which one?" he asks.

"All of them." She shoves up her sleeves and steals the six oysters I have ready for her. "We're doing a tasting tonight so that I know which one goes best with dinner for Noah."

"Wow. This is getting intense," he says.

"Sure is," I say. "And you should try being on shucking duty."

"That sounds kind of dirty," he says, and moves over to me for a kiss.

J.J. is not your average kisser. He does not introduce tongue too early or open his mouth a million miles wide like they do in the movies and leave a ring of slobber around my lips. He is into a kind of kiss that can only be described as a slow motion peck. Lean in, brush lips over mine, press them there for a millennium, drag them away. It takes about twenty minutes of these kinds of soft, intense little smooches before he slips me the tongue, but hey, it is better than the opposite. I have learned that when he kisses me, I must be patient, and that's incredibly sexy.

But today there isn't time for the whole deal. The oysters are in the fat now, and I notice that Janey is standing as far away from the pot as she can while still staying within reach with her strainer spoon thingy, because the pot is hissing and spitting hot oil in every direction. I look up, and, sure enough, the ceiling is glistening with yellow specks of oil.

"Um, hey, is that supposed to happen?" I ask, pointing up.

"I thought they were dry enough," Janey is muttering, but she looks very afraid of the pot. "I don't know why anyone eats these stupid things. They don't even look like food."

"I'm sure they'll be great," J.J. says, carrying the wines to the table. "Noah will love them. He'll love any of the things you've cooked so far."

"But which one will he love best?" she asks. "The ceviche? The filet mignon? The crab cakes? The roast Cornish game hens?"

J.J. shrugs indifferently, but Janey doesn't see. She's fishing out the oysters with a pained look, holding one arm over her eyes as she leans closer to the angry pot.

I sigh. "Why don't you just make everything, and let him decide." Honestly, I am getting a little tired of these cooking marathons. She is so focused on food right now that she hardly listens when I try to tell her about J.J. And being head over heels in love is pretty much pointless without a girlfriend to share it with.

"I can't do that. He'll think I'm desperate."

I say nothing in response to this, showing my great maturity and restraint. Janey flings another set of breaded oysters into the oil and then flees the area, arms waving. "Everyone, to the table. Get Aunt Midge. Dinner is on in five."

When we are all seated and munching on salad, Janey asks J.J. what food he would want if he could have any meal at all.

"Pork chops," he tells her around a mouthful of watercress.

"No, I mean, a food that would make you fall in love with the person who cooked it."

"Pork chops," he says again.

Janey tips her head back in frustration. "You can have pork chops any time. What would be the fancy meal? You know, something truly special."

J.J. thinks for a moment, and then replies, "Fancy pork chops? Pork chops in fancy sauce?"

Janey growls. "I can't just invite a person over for pork chops. It's too simple."

Aunt Midge sets down her fork with a clatter. "Maybe you are making this too complicated, Janey. If the men want pork chops, give them pork chops. Pork chops, mashed potatoes, and applesauce. That's what Albert liked to eat." She smiles as she invokes the memory, and I imagine what life must have been like around Aunt Midge's table back then. There would have been lots of music, I'm sure, and laughing and raunchy jokes. She and Albert would probably gobble down their pork chops by candlelight and then push back the dining room table so there was enough room to dance.

"I miss Albert," I say, and then immediately feel idiotic. I've never met the man, never will.

But Aunt Midge just smiles and nods. "Me too. He was a great guy. He would have gotten quite the kick out of you, Nean. He loved a good story."

My stomach lurches for a moment, and I look from Aunt Midge to Janey, hoping she doesn't catch Aunt Midge's insinuation. Her face remains blank, but J.J. looks at me quizzically over the table and frowns. He has been urging me to be more honest with Janey, but he has no idea about the whole bullshit story that got me into this house in the first place, and I have absolutely no intention of telling him. What would be the point? He'd dump me in a heartbeat, but it wouldn't undo the lies I've told to Janey. Nothing can fix that at this point.

"Janey," I say slowly, trying to think of what to say while I'm talking. "Did you ever meet Albert?"

She smiles. "When I was very little, yes, but I hardly remember him now. All of my memories of him are re-created from photos Aunt Midge used to keep around the house. But my mom talked about him all the time. He was kind of a father figure to her. He taught her how to drive, and he did quite a job. She was notorious for her penchant for speed."

"He taught me how to drive too," pipes in Aunt Midge, her voice dreamy. "But most of our lessons ended up cut short by a detour to the nearest lovers' lane. Oh, that Oldsmobile he drove. Such a spacious backseat."

J.J. has just gotten a mouthful of red wine when she says this, and he snorts and starts coughing. "That explains so much," he says, when his airway is clear. "Obviously you never made it to the part of the lessons that covered turn signals."

Janey sets down her wineglass with a thud. "How does J.J. know you don't use turn signals?" she asks imperiously. "You haven't had a driver's license as far as I know the entire time you've been in Maine."

Uh-oh. Cornered, Aunt Midge sticks out her chin and says, "I am trying to stay in practice, not that it's any of your business what I do or don't do."

"Nean, are you giving her the car keys?" Janey demands. I color, knowing I'm in deep doo-doo.

"Well . . ." Surely Janey has tried to resist the persuasive wiles of Aunt Midge before. She must understand what I'm up against.

Janey smacks the table with both hands, sending the silverware clattering. "What are you thinking? She's an old woman with failing eyesight who lost her license nearly a year ago. She's going to be eighty-nine years old in a month, for God's sake."

"I'm sitting right here," says Aunt Midge, voice shrill. "I know you think I've got one foot in the grave, but you don't have to talk about me like I'm already gone."

Janey turns to her, softening, and puts a hand over one of hers, the smooth and the wrinkled in a little pile together. "I'm sorry, Aunt Midge. I don't think you have one foot in the grave. But you just should not be driving. It's too dangerous. And Nean is an idiot for letting you have the keys."

"I was always right there with her," I protest. "I didn't just send her into town for a gallon of milk or something."

"I wouldn't put it past you," says Janey. She makes a face like she just drank a glass of vinegar. "Your irresponsibility never ceases to amaze me."

"My irresponsibility?" I gesture at Aunt Midge. "She's a grown woman who knows her own mind. She is responsible for her own actions. Besides, you try saying no to her."

"That's right," chirps Aunt Midge. "I'm not a child and you can't try to control my every move."

"You are acting like a child," Janey says. "With your bratty behavior."

"Oh, why don't you lay off and mind your own beeswax," Aunt Midge cries. "I'm not some decrepit old bag waiting for death to come and take me home. I'm fit as a fiddle and I have eyes like a hawk. If I want to drive a perfectly safe automobile along some old country roads with not another human in sight for miles, I will, and you can't stop me." Now she truly does sound like a child. A child with a nineteen-twenties vocabulary, but still.

"I *can* stop you, and I will. Nean, your car privileges have been revoked."

"Oh for fuck's sake," I say. "Are you going to dock my allowance too?" I throw my napkin onto the table and stand up. "Aunt Midge, don't let her talk to you like this. You are a capable person and she's not the boss of you." I don't know why I'm saying this—I know in my heart that Janey's right—it isn't safe for Aunt Midge to drive anymore and it was stupid of me ever to let her. But I can't bear to agree with Janey now that she's being such a pain in my ass.

Aunt Midge rises too. "You sit down," she says to me, pointing a shaky distraught finger at my chest. "I am storming off right now, and you'll just have to wait until I'm done." She pushes back her chair and does her best to dramatically sweep out of the room even at her usual snail's pace. "Harrumph!" she says. "Phooey to all of you." Then she disappears from the kitchen.

I sit there, dead silent, while I wait for Aunt Midge to get her head start. When I hear the poolside door open and shut with a hard slam, I get back up and say, "J.J., are you coming with me?"

He has a mouthful of fried oyster and looks a little sad at the thought of leaving the grub behind, but he shrugs and stands up slowly. "Janey?" he asks, after he swallows.

"It's fine," she says, quietly shaking her head at the table still groaning with food.

"Okay, if you're sure," he says, a little hesitant. "I liked the third wine best, if it's any help."

"It is," she says sadly. He grabs one more oyster and pops it into his mouth.

"Remember what I said about pork chops." He comes around to me and takes my hand and we walk up the stairs to my bedroom together.

"See why I can't tell her anything?" I say the moment we're in the room with the door closed, jumping on the opportunity to justify myself to J.J.

"I guess," he says with a shrug. "Hey, where's Janey going?" He moves to the window but can't seem to get a look at what he's after.

"What do you mean?"

"I just heard a car starting. Is Janey going into town? It's almost nine on a Tuesday, everything will be closed."

"That's weird," I say, until I realize it's not weird at all. "Shit, it's Aunt Midge!" I throw open the door and start galloping down the stairs. "There's no way she can drive at night. What is she thinking?"

Sure enough, Janey is standing at the front window peering out at the pair of headlights we now both see backing out of the driveway. "God dammit!" I hear her cry, and she throws open the door nearly hitting me square in the face. "What is it with this family and stealing cars!?" I file that away to analyze in a more leisurely moment and go running after her onto the driveway. I am barefoot, and the driveway rocks cut my feet, just as they did that very first night when I tried to make a break for it in the U-Haul. I think of how dark and unfamiliar the roads were that night, how there wasn't a single streetlight or road sign, and how quickly I became lost. Aunt Midge should know the roads better from all the times she's driven with me to the shelter, but the way she steers. . . . I shake my head, images of our wild rides into town flashing before me. Janey, running flat out, nearly catches up to the Subaru when it gets to the road, but then has to back away when Aunt Midge throws the thing around the corner wildly and then guns the engine down the street, leaving in a squeal of tires like she's Vin Diesel. I catch up to Janey just in time to watch the taillights disappear into the darkness. The expression on her face is heartbreaking. I know mine is the same.

"Is this what you felt like when you saw me make off with the U-Haul?" I ask her quietly, putting my hand softly on her back as she leans over to get a breath.

"Pretty much," she says.

"I'm sorry I gave you the bird."

"It's okay." Her voice is utterly defeated. I could shoot myself for not taking her side with Aunt Midge. "Is it okay if I call the police? I mean, you better lay low if they come over . . ."

"God yes! You call them; J.J. and I will go out in his truck and look for her. Don't worry." Don't worry? What a freaking ridiculous thing to say. But what else is there? Oh, yeah. "I'm really sorry."

Before she can tell me to go to hell, I turn and run back to the house and tell J.J. to go for the truck. I've never in my life been so glad to see a man run as fast as he can away from me.

In J.J.'s truck we are silent. We have driven the obvious roads twice now, and there is no sign of Aunt Midge. We should have found her by now—it's been nearly an hour. I am crying a little bit, since I know this is all my fault. J.J. is on edge, surely thinking this is all my fault too. We start to bicker, first over where we should be looking, then over the manner in which we look.

"We should head toward town," J.J. says. "She could have gotten a long way before we got on the road. If she's in a ditch we're not necessarily going to find her just driving around the cape. We probably won't even find her 'til morning."

"She's not in a ditch," I say, frantic. "She's probably just parked in some dead end looking at the stars or something." I'm not sure I actually think that, or just want to. It is what I would have done if I'd been in her shoes. The moon is a little sliver tonight and the stars are bursting with light in every direction. "In which case she probably cut the lights and the only way we're going to find her is if we slow down and check every private drive."

J.J. grumbles as he turns into a little side road, one I know we've walked down hand in hand not very long ago. "What is that batty old lady thinking? Doesn't she know what she's putting us through?"

I bristle in defense of Aunt Midge. "But can you blame her? Wouldn't you get sick of Janey being on your case all the time too?"

"Not sick enough to worry everyone like this," he mutters. "Besides, Janey is right. She uses a magnifying glass to read *Us Weekly*. Why on earth would she think she can still drive?"

"That doesn't mean she can't see far away just fine," I say.

"Oh please. The woman thought I was a serial killer from ten feet away. Me!" It's true. There's no missing his bright, friendly good looks—even miserable and stressed, he looks like a choir boy. "She's as blind as a bat."

Of course he's right, but I feel guilty enough as it is. I try to lighten the mood. "Bats are terrific navigators."

"Stop it." His voice is cold and for the first time since meeting him I feel scared. "Just stop talking." He stomps on the brake in the middle of the road, making me rocket back in my seat, then throws the truck into a three point turn. "We're going into town," he says. "If she's still out here, hopefully she'll stay in the car until someone comes along."

I think of her stuck out alone in the dark, dark night, and my fear grows higher. "What if she was hurt?" I ask, my voice shrill. "What if she got into an accident and needs our help? What if she got lost, or drove off the road, or hit a deer?" I feel my armpits dampen as I start contemplating all the things that could go wrong. In my hands the fabric of my dress is wadded tightly and I feel helpless to let go. I can't think of the last time I've felt so guilty and afraid.

J.J. doesn't say anything at all—no comfort, no soothing, no promises. But his hands clench tighter around the steering wheel; I see his knuckles bulging like the blood inside is having trouble working through the veins. After nearly a mile of silence, he speaks quietly. "You should have thought of that before you let her drive all the time."

His words don't hurt. They are what I'm thinking anyway. I am just surprised he's mad enough to say them.

We drive in miserable silence for ten minutes, while we make our way up the familiar road to Damariscotta. I have no idea where we're going, but I've also lost any understanding of where we should look. *Please let her be fine,* I find myself praying. *Please.*

After a while J.J. lets go of the steering wheel with his right hand and moves it to my knee, where he gives me a little squeeze. "Hey, I'm sorry I said that, before. This isn't your fault. She is a grown woman, just like you said at dinner. And I know you love her and would never want her to get hurt."

I don't speak, afraid I might go from quiet weeping to a full-on snot-fest. I don't bawl very often, but when I do it's like something out of *The Exorcist*. But then I look over and see J.J.'s eyes are shiny too, and he's making a face like he's about to sneeze. I know that face. It's the "I'm trying to shut down my tear ducts" face, and it never works.

"Are you crying?" I ask him, my voice a little squeaky.

"Obviously not," he says, but speaking makes him relax his face and two teardrops come rushing down his right cheek.

"Why are you crying?" I demand. "You didn't say anything I wasn't already thinking."

He clears his throat. "It's not that. It's . . ." his voice trails off and he squints into the dark like he can see into the future. "I'm just frustrated, okay? I know I shouldn't be taking it out on you. You're upset too. I should be there for you right now."

I sigh in frustration. "Relax, okay?" I say. It's not that I don't appreciate his sentiment. It's just that it's me who should be feeling bad right now. Me who should be feeling guilty.

J.J. sniffs and nods, and then yanks his hand off my leg and jerks the steering wheel to make a hard left into Little Pond. "I know where we should look," he says. He pulls up to the tiny little downtown area, a four-way stop, and points around at every corner.

"Bar," he says, pointing to the left. Then he moves his hand clockwise. "Bar, bar, bar. Don't tell me this isn't where you would go if you were feeling downtrodden."

"I would go to you," I say, with a hint of a smile, meaning it. "But Aunt Midge would go to a bar."

"Right? Let's hope she made it this far," he says, and then pulls into one of the bar parking lots. No sign of Janey's Subaru there. He cuts across the street to the next lot. Nothing.

But in the third lot we hit pay dirt. The little blue car, not parked so much as stopped suddenly in the middle of three spaces, hazard lights on. I look at J.J. and he looks back at me with a huge grin on his face. "Thank God."

I exhale in a whoosh. "We were worried over nothing."

"Not nothing," he says, gesturing to the front bumper of the car. Sure enough, it's got an inexplicable dent in it, right in the middle, about the size of a basketball. "That's new."

I shake my head, relief and exasperation fogging me up. "Sure is." I unbuckle my seat belt and start to get out of J.J.'s truck when he grabs my shoulder and says, "Wait."

"Wait what?" I ask, eager to get Aunt Midge home where the three of us can yell at her together.

"She's fine. She's in there having a beer with Nancy and bitching about how we treat her like a child. And probably trying to get the number of an all-night body shop. Leave her be for a second."

"But Janey will be in a white-hot panic."

"I'll text her," he says, his thumbs already working the keys. When he's done, he puts his phone away and parks properly in the back of the lot, where we can see the door of the bar and the Subaru at the same time. I sit tight as he hops out of the truck, opens the door of Janey's car, turns off the hazard lights, and slams the door. Then, quite stealthily, he goes to a side window of the bar and peers in for a moment. I see him turn back toward me and give me a big thumbs-up in the gray light of the parking lot, then he jogs back to the truck. When he's back inside, he tugs me toward him. "C'mere."

I scoot across the truck cab so I'm snuggled into his arms and the two of us stare out the windshield for a second, as if Aunt Midge could make her getaway at any moment. Then J.J. says, "I have to talk to you."

My stomach plummets. The wash of relief at finding Aunt Midge is instantly replaced by the terror that phrase strikes. "Oh?" I say, wondering how long I can keep him from saying what it is he needs to say. "Would you rather talk, or . . ." I run my hand up his legs, feeling the rough denim against my sweaty palm and hoping the sensation feels more enticing to him than it does me.

He stills my hand. "Talk," he says, and rearranges us so I face him, my knees up on the bench, our shoulders squared to each other. "I want to talk about what's going to happen this fall."

I am expecting bad news, but this particular lead-in has me stumped. Am I about to discover that our relationship, like Noah's tomato selection, is seasonal? "Um, you mean like, how the trees are going to shed their leaves and the days get shorter?"

"No." He holds both my hands in both of his and I reel. "I mean like, when I go back to school for my senior year. I'm in college, Nean."

I start. "What?"

"I go to Dartmouth, in Hanover."

"Dartmouth?" I gasp. My eyes narrow. "You go to *Dartmouth*?"

"I do."

"As a student?" This can't be right. "You're the gardener there, right?" I ask, to be one hundred percent clear on what he's telling me.

"Um, no. Landscaping is my summer job, to save up money for the school year."

I pull away and blink at him several times. Somehow in just seconds, I've gone to sitting nose to nose with J.J. to pressing my back against the passenger-side door. At the same time I've changed from being his girlfriend to being the trashy girl he's wasting the summer with. The divide now between us feels epic. "Why didn't you tell me?" I ask. I feel enormously betrayed, and also foolish for feeling that way.

"I didn't tell you at first because I didn't want you to think I was some idiot frat guy or something," he says. "And then I didn't tell you later because you seemed . . . touchy about class issues." I suck in air. "Plus, you weren't being terribly forthcoming with me, so I thought maybe . . . you wouldn't care."

I sneer. "Why would I care?" But I care very much.

J.J. shrugs. I squeeze my eyes shut tight.

"When are you going back?" I ask him. "To Dartmouth?" I add unnecessarily, just to try the word out again and see if it seems more normal this time. It doesn't.

"In two weeks," he says.

I burst into tears.

Yes, I've been crying all night. But now I am doing the scary, mucus-based, exorcist cry. My face is immediately sopping wet, and the tears come so hard they are dripping off the edge of my chin into my lap. I start gasping for air through my mouth, because my nose is instantly jam-packed with viscous snot. It won't be long before it starts running down my face too. My shoulders shake.

"You lied to me," I moan pathetically. The thought of him going in two weeks is too much.

J.J. opens his hands to me, like I'm a wild animal. "I never actually lied. I mean, I lied by omission, but you . . ." he shrugs helplessly. "You weren't exactly being straight with me either."

"It's different," I sob, though I know that doesn't make any sense. "I knew *I* was lying," I add, getting stupider as I go.

J.J. smiles a little sad smile. "I honestly thought you would figure it out, sooner or later," he says. "Or ask. I mean, I'm twenty-two. Didn't you wonder what I was planning to do with the rest of my life?"

I cough and choke on my own tears, wondering why I didn't think about that. Probably because I never thought about that question in relation to myself, and I assumed J.J. was just like me. "Mow Janey's lawn?" I say, idiotically.

J.J. shakes his head at me but he's smiling. "I'm sorry, Nean." He snakes his right arm around me and scootches me closer so he can hold on to me. "I should have explained sooner." He puts a hand in my hair and combs through it gently with his fingers while I cry. I know I should push him away and keep my dignity, but that simply isn't happening. I'm staying here, where I'm safe, until the very last second.

I think of all the stupid things I've said to him, of how quickly I assumed he was from the exact same world as me, despite the little clues that told me otherwise. His house—a little split-level way inland with a one-car garage, but still well taken care of, and with both mother and father inside, and married to boot. The way he seemed so comfortable at the fancy lobster restaurant. The books he is always toting around in a back pocket or on the passenger seat of this truck. Not thrillers and mysteries, but skinny green-covered classics. The sort of thing you might be assigned as summer reading.

My head hurts. He must think I'm a complete idiot. How do I stack up against the sort of girls who go to an elite Ivy League college, I wonder? I bet they don't steal tampons from the bathrooms of fine-dining establishments. They probably don't even have periods. Too messy.

With the memory of that dinner, my embarrassment becomes so intense it distracts me from my grief. My crying becomes snuffles and then stops. J.J. stops stroking my hair and pulls out a hanky from his back pocket and holds on to it as I blow. I take a big breath in through my newly clear nose and let my shoulders fall back down to their normal position and in general just unwind a little bit. "I'm okay," I say, my voice a little raspy. "Sorry I lost my shit."

"Understandable," says J.J., rubbing a last tear off my cheek. "Listen,

Nean, I was thinking. This doesn't have to be a bad thing. Hanover is not even four hours away. We can see each other whenever. Or . . ." I watch him as his eyes dart around the cab of his truck. "Maybe you'd want to try out life in New Hampshire? I mean, it's a college town, so there are lots of entry-level jobs you could try, if you wanted to. You could live with me, just for the first semester, and see how you liked it . . ."

I think about living in his apartment, working as a bartender or drugstore clerk while he carves open cadavers or solves physics or whatever it is fancy senior-year college students do, and shake my head. "No," I say. "No. It's not like that," I tell him, surprised by the flash of disappointment I catch on his face, and then skeptical of it. "I think it's better if we just enjoy these two weeks"—I look up at him and lock eyes as I say this—"and then say good-bye."

J.J. looks right back into my eyes. He doesn't break eye contact, but stares at me, like he's trying to see through to the back of my skull. Then he shakes his head and looks down, and I feel the incredible loss of his gaze. After a long time in silence, he shrugs. I shrug back, just so he can know for once how impenetrable such a little gesture can be.

"I agree to nothing," he says, though we both know this isn't something we both have to agree on. "I'm not saying I will let you go."

I ignore him and take a deep breath and sigh loudly, exhausted by the repetitiveness of my life. First the house. Now J.J. Nothing that I think is mine ever stays that way. "Let's go get Aunt Midge," I say. "It's time for us all to go home."

JANEY

"[A] sit-down lunch, even when it's light and simple,
is an immensely civilized respite from the rigors of the day."

—IRMA S. ROMBAUER,
Joy of Cooking

The day after Aunt Midge's jailbreak I meet up with Noah for our standing lunch date, this time for a picnic with sandwiches made on a fresh loaf of Nean's bread. I had to help her make it this morning, so I feel not at all guilty about skimming some slices off the top. Actually, Aunt Midge and I both did. We came downstairs this morning and found her staring at the dough listlessly. The two of them, she and the dough, just one lump regarding another. For some reason, that girl has been acting weird ever since she got back with Aunt Midge and my car last night. Maybe I came down too hard on her. I tried to tell her it was no harm, no foul, but nothing I've said to her seems to sink in. She seems interested only in her loaves, kneading and kneading until I had to take them away from her to save the bread.

I've been so busy with preparations for our big dinner date that I hardly put any thought at all into the picnic menu, so I bring only fruit salad and cookies on the side, but Noah makes a fuss anyway. He tells me I make the best fruit salad he's ever tasted, and eats about thirteen cookies. Then he leans back dramatically and clutches at his stomach like he's expecting an alien to burst out of it.

"You're amazing," he tells me, and I flush with pride. "The things you do with dill . . ."

I smile. "Ever since I learned to cook I've been waiting for someone like you to cook for."

"Ever since I learned to eat, I've been waiting for someone like you, period," he says lightheartedly. Even with his singsong voice and silly face, the words make me melt.

This is my opening—my big chance to invite him over at last—but I balk. Yes, yes, I haven't invited him over yet. I know if I don't say something soon I'm going to have a repertoire of date-night food as long as my arm and no date to show for it, but the tiniest chance that he'll say no and everything between us will just fall through my fingers like a broken egg yolk into a meringue keeps me quiet. Instead I lean back on the picnic blanket next to him and look up at the cloudless sky.

The day is perfect. We're north of Little Pond, where the Atlantic beats hard at the cliffs, with no capes or coves to tame its ferocity. The park Noah chose is set high on the rocks and the ocean seems so far below us—just a sound track of an ocean more than an actual body of water. To the other people in the park, it is clearly not the main attraction either. There are tire swings, and a wooden castle with a rickety bridge, and a lighthouse about five hundred feet down the coast that is surrounded by gray-haired women taking photos of balding men in the foreground, and then the reverse. The grass around us teems with people noises. I am utterly in public, and yet I feel absolutely fine.

I sigh deeply.

"Are you bored?" Noah asks, propping himself up on his forearms and looking down his nose so his chin multiplies several times on his chest.

"Not at all." I think of what to tell him. "I'm people watching."

He sits up the rest of the way and bends his knees in front of him. "There's quite a crowd out today, isn't there?" We both sit and listen to the sound of shrieking little pirates storming their fortress for a moment, and then Noah shoots out his hand suddenly and grabs one of my wrists like a doctor looking for a vein. "Let me see those arms."

I stretch them out to him happily. "Nothing," I say. "They're not even itchy." Then, indelicately, I lift up the arm that's free and gesture to the armpits. "Not sweating, either."

He smiles. "Well, that's a little weird, considering it must be eighty-five degrees out here."

I lower my arm, suddenly embarrassed. "I just mean . . . I think I'm cured."

He loosens the hold on my wrist and moves his fingers around to my palm, tracing gentle lines absentmindedly. "I hope not." He clears his throat. "I mean, I'm glad you're not breaking out in hives every time someone walks too close to our picnic blanket . . ." he looks up at the bright blue sky as if there's a teleprompter up there. "But I'm also glad you still have your quietness. Your bottomless capacity for listening. All the other things I love about you that came from you being so shy . . ."

I feel my throat close. This is it. I have to ask him now. The moment is slipping away.

"I have been working on a recipe for clafoutis," I begin unsteadily. He looks at me puzzled. "It's a cherry custard thing. You make it in a Dutch oven—the oven has to be screaming hot. Actually I've heard it's good made in the fireplace. It's hundreds of years old."

His eyebrows arch inward. He has no idea what I'm talking about.

"It tastes better hot?" I attempt to move through the script as prepared by Aunt Midge, but all my confidence is eroding away.

His eyes search mine curiously and I stop myself. What am I doing? We are on this blanket, on this beautiful day, with the taste of lemon cookies still in our mouths. He is holding my hand, and I can't feel anything else at all but the touch of his fingers.

I am an idiot.

I stop myself from telling him that traditionally the cherries in a clafoutis still have their pits, and, instead, I lean over to him and touch his face with my free hand and close my other hand around his and kiss him. We are frozen like this for a moment, my lips just touching his, and then he begins to kiss me back, and oh, wow. It is long and deep and makes me feel tight and hot all over. I do not want to stop doing this. Ever.

When we do stop, it is because a shadow is cast over us, and I break away to examine the cause. It is a little redheaded boy who is wearing the better part of a chocolate cupcake on the front of his shirt. He is standing about six inches from our faces, staring, mouth open, with completely unabashed fascination. When he realizes our make-out session is over, thanks to him, he beats it pronto, but the damage is done. I feel the telltale burn on my shoulders, and then the redness flushes up and down both arms and across my chest, and I know the hives are only minutes away.

My head tips back as I roll my eyes heavenward. "Well, at least you know I'm not cured," I tell him on a laugh, because what else can I do but laugh and apply calamine lotion?

He laughs too and lays out flat on the picnic blanket with his arms behind his head, looking like he made all this, the perfect day and the hushed ocean and probably the cupcake on the front of that kid's shirt too. Right now, if he told me he did, I think I would believe him. I lie down perpendicular and put my head on his stomach.

"Do you want to come over to my house for dinner tomorrow night?" I ask him. "I am making clafoutis."

"At your house?" There is just a hint of hesitation there. Enough to make me worry.

"Yes. Well, or . . . I could cook at yours, too, if you'd rather. I could bring the clafoutis over. If you'd like."

There's a pregnant pause, and then Noah shakes his head at me, and for just a second I think I am about to hear a no. Instead he says, "I would love to come to dinner tomorrow night," and his voice echoes through his stomach into my ears. "I love clafoutis. Did you know that the recipe is hundreds of years old?"

I laugh and he does too, and when he laughs, his stomach bounces up and down like a little trampoline for my head. My head bounces up and down, and my eyes close in the brightness of the sun, and the ocean keeps splashing so far below. It is right then that I realize that I am in love.

NEAN

"I've sometimes thought that if my mother had been a baker (she wasn't),
and if she had ever made me this cake (which she didn't),
it would have been my childhood favorite."

—DORIE GREENSPAN,
Baking: From My Home to Yours, on her Devil's Food White-Out Cake

In the days that follow, I tell Janey nothing at all, resolved to enjoy every last second with J.J. and then forget he ever existed. Besides, she is obsessed with the last-minute preparations for her date with Noah. But she must notice me stewing, because the eve of her big dinner, she invents a wild-goose chase to keep me busy while J.J. is off doing the sort of things college students do two weeks before a new semester. Buying condoms and Trapper Keepers, I guess.

It's black truffles Janey wants, but after hours of shopping, I'm still empty-handed. I finally find them when I am inspired to swing by Damariscotta's woo-wooey-est restaurant, a sustainable food place where the daily menu is written by hand on butcher paper on each table. I show up well before the dinner service, looking as respectable as I can, and bang on the window until they let me in. Then I ask them their source for black truffles.

The chef has a good laugh at this, but does eventually lead me back into her kitchen to give me the hookup from her own stash, after I explain that the presence of black truffles could make or break my only friend in town's chances of getting some nooky. I pay almost a hundred bucks of Janey's money for less than an ounce. I tell the chef that at that price, I should get to rub some on my gums gratis, and this cracks her up so much that she sits me down and feeds me for free, along with two waiters and her wine lady–slash–girlfriend.

The crew explains that this is their family dinner, where they taste the specials of the night so they can sell them to the diners. Then over the next hour and umpteen dishes, they regale me with stories of rude customers and knife injuries, and I momentarily forget the sadness that's been clinging to my shirt hem like a spoiled child. The food, which is almost as good as Janey's cooking, I must say, is served with a thick-crusted sourdough loaf that crackles when you slice it and melts when you chew it. When I ask them where they got their bread, the chef tells me about the bakery I've walked by admiringly so many times. It is Bread and Honey, the place with that amazing list of daily breads in the window, always changing and making my mouth water. It's only two blocks away.

After I leave the restaurant, I walk to the bakery and peer into the windows. It's almost five now, and the employees inside, two youngish women with hairnets, are putting the place to bed. There are hardly any loaves left behind the counter, but there's a cake, a round three layer that one of the women is boxing up. It's so beautiful, that cake, that it nearly takes my breath away. The frosting on the sides has been coated with bright white coconut, and on top are the words "Happy Birthday Meredith" in curly orange cursive, studded with pink and red polka dots. Little yellow flowers are sprinkled around the words, their middles rounded and dark. Black-eyed Susans, I realize, the same as grow in the ditches of Iowa.

The cake makes me lonely, and then jealous. I would like to be Meredith tonight. I would like to come home and open the front door and hear the word "Surprise!" and then see J.J. and Janey and Aunt Midge and Noah and maybe even the people I just met from the restaurant, grinning expectantly, gesturing "ta-da" toward that lovely little cake on a table next to a stack of tiny waxed paper plates and plastic forks.

But my birthday is in January. J.J. will be long gone by then. Janey and Aunt Midge will have tired of me. There won't be any surprise, or any cake. It's not fair.

All at once, I think of walking in, telling them I'm here to pick up the birthday cake. I can pay for it with the extra truffle money Janey gave me. I'll tell them that Meredith is my coworker over at the bead store in Boothbay Harbor, and that she has no idea there's going to be a party—that we told her that we had to stay late in the store and do inventory so she wouldn't suspect. They probably took the order over the phone. They'll never be the wiser.

Until the real friend of Meredith shows up wondering what happened to her cake. God, what is wrong with me? Stealing birthday cakes? I shake my head in disgust and turn to leave when the door of the bakery pops open with a jingle.

"Hey," says the woman, the dirty-blond one I saw sweeping a moment ago. "Do you need anything? We're getting ready to close but we can still find you a loaf of something if you're desperate . . ."

"Um," I stall, feeling guilty just for thinking what I was thinking. "I was wondering, um . . ." I can't think of a thing to say that doesn't involve stealing a cake.

"We still have a stollen," the woman supplies.

"You do?" I'm not entirely sure what "stollen" means when it's a noun.

"Sure, come on in."

I follow her into the bakery, which smells overpoweringly of blooming yeast and vanilla, and look around at the empty racks and tidy back counters. Usually when I pass by someone is back there, kneading up a cloud of flour on the long metal table behind the cash register. Now the table is pristine.

"When do you make tomorrow's bread?" I hear myself asking, as she wraps up a yellow braided loaf that is so shiny on top it seems to be made of plastic.

"Depends on the bread," she says. "Most of it gets going tomorrow morning around four-thirty."

"A.m.?" I ask, incredulous.

She grins, clearly used to this response. "Believe it."

"If you hired me, I could do some of that early work for you," I say, and then wonder if my eyes are going to turn around in my head and give myself a dirty look for saying such a thing. I mean, four thirty in the freaking morning? I have lost my mind.

But before I can backpedal, the baker tilts her head. "Do you know how to make bread? Good bread?"

"Yeah," I say, too proud to shut up. "I do. Not as many kinds as you guys have. But I'm a fast learner. And I make, like, four loaves a day, so I get plenty of practice."

She looks around the kitchen for a moment, like there's someone she can consult about this. But the woman who was boxing the cake is gone, and so too, I realize, is the cake itself. Is Meredith one of her friends, I wonder, or is she just delivering it to the real buyer? Either way, there would have been no asking for work had I come in here claiming that cake as my own. And now that I've asked for a job, I realize how badly I want to work here.

"I'll tell you what," the baker is saying. "Why don't you bring in your best loaf for me on Friday. We'll have a taste, and if it's a hit, then you've got yourself a job. I can't pay you more than nine an hour," she says with an apologetic shrug. "But it comes with all the bread you want."

"Seriously? Four loaves a day, if I wanted?" If she says yes, I could work the job without affecting the shelter supplies at all. I gotta think that's some kind of good sign in favor of working for a living.

She pauses. "If your bread's that good, sure. Consider it your bonus." Then, she adds, "But not the chocolate cherry loaf. That shit's expensive."

"It's a deal!" I say. I drop a five on the counter and snatch up the paper bag of bread she's readied for me, fighting the urge to stick my nose in and see if that light saffron smell is coming from the bread. "See you Friday."

"Friday. Hey, I'm Kim, in case I'm in the back when you show up. But everyone calls me Honey. What's your name?"

Without thinking, I blurt out, "Nean Brown."

Just like that, I tell her the truth, without even trying.

JANEY

My date with Noah is tonight. I have prepared the following:

Cold melon soup with prosciutto croutons
Ceviche scallops on watercress
Maytag-stuffed pork chops with cherries and balsamic caramelized
    onions
Mashed potatoes with black truffles (*thanks, Nean*)
Wine-braised artichokes
Baked grape tomatoes

And then, in case he doesn't eat pork, I whip up tuna crusted in herbs
with smoked paprika grits from my Charlie Palmer book.

And fine, I will admit it, I also have a lobster risotto standing at the
ready for emergencies.

For dessert I have toiled over the clafoutis, that beautiful gingham
pudding of cherry and custard, and it does taste better warm, at least to
me, under a scoop of homemade vanilla bean–flecked ice cream, which
is hardening in the outside freezer right now. In my wildest imagination,

though, we linger over dinner, lost in light conversation and bright red wine. Then, perhaps as we sip on the second bottle, we are overcome by passion and rush upstairs before dessert is even served, and wind up eating the clafoutis hours later and cold anyway, and neither of us cares a whit. The thought of it—and I don't mean the dessert—makes my mouth water.

In the extremely low chance that things go *even better* than my fantasy, I've stocked the refrigerator with the makings of breakfast: smoked salmon and cream cheese and eggs and chives and fresh oranges for juicing. It is my nod to the power of positive thinking. Nean calls it my Fridge of Dreams.

In addition to the somewhat excessive cooking, I have spent hours upon hours in the wine store, trying to sort out what will make all these courses taste best without making it seem like I tried too hard. Which I did. Will he think it odd if I pour a different wine for each course? Or should I try to find one perfect wine that tastes great with artichokes and cherries both? The men at the wine store squint at me when I ask them what to serve with pork, lobster, scallops, and tuna at the same time. After a bit of private discussion, they suggest "something white." The exercise is exhausting.

Add to all this that I'm extraordinarily nervous. Tonight will either make or break this thing going on between Noah and me—this is my one shot at making it happen. If he doesn't like the food and we don't have fun, there's no hope for me. I will never, no not ever, be able to screw my courage up again and start over. And even if I did, which I wouldn't, I would not find another Noah. Noah is unusual in one thousand ways, not least of all being that he talks to me.

Everything is at stake tonight. Jittery, I repeatedly shoo away Nean, who is walking around in a haze anyway, and Aunt Midge, who is determined to make me nuts by draping various accessories around my neck, walking back a few steps, staring at me, then shaking her head and taking back the necklace or scarf or shawl or, in one instance, cloche hat and starting over. I set the table six times, until I feel it's appropriately nonchalant. I change clothes again. Now I am wearing a lapis-colored trapeze dress with big thick straps and a loose waist that makes me feel sort of naked underneath. When I come downstairs I get catcalls from the peanut gallery, so I stick with it.

Seconds before Noah is expected, the phone starts ringing. I go into full panic. What if he's canceling? What if he's changed his mind? What if he's been hurt, or gotten sick? I fall on the phone like it's a bomb I have to diffuse, and yell "HELLO?" into the receiver.

There's a long pause. Maybe he's been in a car accident and he's managed to call me just before passing out. Or bleeding out? "NOAH?"

"Who? No, this is Meghan Mukoywski. Executive producer at the Home Sweet Home Network. Could I speak with Janine Brown, please?"

Oh my Lord I have lost my mind. I sit down at the kitchen island with a gasp of relief. "This is Janine," I say on an exhale.

There's a pause. "Is this a good time?"

I look over at the counters. They are groaning with food. I've never tried to make so much food for an actual person before, and I am glad for the challenge. It gives me something to concentrate on. Something I can control.

"Sure it is," I say distractedly. Should I plate the scallops now, or keep them cold until the last moment?

"You sound different," she says, confusing me for a moment, until I realize, I'm not stuttering into the phone. Not even a little. This is amazing! I can't wait to tell Noah. "I'm just calling to check in, see how things are going. You've been in the house for almost three months. I'm thinking by now you must be mostly settled in."

"What? Oh, yes. Yes, we're all unpacked." I look at the clock. He's supposed to be here any minute now. I should probably get her off the phone.

"You are? Terrific. In that case, this is probably a great time for us to send some cameramen over to film."

I wrinkle my forehead. What? Why would she do that? "I'm sorry?"

"For the montage? Remember, we talked about it on the night of the sweepstakes. Nothing fancy. We're just going to get some shots of you walking through the house. Showing it off."

I tip my head back and remember that evening. Can it really have only been three months since my life changed so drastically? "I'm sorry, Ms. Mukoywski, I completely forgot about all that. Can we, uh, schedule it for September?"

She ignores me. "Let's say Friday. Morning or afternoon?"

Somewhere in the dull recesses of my brain a voice protests. "That's . . . tomorrow . . ."

The producer laughs, uncomfortably. "I know, I know, I wish I could give you more notice. The thing is, we've got a freelance guy we use in Maine, and he's only free on Friday. Something about football season . . . CBS Sports? Ugh. I hate freelancers. But you don't mind, do you?"

I am about to say that I do mind, adamantly, when the doorbell rings. My panic rises. This is a date. This is not a drill. I look around. Aunt Midge is waving at me and pointing up the stairs, and Nean is scooting out the door for her date with J.J. Right this minute Noah is standing at the door waiting for me and only me.

"I've got to go," I say into the phone.

"You'll be home tomorrow then?" I hear Meghan ask as I hang the phone up. I don't answer. I can call her first thing tomorrow and cancel, I tell myself as I rush to the door. The house will be a mess anyway. Or maybe he can just do exterior shots? It will work itself out.

By the time I throw open the door I've forgotten the conversation entirely.

"Hi!" I shout a little frighteningly. Noah is standing there, and he's clearly dressed up for this, and he looks good. His jeans are cleaner than usual, and he's wearing a buttoned-up checked shirt instead of his usual plain blue one open over a tee. Of course, the shirt is rolled up to his elbows, so he still looks ready at any time to mulch out a raised bed, but still. I am flattered. And excited.

"Hi," he says, and steps inside. "I think this is my first time inside your house."

I lean in for a hello kiss but he is already walking through the entryway into the big living room. When I catch up with him he's running a hand along the rock of the massive fireplace in the center of the room. "Wow," he says. "This is pretty posh."

"Yes," I say, already feeling like the evening is out of my control. "Would you like a tour?"

He looks at me, almost as if he is noticing me for the first time. I know that this house, with all its fancy detail and grand décor, might have that effect on guests, but I feel hurt all the same. "Sure," he says.

I wave my arms around me. "This is the big living area," I say unnecessarily. "It's called the great room on the contest website. And over there is the door to the pool where Aunt Midge swims." He walks to the sliding glass door and peers out at the endless pool, and I say a silent prayer of thanks that she's not out there swimming in the buff right now. "And this long room on the back of the house is the three-seasons room. It has a really nice view." I guide him out there and gesture at the round glass table set for two. "I thought we might eat dinner out here, since it's such an exquisite evening." Such an exquisite evening? Who says that?

"Looks nice," says Noah, noncommittally. Doesn't he like it? I wonder. Should I have set the dining room table instead?

"And this door goes into the dining room, and then the kitchen." I hold my breath as we walk through to my glorious, heavenly, palace of a kitchen. Will he see how perfect it is? Will he even care?

"Wow," he says again. "This is really something." It doesn't sound like a compliment. He beelines right for the fridge and points accusingly at the television screen set into the door. "What is this for?"

I feel instantly foolish. "Um, well." I love that fridge. It is my third best friend after Nean and Aunt Midge. But I sell it out in a heartbeat. "It just came with the house. Crazy, right? A TV in the refrigerator?"

Noah shakes his head. "Some people will buy anything." My heart breaks a little.

"But you can watch cooking shows on it, which is kind of nice," I say, just in case the fridge can hear me. "It's just a fun little perk, that's all."

"Hm," he says, and my spirits sink a bit lower. "Whoa." Now he has turned toward the island, where all the platters of food sit waiting for finishing touches or heat. He turns and sees all six burners in service, the lights of both ovens on. "Who else is coming over?" he asks.

I purse my lips. "Just us." My stomach churns. "I wasn't sure what you would be hungry for." I feel like an enormous idiot. I should have never let him into my kitchen. Desperate, I grab the two glasses of wine I've been letting breathe on the buffet and foist one at him. "Cheers!" I say, hearing the mania in my own voice.

He sets it down like it is a dead rat. "Janey, I don't drink. I thought you knew that."

"You don't?" How would I have known that? We've only ever been together during lunches.

"No." He crosses his arms, defensively. For the first time I notice that he is in a horrible mood. Did I do something wrong?

"But I picked this out especially for you. It's a Hudson River Valley wine, from near where you used to have your farm!"

He shakes his head. "Thanks, I guess." He looks downright offended. Have I scared him off with all my cooking and planning? But I thought he liked my cooking. Have I totally misread the signs?

My face falls. "It's no big deal," I lie, wishing I could shut myself up. I take a big swig of my own glass. "I just thought you would recognize the *terroir*," I add, my voice trailing off when I hear how stupid this sounds.

For a while, I stand there silent, feeling moronic. Did I really just use the word "*terroir*" in a sentence? I play the word over and over again in my head, all the while thinking of the four bottles of wine that are breathing on the buffet a few feet away from us. He's going to think I have a drinking problem. But who doesn't have wine with dinner? Only alcoholics, right? Is he an alcoholic?

He clears his throat, bringing me back to this awkward moment. "Let's eat," I say, because where my witty conversation fails me, my food might come to the rescue. "Have a seat out there and I'll get the soup ready to roll. You like cantaloupe, right?"

"Sure," he says, and smiles at me for the first time since he's walked into the house. The smile, that perfectly familiar crooked grin, gives me refuge enough to touch him on the back gently, pushing him toward the back room and the romantic table for two that's waiting out there.

"I'll meet you out there in two shakes." I open the fridge, stroking the television panel apologetically as I do, and pull out the chilled soup and the crème fraîche I infused with mint to dab on top. This, at least, I've done right. This he will like.

When I've plated the two bowls I carry them out to him and find him standing in the middle of the room, looking at the ocean view with a frown.

"What is it?" I ask, as I set down the soup bowls in their matching white chargers.

"Nothing," he says, his face twisting a little as he sits down at the table. "It must be nice to live here, is all."

"It is." I nod emphatically. "Where is your place again?" I try to sound casual about this, but really I am desperate to know these details.

"Up in Little Pond," he says, using the exact same tone he used when he told me he didn't drink. It is the voice of a teenaged boy saying, "Duh."

I try to draw him out, get him on familiar footing. "Close to the shelter?"

"Not far." A silence falls. I watch him intently as he spoons up a mouthful of soup, tastes it. "Mmm," he says, but none of his usual enthusiasm is there.

I smile wanly. "Tell me about your place," I say, wondering if I added too much mint. "Does it have a view?"

"Not really."

"So it's inland."

His eyes cut back out to the ocean. I realize I've never seen him in a mood like this. "Right," he finally says. "No place as nice as this," he adds.

I think of Nean, of her great impatience with people who have money. Is that what Noah is feeling right now? Is that why he seems so grouchy?

"Winning a house like this is about as good as it gets," I say, trying to remind him that I didn't buy this place, that it fell into my lap. "I feel very lucky."

"I can't imagine what the property taxes are like."

I recoil, not sure what to make of that. It seems like a crass thing to say. But then, I have heard that New Englanders are more open about affairs of money than we Iowans are. It would be hard not to be. Attempting to do as the Romans do, I answer him honestly.

"I'm planning to pay them with an inheritance I came into many years ago," I say.

He snorts. "Some people have all the luck."

I drop my spoon. I've had enough. "Excuse me? Luck? I would much prefer having the living man to the inheritance, thank you very much." I'm so offended by his statement that I forget that I've never told him about Ned. When I realize that it's the first time I've mentioned him to Noah, I feel nauseous.

He has the decency to look good and ashamed now. "I'm sorry," he says softly. "I'm being a jerk."

"Yes, you are," I agree wholeheartedly. "You didn't even say if you like the soup."

He pulls the napkin out of his lap and stands. "I need to go."

"What?" I think of the pork chops, stuffed and seared, finishing in a low slow oven right this moment. "Now?"

"I don't think this was a good idea." His voice is low and expressionless, but I can tell he's not talking about the cantaloupe soup. He starts to back away from the table.

"Wait," I stand up so fast my soup bowl clatters off the charger. "You can't go. I made pork chops. I made mashed potatoes and braised artichokes. I baked a clafoutis." I hear how desperate, how pathetic I sound, but I can't seem to stop.

"There's homemade ice cream in the freezer," I shout after him, as he starts walking into the living room. "Noah!" He's just walking away from me now, and I feel the tears start to build up in my eyes at the sight of him retreating. Tears of anger. "Do you know how long it takes to clean an artichoke?" I cry.

Midway through the living room he stops and turns back to me. I am chasing him so fast I nearly bump into his solid body. I put my arms out to steady myself, then grab onto his shirt. "Noah?" I ask. "What's happening?"

He looks at me, his eyes still warm though his face is frozen. "Janey, you're wonderful," he says, and I know from dating in high school that this is it. "Really you are."

I lose my head right then. I start to cry and I clench tighter onto his shirt. I tip my head into his chest as if I can hide from this.

"But really, I'm not right for you," I hear him saying, from another room, another house even. Is he even talking to me? Or is he saying this to someone else, in another life, in some other dimension?

"I'm not right for anybody," I say softly into his shirt, and force my tears back up inside my head. I straighten and let go of his shirt. "I should never have made so much food," I add, knowing as I say this how crazy I've been. I've fallen in love over a series of meaningless lunches and picnics and, and . . . *rides in the car*, for God's sake. I've cooked enough dinner tonight to feed an entire relationship, beginning, middle, and end. But there has never been any relationship to feed. Only the one in my mind.

His shirt, where I am staring now, is wet in splotches: two eyes, a nose. There are two wrinkled patches where I was holding on for dear life. "Thank you for coming over," I say, though I have no idea what I'm thanking him for.

"I'm so sorry about this," he says, and leans over and kisses my forehead. I hold my breath, pinch my lips together tightly. "Good night, Janey," he says, and then leaves me standing there, my eyes getting drier and drier, my thoughts going farther away. I think of everything I risked tonight. I think of everything I've lost. I don't know how long I stand there before I cross into the kitchen and turn off each oven, kill the heat under each burner.

Then I clean up the soup bowls, put the spoons in the dishwasher, and throw the napkins in the laundry. When there is no trace of Noah ever having been here, when it is like the whole thing never happened, I go outside. Down to the rocks, to wait for the dark and the stars and the moon, and the only time I can talk to Ned.

NEAN

"The most underused tool in the kitchen is the brain."

—ALTON BROWN,
I'm Just Here for the Food

While Janey woos, I wander through the woods looking for J.J. We have made a date at that same pine needle forest that we first got down on, and I am looking forward to it with my whole heart. I've filched a bottle of wine from Janey's expansive lineup, and J.J. is in charge of bringing paper cups and a blanket. What more do we need?

We need him to not be leaving. But that is not going to happen.

When I finally make it to our spot, he is waiting there, looking utterly relaxed. Now whenever I see him I imagine he is in the movie *School Ties*, moving confidently through the hallowed halls and grassy quads of Dartmouth with leather-bound books tucked under his arm. Apparently, in my mind, it is still the 1950s on every Ivy League campus.

I try hard to replace that image with J.J. the part-time gardener, wearing battered jeans and pushing a wheelbarrow. It's hopeless now. To me, he will be preppy forever more.

"Nine more days," I tell him, by way of hello. I've gotten into the habit of reporting to him on how much time we have left together—

maybe because he is moving toward something, whereas I am being left behind, and I want him to feel guilty about this.

"Hello to you too," he replies. "Is Noah at the house right now?"

I nod. "I got a peek at him as I skulked off. He looks cute, in his farmer way."

J.J. cracks a big grin. "You Brown girls," he says, lumping us together in his infuriating way. "Just can't get enough of men who till the soil."

"How many times do I have to explain this? We are not related. We just happen to have the same last name."

J.J. shrugs. "You seem like sisters to me."

I give him a little shove, pretending to be perturbed; secretly I am flattered. "Well, we're not," I say, just as much to myself as to him. "And don't you forget it."

"How about that wine?" he asks. "What did you find for us?"

I produce a bottle of wine with a picture of a French château on it. "Let's see . . ." I squint at the label. "Côte Rôtie. That is French for 'This will make you extra tipsy.'"

"My favorite vintage." J.J. produces a corkscrew—see, this is why he goes to such a fancy college, because he thinks to bring a corkscrew—and soon we are into our first glass. Cup, I should say. The wine is truly wonderful, and for a moment I feel guilty that I took it out of the roster for Janey's big dinner—but then, she did buy two bottles of the stuff. And it seems to pack a much bigger punch than the usual nonfancy wines. So I probably did her a favor.

J.J. seems to be following my thoughts. "I wonder what Janey and Noah are doing right now."

The night is warm. I stretch out my legs in front of me and slip off my shoes. "Probably eating pork chops," I say.

"Maybe . . ." J.J. curls up behind me, forming himself into a sort of lounge chair for me to lean on, and starts running his fingers through my hair. "Or maybe they're too consumed by desire to eat . . ." He puts down a little trail of kisses on my neck and my whole body gets heavy.

Then I think of Janey consumed by desire and laugh. "Yeah right. Like Janey could think about anything besides the cooking. You should have seen that kitchen. Everywhere you look, food on top of food. It's like going to the Old Country Buffet." As soon as I say that I blush. I bet J.J. has never been to the Old Country Buffet in his life. Too busy eating lobster.

But J.J. laughs and his laugh is warm and inclusive. "I once went to the Old Country down in Portland when I was on a Cub Scout trip. We had a contest to see who could eat the most cottage cheese. I won. It was a weird feeling, riding home in the back of the school bus with my stomach full of cottage cheese."

I snarf at this. "Why cottage cheese? Why not fried chicken, or chicken-fried steak, or something else yummy?"

"Because," he says matter-of-factly, "unlimited cottage cheese is free with purchase of the salad bar," he says, like it's the most obvious thing in the world. "And the salad bar is way cheaper than the full buffet." He leans in to whisper in my ear. "We also ate a lot of bacon bits."

I tilt my head. "Seriously? You didn't splurge for the $6.99 kids' all-you-can-eat special? I don't get you. Are you rich or poor?"

Another warm laugh. "I'm not sure. What's the right answer here?"

"Poor," I say with confidence, turning my shoulders so I can face him.

He shakes his head. "Nean, you are so weird." Then he takes my face in his hands and kisses me.

A long while later, when the blood supply has returned to my brain and the wine is a distant memory, I talk J.J. into going back to the house with me. I am tipsy and well-loved, after all, and therefore starving. I think of the piles of food that were sitting on the island when I left—potatoes, fresh lobster, scallops, grits—and realize there's no way I'm going to be able to resist a chance at leftovers. When I remind J.J. that Janey probably cooked plenty of extra pork chops, I practically have to run to catch up with him. He makes quick time back to the road and up past the farm, then cuts through the woods toward his gardening shed. When we get to the tree line about a hundred feet from the house I grab at him, using the full weight of my body to stop his meat-induced stampede.

"Wait," I hiss, whispering as though the lovebirds inside might hear us approaching from this far away. "We've got to be stealthy or we might cramp their style."

J.J. nods solemnly and we loop around so we're on the ocean side of the house and start creeping toward the kitchen door, low, so that even if they're in the back room they won't see us. J.J. starts humming the theme from *Pink Panther* as we approach, and suddenly I get a fit of giggles, which I try desperately to stifle. "Hush!" I stage-whisper. "We must remain undetected. The future of your pork chops are at stake."

This only makes J.J. creep more dramatically, and the sight of him up on his tippy toes, head bent low, with his index finger pressed to his lips, is my undoing. I clamp my mouth shut to push back the giggles but they escape from the sides of my mouth, and out my eyes.

He hugs me close to him, using his chest to muffle my giggles, but then I feel him start to laugh too, and soon we are both shaking with the laughter we're trying to keep in, holding on to each other for dear life.

"Quiet," I try to say, but it comes out on a gasp. "Think about Janey!" In an attempt to stop my giggles I imagine the look on her face if she saw us collapsed against the side of the house practically peeing ourselves with laughter. The thought of her furious expression actually makes me laugh harder.

J.J. shakes his head, hysterical. "I'm sorry, I'm sorry." He takes a huge breath. "Seriously, if we ruin her groove with Noah she will have us both killed, you know." He sobers up a little and straightens me up by the shoulders.

"You're right," I say, nodding and panting. "All that cooking and prep work . . . if we screw it up for her now who knows when she'd get another chance to get laid."

"Not until the grocery stores are able to restock, at least. Come on,"

J.J. stands up to his full height and peers in the high kitchen window. "There's no one in the kitchen." He slowly, slowly creeps up the stairs to the kitchen door and turns the handle. There is no sound from within. He pushes it open about an inch and pokes his nose inside.

"The coast is clear!" he whispers excitedly. "And I see pork!"

The two of us tumble inside. I watch J.J. as he looks around at the spread of food, and then falls upon a metal pan sitting on a hot pad, where six enormous beautifully browned chops sit completely ignored and untouched. He pulls one up with his fingers, holding on to the bone, and takes an enormous bite like he's eating a leg of mutton at the Medieval Times.

"Mmmm . . ." he says enthusiastically, if very softly.

I find my jackpot, a cold pot of lobster folded into thick, creamy rice, which also looks completely untouched. Using the wooden spoon from the pot, I bring a scoop to my mouth. The creamy sweet deliciousness makes my eyes roll back into my head and I moan around the mouthful. "Ohmmmphf." When I swallow I add quietly, "Oh my *God* this is good."

J.J. comes over and I hold out a spoonful of lobster for him. He tries some and his reaction is similar to mine. Then he looks over at the sideboard and his eyes get big.

"Wine!" he whispers. He starts for the line of bottles, but I stop him with an arm to the chest.

"Wait. Where is the happy couple?" I ask.

"They must be upstairs," J.J. says with an eyebrow wiggle. "I haven't heard a peep . . ."

I peer out the kitchen entryway and see nothing. Emboldened, I creep into the main living room. Nobody. No one in the three-seasons room either. To be extra safe I make sure they're not out by the pool, but there's nothing to see but the growing darkness outside. Jubilant, I rush back to the kitchen and give J.J. a giant smack on the lips. "No one's down here!" I tell him, letting my voice get just a hair louder. "They must be upstairs getting it on!"

J.J. grins. "That means . . ." he gestures to the appetizing food that surrounds us in every direction and looks at me questioningly.

"Oh yeah, baby," I say back, and go to the cupboard to fetch the largest plates I can find. "All this is ours."

Now we truly dig in. We each grab forks and big soup spoons from the drawer by the sink and lug pans and platters full of lobster, bright orange-yellow spiced grits, bursting red tomatoes, tiny little toasts heaped with prosciutto, and massive amounts of mashed potatoes to the breakfast bar. J.J. brings over serving plates heaping with thin-sliced scallops and salad, artichoke leaves around a little tureen of creamy dip, and of course his pork chops still in the pan, and then pours us both big glasses of wine in the fancy bowl-shaped goblets that came with the house. We pull up stools at the kitchen bar and tuck in like wild beasts, straight from the dishes. I am two bites into the mashed potatoes, which, even cold, taste of heaven and earth both, thanks to those spendy black truffles and a generous topping of butter, when J.J. points to a large red enamel pot covered with a lid that stands on the bar about two feet out of reach.

"What is that?" he asks. His eyes are large and greedy, like a toddler spotting his first Slip 'n Slide.

"No idea." I stand up on the rungs of my stool to reach the pot in question and drag it toward us. "I don't remember seeing her make anything in this pot . . ."

Slowly I lift up the heavy lid. We peer inside and are silenced with awe. Within is a beautiful, lush, cherry dessert of some kind. Creamy butter-yellow custard forms the backdrop for vibrant cherry polka dots, painstakingly spaced out over the dessert to give the dish an incredible style and elegance—like something from the cover of a cookbook. One look at this dish and you can taste the bright juicy cherries and feel the silken cream on your tongue. I feel my mouth water.

"Whoa," says J.J. "What is it?" I can see him stagger with the same wonderment I am feeling.

"I'm not sure, but it must be dessert. It looks amazing," I add unnecessarily as I start to lower the lid.

"Hang on—" J.J. says, wielding his spoon toward the pot like a weapon of mass destruction. "I want a taste."

"Don't even think about it." I slam down the lid and start scooting the pot out of his reach. "Did you see that thing? It's gorgeous. We can't spoil that—what if they are planning to eat it later? *After?*" I hit the word with as much significance as I can so J.J. will see what's at stake here.

J.J. lowers his spoon hesitantly, keeping his eyes trained on the pot as it escapes his clutches. "No, you're right," he says slowly, as if he doesn't quite believe it, turning back to his pork chop with lessened interest. "It's too perfect."

We sigh together, as if on cue. "Exactly. Too perfect for us," I say. "Pass me some more wine."

J.J. and I linger over our food and drink for at least an hour, maybe more. The rich meats and creamy starches make us lose track of time. I eat slowly, despite my ever-growing good wine buzz, tasting everything as carefully as I can, cherishing every bite, until it becomes painful to eat any more and I feel spacey and warm all over. All the while there is not a peep from upstairs, and I find myself goggling at J.J. in wonder when I realize how much time has passed. "Noah must be a stallion," I say around a mouthful of wine.

J.J. looks at the big kitchen clock and then at me. "Holy cats. It's almost eleven. I didn't even realize how long we'd been in here."

"Me neither. What do you suppose is going on up there?"

"I don't know, but you should find out from Janey so we can try it," he says, eyes bright. He has been drinking as much as I have, I can see. We both have adopted a certain precarious lean on our stools.

"Maybe we should practice our technique a little first," I say, slurring my words just a bit and flipping my hair as sexily as I know how. "Before we add anything new to our repertoire." I put my hand on J.J.'s thigh so he will know this is an invitation and not a dig on his skills. He grabs my wrist and moves my hand upward on his leg. I purr.

"Maybe we should," he agrees, and then stands—or rather tips off from his stool—and lifts me off of mine. He gives me a loooooong with six *o*'s J.J. kiss and then surprises me by breaking away, looking me up and down, and then kissing me again right away, this time harder and more frenzied. I feel my already wine-addled brain melt. "Oh, my," I moan.

The next thing I know we are up against the countertop, with my back to the acres of serving platters, my arms splayed behind me for balance, and my legs wrapped around his waist for dear life. I've never had this kind of crazed sex before, and I swear my eyes have burned up in their sockets, it's so hot. I can't see or hear anything and feel like a giant ganglion of exposed nerves. Things move fast and get more and more intense. At some point I swear I black out.

And then a sound does cut through the fog. It's a cry. An anguished cry.

Oh shit.

My eyes spring open and I look over J.J.'s shoulders right into the red, unblinking eyes of Janey. My mouth pops open. "Oh shit." I say, loud enough for J.J. to stop his movements instantly.

"What is it?" he asks, looking at my face and trying to hold my legs in place even as I go limp.

"Oh shit," I say again, helpless for words, desperate to push J.J. away. "Oh Janey, oh my God." I manage to wriggle away and get my skirt pulled into place at about the same instant, and quickly step out of my underwear, which are down around my ankles anyway, so I can run toward her. She is staring at me still, speechless. The look on her face is completely inscrutable.

J.J. by now has also figured out the situation and is scrambling for his jeans, but Janey isn't staring at his bare naked ass as I would probably be doing in her shoes. She's scanning the room with her eyes, taking in the empty bottles all around us. The stains from the wine I spilled on the floor. The missing bites from every platter and bowl and pot. The plates at the bar covered in half-eaten potatoes and pork chop bones. Surely it looks like a couple of animals got loose in here. The room spins. "Janey, I'm sorry about this, and the mess," I say, frantic. "I'll help clean it up. We thought . . ." I stammer to explain somehow. "We thought you and Noah were upstairs. We didn't think you would mind."

"Not mind?" she cries. "Not mind?" Her voice is high and panicky and I can tell she's about to cry. I start sweating bullets, wondering what I should do to make this right. Should I hug her? Start cleaning? Put my undies back on? I'm afraid to approach her while she's this upset. "This is my kitchen!" she shrieks, and I remember with horror that the last time she said that to me she attacked me with a duck. "You can't just come in here and talk me into humiliating myself and then screw your boyfriend in my kitchen while I cry!"

I stumble backward. Nothing makes sense—least of all that I was thinking to drop my panties on Janey's travertine tiles. All of a sudden I can feel how drunk I am, and I want nothing more than to stumble upstairs and lie down and close my eyes. "Janey, I really am sorry," I say, exhaustion telegraphing through my voice.

"It just happened," J.J. pipes in. "We didn't mean to . . ."

But his words fall on deaf ears. Janey has switched herself off again. Her eyes have gone cold and her whole posture is defeated. In the silence it hits me. Noah's not upstairs. He's gone. All that food wasn't leftovers—it was never served. The date was a flop.

Automatically I move to her and touch her arm, but she pulls away from me. Who can blame her, considering I am all covered in sex germs? I'm such an idiot—in my drunken lust I've only made a bad situation much worse.

"What happened?" I ask her, but she doesn't seem to hear. She is staring at the floor. "What happened with you and Noah?" I say again, louder this time, almost shouting, and she tilts her face to me and I see the heartbreak written all over it.

She looks at me carefully, unsure. I want to hold my arms out to her and let her collapse on me, but I feel disgusting, filthy, and I'm sure she sees me in that exact same way. "He left," she says at last, her voice still shaky from the anger and sadness. "He didn't even eat anything. He just got up and left in the middle of the soup—" She stops herself suddenly and steps away from me.

"What?" I ask, but she is walking to the counter where I was leaning just a minute ago. She is kneeling by the counter and looking down at something I can't see behind her body. "What is it?" I ask again.

She stands up slowly, and I see that her whole body is vibrating with fury. "Get out of my house," she says, low and hard, and with utter seriousness.

I know I should turn and run, but I'm too stupid to move. "What?" I say, dizzy and confused. "Why?"

She steps to the side and points down. Behind her, on the floor where I must have accidentally knocked it when J.J. and I were . . . well, doing what we were doing, is the red dessert pot I had protected so carefully from J.J.'s spoon an hour ago. The red enamel of the pot is cracked in a thousand places, shattered all over the dark tiles. Around it, like the splattered brains of a suicide jumper, are the contents of the pot: custard in lumps and those big bright cherries, looking limp and useless now all over the floor, no longer the stars of a perfect showstopper. Just ruined red clumps in a yellow pool of goo.

One of the cherries has been smashed—the unmistakable tread of J.J.'s work boots crisscrossing its mangled carcass. I wish ardently to switch places with that cherry now.

"I'm tired of you screwing up my life," Janey says, crying, and I know why she's saying this. She was perfectly happy living her quiet life before I came along. I came here, and got in her way, and never shut up, and pushed her and pushed her, and now she's heartbroken and miserable. I know all at once this is true: she would be happy if it wasn't for me.

I start to cry too. It all makes me so incredibly tired. I'm tired of making such stupid decisions, day in and day out, and ruining all the good things in my life.

"It's time for you to go," Janey says, but I stand there, mute, wishing I wasn't such an idiot, wishing I wasn't so drunk, wishing, mostly, that I had never come to Maine in the first place.

When I don't move, she gets angrier. "I mean it. Get out of my house," she says, pointing again to the mess where her perfect dessert lies ruined, and then the door. "Just get out."

I look down at the floor. There is nothing I can say, so I take J.J.'s hand and pull him toward the kitchen door. "Come on," I say to him quietly, for all the fight to stay has gone out of me in a cold bath of pity and shame. It's time for me to let Janey have her life back, to let J.J. go, to move on from here and find a new set of lies to tell and lives to screw up. "It's time for me to go."

JANEY

"As in cooking, so in life: We muddle through as best we can . . ."

—NIGELLA LAWSON,
Nigella Express

That night is awful.

I go upstairs and lie down on the top of my still-made bed, which is too empty now with only me in it. Why did the designers put such a big bed in here? It's not even the master bedroom. I stretch both arms out to try to fill up the space and lie there feeling foolish and wishing I could sleep.

After a few hours I give up. There is too much shame and disappointment inside me to ever sleep again. I pick up my favorite Nigella Lawson book from the nightstand, but she is too cheery as she advocates the use of infused vinegars and tuna packed in oil. I put the book back down again on the bedside table and scooch to the edge of the bed where my legs can dangle over. I'm still dressed, still in my blue trapeze dress that felt so sexy and carefree this afternoon. Now it is too much fabric under my arms, too much movement around my legs. I stand up and spin around and feel the dress go out like a parachute, and then fall back into me. When I stop spinning I am facing the slightly ajar door of my bedroom, and I see a pair of eyes peering in.

"Baby," says Aunt Midge, when she sees me seeing her. "Oh baby."

She pads into my bedroom in her frilly pink housedress and ridiculous fuzzy Einstein slippers and wraps her arms around me tight. "I heard everything. I'm so sorry."

I start to cry right away. "Noah left, and then I kicked Nean out," I say.

"I know, honey, I know."

I grow too warm in her arms and wriggle away. "I'm okay," I tell her, because what else should I say?

But she is ignoring me, moving toward the bed, where she pulls back the covers invitingly and piles the pillows up high. She sits down on my side of the bed and leans back and pats the side opposite. "Come here and cry on my bony old shoulder."

I sit down on the bed, rigid, afraid that if I let my body relax, the big tantrum I sucked inside earlier will flow right back out of me. But Aunt Midge is on to me; she tugs on my arm to pull me around and at the same time rubs my back like I'm a colicky baby. The sensation is so comforting I know it won't be long until I'm sobbing in earnest.

"I'm sorry, Janey," she says, still patting my back. "I put so much pressure on you, and I egged Nean on to do the same." I curl up on the bed and rest my head on the pillow right next to her, so she can stroke my hair like she did when my mother died. "I wanted you to find someone—I didn't want you to be alone. But you don't have to look anymore if you don't want to. I won't bring it up ever again."

I let myself cry now in earnest. "It's not your fault, Aunt Midge," I whine to the ceiling. "And it's not Nean's either. It was me who wanted him. I let myself get so carried away . . ." My voice drifts off in a miserable wail.

Aunt Midge sits up straighter and looks down at me, lying there like a wet mop. "Listen to me, Janey Brown," she says, after she's let me sob for a little while. "If you want him—if you love him—you can have him, do you understand?"

I nod a little, because I know it is the only way Aunt Midge will go back to stroking my hair, and because she can't know how wrong she is. She wasn't there—she didn't see how he looked at me.

She jerks her hand away. "Don't you humor me just because I'm an old woman," she says, as sternly as she can.

I shake my head. "I'm sorry, but—"

"Sorry is as sorry does," she tells me, a saying that makes no more sense this time than it has any of the other thousands of times she's said it to me in our thirty-five years together. But it does stop me from crying a little, just trying to puzzle it out.

"There. That's better," she says with a sweet little smile. "Nothing like the wisdom of your wise great-aunt Midge to make you feel better."

I nod solemnly and let my face relax. Her self-aggrandizing silliness never fails to cheer me up, and she knows it.

"There are things you learn in eighty-eight years," she tells me in her queenly way. "Things that make life a little easier." She pauses, searching her memory, and I wait for her wisdom. "Like, for example . . ." I watch her reach for the right words. "Like, you can't always get what you want."

"Aunt Midge, that's a Rolling Stones lyric." As well she knows.

"I think I actually said it first. What else did I say? Oh yes: if you try sometimes, you just might find . . ."—she breaks into full voice—"you get what you neeeeeed!" She is, needless to say, also air guitaring.

I give her a tiny smile—her rendition makes it impossible to keep up my melodrama. "Better," she tells me when she sees. "But seriously, here is what you learn when you are eighty-eight years old." Now she has a voice as solemn as I've ever heard from her. "You learn that houses—big old houses like this one especially—are just like hearts. They're for putting as many people as you can inside." She slides down a little lower under the covers and I can tell she's going to keep me company in my room for the rest of the night, and my heart fills with gratitude for this. "Don't forget that, okay, Janey?" she asks me, as she fluffs her pillow under her head.

"Okay, Aunt Midge," I tell her.

"Now turn out that light so I can get my beauty sleep," she says with a wave of the hand. Before I am even back in bed, she is fast asleep and snoring. Though I know I should stay up all night and feel miserable, I am not far behind.

NEAN

"I think of breakfast not as a way of starting fresh
but as continuing what happened the night before."

—ROY FINAMORE, *Tasty*

That night is awful.

J.J. leads me back to his truck, and then to his house where he fixes me
a clean pillowcase while I stand waiting, speechless. He takes himself
off into the TV room to crash on the couch. I pass out on his bed, under
his polyester Snoopy comforter.

A few hours later I wake up, jolted awake by the return of sobriety. For
a few moments I lie there confused, and then it all comes back to me: the
kitchen, Janey, the Snoopy comforter. Then the rest: J.J., college, Noah,
my promises to Aunt Midge, and the Big Lie that started it all. I feel
nauseous, rich food and expensive wine plus shame giving me a leaden
stomach. My mouth is too dry. I hoist myself out of bed to go for water.

In the kitchen I find J.J. sitting at the kitchen table with the newspaper, working on the Jumble. He is clutching a Big Gulp of orange juice
in one hand like it's his only hope for survival.

"Good morning," I grunt, rustling in his mother's cabinets for a water glass. "Parents still asleep?"

"As far as I know. God, I feel awful," he says, clutching at the back of his neck.

"Me too," I say, referring to my fight with Janey, not the hangover, which feels like a natural extension of my guilt.

"What should we do?" J.J. asks me, apparently talking about the same thing. "Go over there and apologize?"

I shake my head slowly. "I can't go back there, J.J.," I tell him. "And I'm not staying here, either. It's time for me to move on."

He frowns and furrows his forehead. I can see the pounding headache in his eyes. "Move on? You sound like a drifter or something."

I sigh and sit down at the little wooden table next to him. "I am a drifter," I say heavily, saddened by how perfectly the word fits me. "I came to Maine because I thought I had won Janey's house in the sweepstakes. I broke in and squatted there illegally until she showed up. Then I told her an enormous lie so she would feel too guilty to kick me out and have been taking advantage of her generosity—and gullibility—ever since."

J.J. blinks at me several times, shocked. "Wow," he says after a long silence.

"Yeah," I say glumly. "Wow." I take a big swig of water, and I swear I can feel it coursing through me.

"What did you tell her?" J.J. asks. Of course he would ask.

"I told her I killed someone," I say as nonchalantly as I can. Not that delivery matters at this point.

J.J. reels at this, just as I knew he would. "And she believed you?"

I smile just a little, a sad smile. "I know, right?"

He shrugs. "Man." He is quiet for a very long time, and I realize during this time that I am holding my breath. Even though I know it's almost over between us, I can't help wishing he will go on liking me now that he knows everything. A forgiving word from him could make this all so much better than it should be.

"Well," he says finally, standing up from the table. "Here is what we will do." His voice is all business, and I don't know if he's furious with me or just thinks I'm worthless. Either way . . .

"I'm going to make pancakes, and we're going to eat them with a whole bunch of syrup and about eight cups of coffee. And then we are going to go over there and you're going to tell Janey the whole truth—everything, not just the boiled-down version you told me, but the beginning, middle, and end. Well, not the end. We don't know the end yet, do we? But we will soon. Either she'll let you stay, or she won't, and we'll go from there."

Oh, J.J. "I'm up for the pancakes," I tell him, as if anything in the world could stop him from his syrup fix, "but I'm not telling her anything. I've made her miserable enough. She deserves to be left alone now."

"She *deserves* to know the truth about you," he replies, already stirring up pancake mix from a Bisquick box. "You are her best friend now, like it or not, and when your best friend gets her heart broken, you don't 'move on.' You go back, with your tail between your legs, and you apologize for having sex in her kitchen, and then you tell her the truth so she has someone to talk to."

This is not phrased as a question, I notice.

"Hmm," I say, because in the end I will do as I please, and J.J. should understand that by now.

"No hmm," he snaps back, slamming the refrigerator door with more force than necessary. "Don't blow me off. This is what is happening. This is what you have to do. Deal with it."

I don't have to do anything, I think. "Well, I—"

"Shut it," he says with surprising menace, and I clap my mouth shut, cowed, a flash of Geoff coming across my mind and then vanishing just as fast. "Don't say another word. Just sit there and think about what you're going to say to Janey, do you understand?"

I nod, stunned stupid. I've never seen J.J. insist on anything before. He is usually way too easygoing for that. He returns to making the pancakes with renewed vigor, and we are both silent while he melts butter on the big griddle built into the stove and starts pouring out circles of batter. Maybe I should consider what he's saying, I think, after a while. Maybe Janey would forgive me. Maybe she really does need someone to talk to right now . . .

No. That is just a way of justifying the whole thing to myself. An excuse to get everything off my chest and start new at Janey's expense, like I'm one of those asshole cheating husbands who spill the beans ten years after the fact. That is the last thing she needs right now.

In the tense silence J.J. serves us plates of pancakes stacked so high that I am reminded of last nights' feeding frenzy and what followed it. My stomach clenches up. I manage to eat two bites before I give up and push my plate away, anxious from thinking of all of the possible reactions Janey would have if I told her the truth. Anger, that one's for sure. Betrayal. Disappointment? Maybe not: she should not be expecting any better from me.

When J.J. has finished all his pancakes and the rest of mine too, and the previously half-full bottle of syrup is sitting empty and sticky on the countertop waiting to be rinsed and recycled, he pushes back from the table and says, "Are you ready?" He sounds a little more gentle now. I know he can see how hard this will be, if I do it.

Then he holds out his hand and takes mine and leads me to his truck. It is not quite 6:30 a.m., still too early for most people, but there is a decent chance that Janey will be up soon—will she have to make the shelter bread in my place?—and a sure thing that Aunt Midge will be splashing away in the pool. So at least I will have a chance to say good-bye to her, no matter what.

Because I haven't decided for sure that I am going to talk to Janey, even though I don't plan on letting that on to J.J., who is holding me captive to what he thinks is best. After he drops me off, how is he to know if I actually spill the beans or if I just lurk behind the house for a reasonable amount of time and then run for it like a coward?

It is only that plan that makes it possible for me to get into the truck with him and let him drive me to Janey's house. He turns into the driveway, but I stop him before we get to the tree line. "I'll take it from here," I tell him, as though my mind is made up. "It's better if I do this alone."

J.J. nods, and puts the car in park. "I'll wait here," he says, pulling a book of Raymond Carver stories out of his glove compartment. "Good luck."

I hop out of the truck and crunch down the gravel driveway. With the sun coming up behind it, the house looks more beautiful than ever. Each shingle seems to glimmer. The front porch looks cool and inviting. The bright red front door promises so much. I see the large upstairs window that opens to Janey's bedroom—the light doesn't seem to be on, but the sun is so bright it's impossible to tell if there's any movement within.

The hedgerow that J.J. keeps so perfectly straight and flat beckons me. I'll just go around and say hi to Aunt Midge, I think, and then I'll decide what to do. Maybe she'll give me some clue about my chance of success. Maybe she'll give me some words of wisdom.

I walk past the flowerbeds that flank each side of the driveway and up to the small gate that leads to the pool. The sun is going to be hot today, I know. There's not a cloud in the sky. It's not exactly ideal hitchhiking weather. Maybe I should talk to Janey. Maybe she will understand. I groan, exhausted from turning this over in my head. I am no closer to making my decision than I was when we were back in J.J.'s kitchen eating pancakes. Only now there's no more time. I have to decide now. Just as soon as I've talked it over with Aunt Midge.

I push the gate open, and that's when I see her. She is naked, as she is every morning during her swim, but she is not swimming. She is lying beside the pool, crumpled, utterly still. I run now, drop down to the grass next to her and shout her name, but she doesn't see me. She isn't breathing. I stop breathing too, for what feels like a very long time.

"Aunt Midge!" I scream, pushing the last air out of my lungs. And then, because I know Aunt Midge is not going to answer back, I scream, "Janey!" I grab Aunt Midge under her arms; she is heavy like sand. I touch her neck for a heartbeat, I feel the air by her nose for movement; there is none. "Janey," I cry, but now there is not much sound coming out of me. Now there is just crying and fear coming from every pore. "Janey!" I hear myself whisper.

I feel myself gathering up Aunt Midge in my arms, holding the full weight of her body, trying to lift her to sitting somehow. Like if I can just sit her up, her eyes will pop open and she will talk to me. My tears feel hot and my head swims around in search of some reasonable thought. She was supposed to tell me what to do. Aunt Midge, wake up! I need you to tell me what to do!

The glass door slides open, and Janey is there, wearing the same blue dress she had on yesterday, her eyes half closed and crusty. I look at her for just one long second, just so I know she knows what has happened, and then I turn back to Aunt Midge's body in my arms. For the first time I realize her eyes are open. She is looking up at me.

Then I feel Janey's body next to mine, her arms around us both, hear her cries, see her shiny wet face. She touches Aunt Midge's cooling cheek and then pinches her lips together in painful understanding, but she doesn't let go of us. We stay there for a very long time, Janey hanging on to me, while I hang on to Aunt Midge. After a while I realize that Janey is talking softly over my cries.

"It's okay," she's saying, as she cradles me. "It's going to be okay."

PART THREE

Serve

JANEY

"Not all of our food history is set down in cookbooks."

—JAMES BEARD,
James Beard's American Cookery

We sit like that for a very long time, me, Nean, Aunt Midge, all together one more time. Then J.J. shows up, and we come back to our
senses, and stand up, and stretch our legs, and I am surprised at just how
achy mine have become. J.J. tucks Nean under his arm and lets her cry
on his shoulder, his broken expression and leaking tears hidden from
her view, but not mine. I go back into the house, to call someone,
someone who can come and declare my great-aunt Midge dead.

Then we three sit on the leather sofas around the fireplace for a long
time, waiting. Nobody says anything. Nobody cries either. I sit straight
up on one end of the sofa and stare into space, thinking about nothing.
Nothing at all. Nean curls up in a tight ball on the opposite side, her
head on J.J.'s lap. If Aunt Midge were here, she would make fun of
them for being so clingy. But she is outside, by the pool, and not coming back in.

After who knows how long, a thought hits me, the first one I've had
since I saw Aunt Midge was gone. A rational thought. So strange that I
should be thinking so clearly.

It's all so strange.

I ask J.J. to excuse us for a second, to go into the kitchen and have some coffee. When he's gone, I sit down next to Nean and put my hand on her arm, to show her that I'm not angry anymore.

"Nean, when the coroner gets here, you have to go upstairs. You can't be down here, giving a statement."

Nean looks up at me for a moment, her face completely blank.

"It could go into the system—your name, I mean—if you tell them you're the one who found her. And then the police could find you."

She shakes her head at me, like she doesn't know what I'm talking about. Then she squeezes her eyes closed tight. When they open again, she inhales deeply and says, "Janey, I have something to tell you."

"Now?" I say, I don't know why.

"Yes, now. It has to be now. It should have been months ago. It's about the police. No, it's about me. It's about how I'm a big fat liar."

I sort of knew this already, but it doesn't seem pertinent. "Okay . . ."

"I lied to you about killing my boyfriend. I didn't kill him. I hit him in the head and knocked him out. With a coffee cup."

I stare at her.

"Then I stole his car and made a run for it."

I still stare.

"I just told you the whole story so you and Aunt Midge would let me stay."

I blink a little. "But Aunt Midge said . . ." My voice drifts off as I think back to exactly that conversation, to how Aunt Midge looked that day, to the sound of her voice. "I didn't believe you. But then she said she checked you out online and saw your boyfriend's name in the paper."

"She knew everything," Nean says, shaking her head, and I can tell she's thinking of Aunt Midge's voice too. "I'm sure Geoff's name was in the paper. For a DUI or something. She was doing one of her classic lies by omission. To protect me."

Well. That makes some kind of weird sense. "Huh," I say. Somewhere inside I know I should be angry, but how can I find the will to be angry right now? It's buried, way past numb, behind devastation,

THE GOOD LUCK GIRLS OF SHIPWRECK LANE   257

under a huge stack of heartbroken. "I guess that explains why no one ever came looking for you." My head feels muddy as it tries to wade through all this new information.

"Yeah," she says.

"And I guess you figured you couldn't come clean even after we got to know you, because you thought I would kick you out."

"Sort of," she says.

"Which I guess makes sense, considering I did kick you out last night over something much, much less significant."

Nean looks at me a little apprehensively. "I guess so."

I shake my head. *Hearts are like houses . . .* "I shouldn't have done that," I say.

"I shouldn't have done . . . all the things I did either."

We sit there for a moment. "I'm glad you're not a murderer, I guess," I say.

"Yeah," she replies. "Me too."

I frown. "I think I would be really upset about this, if it wasn't for Aunt Midge being dead." *How can she be dead?*

Nean says nothing. Her face is all crumpled.

"I would have kicked you out, you're right about that. I would have been furious."

She watches me carefully through wincing eyes.

"But I can't feel anything right now."

Nean swallows and lets her face relax and circles her arm around my shoulders. "You don't have to feel anything right now," she tells me. "You don't have to decide if you're mad or whatever. You get a rain check on hating me, okay?"

"Yeah," I say, and my voice cracks. "Okay."

"When you are ready to hate me, just give me some sort of signal," she goes on, "like, change the locks or something."

Even through the numbness I know I will never get around to hating her. I don't have the luxury anymore. Aunt Midge is gone. Nean is all I have left. Without her, I would have no one to cook for.

•   •   •

The coroner comes and goes. The guys from the funeral parlor show up and I sign ten thousand sheets of paper. Aunt Midge drives away in the back of a bright yellow pickup truck—apparently the hearse is doing a funeral in town today. I know she wouldn't mind about the indignity. She'd be happy for the view of the sky, if she wasn't all zipped up in that awful bag. Of course, she would prefer to be driving the truck herself, I'm sure.

Nean notes the same thing as we watch her back down the driveway, but then adds that she's probably not that much more dangerous driving dead than she was driving alive. She's not wrong, I think as we return to the great room, flopping back onto the sofa, aimless, restless, at loose ends.

I'm not sure how long we've been sitting there when suddenly Nean sits up perfectly straight, alert. "Did you hear that? Someone's walking around outside."

"What? Who?" Before I can get hold of my thoughts, I find myself thinking, hoping: *Noah.*

"Stay there. I'll take care of it." Nean disappears into the entryway for a moment, and then I hear, "What the hell?!"

I find myself moving surprisingly fast, inventing any number of possibilities as I go. None of them involve a hugely fat man unloading thousands of dollars of camera equipment from his nondescript van.

"What's going on?" Nean asks me.

"I have no idea," I start to say, but stop myself mid-sentence. "Oh no. Not now. Not this." My stomach clenches. I try to breathe but already feel faint.

"Which of you is Janine Brown?" the man asks, a humongous camera propped up on his shoulder. He's wearing a gray sweatshirt and sweating profusely in the morning heat.

"We both are," I hear myself tell him. There's a red light flashing on his camera. He's filming already. I start to shake.

"What now?" he says, glancing down at a clipboard he's somehow attached to his pants. "I'm here for a Janine Brown and a Maureen Richardson." He looks from Nean to me. "Which is which?"

The mention of Aunt Midge seems to choke me. I try to speak but nothing comes out.

Nean has no such problem. "I don't know who the hell you are but you better turn that camera off right now, buddy," she says. She's down off the porch and headed toward him like a guard dog. I half expect her to growl.

The man hesitates, but doesn't turn off the camera. "Easy there," he says slowly. "I'm just here to film for the Home Sweet Home Network. They were supposed to tell you I was coming. Won't take long."

"This is not a good time," Nean tells him. "You go on home now."

"No can do," he says. "Gotta do it today or it won't get done."

"Then it won't get done," Nean says. "Wait, are you still taping?"

"Lady, I'm sorry, but I don't take orders from you, whoever you are." He looks her up and down. For a moment I see what he sees, the matted hair, the gaunt cheekbones, the slept-in clothes, the tear-streaked face. She is not the same mangy girl who I first met three months ago, but the shadows of that girl still remain. "I'm gonna have to talk to the person who actually lives in this house."

Without a moment's hesitation I step out of the house. "You already are," I hear myself tell him, in a voice clear as a bell.

He looks from her to me. "You're telling me she won this million-dollar pad? Doesn't it have a shower?"

I cross the porch and climb down the stairs, holding my back rigid, forcing my lungs full of air. "We both won it," I tell him. "And we're both telling you to go."

"You can tell me whatever you want," he says with an unconcerned shrug. "I drove an hour out of my way. I'm doing this taping today." He starts advancing on us again. The camera is still on.

I set my jaw firm. "You want to do this taping today? Fine. Knock yourself out. You'll want to avoid close-up shots of the garden, though. The coroner was just here removing our great-aunt's dead body, you see, and I'm afraid he may have trampled some of the flowers."

The guy looks at me for a second. I watch as he digests what I just said, and his face turns the same pale gray of his sweatshirt. "Are you serious, lady?"

"Does this seem like a joking matter?"

"Christ," he says, waving his free hand in front of him. "I'm so sorry. You should have just told me this wasn't a good time."

I ignore that as best as I can. "Come on, Nean. He's leaving now." Sure enough, he's scrambling into his van without another word.

Nean climbs up the porch and stares at me in silence for a moment. We listen to the sound of the van starting up, backing away in a hurry.

"Holy shit, Janey. You just told off a stranger."

Did I really? "I guess I did."

"You sounded just like Aunt Midge."

Despite everything, I smile. "So did you."

We both look at each other for a long moment.

"She told me to take care of you," Nean says. Her lower lip is shaking.

"She told me to take care of you too," I realize.

Nean swallows hard. Neither of us says anything for a while. Probably because we are both trying so hard not to cry.

Of course, it is Nean who breaks the silence. "Hey. What was Aunt Midge's favorite food?" she asks me, out of nowhere.

I shake my head. "I'm not sure," I say, but when I think about it for a second it comes to me. "No, I do know. It was egg salad." My voice is shaking now. "Egg salad. How annoying is that? I cooked everything for her, fancy roasts, elaborate fish dishes, homemade pastas. But every now and then I would catch her in the kitchen in her bathrobe with two eggs on the boil and a blob of store-bought mayo at the ready." I sort of cough and laugh at the same time thinking of this, thinking of how she was pulling such a stunt just a couple of weeks ago when she thought I was out with Noah. When I caught her, she actually tried to hide the mayonnaise jar behind her back like she'd been caught stealing. How did she keep getting jarred mayo into the house without me knowing?

"The whole thing seems gross to me. I mean, mayonnaise *is* eggs. Why would you stir more eggs into it?" I shake my head again. Everything happening now seems so foggy. But that day seems so clear . . .

"What did she put it on?" Nean asks. "I mean, what kind of bread?"

I think back. "Anything. Pumpernickel, I know she liked that a lot."
Nean frowns. "I'm not sure I know how to make pumpernickel bread."

Now I understand why she is asking. "I do, at least vaguely," I say. "You will be very good at it. Better than me." This is true—she has developed such a gift for bread that I am starting to prefer her loaves to anything I can get at a bakery. "And she liked to eat the egg salad with potato chips," I go on. "We can make potato chips." We can cook up Aunt Midge's entire life history. Maybe we can cook up just a tiny bit of her spirit.

"What else did she like?" Nean asks, and then answers herself. "I know she was crazy about your pot pies."

"Oh yes. Chicken pot pies. I have been making those for her for years. Before we came here, to Maine, I would make a huge recipe and freeze little individual pies in ramekins so she could eat them on nights when I didn't come over. One time she told me that mine were almost as good as the Stouffer's ones. I wanted to smack her."

"She would have smacked you right back."

I nod. "I know." I think about the little pies I would assemble for her, no bottom crust, but a big towering top of buttery puff pastry.

"We could make the puff pastry lids ourselves," I say, gaining momentum. "It would take hours. Hours upon hours."

"Perfect," says Nean, nodding. "And what about seafood?"

"Lobster, definitely. Lobster macaroni and cheese. She saw it on Paula Deen and wouldn't shut up about it until I made it. I thought it was like eating money, but she loved it."

"Good," says Nean, and I see that she has materialized a pen and paper, and is making a grocery list now. "Perfect. Fish, chicken . . . any favorite kind of red meat?"

"Mmm," I search my memory. "One time she made me buy a share in a cow. Cow-pooling, she called it. She bought half the cow, I bought the other half. It was ridiculous—a whole heifer for two women! I don't know what she was thinking." I smile thinking of it and realize that the muscles on my face are aching from being bent into so many shapes.

"We went to see the cow—she said she wanted to know what she was investing in—and of course she fell in love with it. Those big doe eyes. I told her she should never ever name something she was going to eat, but she didn't listen. As a result, she lost her stomach for the whole enterprise, and in the end I gave most of the meat to the food bank."

"What did she name the cow?" Nean asks me, leaning in.

I roll my eyes. "I can't tell you. It's too ridiculous."

"You have to tell me right now," she says.

She's right, I do have to tell her. "Timberlake."

"Timberlake?"

"Right."

"As in Justin?"

"The very one. She said they were alike in that they were both delicious."

Nean shakes her head. "The dirty old bird." The way she says it it's clear it's the highest compliment.

"Wasn't she just?"

"Justin Timberlake could have done a lot worse, though," she says on a sigh. I nod. A lone tear leaks out, the first in almost an hour.

"Don't cry," Nean says, though she is crying too. "She was a happy old lady who lived a very long life. She wouldn't want us to be sad right now."

I laugh over a sob. "Oh yes she would. She would want us to weep and gnash our teeth and carry on like we won't be able to get through another day without her. Which maybe we can't, being such a sorry pair of liars and outcasts." I shake my head and then, when a thought hits me, I look back up at Nean. "And then she would want us to drink."

Nean grins back at me, her face bright through the tear marks running down her face. "Well, we should at least oblige her there. It's almost ten o'clock. We can cook tipsy, right?"

I nod. "I can cook in any state at all. I can cook through anything." I know this for sure. And it hits me: I've done all this before.

"Good." Nean lifts her voice just a little notch and leans her head into the house. "J.J., I know you are eavesdropping so just get your ass out here."

"What's up?" J.J. asks in the microsecond it takes him to appear from wherever he was lurking.

"We need you to do us a little favor. Just a quick run to the grocery store." She holds out the list and I see it's miles long. Smart woman. "But first, can you grab us a bottle of scotch?"

At one o'clock, we sit down at the breakfast bar for egg salad. We rush over our lunches, eating quickly so we don't lose our rhythm, maybe, or so we don't sink into the gloom that seems to wait right outside the kitchen door. From my perch I look at the kitchen and see the mess—not from the night before; cleaning it up is the first thing we did after we filled two rocks glasses with what Aunt Midge used to call a "vertical finger" of Scotch. This is new mess, from all the recipes we've started in the last hour, while waiting for J.J. to return with groceries. It calms me, to see the sink with a pot soaking in it, the granite countertop still dusted with flour from my messy pasta-making process, Nean's bread rising in a warm corner and filling the room with its comforting smell. I hasten to return to its midst and use a dinging timer as an excuse to scramble off my stool and get back to work.

It is around dinnertime when we finish our first set of dishes. We eat creamy lobster macaroni and cheese standing over the saucepan while we wait for the pot pies to bake. I start to think of more things we could cook, and after running them by Nean we set to work again, sending J.J. out to the market once more. We decide on knishes, to celebrate Aunt Midge's two exciting years living in New York's East Village, and paella for the twenty-fifth anniversary trip she took with Albert to Spain. Then there is Irish soda bread, for her father's side, and chicken schnitzel for her mother's. Each new recipe we pick leads to more stories, and I find myself educating Nean over the hours on everything I know about Aunt Midge's life, from time to time stopping and wiping my hands down on the towel I keep tucked in my waistband to go fetch a photo album. I show her Albert in a bullfighter's jacket with the cape unfurled in his hands and Aunt Midge five years ago when, on a bus trip to Branson, she had a brief affair with the string bass player in a jamboree show. Later, while I am pounding out thin layers of chicken between two sheets of plastic wrap, Nean rummages around in an album and pulls out a picture of me as a toddler, sitting on Aunt Midge's lap with one of my fingers lodged up her nose and a look of great distress on my fat little face. She holds it up to me, speechless.

I shake my head. "Of course you would find that. She loved that picture, and I was always trying to destroy it, but she must have had the negatives squirreled away somewhere."

"Um, why are you picking her nose?"

I look heavenward. "She said I went through a phase where I was always trying to put my fingers in everyone's noses. Strangers, family, it didn't matter. My mother was at loose ends over it. Everyone else batted me away, but Aunt Midge figured the only way I'd learn the error of my ambitions was to actually succeed in them, and boy was she right. She had a nasty cold at the time."

"Ew."

I nod. "I was most displeased, apparently, and threw a monster fit and never tried to pick a nose again."

"Well, thank goodness for that," Nean says. "Let's put this one in pride of place to remind us all of that important lesson." She takes the photo to the refrigerator and affixes it with a magnet right in the middle of the freezer door.

I find with surprise that I don't mind at all. In fact, I like the picture all of a sudden. The young version of me is wearing a fussy pink ruffled dress, and Aunt Midge is sitting on an avocado green easy chair wearing an outrageously large hat festooned with plastic flowers. It must have been Easter, I realize. Easter was, as far as I can remember, the only day that prompted Aunt Midge to cook. She made the same thing every year.

"Nean, would you call J.J. and tell him to pick up a ham, too, and two cans of sliced pineapple rings? Oh, and a jar of maraschino cherries."

"Um, sure," she says. Then she looks at the clock. "It's nine," she

says. "This will have to be his last trip; the stores close at ten on Fridays."
She stops work suddenly and turns to me. "Oh SHIT. It's Friday."

"Yeah? So what?"

"I was supposed to take some sample loaves up to Bread and Honey,"
she says, her voice getting shaky for the first time since this morning.
"I'm trying to get a job there."

"You are?" I ask. "You don't have to do that."

"I do, Janey," she says, resolute. "If you decide to let me stay, I have
to start doing something real. I can't just keep waiting for whatever to
happen."

I furrow my brow. I know she's talking about herself, not me, but
still I wonder if I am doing that very thing by staying home all day
shortening hems and frittering away Ned's money on groceries. I know
what Aunt Midge would say about that, as if she is right here, standing
in the room with me. I turn to Nean and say those words to her.

"If you want a job, then you'll get a job." I walk over to the cabinet
and start pulling back down all the flours I can find and loading up the
countertops with them. "Start working on your flax pullman and
maybe those incredible pretzels you make. Oh, and the asiago cheese
bread, that is your very best loaf. We'll take them in tomorrow, first
thing, and explain why you couldn't make it in today."

Nean looks at me. "But I'll have to stay up all night," she says. "It'll
take me hours."

"Then we'll stay up all night," I reply—the "we" part popping out
automatically. I open my arms wide to the kitchen around us. "At least
we have plenty of sustenance."

Nean looks around at all the food and smiles, but then she scruti-
nizes my face. "Are you sure?"

Since the moment that I saw Aunt Midge—saw her body—by the
pool this morning it has felt like the world has been tilting, shifting
wildly, leaving me desperate to right myself. But now, after hours in the
kitchen with Nean, I feel safer, more sure. Like I have found a small
island of solid ground.

"I am positive," I say. "On the condition that we do not have to talk about boys."

It is four in the morning when Nean pulls her final loaf out of the oven. It's a fine Italian specimen with beautiful crusty slashes on the top cut to look like a sprig of rosemary. Gratified by the results, we both fall asleep on the leather sofas in the living room, then roust ourselves again an hour and a half later to start packing up the car. I am going to take everything but a few knishes and the ham into the shelter first thing. The knishes will be lunch; the ham, which is now overwrought with pineapple and cherry "flowers," will keep in the fridge until the funeral.

Nean's pointed out that by stopping at the shelter so early, we'll avoid Noah altogether. And I've pointed out that by arriving at the bakery at the crack of dawn, we'll make a good impression on the owner. So we split up. A groggy and confused J.J. takes Nean to Damariscotta, while I schlep the food to the shelter in Little Pond.

But our plan has one major flaw: The quiet drive all by myself, with the sun so low in the sky turning everything pink, gives grief a window to find me, and grief is nothing if not opportunistic. By the time I pull into the parking lot of the shelter I am mired in sadness, under its thick cloudy spell, having trouble getting a good breath of fresh air.

That overwhelming ache is probably why I don't see anything unusual in the lot. I load myself down with Tupperware containers and crocks and make three trips back and forth to the walk-in refrigerator in the kitchen, a trek I've made enough times I can do it blindfolded. All this time I don't see or hear a thing, lost in the memory of Aunt Midge, tucking herself into my bed, singing the Rolling Stones to me, stroking my hair. The fourth trip inside, which I am determined shall be the last, is two paper sacks full of bread and a big Pyrex dish of chicken pot pie, and the balance is so precarious that it forces me to slow down and enter the kitchen, which has industrial-style swinging glass doors, butt first. And that is when I see him.

Sitting in the dining room, wearing a plain white T-shirt and clean jeans and leaning over a bowl of cold cereal, is Noah. He looks sleepy, and his hair is wet and shiny, like he just got out of a shower two minutes ago. I'm shocked to see him. I know Noah enjoys his work, but coming in at—I look at my watch—six ten in the morning?

I stare too long and he looks up, sees me juggling my bags and dishes and gaping at him openmouthed. He stands, so I quickly back into the kitchen and put down the food, start looking for an exit. My face feels on fire, and my arms like they are being tickled by porcupine quills. Desperate and out of my head, I run into the walk-in and let the door close behind me and feel the cold rush over my flushed face in a whoosh.

Through the small foggy window of the cooler, I see the kitchen doors swing open, and then Noah appears. The sight of him brings the hurt from two nights ago heaving back and my heart starts to ache even more than it was aching already. I want to run out of the freezer screaming, catch him by surprise, smack him in the face and pound on his chest and cry. Mostly, I want to tell him about Aunt Midge.

Instead I hold completely still and try not to breathe. I watch as he spots the bags on the counter and pulls one closer to look inside. He lifts out a loaf of Nean's bread then sets it back in the paper sack. Then he picks up the pot pie and starts looking around in circles. He shakes his head in confusion, his wet hair getting loose and draping itself over one eye. Before I know it he's opening the cooler door and walking inside.

"Hi Janey," he says, just as casually as that. "What is this?" He is holding out the pot pie.

"It's a pot pie," I squeak out helplessly. There are ten million questions in my head right now: Why did you leave my house like that and break my heart? What are you doing here at six a.m.? Do you understand that I love you?

Instead I tell him about the pot pie. "It goes in the freezer. I taped heating instructions to the bottom of the pan."

Carefully he lifts the pan above his head and finds the index card I've scotch-taped on. "I see."

I stand there like an idiot, feeling lost for words. I look up above his head, and then, when he sets down the pie on a shelf of the cooler, I move my eyes to the floor. I am looking for a way to tell him that I was trying to avoid him, that I didn't want to see him today, without saying exactly that. Then I notice his feet—they are bare except for white tube socks. "Where are your shoes?"

Now, in Noah's eyes, I see the very same look I saw in Nean's yesterday—was it just yesterday?—morning. The look is guilt. A revelation is coming, I understand, and my gut clenches up. Not another revelation, *please*. I can't take any more surprises, not today.

Noah looks into my eyes—maybe he sees in them the fear coursing through me—and then down, as if noticing his socks for the first time. "Let's go back into the kitchen. It's cold in here."

"No," I say stubbornly, tears welling up. "If we go into the kitchen where it's warm, I'll tell you about Aunt Midge and you'll be kind to me and I'll cry and you'll use it as an excuse not to tell me the truth and then I'll never know why you are looking at me that way. What are you doing here? Tell me."

"What about Aunt Midge?" he asks me, not moving from the icy room.

I sniff and cough. "Nothing. Well. Something. She died," I say, as solidly as I can.

"Oh, Janey," he says. "I'm so sorry—"

"Yes, yes," I say, desperately wanting the consolation, but not from him, not right now. "What are you doing here?"

He takes a deep breath. "Janey, I should have explained my situation a long time ago," he says.

"What situation?"

"My living situation. I live here, in the shelter," he says, but by now I already know this. Somehow I knew it the moment I saw him sitting at the dining room table, where I've seen and fed so many people over the last months of lunches.

"You work here," I say, stupidly. It is cold enough that I can see my breath in here, and it looks thin, like it could falter and stop at any time.

"Yes, but I also live here."

I grab a shelf full of milk jugs for stability. "I don't understand," I say, even though I do.

"I came here, to this part of Maine, just before you did," he begins. "I was homeless, and I had been living in my car. I heard they needed someone to run the shelter garden, so I asked for the job in exchange for being allowed to stay for more than the usual eight consecutive days. I needed the time to get back up on my feet."

I shake my head. "But you said you had an apartment in Little Pond," I begin. "You told me that you were saving up to buy a new farm." The realization that he has been lying to me all this time hits me and makes my stomach churn more.

Noah shakes his head. "Even when you declare bankruptcy," he tells me, "there are still lawyer's fees to pay. And I owe money to friends, cousins, anyone fool enough to give it to me. I couldn't have told you that—you would have hated me. I had to tell you something."

His lies roll into a snowball with Nean's, and together they hit me hard enough that I feel beat up. I flail back in defense. "Are you a drunk?" I demand, thinking of the way he declined the glass of wine at dinner despite my protests. "Is that why you went bankrupt?"

"No," he says back quickly. "But one of the rules of the shelter is that you can't drink—not a single sip—if you want to spend the night here."

Of course. It all makes sense, but it doesn't stop the feelings of betrayal. "You should have explained," I say. I can't believe he wouldn't have told me sooner. Instead he's twisted it so that every minute we've spent together has been based on pretext and lies. "I would have understood."

"Really?" Noah asks, his voice growing just one hair louder. "Would you have? Or would you have assumed, as you just did, that I was an alcoholic, or an addict, or a criminal of some sort?"

His raised voice feels like a slap in the face, like this is somehow my fault, instead of his. "Well, why else would you be living in a homeless shelter?" I say defensively.

Noah shakes his head. "Would you listen to yourself?" he asks.

"I'm not the one who has been lying all this time," I cry. I lean against the shelving, my legs losing their sturdiness in the cold. "You lied, and lied, and you made me fall in love with you."

At this, Noah at least has the sense to lower his eyes. But I want to punish him, so I go on. "No, not you. I never fell in love with you. I fell in love with someone you invented."

It works. His shoulders slump and I see I've hurt him, and the shame of it heats me back up, even in this freezing cold walk-in. Somewhere inside me there is a tiny, rational voice telling me to apologize, to talk to him, to hear him out and try to understand why he wasn't more honest with me. It is telling me that this is real life, this feeling-out of other people, this litany of surprises, this flailing around for the truth. And missing it most of the time.

But I hate that voice. I hate the insecurity and the uncertainty and the opaqueness that comes with it. Noah is a liar. Nean is a liar. Aunt Midge—even she lied to me. She promised me she'd make sure I was taken care of. She said she'd stick around.

I shake my head, feel my body shudder with cold and anger. I want everything to be clear, and make sense, and stay the same. I want to get out of this freezer.

I angle my body so I can push to the door without touching Noah. I know even the brush of his shoulder against mine would crack me wide open in this cold room. But I avoid him and remain intact. When I reach the handle I don't turn around, I don't take one long last look, I don't apologize for my shortcomings or forgive him for his.

I just beat it the hell out of there and head straight for home.

NEAN

"Bread is like life—you can never control it completely."

—ROSE LEVY BERANBAUM,
The Bread Bible

It doesn't seem right that Aunt Midge should have turned out, despite her big talk, to be mortal. And it's weird that the person I most want to discuss her death with is, well, her. If this world made any sense, any sense at all, I would find her now, and we would sit out by the ocean and stare, and she would tell me a story that would explain everything in an incredibly roundabout way. One that would tell me what to do without her.

J.J. is doing his best to comfort me, but I can hardly hear a word he says over the shock that he is still talking to me at all. That he is here, still, despite everything, driving me to and from the bakery in his truck with his arm around my shoulder is just too goddamn unbelievable. He hasn't yelled at me once. Hasn't balked at the back and forth of grocery trips we put him through yesterday, or the ridiculously early hour he was called upon to chauffeur me this morning. Hasn't even complained.

And then there's Janey. Did she really mean what she said to the cameraman yesterday—that we were sharing the house? How could she possibly, after everything I've done? But she and I have cooked and cried together for nearly twenty-four hours, and she hasn't mentioned kicking me out once in all that time. In fact, she's been filling me in on Aunt Midge's life, helping me know her as well as she did, like I am some long-lost sister that needs to be caught up on the family history she's missed out on. Like I will be staying, in that house, indefinitely.

Out of sheer gratitude I convince J.J. to swing by the funeral home on the way back from the bakery. I know, from watching *Six Feet Under*, that planning a funeral is a huge pain for the survivors, and last night while we rolled out knish dough, Janey told me all of Aunt Midge's wishes, so I feel pretty qualified to take over this miserable duty. She wants to be cremated and live in an urn on the mantelpiece so she won't miss any of the action. She wants a good-bye service down by the boat put-in, and if anyone sings "Nearer, My God, to Thee" she has vowed to come back and haunt them.

After filling out six million forms, it is all arranged. The service will be on Monday, and the director will post something in the Damariscotta paper so people know to come. He, a kind old guy with Santa Claus reading glasses, also volunteers to call the shelter and let everyone there know the news, just in case Janey didn't feel like spreading the word this morning. The wake will be at our house, and he reminds us to stock plenty of food and drink. I promise him this won't be a problem.

Then I go home to tell Janey the news. She is upstairs, lying in bed, her eyes rimmed with pink from all the crying. She looks like hell, and I can see that things are hitting her very hard today, so I sit down on the side of her bed and tell her everything is going to be okay. She squints at me like I've lost my mind. Maybe I have. I know the grief is going to catch up to me, just as it has with her, but right now I feel a strange buoyancy, the lightness of confession, I guess. Just for now, for this brief moment in time, I have no secrets, from anybody. Aunt Midge would be damn proud.

When I come downstairs I find J.J. leaning over the dishwasher, pulling out clean dishes and trying to figure out where they go. I take the stack of plates he's clutching and put them away. "You don't have to stay here, you know. You can go home whenever."

"I'm just trying to make sure you're all right," he says, sounding a little hurt.

"I'm going to be fine," I tell him. "It just takes time," I tell myself.

"Well, I have time," he says stubbornly, taking a wad of silverware out of the dishwasher baskets and opening first one wrong drawer, then another.

Not really, I think, but instead I ask what I've been dying to know since the moment I told him about my horrible lie to Janey. "How come you're being so nice to me?" I point him toward the flatware drawer. "How come you aren't telling me where to go?"

J.J. tilts his head at me confused. "Why would I do that?"

I look at him aghast. "Have you been unconscious over the last few days?"

He shakes his head and clangs a pile of forks into their drawer. "No. Have you?"

I stop unloading dishes. "What do you mean by that?"

"Have you somehow not noticed in all the time we've spent together that I am a good guy? That I am not the sort of man who will just abandon someone he cares about because she's done some stupid—some very stupid—things?" He slams the drawer closed hard enough to rattle all the cutlery within. "That when the chips are down, I'm the sort of person you can count on?"

I stand mute for a moment, duly admonished. "Of course," I say. "Of course I know that."

"Do you really? Are you sure you don't think I'm going to dump you the moment Aunt Midge is in the ground and go find some Dartmouth girl to replace you?"

I am dumbstruck. That is exactly what I think. "Well, maybe . . ."

J.J. groans. "See?" he cries. "Nean, you drive me crazy. Is it so hard to believe that I'm going to forgive you for all your bullshit?"

I bite my lip, unsure if I am in trouble, or what.

"You have to start believing it, you know," he tells me, as forcefully as I've ever heard him. "If we are going to make this work long distance, you have to believe in me."

"But," I begin, trying to think how to tell him that it's okay, that he doesn't have to stick with me after next week, when school starts. That maybe that's not even what's best. "But I'm not sure that I—"

"Don't even start with that," he growls angrily. "Don't try to give me an out I don't want."

I grab his hand. "It's just that . . ." I go hunting for the right way to explain, something that will show him how I do appreciate him, do see how special he is. "It's just not possible that you are as good as you seem," I say at last. "And if you are, you deserve better."

J.J. shakes his head. "If that's what you think, Nean, I'm not sure I'll ever be able to talk you out of it. But if you think you might be worthy of a decent guy, that it might just be your turn to be treated well, that someone good might actually be out there waiting to be with you, you know where to find me, okay?"

Then he faces me and puts his hands on my shoulders. He kisses the top of my head and repeats himself a little more quietly. "You know where to find me?" The way he says it, I only hear good-bye.

I nod, a little dazed, a little unsure of the right thing to say. "I'll find you," I choose at last, but I am saying it to his back; he has already headed out of the kitchen and is opening the front door to leave.

JANEY

"Cooking, preparing food, involves far more than
just creating a meal for family or friends:
it has to do with keeping yourself intact."

—ALICE WATERS,
Chez Panisse Menu Cookbook

The funeral, or wake, or whatever this thing is that Nean has arranged, is as grand a success as it can be without the dead actually coming back to life. It starts officially at 5:00 p.m., but by 4:45 the seashore is crowded with people—all the bartenders at every bar in Little Pond (and there are more than you'd think) apparently had a chance to form a close attachment to Aunt Midge, and so did the folks at the farmer's market and the local shops. J.J.'s parents are there shaking hands with Nean, and I see Nancy the Geoduck Perpetrator blowing her nose into a tissue. The neighbors on the cove, most of whom I've never met, all seem to have known her somehow, and of course all the staff members of the shelter are there with bright tears hovering in their eyes. The shelter director, a graying man named Rupert who is much, much more bereaved than seems proper, points out people from the amassing crowd who met Aunt Midge during their stays at the shelter, but have since moved on to more permanent housing situations. I am impressed with just how many people passed through Aunt Midge's life in search of help during the last few months. To think that all this time, I thought I was the only one.

Five minutes before the service starts, a rental van full of the shelter's current patrons arrive, a mixed bag of men whom I now see, with clearer eyes, are from all walks of life. I find myself looking desperately for one particular face, but of course he isn't there. I know how badly I reacted to his situation, how incredibly cold and bitter I was to him, and how I've said things that there just aren't take-backs for. But I can't help hoping he might remember the other things about me that he praised so often and so earnestly and forget the meanness I showed him one day in a freezer. And I tell myself over and over again that my bad behavior shouldn't taint his memory of Aunt Midge. But it doesn't matter what I tell myself. He isn't there. He isn't coming.

The service is short. I've made Nean promise to do all the public speaking for both of us today—I tell her that even though, thanks to Noah's "immersion therapy," I am feeling just fine in this large crowd of people, having them all stare at me at once is still more than I can handle. I've given her the large yellow envelope Aunt Midge kept in her underwear drawer and reminded me about every now and then; there's no mistaking it for anything else. In her shaky old-lady cursive it is marked in blue ink: "Read to my fans when I croak." And I've suggested some appropriate songs to play on the iPod Nean has connected to a tinny indoor/outdoor speaker that shouldn't offend Aunt Midge's ghost too terribly much. Nean tells me she'll take it from there. I nearly cry with gratitude for all she's done to make this easier on me.

At 5:35, when we've finally managed to stop the milling and gotten everyone to stand quietly on the grassy part of the beach, facing Nean where she stands with her back to the ocean and a gaudy plastic urn next to her on a table, she begins.

"Everybody," she starts, "we are gathered here to say good-bye to the living incarnation of Janine Brown's Great-Aunt Midge," she says. "Janey and I want to thank you all for coming to support us today. We know wherever Aunt Midge is now, she is smiling down on us." I shake my head. Nean has no idea.

"Aunt Midge prepared a few words to guide us today as we mourn our loss and celebrate her life at the same time."

She stops to open the envelope and reads a few sentences to herself before she launches in. I see in her face just a hint of surprise, and I smirk.

Nean clears her throat. "Maureen 'Midge' Richardson was a fashion icon and a pillar of society," she reads with a straight face but just the slightest cough at the end of the sentence. She presses on. "She was the inspiration to many, and beloved by all. In her too brief life here on earth, her accomplishments are almost too many to name, but let us attempt to highlight a few of the most momentous achievements of this remarkable woman." I watch Nean's eyes bug out as she reads this. She has no idea what's coming.

"Who can forget how, in September of her nineteenth year, she ate seventeen corn dogs at the Hog Wild Daze Festival in Hiawatha, Iowa, to win the eating contest and be crowned the Hog Wild Daze Pork Princess? But that was simply a foreshadowing of future accomplishments. Just a few short years later she had the distinction of being prohibited from reentering no fewer than eight of New York City's finest drinking establishments and spent a total of three nights in the tank, each on separate occasions. In her middle, more moderate years, she was known for experimenting with life as a vegetarian, a communist, a macramé artisan, and, most memorably, a student of transcendental meditation. She could roller skate, dress a deer, and shoot a gun. For her fiftieth birthday she went bungee jumping and did not pee her pants on the bounce. She was married once, to the late Albert Richardson, who was a great man and a better lover." Nean swallows hard at this last bit, and I look around taking in the slightly confused—or dare I hope amused?—faces of her mourners.

"Over her lifetime she amassed more than twenty-five traffic tickets, was tattooed three times, accidentally stole two husbands, and was featured once in an adult video. She fell in love seven times, twice with astronauts." Nean stops, looks up at me as if to ask if she has to read the rest. I give her a solemn nod. "Also, she cured cancer, swine flu, and feminine itching."

Now the audience is tittering, in, at last, on the joke. Nean looks up, helpless, and raises her voice to be heard. "She will be greatly missed, and is survived by her two favorite girls, Janey and Nean Brown."

She drops the letter to her side and looks right at me, shaking her head and smiling just a little. Then she mimes putting a gun to her head and firing and I smile back and shrug. What can you do? I ask her with my eyes. She shrugs back.

"So everyone," she calls over the murmurs of surprise and laughter, "That's it. Please join us for punch and chow at the house." Then she goes to the iPod and hits play, and "November Rain" by Guns N' Roses starts playing softly as the guests begin to mill again in earnest.

I make my way across the throngs to Nean. "Really? 'November Rain'?" I ask.

"Really?" she mimics. "You didn't see fit to tell me to read the letter first?"

I smile. "I knew you could handle it. Besides, I think it sounded better with the element of surprise. Gave it that certain spontaneous quality Aunt Midge was always so good at."

"Damn straight," she says. She puts her hand on my arm and gives me a tug. "Let's go slice up the ham," she says, and the two of us start up the path to the house together.

Five hours later we are crowbar-ing the last of the masses out of our house. Though I have cooked more than I've slept in the last few days, digging for solace with wooden spoons and silicone spatulas, I find that we've been picked clean of every last bite—all that remains in the fridge are three kinds of mustard and some ginger ale. The kitchen is a train wreck, and there are plastic cups on every surface that's not already covered by wadded-up paper napkins. In all, the place looks like it's been crammed full of drunken coeds, not somber mourners, and I figure that would have pleased Aunt Midge to no end.

Just as I'm taking stock of the mess, I hear steps in the hall. "It doesn't exactly scream 'funeral' in here," calls a voice from the front door, which has been standing wide open for hours. It's a voice I would know anywhere. A voice that makes me vibrate through like the Jell-O dessert that Nancy brought. I drop the Bundt pan I'm rinsing and grab for a towel to dry my hands.

But Nean beats me to the door. "What are you doing here?" I hear her ask snappishly. "Janey's not here."

"I'm right here," I call, trying not to sing the words. Noah is here! "Let him in."

I rush to the archway of the kitchen just in time to see Nean staring Noah down dangerously. She has a hand on each hip and the readied stance of a lioness, and Noah looks cowed, but still achingly handsome, with his floppy hair tucked back behind his ears and a tie knotted clumsily at his neck. He's dressed up for the funeral, I realize, as I watch him try to scooch past Nean without starting some sort of brawl.

"It's okay, Nean," I say, waving Noah into the kitchen, onto my home turf, and holding out a hand for the foil-wrapped paper plate he's brought along.

She sneers disgustedly as he hands it to me but still follows us into the kitchen. Of course she's protective—she only knows what she must have inferred the night after our ill-fated date. I'll have to fill her in later. But now, I need to apologize to Noah, and so I give her my very best bug-eyed, eyebrows-lifted "go away" look.

She ignores me. "He's a little late if he wanted to pay his respects to Aunt Midge," she says, as if he's not standing right there next to us. "The service was at five."

"I know," he says, hands open to both of us in apology. "I just didn't know if . . . I mean, Janey already had her hands full, I figured. So I waited, parked down by the water, in my car. I didn't want to upset her."

I feel light when he says this—*he's been here, waiting nearby all this time*—but Nean snorts. "So you come over as soon as the last person leaves to try to make a hard day even harder?" she demands. "What is wrong with you?"

"I'm sorry," he tells Nean, "but I had to apologize." He looks helpless, but he has just uttered the magic words, the words I needed for all the world to hear. I inhale and close my eyes just for a moment, basking in this tiny moment when we might have another chance. "I couldn't just leave things the way they were."

Before I can apologize in return, Nean snaps back. "You could, actually, but maybe you're just too selfish."

I put my arm out in front of her, like a crossing guard at a stoplight. "Nean, let's just hear him out, okay?" I say. I know I should rescue him from Nean's interrogation altogether, but it just feels so good to have her looking out for me. She's a security blanket. Who would have thought I would ever say that about her?

"Fine," she says, not disguising any of the bitterness in her voice. "But let's talk about this outside, where it won't make a mess if I have to knock out a few of his teeth."

Noah gives a stilted chuckle at this, like he's not sure if she's serious or not.

"Nobody is knocking out any teeth," I say, surprisingly evenly, considering how dizzy I feel. "Not yet. Noah, I'm so sorry about the way I reacted yesterday," I recite, repeating the words I've practiced over and over again in my head in the hopes that I would get this chance. "I was overwhelmed and I didn't handle the information well. It seems like I had been getting a lot of bad news in just a few days and yours . . ." I drift off. What's the nice way to say *shocked the shit out of me*? I know I had it figured out last night.

"You don't have to apologize," he says, though of course I do. "My news was a big surprise, to say the least."

"Wait," interjects Nean. "You saw him yesterday?"

I turn to her a little impatiently. "At the shelter. Where he's living right now."

Nean's eyes widen. "Seriously? You're homeless?" she asks Noah.

Noah looks down and I fill up with regret. I should have kept Nean out of this, so he could be spared this embarrassment, but before I can get a chance to remedy this he looks her right in the eyes and says, "Yes, it's true that I don't have a place of my own to live right now."

"No kidding?" asks Nean. "Well, well, well. I guess there had to be something wrong with you eventually." She turns to me. "It could be a lot worse, Janey. What's the big deal?" Bless her heart, she's more adaptable than evolution. I wish I could have reacted that way when he told me.

"The big deal," he goes on, "is that I lied to Janey about it, because I was too ashamed to admit the truth. Then, when she went to all the trouble to have me over to dinner, I panicked. I was embarrassed. And jealous, too, of this beautiful place. Most of all, I was sure I would be caught out in the lie, and I ran for it rather than let that happen." He sighs. "But she found out eventually anyway, and it was a big mess."

Nean nods her head. "I can relate," she says, sympathetically. "I lied to Janey too, so I'd have a place to live."

Noah looks at me, one eyebrow arched. "Really?" he says, taking just a tiny step closer to me. I nod, not trusting myself to make any human sounds. "Poor Janey. No wonder you were so upset." Gently, he takes the paper plate out of my hands—I've been clenching it all this time—and sets it down on the countertop beside us. Then he puts his hand over mine, and I follow the movement with my eyes, loving the sensation that it sends up my arm.

"Yeah, yeah, poor Janey," Nean interjects. "You'd think people would be glad I didn't kill anybody." Noah looks at her quizzically, and I mentally thank her for once again putting my life in some kind of perspective. "So," she says. "Spill. What happened to you that you ended up homeless?" I'm glad she asks this, because I'm wondering too, but of course I don't want him to know that I want to know. I try not to look at him too curiously while I wait for a reply.

Noah smiles wanly, seeming not at all put off to be explaining this not only to me but also to my somewhat lunatic friend. "Nothing exciting, I'm afraid. I got in over my head in the farm," he begins, and then turns to Nean, "I used to own a small farm, Nean." She nods. "It was supposed to be a fancy organic boutique sort of farm, salad greens for four-star restaurants and spas, but the yield I got wasn't good enough, and oh, God, the bugs. I had borrowed to the hilt to buy the property in the first place, and within a year I was losing money hand over foot, but instead of giving up and getting out while I still had something to get with, I kept pushing it, borrowing more and more money, spending down all my savings and racking up my credit cards in the hopes that the enterprise would one day work out. When I finally accepted that I needed to sell the property, it was too late, it had lost too much value and I had borrowed way too much on its equity. I couldn't sell it fast enough and got into more and more trouble with my mortgage, but instead of facing down my problems, I did everything I could to avoid them." He sighs, and I find myself a little dazzled at the ease with which he is recounting this sad story. He's over it, I realize. He's already forgiven himself. Realizing he can do that makes me love him even more.

"In the end, I declared bankruptcy and, eventually, the farm was foreclosed. I ended up living in my car for months, working hard to pay off the settlements I owed my creditors, until the shelter job came up and gave me a chance to get back on my feet."

"Oh my God," I say, my heart aching to think of Noah in such a horrible position, contemplating what could have happened if all the chips hadn't fallen into place as they did.

"Don't be upset, Janey," he says. "I got myself into a dire situation, yes, but I'm making up for it now, and I even have a farm of sorts again. Things can only get better from here." He pauses. "Except . . . well, things with you were already pretty darn good."

I sigh and look up into his eyes. "They were, weren't they?"

"I'd like them to get better."

"Me too," I hear myself say softly. I angle myself toward him, tipping my face upward, praying against prayer for what I want to happen.

It does. He kisses me gently, putting one hand on my cheek as he does, then angling my face so he can kiss first my left eyelid, and then my right. Then he pulls back and locks eyes with me, his hand sinking down my neck, just to my clavicle, where it warms me through.

"Janey," he says. "I've made a lot of stupid mistakes in my life, as you well know. Debt, denial, bankruptcy. But believe me when I say this: not finishing your cold cantaloupe soup was one of the stupidest."

I clasp onto his upper arms, one in each hand, heady with the knowledge that I don't have to let go. "All stupid," I agree quietly, forgetting that anyone else is in the room, as I sink my head onto his chest. "But also, all reparable."

I close my eyes and breathe in the comfort, the safety, the feeling of home I find in this kitchen, near these people. Then I open them again, looking from Noah to Nean plaintively, wanting them to know just how much I need them both.

Nean looks back, and then she frowns. "I'm not going to the grocery store, if that's what you're thinking."

I smile. It was exactly what I was thinking, but when I look at Noah again, cooking becomes the last thing on my mind.

December

NEAN

"The sharing of food is the basis of social life, and to many people
it is the only kind of social life worth participating in."

—LAURIE COLWIN,
Home Cooking

Believe me when I tell you that Janey and Noah getting together has
been one of the more disgusting developments of my life. Who knew
Janey would turn out to be such a lap sitter? Every time I walk into a
room she's sitting on Noah's lap playing with his hair or kissing the top
of his head. Blech. It's not safe in here anymore, ever since he moved in
after the first freeze in October.

Luckily I have a place to escape to: the bakery. Though it was a
shock to the system at first, over the last few months I've gotten pretty
good at getting up at the dawn of time and driving in the dark to town
to get the daily bread going. With coffee, all things are possible. I like
the ritual of it, and I'm making real money—which is a good thing,
because soon, when Janey starts her long-overdue student teaching in
January, we're going to need a second car.

The doorbell rings, and, speak of the devil, it's Honey, holding an
armload of the long skinny paper bags that we sell baguettes in. I give
her a big one-armed hug when she's inside, then take the bread off her
hands. "I baked this, didn't I?" I ask, laughing. I've only been home

from the bakery for a few hours, and my work seems to have followed me home.

"You did," she admits with a sheepish shrug. "But I also brought a cake—it's in the car. You're going to love it—it's practically dripping with frosting flowers."

"Sounds fabulous. J.J.!" I call. "Come meet Honey."

From the living room J.J. lumbers over, holding a glass of red wine and one of Janey's cheese puffs. He looks exactly the same as he did when he left in August, only less tan. And he's experimenting with a beard, with limited success, though don't tell him I said that. "Hey," he says, popping the puff into his mouth to free up a hand. "Nice to meet you."

"You too," says Honey. "Though I've never heard of you," she teases.

"Really?" J.J. looks taken aback.

"I wish," Honey says with a smile. "Unfortunately, Nean has it kind of bad."

"It's true," I tell him, angling up for a kiss. "I do."

"I heard there was cake," says J.J., after he's obliged me.

"It's in the car," Honey says, and before she can go on, he throws open the door letting a burst of cold air in, and trots outside in his socks, calling, "Be right back."

"Nice guy," Honey says to me with a smile.

"Right? Who knew they existed?" I say, because even now, the idea takes some getting used to. But damned if I'm not up to the task.

J.J. returns with the cake at the exact moment that Janey starts calling for dinner, and we all obediently march to the formal dining room, a room we are actually using for the first time tonight, because it's way, way too cold to sit on the sun porch, and there are just so darn many of us. Nancy is already sitting at the long table next to Rupert and two other staff from the shelter who are off work tonight, and so is Danette, the chef from the fancy restaurant in Damariscotta, and her wine steward girlfriend Angie. Danette and Janey met at the farmer's market when they were fighting over a good-looking slab of bacon, and when they found out that Danette buys some of her produce from Noah, a fast friendship was formed. I'd be jealous, except I was too damn happy for Janey when I heard she'd managed to make a new friend without puking in the bushes or breaking out in a rash. That's a real breakthrough.

Besides, it makes me feel good to know she'll have lots of friends around when I go away to pastry school next fall.

Yeah, yeah. Look at me making something of myself. It was J.J.'s idea. Now he's looking for jobs for after graduation near the culinary institute, so I think I'm stuck with him.

Janey's made noises about missing us, but we'll be just over in Vermont, so I'll never be far if she needs me. And it won't be long until I am back, I can promise her that. This house is my real home. I couldn't stay away for long.

We all take our seats, and I smile as the newcomers to the Janey experience gape at all the food weighing down the table. It's Christmas Eve, so we're doing the feast of the seven fishes, but I don't think Janey was able to stop with just seven. Everywhere I look there are dead things from the sea. Most are looking scrumptious, and a few things look nasty, like the eel stretched out on a long skinny platter and the stuffed squid bodies, tentacles long gone but probably lurking in one of the other dishes somewhere. Not that I won't eat them all anyway. At least nothing's still alive. You should have seen that eel go down.

When we're all assembled, Janey brings out the big showpiece, a huge, steaming pot of creamy oyster stew, and Noah trails behind her with a smaller crock of corn chowder and a platter of portobello steaks for Honey, who is annoyingly vegetarian. Janey moves around the table, ladling our bowls full of stew, and when she comes to me I see that her eyes are glinting in the light of the candles. I know right then that neither of us has ever been happier.

When we are all served, and champagne is bubbling in all our glasses, Noah rises to make a toast. In the back of my mind I hear him thanking us all for being there, complimenting Janey's cooking, praising her decision to become a home ec teacher and the bravery to see it through. I hear him wishing us love and joy in the New Year, and friendship and a place to call home for the rest of our days. But I'm not really listening. I'm looking at the wall behind him, where Janey has framed Aunt Midge's funeral speech, and remembering that day when we told her good-bye. She would be proud of us, crowded around this big table, getting ready to eat and drink like there's no tomorrow. I know she would. And though I can't see the words from this far away, I remember by heart the little postscript she must have added toward the very end of her life, the one she marked "Confidential" in block letters at the end of her letter.

"CONFIDENTIAL, to my girls, my family, Janey and Nean," it reads, in the jittery cursive I will never forget. "Don't forget, I'm watching you. So keep it interesting."

THE GOOD LUCK GIRLS OF SHIPWRECK LANE

by Kelly Harms

About the Author

- A Conversation with Kelly Harms

Food for Thought

- Recipes Inspired by the Novel

Keep on Reading

- Recommended Reading
- Reading Group Questions

A Reading Group Gold Selection

For more reading group suggestions,
visit www.readinggroupgold.com.

ST. MARTIN'S GRIFFIN

A Conversation with Kelly Harms

Could you tell us a little bit about your background, and when you decided that you wanted to lead a literary life?

When I finished college, I went to intern at a magazine that still had a books section (quaint!). There, I started rubbing up against the business side of books: publicity, marketing, uncorrected proofs. That was the first time I truly understood how many people were involved in getting a book to the shelf, and started to believe there was room for me among them. I didn't allow myself to hope I might be a writer myself, but I believed I could hang with the writers. That led me to New York, and to the doorsteps of literary agents.

"I didn't allow myself to hope I might be a writer...."

Is there a book that most influenced your life? Or inspired you to become a writer?

I read *The Girls' Guide to Hunting and Fishing* the year I turned twenty—one and the new millennium rolled in. Some combination of those things changed my life. If it weren't for that book I would probably be a doctor now. Thanks a lot, Melissa Bank.

What was the inspiration for *The Good Luck Girls of Shipwreck Lane*? And can you tell readers how you came up with the title?

The title just came to me exactly as it is. I had to go back and change the house's address to suit it. I think the girls originally lived on County Road B.

The inspiration was, of course, HGTV. A potent brew of my tiny NYC apartment, wishful thinking, and a cable subscription.

**Take readers into the process of writing your novel.
What challenges did you face in terms of plotting
and structure, for example? How did you manage
to create the distinct voices of each of the main
characters?**

Erm...process? My process was to sit in the same
chair every day until a book came out. And then
revise. And revise. And revise. Oh, and there was
some crying in there, too.

**Do you have a favorite scene from *Good Luck
Girls*—a setting or incident that's especially
meaningful to you?**

Yes I do, and it's on the cutting room floor! It's a
scene where Nean accosts the network's lawyer at his
office after swiping the U-Haul sans pants. It didn't
serve the book, but it made me laugh. It was fun to
write, and character-building to delete.

**Are you currently working on another book? And if
so, what—or who—is your subject?**

I find once again I am telling the story of women
who must make drastic changes to their lives to find
their passions and purpose, and who need to let new
friendships in to show them the way. To me, there
is nothing so appealing as a fresh start, and nothing
so transformative as the power of friendship. And,
because I can't seem to help myself, there will be
food. Breakfast food, specifically. Scones, mimosas,
crêpes, quiche, pancakes, caramelized bacon, and
perfectly poached eggs over a bright fresh green
salad...the research for this one has been positively
scrumptious.

How to Make Fresh Pasta Janey-Style

I learned how to make fresh pasta from Lidia Bastianich's cooking show. This was in a time before iPads, so I never paid much attention to the precise quantities of flour, and had no room in my Upper West Side studio apartment for a pasta machine either. That's why Janey, a figment of my imagination, after all, uses the volcano method and a rolling pin. But, I will grant that you can sometimes end up with a floury waste if you just eyeball it, so I have bent to the pressure and herewith provide vague measurements that should be taken with a grain of (kosher) salt. What you'll do with these ingredients is even more vaguely elaborated on below. Stumble through it at least twice for great results. I have never met a fresh pasta I didn't like. (Of course, the same goes for donuts, so consider the source.)

1¾ cups flour
2 eggs
¼ cup olive oil
Aforementioned pinch of salt

Sift the flour with the salt out onto a clean counter where you have plenty of room. A dream home kitchen really helps for this recipe. Failing that, banish your family from the kitchen and take over the table.

Make a well in the middle of the pile of flour, and crack the eggs into it. Add half of the oil. With a fork, get to beating the egg mixture and let some of the flour join the party. Invite more and more flour until the well is gone and the dough is forming in its place, and then toss the fork and get kneading with your hands.

After some time you will have smooth and shiny dough that wants no more flour or oil. Make a disk and go read a good book for fifteen minutes. When you come back gluten will have formed, and you can go back to kneading and soon, in 5 to 10 minutes, the dough will feel springy and less willful.

Now you must roll all this out into a very thin disk, which may take breaking things into three batches. How thin must your pasta be? The thickness of one skeptically arched eyebrow (or an eighth of an inch). You'll need the leftover flour for this and some patience, and, if you have a toddler, a video of a tractor driving around a field for thirty minutes. Eventually you will have this lovely vinyl record-sized pasta round before you, and you will flour it some more, fold it into thirds, and use a pizza cutter to make skinny tripled ribbons.

Those ribbons can be dried by hanging on a coat hanger or chair rung or any old place you can keep clean for three hours. Or they can be dried for much less time—for me I can only bear an hour or so— and then thrown into boiling water for two or three minutes.

Top your homemade pasta with thin slivers of La Quercia prosciutto, fresh peas, parmesan, ground black pepper, and reserved pasta water for a dish worth scaling a cliff for.

Aunt Midge's Most Perfect Egg Salad Sandwich

"The whole thing seems gross to me. I mean, mayonnaise *is* eggs. Why would you stir more eggs into it?" So says Janey, but I couldn't feel more differently. I craved egg salad and deviled eggs so ferociously during my pregnancy that I started to worry that I was gestating an oviraptor. (And there are days now when I think maybe I did.) The secret, I think, to a really good egg salad is to rely not at all on the bread for flavor, and instead to put your whole heart into the filling and then scoop it into the softest loaf you can find so as to avoid smooshing. Nean would be outraged, but I like the filling so much I don't even top it with that second slice of bread but eat it open-faced with one singular piece of curly leaf lettuce perched on top. Here's my recipe:

If you don't grow your own chives, first, start growing your own chives. While you wait to harvest, you may use dill instead, and/or a squeeze of lemon for brightness.

4 eggs from The Farm or the store. Eggs that have reached a certain age are best.
3 tbsp. good mayonnaise. So, Hellman's. Even Janey will eat Hellman's in a pinch.*
¼ tsp. dry mustard, or failing that, a teaspoon of the dark brown prepared stuff
The eeensiest dash of Worcestershire sauce
1 tbsp. chives, cut into dots with shears. Chopping chives with a knife is a fool's game.
Paprika for garnish

Serves two

Add an inch of water into a lidded pot with a steamer tucked inside. Bring the water to a boil, add the four eggs to the steamer basket, cover the pot, and turn down the heat to a simmer. Come back in 12 minutes to perfect boiled eggs, and feel smug.

Move the eggs into an ice bath to stop the cooking, then peel. With a pastry blender, dice the eggs into nice rough chunk-lets.

In another bowl, mix the mayo, mustard, and Worcestershire.

*Typically Janey would make her own mayonnaise. I've done so myself a time or two, and find it results in stunning arm definition and great mayo, but also an intense feeling of martyrdom unless at least thirty people call you spontaneously to congratulate you on making your own mayonnaise. Which doesn't happen very often, to me at least.

Marry the mayo mix to the eggs and stir. Add chives
and salt and pepper to taste. Aunt Midge likes it salty.

Dollop onto some dark soft bread, and top with a
sprinkle of paprika, and, should they be lying about,
some greens. There, don't you feel virtuous?

Pork Chops for J.J. and Noah

I am an Iowa girl, and thusly know my way around a
pork chop. But somewhere along the line I stopped
liking them. Then, the FDA, in their infinite wisdom,
announced that we could stop cooking the bejesus out
of them, and lo, pork chops were redeemed in my eyes.
This perfectly simple recipe cooks up between the time
the doorbell rings out "La Cucaracha" and you answer
it, because you've bisected the chop and stuffed it with
more Iowegian goodness: Maytag blue cheese. And since
blue cheese loves fruit, how about some cherry pan
sauce down over the top? Be careful who you feed these
to, as they are manbait.

Two bone-in pork chops, 6–8 ounces each, trimmed
2 tbsp. salt
A few peppercorns
1 smashed clove of garlic
2 ounces of good blue cheese, crumbled a bit
A large handful of dried cherries or cranberries,
    covered in hot water to plump
A glass of nice red wine, most of which is for the cook
Butter

Serves two

Put the first four ingredients in a plastic bag or glass dish
with a lid and cover with cold water. Put the whole thing
in the fridge and go write a favorable review of this book
on Amazon.

Thirty minutes later, pat the chops dry, toss the brine, and make a slit in the non–bone-side of a pork chop lengthwise, leaving one–inch borders on either end. Forcibly cram half the blue cheese in there with a fork. Repeat with the other chop. It's not elegant. It's pork chops.

Heat a cast–iron or other serious pan on the burner with a little pat of butter. Cook the pork chops for three minutes per side or until the meat—not the cheese—reaches 145 degrees. Put the chops aside to rest and add more butter, some red wine, and the drained dried fruit to the pan. Scrape any fond from the pan into the sauce and simmer until the boozy smell is cooked off.

Serve the chops with a good drizzle of sauce and a flirtatious wink.

📖 *Recommended Reading*

A Glimpse into Janey's Cookbook Collection

The Perfect Recipe by Pam Anderson

James Beard's American Cookery by James Beard

The Bread Bible by Rose Levy Beranbaum

How to Cook Everything by Mark Bittman

I'm Just Here for the Food by Alton Brown

The Way to Cook by Julia Child

Home Cooking by Laurie Colwin

Tasty by Roy Finamore

How to Cook a Wolf by M. F. K. Fisher

The Barefoot Contessa Cookbook by Ina Garten

Baking: From My Home to Yours by Dorie Greenspan

A Real American Breakfast by Cheryl Alters Jamison
  and Bill Jamison

The Splendid Table's How to Eat Supper
  by Lynne Rossetto Kasper and Sally Swift

How to Be a Domestic Goddess by Nigella Lawson

Pass the Polenta by Teresa Lust

On Food and Cooking by Harold McGee

Practical Guide to the New American Kitchen
  by Charlie Palmer

The Silver Palate Cookbook by Julee Rosso and
  Sheila Lukins

Joy of Cooking by Irma S. Rombauer,
  Marion Rombauer Becker, and Ethan Becker

The Art of Simple Food by Alice Waters

Cooking from New England by Jasper White

Reading Group Questions

1. The title of this book tells us luck is important to the story, but in fact both of the narrators have had a few hard knocks before even reaching page one. Do you think one huge turn of fortune can make up for a lifetime of bad breaks? Would you describe these two women as "lucky?" What about yourself?

2. Early in the story, the producer of the sweepstakes asks the winner if she plans to actually live in the house. Did this question take you by surprise? What do you think happens to the real-life winners of such windfall contests? What would you do if you won a million-dollar house hundreds of miles away?

3. Each chapter of this story begins with a quote from a real cookbook chosen from Janey's imaginary collection. Which piqued your interest the most?

4. Janey and Nean put their hearts and souls into telling Aunt Midge's story to each other through food. What would a culinary history of your life look like? Are there certain meals you'd like to add? Delete?

5. Both Janey and Nean begin this story with unique—and debilitating—flaws. Did you relate to one character or the other more? Find one or the other more likable?

6. How did one woman's weakness pair together with the other woman's strengths? Are there relationships like that in your own life?

7. The truth about Noah's situation takes many readers by surprise, as it does Janey. Nean, however, hardly bats an eye. Why do you think that is?

8. If you could have one meal from the book served up on a plate, which would it be? And with which character would you eat it?